PALE PLEASURES

'What's going on? What's wrong with the yoghurt?'

Gwen held the back of the container up for her. 'Read it. Translate it.'

Anna frowned. 'What? You mean . . .'

'No. I don't mean. The container means. The containers mean. The whole lot of them. He's made yoghurt from us. From our milk.'

'When?'

'When we were in the hothouse. Don't you remember? I told you. He did it to me.'

'N . . . no. I can't.'

'You can. I think we all can. He's been milking us. Turning the milk into yoghurt.'

PALE
PLEASURES

Wendy Swanscombe

This book is a work of fiction.
In real life, make sure you practise safe sex.

First published in 2002 by
Nexus
Thames Wharf Studios
Rainville Road
London W6 9HA

www.nexus-books.co.uk

Typeset by TW Typesetting, Plymouth, Devon

Printed and bound by
Mackays of Chatham PLC

ISBN 0 352 33702 8

Some commend the exposure of these orders unto the western gales as the most generative and fructifying breath of heaven. But we applaud the husbandry of Solomon, whereto agreeth the doctrine of Theophrastus: 'Awake, O north wind, and come, thou south, blow upon my garden that the spices thereof may flow out.' For the north wind closing the pores and shutting up the effluviums, when the south doth after open and relax them, the aromatic gums do drop and sweet odours fly actively from them.

The Garden of Cyrus (1658), Sir Thomas Browne.

Mme de Saint-Ange: Elle en pourrait avoir sous les aisselles et dans les cheveux, elle devrait en avoir trente autour d'elle s'il était possible; il faudrait, dans ces moments-là, n'avoir, ne toucher, ne dévorer que des vits autour de soi, être inondée par tous au même instant où l'on déchargerait soi-même. Ah! Dolmancé, quelque putain que vous soyez, je vous défie de m'avoir égalée dans ces délicieux combats de la luxure . . . J'ai fait tout ce qu'il est possible en ce genre.

La Philosophie dans le boudoir (1795), *Quatrième Dialogue*, D.-A.-F. de Sade.

'Good moaning.'

Catchphrase of mock French policeman in *'Allo, 'Allo*, BBC wartime comedy serial (1984–92).

One

Black leather boots. First rapping on the bare marble floor, then crunching on the rime of evaporated piss that lay beneath the three of them like a broad yellow flower. The three of them turning in the hothouse air, hanging naked and horizontal in harnesses of transparent plastic on bright silver chains from three-pointed silver stars. Crunch. And crunch. And crunch. Until his black leather boots, and his black leather body, were standing where she would face them every few seconds, turning and turning in her harness of transparent plastic from her three-pointed silver star.

On the next turn his black leather arms came up and his hands, in their black leather gloves, caught hold of her cropped, black-furred head, holding her gently by the ears, so that she stopped turning and hung in front of him, sleeping face pointed at his black leather midriff.

'Gwen.'

A bass voice rumbled out along the walls of the hothouse from two or three dozen concealed speakers, its notes trembling in the humid air, shaking the bright little heads of the orchid flowers so that they nodded or negated the name.

'Gwen. Wake up.'

The bass voice again. His voice? He was pinching her earlobes gently.

'Gwen. Gwen.'

And her eyes were flickering, blinking, opening, widening. Brown eyes in a white face beneath that cropped,

1

silkily furred skull. His right hand released her ears and began to roam across her scalp, black leather fingers ploughing through black silk.

'How are you, Gwen?'

'Master?'

Her voice now. Weak and uncertain, and insubstantial anyway after the rumbling bass of his voice.

'Yes, Gwen. I am here. How are you? How do you feel?'

She blinked, trying to look up at his face. A red tongue-tip crept from one corner of her mouth, slid along her lips, paused midway, carried on. He let go of her head and stepped back, crunch, crunch, so that she could see his face. Only it was no face. Only a blank black mask: eyeless and noseless and mouthless, but horned on either side.

'How are you, Gwen? Come, tell me. How are you?'

When he had let go of her she had begun to turn again, carried away from him, her head twisting as she tried to keep him in view.

'I'm well, master. But I don't . . .'

'I know you don't. I don't want you to, yet. It's time for your shave.'

There was a flat, square holster on his right hip. His hand dropped to it, flicked it open, and as she was carried back towards him again his hand lifted a fat black silver-denticled razor trailing a sinuous length of electric flex.

'Time, Gwenchen.'

His hand didn't seem to move but the razor buzzed awake, its row of minute silver teeth gnawing at the air. She was being carried away from him again, body turning flat and horizontal on the warm air, her belly curdling with fright at the buzz of the razor. Like a wasp. A huge, black, hungry wasp. At the thought her bladder let go, pissing out her fright in a golden curve to the marble floor and the golden crust of evaporated piss that she and her two sisters, turning like her in their harnesses from their three-pointed silver stars, must have laid down over days. Maybe weeks. Turning and turning and turning.

Carried back towards him, she heard his boots crunching in the evaporated piss, and his left hand caught her head again, holding her to his stomach, cool, smooth leather beneath her cheek. A final spurt and dribble and she was pissed out. Her nostrils wrinkled. There was a smell of hot piss. Boiling piss. She could feel steam rising against her body from beneath. Her fresh piss was being boiled away, scalded from the marble floor. The buzz of the razor seemed to be inside her head, harsh and skull-filling, and she jerked as the razor touched her and began its first long sweep across the black field of her hair. Wisps of it fell past her face into the rising steam of the piss.

'Your weekly shave, Gwenchen. For I have need of more of your hair. Of yours, and Beth's, and Anna's. Three good little girls who willingly sacrifice their locks to their master, knowing that he will one day soon restore them to them.'

His voices rumbled through the buzz of the razor, like the contented rumble of a bear as it raids a hive of giant electric bees. It made her feel dizzy. More hair falling into the rising steam of the piss. Boiling piss, singeing an acrid blare of uric acid into her nostrils. Acrid acid. The golden blare of a melted trumpet, lying flat and steaming on the floor while its note pours on. Piss-trumpet. Piss-strumpet. Shaved by the cruelly gentle, gently cruel black-leathered hands of her master. Hair falling past her face into the rising steam. Into the boiling piss.

But then why wasn't she smelling scorched hair? No, he was catching it somehow. Catching her hair as it fell from her widening white scalp. Cruelly gentle and gently cruel. Buzz of the black razor and blare of the golden piss-trumpet.

'There. That's better.'

He released her and stepped back, crunch, crunch, and she began to turn again, the air sliding across her skull more intimately now, more caressingly, kissing her bald skin. She sniffed and realized that her eyes were welling with tears. She sniffed harder, closing her eyes tight, trying to force the tears back in, suck them back into her head. She wouldn't let him see her crying. No. She couldn't let him see that. And there he was again, carried back into

view as she turned, black leather boots and body, blank
black mask, black razor still in his hand, and in a pannier
of transparent plastic hung around his hips, a few handfuls
of her black hair. At the sight of it, clustered on the smooth
curve of the pannier, the tears were back again, welling
thicker and faster than ever, too thick and too fast to hold
back, so that she had to let them flow.

Then there was nothing again.

Two

Black leather boots. First rapping on the bare marble floor, then crunching on the rime of evaporated piss that lay beneath the three of them like a broad yellow flower. Crunch, and crunch, until as before he stood where she would face him every few seconds, turning in her harness of transparent plastic from a silver three-pointed star. Her scalp was silkily furred again, white skin shaded and concealed by fresh black hair, but this time there was no holster on his hip.

He stepped forward, crunch, and crunch, and caught her head as she turned.

'Gwen.'

The bass voice rumbling out from the walls again, vivid little orchid-flowers nodding or negating the name.

'Gwen. Wake up.'

Black-leather fingers squeezing at her ear-lobes again, and her eyes flickering, blinking, opening.

'How are you, Gwenchen? Do you remember last time?'

Red tongue-tip between her lips, moistening them again.

'No, master. I don't remember . . . anything. Anything, master.'

Her eyes widened for a moment, opening on the darkness inside her skull, probing at it in vain. Nothing. Or almost nothing.

'No, Gwenchen. Not strictly true. You remember three things. You remember me and you remember yourself and you remember the relationship between us. Don't you?'

'Yes, master.'

'Who am I?'

'My master, master.'

'And what are you?'

'I am your . . .'

She broke off, swallowing.

'Yes, Gwenchen?'

'Your slave, master.'

'Good girl. So you remember all that is vital in the universe. You and me and our relationship. Master and slave. All else flows from that. Time flows from that. It is my gift to you. Do you understand me?'

'No, master.'

'Then I will give you something else. Knowledge. Understanding. Watch.'

He let go of her head and stepped back, crunch, crunch. She started to turn from him, the touch of his fingers preserved in the nerves and flesh of her ears, and the truth of what he had said to her glowing in her nipples and stomach and cunt. But not the whole truth. She knew four things, not three. She knew him and she knew herself and she knew the relationship between them. Master and slave. But she also knew that she wanted to overturn that relationship. Not just slave: rebellious slave.

And now she was turning back to face him again, twisting her head to see him before her body had quite turned far enough. He was standing ready for her, cradling something flat against his black leather body. Almost like a door. A door through which she could see beyond him. One wall of the hothouse, crowded with orchids and with . . . three girls hanging in the air in front of it. Because it wasn't a door. It was a mirror. He was holding up a tall mirror, cradling it against his body so that she could see herself and her sisters, Beth and Anna. Something else she knew. Something else that he hadn't given to her. Or had he?

'Do you see, Gwenchen? Do you see yourself?'

She had turned level with the mirror now, gazing full-face into its silver depths for a moment before her

6

turning body began to carry her away again. Her strapped and harnessed body hanging from silver chains, breasts held flat beneath her, cropped skull above a white face.

'Yes, master,' she said, speaking into the air now, carried away from him and the mirror, reaching the zenith, beginning to fall towards the nadir and another deep glimpse into the silver depths of the mirror.

'How long was your hair, Gwenchen?'

'Not long, master.'

'Recently cut then, Gwenchen?'

'Yes, master.'

'And how long is it *now*, Gwenchen?'

She was swinging to face the mirror again, twisting her neck to look into it, to see herself and her two sisters. And Anna's blonde hair was brighter, because it was longer, and so was Beth's, and so ... so was hers. It was the same white face gazing into hers, the same strapped and harnessed body on the same silver chains, the same breasts pressed flat beneath, but the hair was longer. A week's growth longer. A fortnight's. She didn't know. Only that it was longer. Much longer.

'How long, Gwenchen? How long *now*?'

'Longer, master.'

She was turning away from him again, turning away from the mirror, rising towards the zenith.

'How much longer? A week? Two weeks?'

'Yes, master. Maybe two weeks.'

'But how can that be? How many times have you turned?'

'Twice master.'

She had reached the zenith of the turn, was falling again towards the nadir, turning to face him and the flat, time-annihilating mirror.

'Then this would be your third turn, Gwenchen, *hein*? And how long is your hair *now*?'

She saw Anna and Beth before she saw herself fully, and their hair was neck-length, spilling down and round their sleeping heads, bright blonde and glossy copper, two or three weeks or a month longer than before. Like hers.

7

Because she was facing full into the mirror again, and there was her hair, neck-long hair framing her white face as it hung downwards, half-concealing her pressed-flat breasts.

'How long, Gwenchen? Tell me: how long? How long *now*?'

'Neck-length, master.'

'There has not been time, Gwenchen. Has there?'

'No, master.'

'Not unless I can give you time and take time from you at will. At a whim. As a tithe or as a gift. Do you not agree?'

'Yes, master.'

'Good girl. Very good girl. And how long is it now, Gwenchen? How long *now*?'

Past the zenith, falling to the nadir, falling towards the vertical face of the mirror, the white bodies of her sisters and herself, their bright, re-grown hair. Fully re-grown. Shoulder-length or longer. Anna was blonde again, Beth redhead, she raven. She gazed into herself as she turned full to the mirror for the fourth time. Two black silky wings down either side of her face, framing it, heightening its whiteness. She was back again, because she was black again.

'How long, Gwenchen?'

'Fully grown, master.'

'But there has been no time, Gwenchen. No time for it to grow. Unless time is mine, not yours. Mine to give, yours to receive. Is that not so?'

'Yes, master.'

'Good girl.'

She was turning away from him again, but she heard his boots crunching towards her on the rime of evaporated piss. A gloved hand on her left buttock, kneading it for a moment, squeezing the plump, firm flesh up, presenting it to some unknown attention. She gasped. A sharp, momentary sting and then nothing.

Three

Black leather boots. First rapping on the bare marble floor, then crunching on the rime of evaporated piss that lay beneath the three of them like a broad yellow flower. Crunch, and crunch, until he was standing as before, where he would face her as she turned. This time he did not step forward and take hold of her head; rather he waited, watching as she turned, her long black hair riding back a little on the air she moved. Then he spoke, bass voice rumbling, the bright little orchid-heads nodding or negating to its notes.

'Gwen. Wake up.'

She was facing away from him as he spoke, but from the sudden change of tonus in her long slim back and buttocks he knew she had awakened at once and that her eyes would be open as she was carried back round to him in her harness.

He waited. She was carried. Her eyes were open. Now he stepped forward to her. Crunch, crunch. Stepping to stand beside her, within the circle of her turn, almost at the axis of it, one black-gloved hand resting lightly on her flank.

'Are you well, Gwen?'

His boots were shifting, turning him with her.

'No, master.'

'Your tits?'

'Yes, master.'

'Do they hurt?'

9

'Yes, master.'

'Good. Then I will milk you.'

She felt him loop something over her shoulders, reach beneath her, adjust something, clip something into place, then tug at the straps of her harness, release something with a click, so that her breasts suddenly came free and hung bare to the air, fat and swollen and aching.

'Milk you, Gwenchen. Like this.'

His hands closed over her breasts, probing, squeezing, and breath shuddered from her mouth. Something hot seemed to begin trickling down her spine and between her closed thighs; the lips of her cunt began to swell and unfurl.

'So . . . and so . . . and so . . .'

His index and forefingers had closed over her nipples, left and right, his feet still crunching on the piss-rime as he turned with her. Now he began to milk her, left nipple then right, his fingers tugging at them, stretching them, drawing them out, milking them. She felt the fluid in her breasts spurt, a little jet from the left nipple, a little jet from the right, landing in whatever he had hung beneath her breasts with liquid sounds, left nipple and right nipple, index and forefingers tugging, stretching, drawing, milking. *Split*. *Split. Split*.

Her spine was incandescent down its full length, rooted in the fire that had spread from her cunt to overwhelm her buttocks and thighs. Her cunt was straining to open between her closed thighs, seething with hot yelm, and her clitoris was like a fiery splinter. Christ, it hurt, and it was good, strong fingers milking her aching breasts, *split*, *split*, *split*, relieving their congestion, drawing off the hot milk that filled them, *split*, *split*, *split*.

'Thank you, Gwenchen.'

It was over. God. It was over, and she hadn't orgasmed. Her cunt was overflowing and her spine was on fire and her clitoris itched and she couldn't get her hands free and he was leaving her like this. How could he do it?

Crunch. Crunch. He was moving down her body, his fingertips brushing her back, stroking her buttocks for a moment, leaving them as an equine shiver passed through them. Chains clinked and catches snapped open and the seal of her thighs suddenly loosened. He was swinging her legs apart, exposing her ripe cunt to the air, a juicy, overflowing fig, swimming in rich, hot sweetness.

'Excellent.'

The rumble of the word was underlain on the second syllable with a dry sucking noise, an electric inhalation from some machine he had switched on. And then it touched her. A thirsty plastic proboscis, passing over the lips and vestibule of her cunt, sucking at her yelm, quivering and tickling, drawing her skin into its mouth, releasing her, sucking and tickling, tugging at the delicate hairs with which her cunt was lapelled, nosing into her culks, riding over every inch of the kingdom of her cunt, thirsty for yelm.

The lake of incipient orgasm inside her, settling uneasily from the turbulence of his milking, began to agitate, to put up waves, to rock and fling spray and steam, rising to the boil, timing itself to the arrival of the sucking proboscis around her clitoris. Maybe on her clitoris. Slipped directly atop it, sucking at it hard, drawing it endlessly up and out of her body. A dry, endless sucking, lashing the lake to frenzy.

The proboscis left her and the sucking stopped. Catches snapped as they were re-fastened; the chains clinked; her thighs were re-sealed, entombing her unsatisfied cunt and clitoris in marmoreal, yelm-smeared smoothness.

'Thank you, Gwenchen.'

She clutched her disappointment and anger to her body as she sank back into oblivion, a white priestess sinking into green depths and clutching useless idols of gold and quartz to herself that only hastened her descent towards the ultimate darkness of the abyss. Crunch. Crunch. His voice came rumbling at her from the walls of the hothouse, trembling in the humid air.

'Beth, wake up.'

Four

She opened her eyes. A voice had been calling her name.
Two voices. Anna and Beth were calling her name. The
wall of the hothouse was sliding in front of her, turning her
towards them, and yes, there, a pair of slim white feet, slim
legs, buttocks, back, shoulders, a harnessed body hanging
from silver chains, swinging like hers, and a red-furred
white head with a white face and a red-lipped mouth
opening 'Gw . . .', then closing as the green eyes met hers.
The mouth opened again.

'You're awake.'

In a whisper.

'Yes. Where's Anna?'

She had whispered too. Why?

'Coming up fast on your right.'

Because of Bärengelt. The other side of Beth's body was
turning away from her, shoulders, back, buttocks, legs, feet,
and then Anna was in front of her, harnessed and strapped,
hanging horizontal from the same silver chains, her blonde
hair cropped tight against her scalp, blue eyes wide on hers
as their faces conjuncted and began to turn apart.

'He's shaved us again,' Gwen said.

'What?'

Still whispering.

She waited. They had to feed each other scraps as their
heads conjuncted, assembling a conversation between
silences, not daring to raise their voices, still frightened of
him. Even she. The rebel.

'He's shaved us again ... our hair had grown back ...
I saw it ...'

'When?'

Waiting for the moment.

'He showed me. It grew back and n ...'

She stopped, startled by the note of a bell sounding from above her.

'What the fuck was that?'

Beth, whispering fiercely on her right.

'I don't know. I can't see.'

They continued to talk, assembling words and phrases and sentences, comparing experiences. Beth could remember being wakened to be milked too, several times, but Bärengelt hadn't shown her the hair-growth trick. Anna was blushing as she described what had happened to her, white face turned bright pink, fading on successive turns to thin translucent rose, for she had wakened six or seven times to find Bärengelt drawing off her menses. Maybe more times than that.

'And what else?' Gwen asked.

'Nothing.'

But her blush was back as fierce as ever when their heads conjuncted again, glowing with the memory of Bärengelt's filthiness and her orgasmic response to it.

'If he did that to you,' Beth said, 'we must have been here months.'

Voices getting gradually louder. More confident.

'Just hanging around.'

'With no particular place to go.'

'Sleeping.'

'We're not asleep now.'

The bell-note sounded again from above them, but overlaid this time by another bell-note, a deeper one.

'What is it?'

Beth again. Voice momentarily re-softened with worry. If there were mysterious noises, could Bärengelt be far behind?

'Nine.'

Anna.

'What?'

13

'Nine. I've been counting.'

'Nine what?'

'It's me. When I turn around nine times, that happens. The bell.'

'There were two notes.'

Beth.

'I know. One for you and one for me. You're turning twice as slowly. When you complete nine, your bell sounds, and so does mine, because I've just completed eighteen. Count. When Gwen completes her nine, *she'll* ring, and it'll be twenty-seven for me, so I'll ring too, but *you* won't, because it will be only fourteen-and-a-half for you.'

Gwen frowned for a moment, then said, 'She's right.'

'So when do we all ring together?' Beth said.

'Um,' Gwen said. 'When it's the lowest thingumajig of nine, eighteen, and twenty-seven. Like eighteen is the lowest thingumajig of nine and eighteen.'

'Lowest common multiple,' Anna said.

'How do you know?' Beth said.

'I don't. I mean, I don't know how. I just do.'

'It's him. It's a message from him.'

'What?'

'When the bells all sound together. Something will happen. We have to be ready for it.'

'And when will that be?'

'On the lowest thingumajig. Lowest common multiple.'

'Which is, Cleverclogs?'

Gwen had been working it out, frowning at the sliding walls of the hothouse.

'Fifty-four,' she said.

'Fifty-four?'

'Yeah. Nine times six and eighteen times three and twenty-seven times two. The lowest common multiple.'

'Or LCM.'

Beth.

'Yeah. LCM.'

'But that could mean Luscious Cunt Melting.'

'Yeah. Or Lickable Cunt Melting.'

'Or Luminous Cunt Moth,' said Anna.

14

Beth asked, 'What's that?'

Gwen laughed.

'It's a moth that's luminous and lives on cunts.'

'Eats them, you mean?' Beth said.

'Figuratively speaking. Licks them. With its long tongue. Probes inside them. Thoroughly. That's right, isn't it, Anna?'

'Yes. *Very* thoroughly,' said Anna, her voice trembling a little. Silence again as the three of them turning in their harnesses, thinking of the luminous cunt moth. Anna's bell-note sounded again and as though this were a cue Beth asked, 'Does it hurt?'

'A little bit,' Gwen said. 'When the moth is licking especially hard.'

'Especially *thoroughly*,' said Anna.

'Yeah. It hurts when it's licking especially thoroughly. Being a conscientious luminous cunt moth.'

'A CLCM.'

'Yeah. A CLCM.'

'Where does it lays its eggs?' Beth said.

'In yelm-stained knickers.'

'Yelm-stained *silk* knickers,' Beth said.

'Why silk?' Gwen asked.

'Because if silk-moths make silk, cunt-moths eat it.'

'Why?'

Anna said dreamily, '*My* moth would lay its eggs in cotton knickers. White cotton knickers.'

'Still warm. Still damp with yelm,' said Beth. Gwen hid a smile, not wanting Anna to see it as they conjuncted. She licked her lips.

'Then it would fly back to your cunt and lick it, Ansie.'

'Wouldn't it have to lick her cunt first? Before laying its eggs?'

'Yes. But it would have licked her cunt first. While she was still wearing her cotton knickers. It would have slid under the elastic and snuggled down into her cunt and licked it thoroughly.'

'Very thoroughly.'

'That's why Anna's knickers would be yelm-stained. She would leak so copiously that there would be enough yelm

15

and to spare. Enough yelm for the moth and to spare for her knickers.'

'They would be soaked.'

'Yes. Soaked with yelm.'

Anna chuckled.

'I don't mind. I would like it.'

'We know you would, you little slut. A big moth in your knickers. Licking. Tickling. Making you leak yelm all over your clean cotton knickers. Then you'd peel them off and throw them on the floor and the moth would fly down and lay its eggs on them.'

'Would it be in the dark?'

'Not necessarily. Why?'

'Because you said it was a luminous cunt moth. I'd like to see it glowing in the dark. Glowing as it sat on my knickers and laid its eggs.'

Anna's bell-note again, melding with Beth's, a strip of silver and gold or gold and silver. Two notes. And they were waiting for three. *Her* note. On completion of her nine turns.

'How much longer now?' she asked.

'Fifty-four for me,' said Anna, 'so that's forty-five to go.'

'And twenty-seven for me,' said Beth, 'so that's eighteen to go, for me. So that's . . .'

'Seven-and-a-half,' said Anna.

'Seven-and-a-half left for you. But less, because it's gone down while I was working it out.'

'While *I* was.'

'I was too. You only said it first.'

'I'm turning slower now. Much slower than I was when Bärengelt was here.'

'How fast were we turning?' Beth asked.

'About the same speed, I think. But we weren't synchro-nized.'

'Syncuntized,' said Anna.

Beth snorted.

'You're being filthy today, Ansie.'

'It's her memories of Bärengelt and her periods. They've excited the little beast. Haven't they? Haven't they, Ansie?'

16

'What did he do to you, Ansie?'

'Shan't tell you.'

Gwen was waiting for her and Anna's heads to conjunct, to see if Anna's blush had flared again, rich and red and desirable in her creamy skin. She said, 'She enjoyed it, whatever it was. That's why her mind is running on such remarkably filthy lines now. Luminous cunt moths. Syncuntized turning.'

'Note the common thread.'

Yes, their heads had conjuncted and Anna's blush was back, weaker than before, but back. She put out her tongue defiantly.

'Yes. Cunt. Cunt is the common theme. She's thinking of her cunt.'

'She's thinking of what Bärengelt did to her cunt. When she had her periods. You never did like talking about your periods did you, Ansie?'

'Remember when we were on *Oprah*?'

Beth laughed.

'How could I forget it?'

Anna blew a raspberry.

'Don't care. Who gives a fuck about that now?'

'Naughty, Ansie. Insolent. Very insolent.'

'So what? What can you do about it?'

Anna's bell-note again.

'That's what we're going to see, isn't it? At the lowest common multiple. The LCM. The luminous cunt moth.'

'In your white cotton knickers, Ansie.'

'Your yelm-stained white cotton knickers.'

Anna snorted.

'In your yelm-stained red silk knickers then, Betchen. In your yelm-stained black silk knickers, Gwenchen.'

Gwen frowned at a sliding wall of orchids.

'Don't call us that.'

'Why not?'

'Bärengelt calls us that.'

'So do I.'

'Then you're a collaborator.'

'A collaboratrix,' Beth said. 'Or *collaboratrice*.'

17

'*Oui. Une sale collaboratrice.*'

'That's shut her up.'

'Yes. She knows she's sinned. Collaborating with the enemy. With the *Boche*.'

'I'll bosh her.'

'Me too. But what's boshing?'

'It's a special punishment for collaboratrixes.'

'What does it consist of?'

Gwen thought.

'It's more a *regime* than a single punishment.'

'That sounds good.'

'It *is* good. Except for the collaboratrixes.'

Anna's head conjuncted and swung away, tongue protruding defiantly.

'For the collaboratrix. Singular. Just Anna. So what does the regime consist of?'

'Well, on day *one* . . .'

Beth took her cue.

'Day one. I like that. How many days?'

'Seven. A whole week of punishments.'

'Yes. And on day one?'

'On day one, in the *morning* . . .'

Beth laughed.

'Getting better all the time.'

'Yes. On day one, in the *morning*, she is stripped.'

'Slowly?'

'Slowly. Very slowly.'

'Then?'

'Spanking.'

'By who?'

'You and me, of course. One holds her down, the other spanks her.'

'Hard?'

'Yes. But not straight away. There is a whole morning for this, remember.'

'The morning of the first day.'

'Yes. Of day one. Because what we want to do is match her spanked bottom to swatches of silk.'

'Match it to swatches of silk?'

'Yes.'

'What are swatches of silk?'

'Samples. Strips of silk for purposes of comparison.'

'Red silk, of course.'

'In the end, but not at first. At first, pink silk. Pale pink, less pale pink, pink, darker pink, dark pink.'

'Dark pink sounds best.'

'Each stage has its charms. Acquires its charms in part from the stage before.'

'Yes, you're right. So what do we do?'

'We spank her gently and then we compare her bottom to the first swatch of silk. Pale pink. If we are satisfied, we proceed. If not, we spank her a little more or we wait for her bottom to fade a little. We must match the swatch perfectly before we proceed.'

'Yes. I like the sound of that. Pink. Pink bottom, pink silk. Pink spanked bottom.'

'Yes.'

'And when we have matched bottom and silk perfectly?'

'Then we spank her again, but this time a little less gently or a little longer. Then we compare her bottom to the next swatch. Less pale pink. If we are satisfied . . .'

'We proceed.'

'Yes. If not . . .'

'Then we spank her a little more or wait for her bottom to fade.'

'Yes. Because we must match her bottom perfectly to the swatch. That is vital. Spanking is an art, but that is not to say we cannot bring scientific rigor to it. We can, and we *will*.'

'Good. I like the sound of that. Rigor. Being rigorous with our little *collaboratrice*. But won't there be a danger of something?'

'What?'

'If we're *rigorous* with *her*, she might get *rigid* with *us*.'

'What do you mean?'

'Her nipples. And her clit. We will have to have regular inspections to make sure she's not enjoying herself. Regular inspections for rigidity.'

'No, nipples and clit are out of bounds. Strictly out of bounds.'

'Why?'

'Because that will frustrate her. Picture it. A slow, scientific spanking. Frequent pauses to compare bottom with swatch. She *will* enjoy it. She *will* get rigid. You know the little slut as well as I do. But she won't enjoy it for long, because her nipples and clit will be strictly out of bounds. Don't you see?'

Beth chuckled.

'Ah, yes, I see now. We will stoke her hunger but not satisfy it. How frustrating for her. How delightful for us.'

'Exactly. A whole morning of spanking, bottom glowing progressively pinker, and not a single orgasm in sight.'

'Except for us.'

'Except, as you say, for us.'

'We can have as many as we like.'

'Yes. And we will.'

Silence for a few moments as the two of them turned, savouring the thought of it.

'And next?' Beth said. 'In the afternoon?'

'In the afternoon we carry on with the spanking. But this time the swatches are red. Light red, less light red, red, brighter red, bright red. Crimson.'

'Scarlet.'

'Vermilion.'

'Yes. Oh, I love those words. Crimson. It's like rolling a rich wine on your tongue. Red wine, of course.'

'Yes, it is. Crimson.'

'Crimson. And scarlet.'

'Yes, scarlet.'

'Vermilion. Just say it. Vermilion. Delicious.'

'Vermilion. Vermilion silk. Scarlet silk. Crimson silk. To match against her spanked bottom.'

'I can't wait.'

Five

'Coming *now!*' Anna said, and it came: her fifty-fourth turn, Beth's twenty-seventh, Gwen's eighteenth: and the bells rang, three notes melding, swelling, an acoustic alloy, filling their ears, filling their heads, so that when abruptly the notes stopped they stumbled mentally, putting out a foot for a tread that was not there in a rising stair of sound. They had reached the top.

'Oh! Something's happening!'

It was Beth, but she was speaking for all of them. Something *was* happening. The chains from which they hung were trembling, slurring the smoothness with which they turned, and suddenly Anna shrieked. They were dropping. All three of them, dropping from the air, being lowered to the floor. Straps clicked and loosened, first Beth's, then Anna's, then Gwen's, as though Bärengelt were striding amongst them, Anna to Beth, Beth to Gwen, releasing them from their harnesses just in time for them to greet the cool kiss of the marble on their skin.

And they were down. Gwen rolled over and sat up, chains jangling, and reached up to pull away the straps around her chin.

'Free, girls,' she said.

'Be careful when you stand up,' said Beth. She was moving more cautiously.

'Why?'

Gwen pulled the last strap away, swung forward onto her knees, and stood up, leaving the harness lying behind her like a discarded chrysalis. She stepped away from it and the chains that still hung from her three-pointed silver star.

'We've been hanging up there for weeks, maybe months. Our muscles must be shot to fuck.'

'Not that I notice.'

Gwen jogged on the spot, lifting one arm, shaking it, lifting the other, shaking it.

'Can't feel a thing, dear.'

She put her hands on her hips, rotated her upper body clockwise, counterclockwise, then bent and touched her toes.

'Not a fucking thing. I feel in excellent shape. Ready to take on the world.'

Beth stood up too. She took a few experimental steps on the spot, jogged, lifted her arms, put her hands on her hips, rotated her upper body, bent and touched her toes.

'You're right. Now that *is* odd.'

'Why odd?'

'Because we can't have been up there constantly. He must have had us down for exercise. But I can't remember a thing.'

'I can remember something,' said Anna from behind them.

Both of them turned. Gwen was frowning a little, looking at the floor.

'What, Ansie?' Beth asked. 'Do you remember what Bärengelt did when you had your periods now?'

'No.'

'Then why are you blushing again?'

'Leave her,' Gwen said. 'There'll be plenty of time for that later. What do you remember, Ansie?'

'I remember being electrified.'

'Electrified?'

'Electric shocks. Just little ones. Baby ones. But all over. I was jerking and shaking all over, like a spastic elastic.'

'Where does she pick up these expressions?' Beth said.

'I blame the teachers,' Gwen said. 'But she's probably right. He must have done *something* to us to keep us supple.'

'And limber.'

'And, as you say, limber. So why not electricity? But there's something else that's odd.'

22

'What?'

'The floor.'

'What about it?'

'Look at it. It's clean.'

'So?'

'I distinctly remember that when he came to milk me, his boots crunched.'

'Crunched?'

'Crunched. They definitely crunched. So there was something on the floor and I think it was dried piss.'

'Whose dried piss?'

'Our dried piss.'

'Anna's too?'

'Anna's too.'

'Well, it's not there now. Look, smooth as a *collaboratrice*'s bottom.'

Beth squatted on her haunches and rubbed a hand on the floor. Then, as she started to rise, she said 'Ow!'

'What is it?'

'A sudden pain. In my arse, for Christ's sake.'

She was reaching behind herself, fingering at her arse, still half-crouched on the floor.

'Let's have a look.'

'A dekko. A dekko at my dell. Ow!'

She had tried to rise and stopped again, face creasing with the same sudden discomfort.

'What does it feel like?'

Gwen walked over to her, bending to touch her buttocks and nudge them up.

'As though there's something stuck up my arse. Just a little way in. It prickles.'

'Put your head down and your arse up.'

She stooped over Beth's white buttocks, feeling a pulse start to beat a little faster in her throat. Smooth hemispheres of cool flesh, milk-white again, long recovered from the cane-strokes Bärengelt had blessed them with. She ran her fingertips down the arse-cleft and felt Beth shiver with pleasure. Fingertips in the arsedell now, lightly touching the arsehole, silkily tickled by Beth's swiff.

23

'How deep?' she asked. Did her voice sound as tight and unnatural to Beth too?

'Just a little way in. Lever me apart and have a look.'

'Okay. Don't worry, I'll be gentle with you.'

She rubbed at the delicate skin of Beth's sphincter, then put both hands into the arsecleft and pulled, widening the gap so that the arsehole smiled fully between it, like a pale pink sun smiling between two white masses of cloud. She slipped her thumb over it and delicately probed.

'Push out,' she ordered.

Beth pushed and she felt the hot skin of the arsehole pulse with effort beneath her thumb, then rise over it as her thumb slid inside.

'Ow. Hurts again.'

Inside Beth's arse now. Tight, moist arse. Dizziness struck her for a moment and she thought she was going to fall forward, crushing Beth beneath her body, her thumb driven hard between Beth's white buttock cheeks, buried deep in Beth's moist warm bottom.

She bit her lip, riding the dizziness down, and delicately rotated her thumb, feeling Beth shiver again.

'Yes. I can feel something. I'll try and hook it out.'

Something was there. Just inside Beth's arsehole, clinging just within the succulent sphincter wall, a strand of something horny. She hooked it carefully up and a little out, slid her thumb free, and peered to look at it. A whitish strand of something organic. Animal or vegetable? Vegetable, she thought.

'It's a bit of plant,' she said.

'Plant?'

'Plant.'

She took hold of it between forefinger and thumb.

'Push again. I'm going to pull it out.'

Beth pushed and she pulled, drawing the strand out of Beth's moist warm arse, through the delicate portal of her sphincter, up and out.

'Ow! Fucking hell, my arsehole is *sore*.'

And it was out. She rose to her feet and stepped back, holding it up.

'It's out.'

Beth rose to her feet and turned, one hand held casually up and across her breasts, trying to hide her stiffened nipples.

'Well?'

She peered at what Gwen was holding up.

'You're right. It's a bit of plant.'

'A big bit of plant.'

'Doesn't look so big now it's out. It felt much bigger up there.'

'I'm not surprised. It's very tight up there.'

They looked at each other. Beth licked her lips. Her hand dropped away.

'I know. But he'll be watching.'

Gwen dropped the strand to the floor.

'Come on, Ansie. Let's be on our way.'

She and Beth began to walk down the aisle of the hothouse, towards the door at the far end. Anna's feet pattered on the floor as she caught up with them.

'Were there curtains across the door before?' Gwen asked.

'Not that I remember.'

'Well, there are now. I'm getting a funny feeling about this.'

'Why?'

'Just wait and see.'

They came to the curtained doorway and stopped, three white girls outlined against the rich purple fabric.

'Come on,' said Gwen. '*Avanti*, girls.'

She stepped forward, one arm going up to open the curtains, her hand sinking into their richness, their softness, floundering for a moment to find the gap, finding it, opening the way for her head and body. The cloth flowed over her skin, almost frictionless, sliding its long lips over her right nipple, but barely awakening a response there. She was through, blinking in the brighter light of the room on the other side, moving forward a little as Beth and Anna followed her.

'This funny feeling of yours,' said Beth from behind her.

'What?'

'I've got it too.'

25

Six

'Because,' said Beth, 'shouldn't this be a corridor?'

'You're right. It should.'

'Thought so.'

The room was bare, with a single curved wall of white marble emphasizing, directly ahead of them, a strip of pink silk hanging beside a recess set into a closed door. The recess was about hip-high, apple-shaped, with double apple curves inside it, and as they walked towards it they saw what it was. The impression of a pair of buttocks. Just in front of the recess was a large white velvet armchair with a small white box resting on the seat; to the right of it, hanging from hooks, was a line of three scrubbing-brushes; to the left of it, hanging from a silver rail, was the strip of pink cloth. Gwen knew before she reached out and twitched it free of the rail that it was silk. A swatch of pink silk.

She reached and twitched. Beth was looking at the white box on the seat of the armchair. The lid popped loose and she lifted it away.

'What's inside it?'

Beth put her hand inside.

'Guess.'

There was a tinkling noise.

'What the hell's that? Crystals?'

'You're warm. Or should I say, you're cold. Catch!'

Something came spinning through the air, small and sparkling, hit Gwen between the breasts, and bounced away to the floor, where it slid until it hit the wall. Gwen rubbed at the spot where it had hit her, the faint impression of cold fading in her skin even as she touched it.

'Is it ice?'

'It's ice,' said Beth. 'Or ice-cubes.'

She held up a handful of them, then dropped them back into the box and casually replaced the lid.

'What do we need ice for?'

'What do we need an armchair for? And what the hell is this?'

She turned away from the armchair and ran her fingers over the surface of the apple-curved recess.

'Buttocks,' she said.

'I can see that.'

'Yes. But whose? Well, I don't think they're mine and I don't think they're yours, Gwendolyn, so I think young Anna has had the honour. Come on, Ansie, let's see.'

She beckoned Anna closer.

'Turn round and see if your arse fits. Come on, it won't hurt you. It's just ground glass. It's not even cold like it would be if it was marble.'

Still uncertain, Anna turned and edged backwards.

'You're not tall enough, Ansie,' said Gwen. 'We'll have to lift you. Make a chair of our arms for you to sit on. Another armchair.'

She dropped the swatch over the back of the armchair and moved to make a chair of her arms with Beth. Anna slipped onto it, and they boosted her to the recess, moving their arms down her thighs so that her bottom protruded.

'Bit higher. Yes.'

Anna's arse slipped into the recess and a smile broke across her face as her arse settled snugly home.

'Bingo,' said Beth. 'Fits like a glove, love.'

Anna gave a sudden small scream and jerked forward, sliding off the chair of their arms, sprawling to the floor. Bright light had filled the recess for a second, spilling round the edge of her arse and followed by a derisive electronic squelch, like a failed answer on a '70s game show.

'What the fuck was that?' Gwen asked.

'*Nuls points*,' said Beth.

'What?'

'Anna's arse wasn't up to scratch.'

'Why not?'

'It's white. It needs to be pink. The exact same pink as that swatch of silk. When it is, the door will open.'

'Yeah. I think you're right.'

'So do I. But if I am, it means tears before bedtime, though not for us.'

'It does.'

The two of them turned and looked at Anna, who was sitting up on the floor. As her eyes met theirs she scrambled to her feet, hands swinging instinctively to shield her buttocks as she backed away from them, shoulders hunched, head lowered.

'Spanking time, Ansie,' said Gwen.

'And it's going to hurt us much more than it will hurt you,' said Beth. 'In fact . . .'

Anna spun and fled, running straight for the curtains, arms up and swinging ahead of her. She ran straight into them and it seemed for a moment that she was clean through them, for they folded open to her racing body and closed behind her, hiding her completely. A moment later, the shuddering cloth told them that she was trapped, frantically searching for the gap that would let her through to the hothouse and a minute or so more of liberty.

'So *that*'s why there are curtains,' said Beth as she and Gwen jogged comfortably after their prey.

'Yep. Chalk one up to that bastard Bärengelt.'

They reached the curtains, peeled them open, entered the soft-walled chamber Anna's struggles had created (the curtains closed behind them too), took hold of her (the shuddering increased), and dragged her out with them, squeaking, swearing, struggling.

'Behave yourself, Ansie,' said Beth. 'Gwen, you tell her.'

'There's no telling her, only showing her. Come on, to the chair.'

They dragged Anna to the chair. Gwen let go of her, lifted the white box off the armchair and set it on the floor, then sat down.

'Oh, this is lovely to sit on. It's going to be a real treat, this.'

She patted the seat, smiling as she watched Beth struggle to master Anna.

'She's an energetic little beast, isn't she?'

Beth had to gasp for breath before she could reply.

'Yes.'

Gwen laughed.

'Come on, let's have her over my lap.'

She slapped her knees and held her hands out. Beth grabbed one of Anna's wildly swinging arms, dragged it behind her back, and forced it up. Anna squeaked.

'Ow! Bitch!'

'Did you hear that, Gwen?'

'Yes. Such unexpected crudeness in one so young and pretty. She looks as though butter wouldn't melt in her mouth and yet just listen to her language.'

'I don't know – ah, stop that, you little beast! – about her mouth, but – no, *this* way – but I'd like to test butter in some other orifices.'

'So would I,' Gwen said. 'But for the time being' – Beth released her hold unexpectedly and, as Anna flailed, off-balance for a moment, gave her a sharp, scientific shove that propelled her neatly onto Gwen's lap – 'let's stick to spanking, eh? Come on, be a good girl. Lend a hand, Beth, before she gets loose again.'

Panting, Beth helped her settle Anna into place on her lap.

'That's right. Kneel on her feet while I hold her neck. Good. Now, we're nearly ready to begin. Where's that swatch?'

'Over the back of the chair. No, the other side.'

Gwen twisted, made a lunge for the swatch with her free hand, missed, tried again, and succeeded. She settled the swatch on the left curve of Anna's bare, presented buttocks.

'What do you think, Bethy? Does it match?'

'Hmmm. It's pink and Anna's bottom is, well, white. So no, in my considered judgment they don't match.'

'I have to agree. What course of action do you recommend?'

'To make them match, you mean?'

'Yes.'

'Well, is there nothing you can do to the swatch? To make it less pink?'

'There *might* be, but do you think it could be made *entirely* non-pink. Because it wouldn't match otherwise, would it?'

'No, unfortunately it wouldn't. Well, if the swatch can't be made less pink, what *is* there we can do?'

'I was thinking the same myself. What?'

'I'm sure the answer's staring us in the face, if only we could see it.'

The draped swatch bounced as Anna wriggled fiercely.

'Get on with it, you bitches,' her muffled voice said.

Gwen clicked her tongue with disappointment.

'Did you hear that, Beth?'

'I did, Gwen.'

'We can't have that while we are considering this colour problem, intractable as it might seem. Fortunately, I have the solution ready to hand.'

She picked up the swatch, seized Anna by the scruff of the neck, and forced her head backwards and up.

'This will keep her quiet while we cogitate. Just be careful not to chew it, won't you, Ansie, or you might make the pink even darker.'

She pinched Anna's nose shut and, as her small mouth opened, expertly looped the swatch into place across it and tied it behind Anna's blonde-stubbled head.

'Now keep quiet and remember, don't chew. I will want it again, shortly.'

She forced Anna's head back down.

'Where were we, Beth?'

'The colour problem. We'd just decided that we couldn't modify the swatch in the direction of Anna's bottom.'

'Oh, yes, I remember. But when you put it like that, a thought occurs to me. I mean . . . no, it's absurd.'

'What?'

'No, honestly, it's too silly for words.'

'I won't laugh. Promise. Guide's honour.'

'You were never a Guide.'

'I always liked the uniform. Go on, tell me. It might give me a good idea.'

'Well, okay. It's like this. If we can't modify the *swatch* in the direction of Anna's bottom, then why . . . no, really, it's just too silly.'

'Tell me. Please. I won't laugh. Promise. Sister's honour. I *am* your sister, remember.'

'Promise?'

'Promise.'

'Cross your arse and hope to cry?'

'Cross my arse and hope to cry.'

'Cross it, then.'

Beth crossed her arse.

'Very well, then. But if I see the slightest *suggestion* of a snicker, even . . .'

'You won't.'

'Okay. I hope not. Well, it's like this. If we can't modify the swatch, why not modify her bottom? On the Mountain-and-Mohammed principle. Do you see?'

'What do you mean?'

'Well, if we can't make the swatch less pink, perhaps we could make her bottom less white.'

'Less white?'

'Yes. Or pinker. It amounts to the same thing.'

'Are you sure?'

'Yes. Almost. I mean, it's worth considering, isn't it?'

'Making her bottom less pink?'

'No, pinker. *More* pink. Or less white. It amounts to the same thing. Don't you see?'

'A moment ago, no, I didn't, but now, I'm starting to. If the Mountain won't come to Mohammed, Mohammed will have to go to the Mountain. If we can't make the swatch less pink, we'll have to make her bottom less white. Or pinker.'

'Exactly. You've got it.'

'Good. But haven't you overlooked the fatal flaw?'

31

'What?'

'It's all very well *talking* about making her bottom less white – or pinker, if you prefer – but precisely *how* are you going to do it?'

Gwen smiled and held up her hand.

'Simple. With this.'

'What? Your *hand*?'

'Yes.'

'*Just* your hand?'

'Yes.'

Beth was silent for a moment.

'Well, either it's crazy or it has the simplicity of true genius. Perhaps both. I can't see it working, myself.'

'To be honest, neither can I, entirely. But there's no harm in trying, is there?'

'I suppose not.'

'Very well then, let us proceed. Have you got her feet firmly restrained?'

'Yes. Everything's ready. It's up to you now.'

'Don't make me more nervous than I am already. Give me a moment to compose myself.'

She breathed in deeply, breathed out, closed her eyes, turned her head away, and poised her hand over the white bottom.

'Say when.'

'When.'

Thwak.

Gwen kept her eyes closed and head turned away.

'I can't bear to look. Did it work?'

Beth peered, putting her head close to the pink hand-mark glowing on Anna's pearly buttock cheek.

'Ye-es.'

'Yes?'

'Yes. It worked. You can look.'

Gwen opened her eyes and slowly turned her head.

'Oh, you're right! It did. It worked. Shall I do it again?'

'If you want to risk it.'

'Well, why not? There's nothing to lose, is there? I'll try the other cheek this time. Do you think it will work again?'

'I hope so. Try it and see.'

'Okay. Say when.'

'When.'

Thwak.

They looked.

'Yes!' said Gwen. 'It's worked again.'

'It has. I admit I had my doubts.'

'Me too,' Gwen said, 'but it looks as though you've hit on the solution. No pun intended. Another one?'

'Say when.'

'When.'

Thwak.

'Yep. We've found it. Mohammed *has* gone to the Mountain. If you can't make the swatch less pink, make the bottom less white. Again?'

'Yes. When.'

Thwak.

Gwen rubbed the spanked bottom lingeringly.

'Yes. She's heating nicely. But do you think the colour is just a touch uneven? Maybe if I . . .'

Thwak. Thwak. Thwak.

'What do you think now?'

Beth peered.

'Better, but you can still see finger-marks. We need an even glow. A blush.'

'You're right. And I think I know the solution. Get me one of those scrubbing brushes, will you?'

'Wh . . . oh, yeah, those ones.'

Beth stood up, walked around the armchair and reached up and took down one of the three brushes. She examined it, bouncing it a little on her palm, put it back, took down another, examined it, bounced it lightly on her palm, put it back, took down and examined the third. She put it back and took down the one she had examined first.

'This one, I think,' she said.

She returned to the chair, handed Gwen the brush, and knelt again on Anna's feet.

'Thank you.'

Gwen rubbed the brush on her palm.

'Yes, I think you're right. Harsh but not too harsh. We don't want to bring her up in lumps, just irrigate her skin healthily with blood, for that all-over pink glow of rude girlish health. Like this.'

She held the brush on Anna's left buttock and began, gently at first, to scrub it, sliding the brush up and down, left and right, circling over the spanked skin, reversing the circles, gradually scrubbing harder, more cruelly. Anna jerked and squeaked.

'Shut up, you little beast. You don't think I'm enjoying this, do you? Well, I *am*, but you needn't think that's *why* I'm doing it. How else are we going to get through that door, eh?'

She began on the right cheek, scrubbing hard, sliding the brush into the arse-cleft, guiding its bristles artlessly into the dell of Anna's arsehole, and tutting as Anna jerked and squeaked again.

'Shut up, won't you? You don't think I did that deliberately, do you?'

She slid the brush back, twirled it over Anna's arsehole, slid it away, scrubbed, and lifted it clear.

'Well, what do you think, Beth? A more even glow?'

Beth peered, pursed her lips, considered.

'Ye-es. I *think* so. But were you perhaps a little harsh? A little too energetic? Because I'm not sure if it's not a little *too* pink now. Almost red, you know.'

'Hmmm. I'm not sure if you aren't right. Perhaps I did get a *little* carried away. Let's have another compare and see how we're doing.'

She rested the brush on an arm of the chair and began to untie the swatch from Anna's mouth.

'It's just that, you know, she's such a little beast and she *deserves* to be treated roughly. Even if I didn't enjoy it – and who could help enjoying it? – I'm sure I'd be just as energetic out of sheer moral conviction. You might even call it *rough*. But can you blame me?'

The knot loosened and came free and she lifted the swatch to lay it against Anna's spanked-and-scrubbed bottom.

'Oh, dear, you're right, Beth. I *did* get carried away. Her bottom's definitely on the reddish side of that pink. What shall we do?'

'Try putting her bottom in the recess anyway. Maybe we don't have to have an *exact* match. I know it's not exactly pink, but it's not exactly red either. More pink *than* red, if you know what I mean.'

'Not really, but I hope you're right. Well, let's do it then. Up you get, Ansie.'

Beth hauled Anna off her lap, Gwen stood up, and the two of them pulled Anna over to the recess.

'Don't be difficult. It might all be over in a moment. Come on, hop on.'

They made a chair of their arms again and Anna slid reluctantly onto it, frowning, her eyes slits of sulkiness and rebellion, moist and dark with incipient tears.

'And *up* she goes!'

They boosted her to the recess, manoeuvring her bottom until it reached the lip of the recess and slid inside.

'Wriggle, Ansie,' said Beth. 'Make a snug fit.'

Anna wriggled and her bottom slid snugly home. The light flashed again, reddened now around the edges of her arse, but the hope that had risen in them was crushed a moment later by the same derisive electronic squelch.

'Oh, dear,' Gwen said. 'As we thought. Too red. Back to the drawing-board.'

Anna suddenly threw herself off the chair of their arms, landing on the floor already running but, casually stretching out her foot, Beth tripped Anna and sent her sprawling. They trotted to her and helped her up, keeping a firm grip.

'You should know by now, Ansie,' Gwen said. 'You won't get away. Come on, back to the armchair.'

They pulled her back to the armchair. Gwen sat down and Beth forced her onto Gwen's lap, then knelt on her feet.

'Back to square one,' said Gwen. She palmed Anna's buttocks, rubbed them, squeezed them together, wobbled them, then released them.

'But look, that's a lovely even glow now. Just too red. What do you suggest? To get the red down, I mean?'

35

Beth shrugged.

'I'm not sure. We could just wait, I suppose. Wait for them to cool down, I mean.'

'Hmmm. We could, but when you say "cool", it reminds me of something.'

'What?'

'I'm not sure. It's on the tip of my tongue.'

'When I say "cool"?'

'Yes.'

'What about when I say "warm"?'

'No, that's colder. Or do I mean warmer?'

'What about "cold"?'

'Oh, that's definitely warmer. Or colder. Yes, colder. That's the word I want.'

'But not *the* word?'

'No. That's still on the tip of my tongue.'

'When I say "cool" or "cold"?'

'Yes.'

'Then how about "frigid"? "Freezing"? "Icy", maybe?'

'That's the one!'

' "Freezing?" '

'No, the other one.'

' "Frigid"?'

'No, the *other* other one.'

'Oh, "icy"?'

'Yes. "Icy".'

'That's the word?'

'No, but it's *nearly* the word. I've remembered it now.'

'Then it must be . . . icicle.'

'No, it isn't. I'm disappointed in you, Beth.'

'Ice-man?'

'No.'

'Ice-lolly?'

'No.'

'Ice-berg?'

'No. Now you're being silly. You know perfectly well what it is.'

'Not . . .?'

'Yes. That's the one.'

'But we've got some of those.'

'I know.'

'Just here. Beside the chair.'

'I know, I know, I *know*. So get them for me, will you? Her bottom will fade of its own accord if we don't hurry.'

The lid popped open again as Beth removed it.

'One box of ice-cubes. If madam would like to make her selection . . .? The shiny ones are cold and the cold ones are, well, shiny.'

'And the triangular ones are nougat?'

'There are no triangular ones, madam.'

'Oh, very well then. I'll have a shiny one.'

'An excellent choice, madam, if I may say so. Perfectly suited to what you have in mind. Look how smoothly it glides!'

Anna gave a muffled squeak. Gwen was rubbing the ice-cube over her right buttock, up and down in unhurried, even strokes. She held it up.

'Look. The heat's begun to melt it already.'

'If Madame will allow me to advise . . .?'

'But of course.'

'Put it up her bottom and choose another one, madam.'

'Very well. But will it go up, d'you think?'

'Yes, madam. It's self-lubricating. It will slip in sweet as the proverbial nut.'

Anna squeaked again.

'Oh! You're right!'

She had slipped the half-melted cube into Anna's arsedell, rubbed it over her arsehole for a moment, then pushed gently and felt it slide smoothly inside and drop away from her assisting finger.

'Now choose another, madam.'

'Certainly. Another shiny one, I think.'

'Then another excellent choice, madam.'

The cubes chinked as she picked another from the box and began to rub it over Anna's reddened bottom. Up and down in smooth unhurried strokes, completing the right buttock.

'Look, it's happened again. Shall I . . .?'

'Yes, madam. As before.'

She slipped the half-melted cube into Anna's arsedell and pushed.

'Ups-a-daisy . . . Yes, it was even easier than before. But won't it make her inside bottom very cold?'

'Yes, madam. Another one? They will melt inside her and fill her bottom with freezing water. It will be most unpleasant for the little beast.'

'Thank you. Another shiny one, I think. And left buttock this time. Most unpleasant, you say? For the little beast?'

'Yes, madam.'

She started on Anna's reddened left buttock, rubbing the ice-cube up and down in smooth, unhurried strokes.

'And do you honestly think it *should* be most unpleasant for the little beast?'

'Yes, madam. I honestly do.'

'Well, perhaps you're right. Do you think it's working now?'

'I know I'm right, madam. Hard to say as yet, madam. After five or six more, then we'll know.'

'Right-oh. Look, she's melted another. I can barely hold on to it. But I've just enough grip to send it . . . yes, that's gone up too. Three of them now, all milling round in her little bottom.'

'Yes, madam. Milling and melting, madam.'

'It must be awfully cold up there now.'

'It must, madam.'

'Then . . . d'you think I could feel?'

'Feel, madam?'

'Yes, feel. With my finger. Just to test the temperature, you know.'

'Oh, but certainly, madam. She's yours to do with as you will, you know. Her bottom's no longer her own.'

'Index-finger, d'you think?'

'An excellent choice, madam.'

'Or ring-finger?'

'Another excellent choice, madam.'

'Or both?'

'Perhaps, madam. But that might be a little over-ambitious, at this stage.'

'I see what you mean. Then index-finger it is. I'll just probe a teensy . . . weensy . . . Oh, it goes in ever so easily. And yes, it's very cold in there. Freezing, almost. You don't think her bottom will get frost-bite, do you?'

'No, madam. But why should we care if it does?'

'You're right, as ever. Why should we care indeed? The little beast deserves everything she gets – and more.'

She withdrew her index-finger, glistening with water, and wiped it on Anna's left buttock.

'The little beast *can* get frost-bite for all I care. It might teach her some respect for her elders and betters. Now, another one. Let's see, it has to be a shiny one again, doesn't it?'

'Yes, madam. You'll find the shiny ones are always best for this kind of operation.'

Gwen chose and rubbed; inserted the half-melted cube into Anna's anus; chose another and rubbed; inserted the half-melted cube into Anna's anus.

'D'you think it's working?'

'Yes, madam. I think it definitely is. One more should do the trick.'

'One more it is then. Yet another shiny one, I think.'

'Excellent choice as ever, madam.'

She rubbed; inserted the half-melted cube into Anna's anus; clicked her tongue with satisfaction; and said: 'There. What do you think? An all-over glow? Pink and crisp and even?'

'Pink and even, certainly, madam. As for crisp, I couldn't say.'

'Pink and even is enough. Where's that swatch?'

'There, madam.'

'Right . . . Well, what do you think?'

'A very close match, madam.'

'Close enough?'

'Could well be, madam.'

'Then let's get her tested. No sense in delaying.'

'Very well, madam. On your feet, you. Madame wants you tested, and you'd better test well or you'll have me to answer to.'

Anna was slow getting off Gwen's lap and Beth nipped her hard, fingers closing over a generous pinch of ice-cooled buttock.

'Ow!'

'Not *there*, Beth, dear,' Gwen said, rising from the armchair. 'You'll leave a mark.'

'Oh, no, madam. Not if I do it right. See?'

Gwen peered.

'Very well. But let's hope she won't need any more encouragement. Come on, you little beast.'

They escorted her to the recess, turned her back to it, formed a chair of their arms, and boosted her into the air.

'Slide, Ansie. Bottom in, like a good girl.'

Anna slid, scowling, fitting her bottom into the recess.

'And snuggle. Snuggle it in. Nice tight fit for the nice light. And . . .'

The light flashed, their hearts leapt, and stayed aloft as there came a congratulatory electronic belch.

'Done it! Off you get, Ansie. The door's opening.'

Anna slid off their arm-chair, one hand already probing resentfully at her anus.

'My arse is freezing, you bitches. It feels like there's *gallons* of icy water up there.'

'It was in a good cause, Ansie. Don't be a whinger. Come on.'

The door had slid open, carrying the arse-recess with it, and the three of them stepped through into the room that waited for them on the other side. Anna gasped with dismay and turned to run, but Beth's strong fingers were already sinking into her shoulder and the door was sliding closed again, blocking her escape.

'If we have to do it again, Ansie, we have to do it again.'

But Anna had relaxed, a smile breaking on her face. The armchair was red, and even from here she could see that the buttock-shaped recess in the door wasn't the shape of *her* buttocks. She laughed.

Seven

Beth's fingers tightened viciously for a moment on her shoulder, as though to punish her for her laughter, then loosened and fell away.

'Shit.'

They walked towards the red velvet armchair, the red box on its seat, the hanging swatch of pink – pinker – silk, the three brushes, and the bottom-shaped recess. Gwen glanced between Beth's bottom and the recess, eyes narrowing.

'I'm afraid it's your turn, Beth. No pain, no gain.'

'Let's make sure that I absolutely have to. Here, help me up.'

She turned her back to the recess and tried to lift her bottom into it. Gwen and Anna hoisted her up, taking hold of her thighs, lifting her, helping her slide her bottom into the recess.

'Snuggle,' said Gwen.

She snuggled. It was her recess, alright. Shaped to her specifications. To her dimensions. The light flashed and she heard the derisive electronic squelch. She slid out of the recess.

'Okay. I'm too white. Pink me up and let's get out of here. But you already know what we'll find beyond the door, don't you, Gwensie? No pain, no gain.'

Gwen frowned briefly.

'Yes. The joke's on us, not Anna. For the time being. But it's going to be on Bärengelt, in the end. I fucking well swear it. Come on, get on my lap.'

She sat on the armchair, arms beckoning. Beth's mouth quirked and she stooped to settle herself across Gwen's lap.

'Be gentle with me.'

'As gentle as I can be. But you're a big girl now, and you know that big girls have responsibilities as well as privileges.

'A *very* big girl,' she added, her voice sinking to a throaty murmur as she stroked the bottom that Beth had presented to her. She swallowed.

'But perfectly proportioned. You have a beautiful bum, Beth. I'm going to enjoy this a lot. Say when.'

'When.'

Thwak.

'Say when.'

'Oh, just get on with it. Spank me, don't tease me.'

'Very well. Brace yourself.'

Thwak. Thwak. Thwak.

Gwen's hand rose and fell in a relaxed but forceful rhythm, moving steadily across Beth's white, firm, well-fleshed cheeks, leaving them reddened in its wake. Anna watched, eyes shining, shifting restlessly from foot to foot, one hand twitching as though it longed to lift and finger her stiffening nipples.

Panting a little, Gwen stopped.

'Well, Anna's enjoying it, little beast that she is. Stop standing there drooling from both mouths and get me a brush. Medium-bristled, I think. And get me that swatch too.'

Anna blinked and trotted off to obey. Brush. Swatch. She handed them to Gwen.

'Ta very muchly. Your verdict, Ansie?'

She laid the swatch on Beth's left buttock. Anna looked. Her throat noded and smoothed. She started to say something and had to cough and start again.

'T– Too red. And too uneven.'

Gwen tutted.

'I'm afraid she's right, Beth. We'll have to brush you up, for consistency, then cool you down, for colour.'

She laid the swatch to one side and picked up the brush. Bounced it on her palm. Rubbed it.

'Here goes. Brace yourself, Bethy.'

She started to scrub, gently at first, gradually harder, frowning a little with concentration, guiding the brush up and down, left and right, buffing the buttocks to an even red glow. Beth shifted, her buttocks tightening and relaxing.

'Does it hurt?'

'No.'

'I see. Do you want Anna's services? There, all done, I hope.'

She put the brush aside.

'Uh, yes.'

'Before the cubes or after?'

Beth lifted herself up and back, propping one elbow on the edge of the seat so that she could look back at her buttocks.

'Before,' she said, slipping her elbow off the seat and relaxing back to her former position. 'I don't see why I need the cubes anyway. Anna can lick my arse instead.'

'But her tongue will be hot too.'

'Not if she's had five or six ice-cubes on it for a few minutes beforehand.'

'An excellent idea. Anna, come here.'

Anna sighed.

'Come on. No slacking. Give me the ice-box. Thank you. Now, kneel in front of us. Open your mouth. Wide.'

The lid of the box came off with a pop. Gwen put her hand inside it and stirred the ice-cubes.

'Such an attractive sound. So cold, so silvery. Wider!'

She picked up a single cube, popped it into Anna's open, unwilling mouth, then chose another, and another, and another.

'Good girl,' she said. 'Just one more ... Okay, now mouth closed tight. Tight. Good. If I hear a single crunch you'll regret it, young lady. Understood?'

Anna nodded.

'She looks so sweet, Bethy. As though butter wouldn't melt in her mouth.'

'It wouldn't, I hope. In a few minutes' time.'

'Figuratively speaking. I do like her when she's being obedient. Come here, Anna. While we're waiting you might as well have a little treat. Closer.'

Anna shuffled closer.

'Chest out. Come on, big breath and chest out.'

Breath whistled through Anna's nostrils and she pushed her chest forward, carrying her small, perfect breasts within comfortable reach. Her eyes narrowed uneasily.

'Don't worry, dear. A little treat, I said, and a little treat it will be.'

The box of ice-cubes tinkled as Gwen chose another cube and reached forward with it.

'There. Is that nice?'

She was rubbing it over Anna's left nipple. Anna wriggled.

'Is it nice?'

Anna started to shake her head, then stopped, and reluctantly nodded.

'Good. And is this nice?'

She swapped nipples, rubbing the diminished cube on the right, leaving the left peaked and glistening.

'Pinch it, Ansie. Pleasure yourself, dear. Squeeze and tickle it. I give you permission. Do it to both of them.'

She lifted the cube from Anna's right nipple.

'Come on, like this.'

She reached forward and took hold of Anna's left nipple, gently rolling it between her fingers, tugging at it, tweaking it.

'Do you like that?'

Anna nodded reluctantly again and swallowed. Her mouth was filling with icy water now. Icy water from the melting cubes in her small, warm mouth. Only not so warm now. Cooling. Chilling. Gwen reached out with her other hand and began to squeeze and tickle Anna's right nipple.

'Look into my eyes, Ansie. Come on. Do you like this? You like it, don't you?'

Anna swallowed again and nodded, feeling her eyes prickle with tears. Icy water sliding down her throat as her

44

nipples were tugged and teased by her big sister. She didn't want to meet the dominant brown eyes fixed on hers, didn't want to gaze into them, but she couldn't help it. Gwen's brown eyes. Shining with satisfaction as they drank in the reluctant pleasure on her face. Nipples teased and tickled by strong, dominant fingers. Mouth icy, arsehole still cold and moist, but bottom warm with the spanking and scrubbing it had received and nipples stiff and delicious, teased by expert fingers.

'How is your pussy, Ansie? Warm? Oozing? Touch it if you like. I won't stop you. I want you to touch it. To play with yourself. Come on, do it. Be a good girl.'

Brown eyes fixed on hers. Strong fingers on her nipples. And Gwen's diagnosis was correct. Her pussy was warm. Oozing. Lips stickily parting and smiling. Clitoris alight and glowing. Like a little tower, a little *pharos*. A little *pharos* with a brazier of aromatic wood glowing atop it. Scenting the winds.

'Touch it. Go on. Touch your pussy. Stroke it. Pleasure yourself, Ansie. You want to come, don't you? Well, come. I want you to come. You know I want you to come. Beth wants you to come too. Both of us do. Before you lick Beth's bottom.'

Her mouth was numb with cold now, her arsehole still cold and moist, but her nipples were stiff with pleasure and her pussy was leaking freely. Gwen wanted her to come. Wanted her to touch her pussy. Rub and stroke it. Delicately touch and tease her clitoris. Wank herself. Wank herself until she came.

She swallowed, feeling icy water sliding down her throat, and began to move a hand, ready to drop it between her thighs, to obey Gwen's urgent voice. But as she moved the brown eyes fixed on hers, widened and flashed with triumph, shining above the cruel smile that lit up Gwen's face.

'No, Ansie.'

The fingers pleasuring her nipples suddenly became harsh, pinching and twisting.

'I was only kidding. You must know that. You are here to serve and suffer. For pain, not for pleasure.'

With a final cruel twist and tweak the fingers left her nipples. Her pussy was still glowing, still oozing, but a lump of *asphaltum* had been tossed into the brazier of the little *pharos* standing above it and the winds were carrying an ugly scent now.

'Mouth open,' Gwen ordered. Her voice was hard again, sour in Anna's ears after the sugared entreaties of a few moments earlier. *Pleasure yourself, Ansie. Touch your pussy.* She opened her mouth, feeling a thread of the icy water that still filled it escape over her lips and slide down her chin, dripping onto her left breast, sharp and chilling.

'Oh, Beth, you should see. Her mouth was red before and now it's a beautiful pale pink. I think it's nicely chilled for you. A nice cold tongue to cool your arse. But let's see. Ansie, lick my hand.'

She held her hand forward, wrist cocked as though for a kiss. Anna licked it, her tongue numb, not reporting what it touched.

'Yes. Her tongue's freezing. Swallow what's in your mouth, Ansie, and you can get to work. Quick, girl.'

Anna swallowed the icy dregs in her mouth and shuffled on her knees to Beth's arse.

'Budge, Bethy,' Gwen said. 'Swing your bottom over to meet her.'

The wide double curve of Beth's arse swung to her, heat radiating palpably from its reddened surface. Spanked and scrubbed.

'Lick, girl. Kiss and lick.'

She put her head forward and kissed it. Kissed the warm, sensitive flesh. Began to lick it. She felt a ripple run through it, a shudder of pleasure.

'It's lovely, Gwen. She can do it to you, too, when we get through the door.'

'We don't know whether she'll have to.'

'She will. It's waiting for you, honey. But it will be worth it. This cold little tongue. It's like chilled velvet. Delicious.'

The warm flesh shivered under Anna's tongue again. She had almost finished the left cheek, licking, kissing, sucking, and she could feel sensation returning to her tongue.

There, just a final sweep left and right in the gluteal crease and she had finished. Right cheek now.

'Hold it.'

Gwen's voice. She stopped.

'Lift your head. Lick again.'

She lifted her head. Gwen was holding her hand out again, wrist cocked. She put her head forward and licked the skin. She could feel it now, smooth and warm beneath her tongue.

'No good, Ansie. You've warmed up. Back as you were, mouth open, and we'll get you filled again. Six ice-cubes oughta be just right. Come on.'

She shuffled back to where she had been and opened her mouth.

'Good girl.'

The ice-box tinkled.

'One.'

Another cold cube on her tongue.

'Two.'

And another.

'Three.'

Another.

'Four.'

Another.

'Mouth wider. Wider. Good girl. Five.'

Jaw aching with the strain of holding her mouth open wide. For the ice-cubes.

'And six! Good girl. Now, mouth closed. Tight closed.'

She closed her mouth on the by-now familiar hardness. Smooth, cold shapes shifting in her mouth, beginning to melt in the warmth, but more slowly this time, because her mouth was still cold. Just not cold enough for Gwen. Not cold enough for licking Beth's bottom.

'She looks so sweet again, Beth. Mouth closed obediently on the ice-cubes. I love her like this. Mute, obedient and suffering.'

Beth wriggled on Gwen's lap.

'So do I. But it's not me getting all the fun of it, is it?'

'It will be. In the next room. If I have to be spanked there.'

47

'You will be.'

'How can you be so sure?'

Anna swallowed the first trickle of ice-melt. Her tongue was numb again, cold enough to complete Beth's right cheek, but she would have to suffer while the cubes melted fully.

'It's the way Bärengelt's mind works.'

'Oh, yeah? Then why didn't you know it would be *your* turn in this room?'

'Okay, I didn't know that in advance, but once it was established, the next step is obvious, isn't it?'

'You're tempting fate.'

'Not my fate, Gwensie.'

'Shut up. All this trouble I'm going to for your sake. Supervising Anna's tongue-chilling. It's not as easy as I make it sound, you know.'

'You were saying a minute ago you liked it. And loved her this way. Mute, obedient and suffering. Mouth full of ice.'

'Arse full of ice too. Though it must have melted by now.'

'Maybe we should go for the hat-trick.'

'What do you mean?'

'Arse one, mouth two, cunt three.'

'Later. Let's not be greedy. Mouth, Ansie. Open for your big sister.'

Anna opened her mouth again but ice rattled as she did so.

'Hmmm. It's slower to melt this time, but I reckon her tongue is nicely chilled. Swallow the cubes, Ansie, and let's see.'

Anna shook her head.

'Do as you're told. At once.'

Gwen's eyes narrowed.

'Okay, then spit them out. Into my hand. Come on.'

She moved her head forward and spat the cubes out onto Gwen's waiting hand. Though dribbled them out was more like it. Her whole mouth was numb, drained of sensation and strength.

'Now turn round. Put your arse in the air and hold your cheeks apart. If you won't swallow them at that end, you can swallow them at the other.'

Anna scowled.

'Do it. You knew I wasn't going to let you off, so why complain?'

She turned on her knees and bent forward, raising her arse, putting her hands back, taking hold of her cheeks, tugging them apart. Gwen's fingers were on her arsehole almost at once, dripping icy water, pressing a half-melted ice-cube at her sphincter.

'One.'

Only it wasn't so bad this time. Her arse was already cold and moist and the icy sting of the cube entering her was much less. Almost not there.

'Two.'

And the cubes were smaller. Half-melted from their time in her mouth.

'Three.'

Smaller and slicker. Sliding up her bum easily, settling between walls already numbed by the cubes that had sat there before them.

'Four. This is fun, too, Bethy. Putting ice-cubes up the little beast's arse. Five.'

'I'll be trying it myself soon enough.'

'I know. There, six. But that fifth one was so small I've decided it didn't count. So . . .' – Anna heard the ice-box tinkle – 'here's a full, fresh one for you.'

The fingers returned to her arsehole, carrying a fresh ice-cube. Much larger, much colder. Her sphincter winced away from it and Gwen had to push hard, sliding it in half an inch, an inch, and it was suddenly sliding smoothly in, fully up her, sinking beyond her sphincter. Gwen's fingers were trapped for a moment as her sphincter irised shut. She pulled her fingers free.

'There, that's cooled your disobedient little arse for you. Now get licking.'

49

Eight

Beth wriggled her arse home into the recess, sat snug for a moment, and grinned triumphantly as the flash of light was followed by the same congratulatory electronic belch that had greeted Anna's pink and even arse. She slipped out of the recess, landing on the floor and turning in the same movement to watch the door slide open.

'After you, Gwenchen,' she said, bowing a little and raising her arm to point into the third room.

'Less cheek, Bethy,' Gwen said. 'This will teach you.'

Beth leapt forward in the same instant, it seemed, as the meaty *thwak* of Gwen's hand landed on her pink left buttock. She stood in the doorway glaring back indignantly, rubbing at the glowing mark, red and vivid against the pink of the spanked, scrubbed and chill-licked flesh.

Gwen grinned fiercely at her.

'No need for evenness now, eh, Bethy? Come on, get through.'

Beth stuck out her tongue, turned, and walked through the door. Gwen followed her, still grinning.

'Bitch,' Beth told her as she came in.

'True. And isn't it fun? Now, what have we here?'

'Your comeuppance.'

'Maybe.'

The third room was furnished in the same way as the first and second: arse-shaped recess in a sealed door; velvet armchair with a box on its seat; swatch of hanging pink silk; three brushes. But there were hand-holds beside this recess, one on either side, and where the armchair and box in the first room had been white and in the second red, in this, the third room, they were black. Black velvet armchair and black box on its smooth, arse-caressing seat. And the hanging swatch was dark pink. Almost red.

As Anna followed the two of them into the room Gwen moved, strolling over to inspect what awaited her. She ran her fingers over the double apple-curve of the arse-recess; fingered the bristles of the brushes; picked up the box and opened it, *pop*. She reached inside it and they heard ice tinkle. She put the lid back on the box, put the box on an arm of the chair, and turned to face them.

'Looks like it's my turn, girls. Come on, let's get on with it. Who's going to do the spanking?'

'Me,' Beth said.

'Okay. How do you want me?'

'On my lap.'

'While you're on the armchair?'

'Yep. Got it in one.'

'I've had enough practice, dear.'

'And I've had none. I want some. Come on.'

Beth walked forward, turned, and sat down on the armchair.

'Nice,' she said. She wriggled. 'Nice and soothing. Come on, then. On my lap and present your arse for spanking.'

'Don't be gentle with me, will you?'

'No. Certainly not. We want a much richer pink this time. I'll have to lay it on hard. Won't I, Ansie?'

Anna nodded.

'Well, say it then.'

Gwen settled herself over Beth's lap.

'Bit higher. Yes, good. Lift bum. Bit more. Good. Come on, Ansie, say it. We need a much richer pink this time, don't we?'

'Yes.'

'Good. I'm glad you agree. Are you ready, Gwenchen?'

'Yes.'

'Say when, Ansie.'

Gwen snorted and half-lifted off Beth's lap.

51

'You keep your mouth shut, Anna. *I'll* say when. Right?'

She settled herself back. Beth raised her eyebrows at Anna and shrugged in mock disbelief.

'This is a spanking, Gwen. *Your* spanking. A spanking delivered to *you*. So *you're* not the one giving the orders. Are you?'

'If I want to be, I am.'

'Shut up.'

'No.'

'Then I'll shut you up.'

Thwak. The first handmark stood out clearly on Gwen's milky cheek, but Gwen wasn't taking it lying down. Beth struggled to keep her in place.

'Oh, no you don't, you bitch. You bloody stay where you are and take . . . ow! Lie down or I'll . . .'

Thwak. Second handmark on Gwen's milky cheek, glowing red and hot. Anna stood and watched her two elder sisters wrestle and giggle on the armchair, white bodies standing out clearly against its black velvet, cropped heads gleaming red and raven. Her cunt rippled with pleasure. With the thought of domination.

Thwak. Beth forced Gwen down for a moment and delivered a third spank, arm stiff, wrist locked. Gwen squealed.

'Ow! You bitch, that was too hard. We want pink, not fucking crimson.'

'Then keep quiet and lie back down, so I can give this the attention it deserves. Only *I'm* calling the shots, not you. Lie down!'

'Over my dead body!'

'No, over your spanked backside. Lie down!'

Thwak. A fourth spank, fourth handmark glowing on Gwen's milky buttocks. Anna felt her stomach roll slowly, then settle. How she longed to be delivering the spanks herself! To be sitting there on the black armchair with Gwen stretched defenceless and submissive on her lap, pleading deliciously for the spanking to stop, then, as her pussy caught fire from the burn in her buttocks, pleading even more deliciously for it to continue.

Beth looked up, her face fierce with will and determination, and Anna jumped guiltily.

'Anna, c'mere, quick. Help me.'

Gwen stopped struggling on Beth's lap for a moment and turned her head to frown at her too.

'No, stay where you are, you little beast, or you'll regret it.'

Beth grabbed her neck and forced her back down, right hand lifting to deliver another spank.

'No, Anna. Don't listen to her. C'mere now or you *will* regret it.'

Thwak. Anna stood uncertain, pussy oozing, longing to join Beth in dominating Gwen, fearful of the consequences.

'C'mere, now! Lie down, you bitch!'

Thwak. Anna's uncertainty broke to the crisp spurt of sound – like a hymen to the thrust of a firm cock – and she ran forward to help Beth, small hands gripping Gwen's firm white flesh, sliding a little on the sheen of sweat that spiced it.

'Good girl,' Beth said.

'*Bad* girl,' Gwen said.

Anna bit her lip. What was best? To obey Beth and disobey Gwen? To obey Gwen and disobey Beth? Neither: what was best was to ignore the future and live for the moment, to live for the pleasure of assisting in Gwen's domination, in the subduing of her struggles so that she lay unwillingly helpless on Beth's lap, buttocks bared and defenceless to Beth's strong right hand.

'Finally we can begin in earnest,' Beth said. She stroked Gwen's buttocks. 'Lie still and suffer, you bitch.'

And the spanking began again, fierce and unrelenting, raining on Gwen's indignant buttocks with a strong, regular rhythm, humbling their pride, reddening and heating them, shuddering juicily in Gwen's body so that Anna's small hands, clutched and straining to help hold Gwen down, caught and reported its weight and its power and Anna's pussy sang with pleasure. Gwen was being spanked: and she was assisting at the ceremony; Gwen's proud arse being humbled: and she was complicit in the humiliation; Gwen's white firm flesh was reddening and glowing under the hand of an oppressor: and she was an ally of that hand.

Her cunt almost bubbled with delight and she longed to have a hand free to lower to it, to stir and stroke her tumid cunt-lips, to tickle and tease her turgid clitoris, to worry and wank herself so that she could groan in rhythm with Beth's pants and Gwen's gasps.

But the spanking had stopped.

'Get me a brush, Anna,' Beth ordered her. 'The stiffest-bristled one you can find. Gwen's bum is nicely reddened, but it isn't nicely even. We want it even. An all-over glow.'

Anna let go of Gwen, stood up, and obeyed. The stiffest-bristled brush. For scrubbing Gwen's arse. Evening and heightening the red glow of the spanks. But how she longed to perform the scrubbing herself. To ply the cruel bristles of the stiffest-bristled brush over those superb cheeks, up and down, left and right, slipping the brush down the arse-cleft, up it again, searching out the delicate skin of the arse-dell, the even more delicate skin of the sphincter, scrubbing, paining, humiliating.

But that was Beth's privilege. As it had been Gwen's privilege to ply the brush on Beth's buttocks, and on hers. She could only suffer, and assist another to inflict suffering, never inflict suffering directly herself. Always passive, never active, like an irregular participle in a decadent erotic tongue. She had selected the stiffest-bristled brush, wishing that the hand she tested it on had been Gwen's arse; now she handed the brush to Beth.

'Good girl.'

And now Beth set to work with a will, the tip of her tongue protruding at the corner of her pursed and smiling mouth, her hand almost a blur as she worked the brush at Gwen's reddened arse.

'I'm going to scrub you until you plead for mercy, you bitch. Oh, no you don't. Anna, get back here. Hold her down.'

Anna knelt back at the living altar, small hands gripping its slick, warm solidity as she helped hold Gwen down for the administration of the scrubbing. Bum beaten; now bum buffed. Gwen struggled and swore.

'I'll get you for this, Beth.'

'Shut up and suffer, you bitch. You've had this coming for a long time and now it's here I'm going to make the most of it.'

Gwen grunted as the brush slid down her arse-cleft and was ruthlessly twirled over her arse-dell, stiff bristles seeking out the delicate pink disk of her sphincter. Anna's heart thumped in her throat. She knew what that felt like. Bristles up your bum. Bristles marching up and down, left and right across your spanked-pink-and-glowing arse. How delicious to hold that knowledge in your own head as you taught it to another, and how all-delicious to teach it to the one who had taught it to you.

But that was not her privilege. Only Beth's and Gwen's. They could both give and receive; she only receive. Though she could feed on the crumbs that fell from her dominatrixes' table, dab up the glistening spots of butter and wine, lick them from her fingertips with a tongue all the more sensitive for its famine. She had not spanked Gwen herself and she did not scrub her now, but she assisted in the spanking and in the scrubbing, and the sound and sight of it were with her intimately.

And the smell of it. The rich odours of Gwen's struggle-sweat and the musks of Beth's and Gwen's arousal. For both were aroused by their battle, by Beth's attempt to impose mastery on Gwen and Gwen's attempts to throw it off, by Beth's success and the spanking and scrubbing that followed. This was sex for Beth and Gwen. Direct sex, flesh on flesh, hand on arse, hand on brush on arse. And one or both were going to require orgasm at the end of it.

'There. Finished. An all-over glow.'

Beth tossed the brush aside and ran her bare hand over the buttocks she had dominated and controlled.

'Thank fuck for that,' Gwen said. 'I thought it was never going to end.'

'But you liked it, dear, didn't you?'

'Yes. I wouldn't have put up with it otherwise. And anyway, it's nice to know what the other half feels, from time to time. Helps sharpen one's own technique. One's own appreciation of dominance.'

'I couldn't agree more. And now . . .?'

Gwen sat up on Beth's lap, effortlessly shrugging off Anna's clutching hands. She looped an arm around Beth's neck and kissed her cheek.

'And now? What do you think? Time for Anna to put her best tongue forward again. My arse is way too red to pass the recess-test, so we'll have the little beast suck on a mouthful of ice-cubes for a few minutes again, and then lick my bum with a suitably chilled tongue. But right now I have another use for that little tongue of hers. You might find this hard to believe, but my pussy is even more on fire than my arse is. I will just *have* to come within the next five minutes or I will not be responsible for the consequences.'

Beth smiled and returned the kiss, lips to lips, and Anna could see their tongues wrestling for a moment before their mouths sealed against each other, finally coming apart with a pop.

Beth sighed.

'You took the words right out of my mouth.'

'I bags her tongue. An active little tongue on my pussy is just what the doctor ordered.'

'Her white little right paw on mine will do quite satisfactorily. In fact, she can use the other on my nipples, seeing as you've bagsed her tongue.'

'Okay. Then let's get on with it. Anna, you've heard what we want: supply it.'

She opened her legs as she sat on Beth's lap and Anna's mouth began to water involuntarily as she saw the glistening cunt that awaited her. The wide smear of yelm up each white, smooth thigh.

'Give me some room,' Beth said. 'Anna, you can wank me with your right hand while you're cunnilinguing Gwen, and work on my nipples with your left. At the same time, obviously. We expect full concentration on all three tasks, of course, or we will be obliged to punish you.'

'Most severely,' Gwen said. 'Come on, my pussy will not wait.'

She reached down between her yelm-smeared thighs, folding back her pussy-lips with a sigh as Anna swallowed hard and shuffled forward on her knees to lower her head and enter the vee of her sister's thighs, at the same time reaching with her right hand for her other sister's cunt, and with her left for her other sister's tits.

Nine

'What about day two?' Beth said. She had been silent for a few moments, savouring the images she and Gwen had conjured of Anna stripped and spanked, allowing herself to turn in the transparent plastic harness, once, then twice, before speaking again. She heard Gwen chuckle.

'Something most uncomfortable on day two.'

'Good. What?'

'A session in the boiler room, under the *château*.'

'We've got a boiler room?'

'Yes.'

'And a *château*?'

'Yes. This is high-class punishment.'

'In northern France?'

'Maybe. But southern is just as good.'

'I like southern too. And think of the sun. The warmth of the evening.'

'Yes. You're right. Those warm evenings are worth bearing in mind. So, okay, the session is in the boiler room, under the *château*, in southern France.'

'And what does it consist of, this session?'

'Water torture. A special kind of water torture. Using a hot-water pipe. A fat hot-water pipe. About three feet off the ground.'

'Not feet, metres. Metres if we're in France.'

'Okay. A fat hot-water pipe, about a metre off the ground. It leads away from the boiler to the rest of the house, and through some vagary of design it bends and curves quite a bit. And we set our little *collaboratrice* astride it.'

'Naked, of course.'

'Oh, of course. And if she's standing on tippy-tippy toes, she can just manage to keep the inside of her thighs and her bottom off the hot steel.'

'And her pussy?'

'Yes. Her pussy too, of course. She can just manage to keep that off the hot pipe.'

'But won't the pipe be lagged?'

'Lagged?'

'Insulated. Wearing a cloth jacket or something.'

'Oh, yes, it was. Definitely it was. But we've stripped all that away in preparation for the hot-water-pipe torture.'

'Good. Forget about insulation. Hang the expense.'

'Yes. Hang the expense. But we can always put it back on again when we've finished.'

'Make *her* put it back on again, you mean.'

'Okay. But at present, there it is, stripped *bare.*'

Beth took her cue.

'Just like her.'

'Yes. Just like her, in that it's stripped. But gleaming steel, unlike her. And we set her astride it and she can just keep her thighs and bottom off the hot steel by standing on tippy-tippy toes.'

'Tippy-tippy tip-toes.'

'Yes. Exactly.'

'But we don't want her to keep her thighs and bottom off the hot steel, do we?'

'Yes and no. Some of the time, we do. Some of the time, we don't. We want her to *oscillate*. To oscillate between discomforts.'

'What do you mean?'

'We hang two heavy weights around her waist. By short chains. Pulling her thighs and bottom onto the steel. And pussy too, of course. If she wants to stand on tip-toe, she has to lift the weights in her hands. But the weights are quite heavy and her arms will get tired, in time. So she will have to let them go, and her bottom and thighs will be pulled back onto the steel.'

'Her inner thighs.'

'Yes. Her inner thighs.'

'And pussy-lips.'

'Yes. And her pussy-lips. Kissing the hot steel. So she will have a choice of discomforts: to kiss the hot steel with her pussy-lips . . . and bottom . . . and thighs . . . or to lift the weights until her wrists and shoulders ache. Do you see how delicious it will be? Her oscillation? How the memory of one pain will fade as the reality of the other pain grows? Her poor pussy, pressed to the hot steel, begging to be lifted away? Her poor wrists and shoulders, aching *so* badly, begging to be allowed a respite?'

'Yes. I see. I see perfectly. But why does she just have to stand there? Won't that be rather boring?'

'It would. Not for her, but for us, perhaps. That is why she won't just be standing there. She will have to move along the pipe, negotiating its awkward curves, lifting those horrid weights, able to rest from lifting them only by hurting her poor pussy and thighs and bottom, able to rest from hurting her poor pussy and thighs and bottom only by lifting them.'

'What does she get for moving along the pipe?'

'She gets to reach the end of the pipe. Where it meets the wall of the boiler room.'

'And what does she get for reaching the end of the pipe?'

'She gets to go back to the beginning and start again.'

Ten

There were hand-holds beside Gwen's arse-recess, one on either side, and she took hold of them, back to the door, lifted herself up in a single movement, and slotted her arse neatly home.

'No need for a wriggle, girls. Watch.'

Light flashed around the curves of her arse; the congratulatory electronic belch sounded; the door began to slide open. Gwen let go of the hand-holds and landed back on the floor, bouncing up and round to watch the door come fully open.

'*Avanti*,' she said.

They filed into the next room, first Anna, next Beth, who wondered for a moment why Anna had gasped and then saw for herself, finally Gwen, who wondered for a moment why Beth had gasped and then saw for herself. The steel pipe. The gleaming steel pipe that stretched ten or more metres from the gallery where they were standing to an identical gallery on the other side, three or four metres above a white marble floor flooded with two or three feet of water that was crowded with criss-crossing fish. Warm water. Tropical fish. The air was warm and humid and sweat was already beginning to gather between their breasts and buttocks.

Gwen stepped to the steel railing that ran along the edge of the gallery. It was arched in the middle for access to the steel pipe. And access meant allowing someone to climb astride the pipe and inch her way across it to the other side.

'Well, girls,' she said. 'We know what we've got to do. Any volunteers? No? And what's that over there?'

Beth stepped forward to the railing too, staring at what seemed to be a large fishtank set into the wall of the opposite gallery.

'The empty equivalent of what we've got here,' Anna's voice said quietly from behind them. Gwen and Beth turned. Set into the wall behind them was another large tank, full of water but empty of fish, while above it, also set into the wall, were three more tanks, also full of water but much smaller and occupied.

In the first was a gleaming silver fish, large-eyed and ugly with an underslung jaw that glinted wickedly with white, serrated teeth. Beth's arm came up protectively over her breasts as she watched it shift restlessly from side to side in its small tank, gazing unblinkingly out at them.

She swallowed and looked at the next tank. Another fish, but how different. It was mud-coloured, fat and complacent, hanging in the water and gazing out at them too, but with an expression of benevolent unconcern on its dim, herbivorous face. She looked at the last tank. A patch of hanging water-weed. She stepped to it, stooped, and peered. Only that. No fish.

Thwak. She jerked upright, spinning and scowling. Gwen had slapped her bending arse as she stepped behind her, to stand in front of the first tank and the restless silver fish.

'Bitch.'

'You were asking for it. Bending like that. Be glad it was my hand and not this little bugger.'

She tapped on the glass of the first tank.

'Don't.'

'Why not?'

'It won't like it.'

'There's nothing it can do about it.'

Reluctantly, still rubbing at her arse, Beth walked to stand beside her and look into the tank.

'What is it?'

'Not sure. But it's familiar.'

'It's a piranha,' Anna said. They both turned. She was at the far end of the gallery, as far away from the first tank as she could get. Gwen chuckled and looked back at the tank.

'She's right. It's a piranha. And what about contestant number two, then Ansie? Move, Bethy.'

'Don't know,' Anna said.

Gwen had stooped to look directly at the second fish, and out of the corner of her eye Beth saw her chance. She shifted carefully, hand coming up, ready to flash down w –

'Ow!'

As her hand fell, Gwen's arm had swung up, blocking the blow. Gwen straightened and blew her a kiss.

'You're *so* predictable, honey.'

'I'll get you in the end, you bitch.'

'We'll see. But first things first. This one is definitely a herbivore. So we've got carnivore, first tank, herbivore second tank, and, er, herbi third tank. There's nothing else in there, is there?'

'No. Just the plant,' Beth said.

'The herbi. And that's it.'

'Not quite.'

Beth had stooped again, but lower, opening a small cupboard set into the wall beside the large empty tank. She looked up as Gwen stepped towards her and stuck her tongue out.

'You're so predictable, honey,' she said.

'I wasn't going to lay a finger on you. What's in there?'

Beth reached inside the cupboard and pulled out a small fishtank, empty of water but holding a folded sheet of paper, a pair of gloves, a small white aquarium net, and a coil of transparent plastic tubing. She put the tank on the floor, took out the paper, and unfolded it. She frowned.

'Wolf, goat and cabbage,' she read.

'What?'

'Look.' She held the paper up. 'Wolf, goat and cabbage.'

'Carnivore, herbivore and herbi,' Anna said.

'What?' Gwen said again.

'Carnivore, herbivore and herbi.'

Beth put the paper on the floor and snapped her fingers.

'By Jove she's got it, I think she's got it.'

'The sooner she gets it the better, as far as I'm concerned,' Gwen said.

'That too, but otherwise she's right. Don't you see? It's a crossing problem.'

'Crossing prob . . .? Oh, yeah, I do see.'

'Yes. How do you and a wolf and a goat and a cabbage get across a river in a boat that can hold you and two other things? If you leave the wolf with the goat or the goat with the cabbage you'll come back to find only one left.'

'And the piranha is the wolf, whatever *that* is is the goat, and the plant is the cabbage. Right?'

'Yep.'

'And that is the river.'

She turned and pointed at the gleaming steel pipe.

'Yep.'

'But where's the catch?'

'I don't know. But when we find it, we know who it catches, don't we?'

'Yes. And so does she, I think.'

Gwen stooped and picked the gloves and net out of the tank on the floor.

'Presumably we fill the tank with this' – she held up the tubing – 'catch the fish with this' – she held up the net – 'put them in that' – she nodded at the tank – 'and take them across.'

'Easier said than done.'

'True. But we still have to do it.'

She dropped the net and tubing back into the tank and tried one of the gloves on, turning her hand, flexing her fingers.

'This is asbestos,' she said. She turned, bent, and touched a finger of her ungloved other hand to the steel pipe.

'And *that* is hot. Surprise, surprise.'

She straightened, pulling the glove off.

'So, water into tank, fish-and-plant into water, tank carried across pipe, fish-and-plant put into tank over there, and *voilà*, success. The door opens and we begin the next stage in the obstacle course. Yes?'

'Yes,' Beth said. 'But how do we get the water into the tank and the fish out of their present accommodation? Any ideas, Ansie?'

Anna had walked slowly to the third tank and was looking intently into it. Or rather around it. She turned her head.

'There's a button here,' she said.

Gwen and Beth stepped over to look.

'Here. See?'

Anna's small, slim index-finger tapped the wall directly underneath the midpoint of the tank.

'Oh, yes,' said Beth. 'A button. What happens if you press it?'

'I imagine,' said Gwen, 'the tank empties into the larger tank beneath, carrying the plant with it. Right, Ansie?'

'Right.'

'And,' Gwen had walked down the wall a little, looking beneath the second and first tanks, 'these have buttons too. So these empty into the large tank. Which means –'

'There must be some way of getting at the large tank,' Beth said.

'Right. And look' – Gwen had slipped her fingers into something in the wall above the large tank and tugged – 'there is.'

A section of the wall folded down and they could smell the sudden humid warmth of the water in the large tank. Gwen put her hand into the wall and a moment later they saw it appear in the water of the tank, splashing, her forearm distorted by the water so that it seemed bent at an unnatural angle.

Anna shivered.

'I wouldn't even put my hand in there,' she said. 'In case the piranha got into it.'

'Don't worry,' said Gwen. She took her hand out of the water, out of the wall, and shook it. Droplets of water landed on Beth's and Anna's skin and Anna shivered. 'It will stay where it is until we press the button that releases it. But when it is in the tank, guess who's catching it?'

She stooped to the tank again and straightened and something went flying through the air to Anna. Anna caught it clumsily, nearly dropping it. The net. She shook her head.

'No. I'm not catching it.'

'You are, Ansie. Once we've decided the sequence of moves.'

'Goat first,' said Beth.

'No,' said Gwen, 'wolf and cabbage first. Might as well get as much over as possible as soon as possible.'

'That might make it go wrong later on.'

'Well, let's see. Wolf and cabbage first. Bring the wolf back.'

'Then the goat over.'

'Yes. Then the cabbage back and then the wolf and cabbage back over. And it's done. Five moves.'

'Great. So let's get it sorted for this lot. Piranha and plant over, piranha back. T'other fish over, plant back. Piranha and plant back over.'

'But then they all end up in that big tank over there.'

'No. We can keep the piranha and the plant in the little tank we've just carried over. It all works out when you apply a little reason. So, let's get the tank filled.'

She bent to the tank on the floor again and picked out the net and the coil of tubing. She uncoiled the tubing and stretched it.

'Should be plenty long enough. C'mere, Ansie. A little job for you.'

She turned and slipped one end of the tubing into the opening in the wall that gave onto the tank, feeding it through until she saw it drop into the water. As Anna walked to her she held the other end of the tubing out to her.

'Nothing succeeds like sucking, Ansie. Away you go.'

Anna stuck out her tongue.

'Bitch.'

'Shut up and suck.'

Anna took hold of the end of the tubing and slipped it into her mouth.

'Suck,' Gwen said.

She sucked.

'Harder. Come on, harder.'

66

Anna suddenly coughed and choked, water spraying from her mouth as she pulled the tubing out.

'Quick, drop it into the tank. That one, you silly cow.'

Anna dropped the tubing into the tank on the floor and Gwen clicked her tongue with satisfaction as water began to flow from it.

'Good girl. What a powerful suck you have on you. Observe the principle of the siphon in action. Liquid can be made to flow uphill under its own weight, when it leaves a tube lower than it enters it. D'you see? But first we need that all-important suck, to get it flowing. Now, we wait.'

'How much are you going to fill it?' Beth said.

'Half-way, maybe. What d'you reckon?'

'Yeah. Sounds about right. But it will be heavy.'

Water was flowing swiftly into the tank on the floor, rising, swirling, and they could smell its heat again.

'Right, that's about it.'

Gwen stooped and pulled the tubing out of the tank, raising it so that the siphoning was cut off. She pulled the rest of the tubing out of the large tank, casually coiled it and tossed it aside onto the floor.

'Okay, now to get the piranha and the plant into it. Put those gloves on, Ansie. If the piranha tries to bite you when you're catching it they might stop it taking one of your fingers off.'

'I'm not catching it.'

'You're catching it, young lady. No arguments. Press the first button, Beth.'

'What, for the piranha?'

'Yep. Then for the plant. Get those gloves on, Anna, and pick up that net.'

'No.'

Beth walked to the piranha tank and pressed the button set beneath it. Nothing happened.

'Put those gloves on, now.'

Beth turned.

'Hey, Gwen, nothing's happening,' she said.

'Well, forget it for the moment. We've got a bit of rebellion to quash among the peasantry.'

'Good.'

Anna backed up to one end of the gallery and was stopped short by the railing. She turned her head and looked over and down to the flooded floor and the silently criss-crossing fish.

'It's jump or be crushed, Ansie,' Gwen said. She and Beth were advancing on Anna, smiling, their eyes bright with excitement and anticipation. Anna turned her head and looked at them.

'Bitches.'

'We're glad you've decided to see sense, Ansie,' Beth said. 'Hands up.'

They reached her and Beth caught hold of her left wrist and dragged her hand up for Gwen to fit one of the gloves over it.

'As ever, Ansie,' Gwen said, twisting Anna's fingers loose of the fist she had made, 'this hurts you much more than it hurts us.'

'In fact,' said Beth, 'it doesn't hurt us at all. It's fun.'

'A lot of fun,' Gwen said. 'You can barely begin to imagine how much fun it is. There, that's better, isn't it?'

The glove was on Anna's left hand, slightly too big for her. Beth let go of the wrist and caught hold of the right one, dragging her hand up for Gwen to fit the other glove. Gwen twisted the fist open and began to fit the glove, the tip of her tongue wiggling at one corner of her mouth.

'There,' she said, 'nice and easy again. In fact, almost *too* easy.'

'Definitely too easy,' Beth said.

'Yes, I'm inclined to agree with you. She's got off lightly for her disobedience. Almost too lightly.'

'Definitely too lightly,' Beth said.

Gwen sucked her teeth.

'Again, Beth, I'm inclined to agree with you. But what shall we do about it?'

'Put her over the railing and spank her. Warm her arse up for the crossing. It's the only humane thing to do, considering.'

'Well, humane is all very well, in its way, but I'm inclined to prioritise fun again. Will it be a fun thing to do? That's the question I have to ask.'

'Yes. That's the answer I have to give.'

'And is it your final answer?'

'Yes.'

'Then it's unanimous. Over the railing with her and let's get spanking.'

Anna made a futile lunge for freedom, but they seized hold of her and mastered her easily, lifting her half off her feet and swinging her to face the railing.

'And *over* she goes,' Gwen said. 'But be careful. We want to drape her, not drop her.'

'No sooner said than done. Draped, not dropped.'

Anna hung precariously over the railing, feet swinging in the air, waist resting on the topmost bar, upper body hanging free as they held her in place.

'Not quite,' said Gwen. 'She's going to fall if we let go of her. Grab hold of something, you little beast. This bar, here, I reckon.'

She tapped the bar with her foot and Anna lunged for it, got hold of it and gripped.

'And put your feet here. Yes, that's right. Now, Beth, what d'you reckon to that bum? Has it regained its pristine whiteness?'

'Not quite. There are traces of the fury that rained down upon it a few rooms back.'

Gwen snorted.

'Hardly fury, Betchen. I was not beating to bruise, merely to erubesce. Remember that the arse-recess demanded pink, not crimson, and a pale pink at that. But now, well, there are no externally imposed constraints, are there? I can really let myself go.'

'And me.'

'Very well, and you. Shall we take it in turns? A cheek apiece? Six to start with, and take it from there?'

'Six each?'

'Of course. Six each. But is that six for each cheek or six for each of us?'

'Both.'

'Then that must be twelve then. Twelve for each of us for each cheek. Twenty-four in all.'

'And then we take it from there.'

'And then, as you say, Beth, we take it from there. Well, are you ready?'

Beth shifted, ready to swing her first spank at the defenceless pinkish cheek that was stretched taut in front of her.

'Yes,' she said.

'Then we shall begin. On the count of three, one . . . two . . . *three!*'

Thwak. Gwen's hand swung and landed heavily on the quivering left cheek and leapt back as *thwak* Beth's hand swung and landed on the quivering right, and leapt back as *thwak* Gwen's hand swung and landed heavily on the red-marked left cheek and swung back as *thwak* Beth's hand swung and landed on the red-marked right cheek, and *thwak thwak thwak thwak thwak thwak thwak thwak thwak thwak thwak thwak thwak thwak thwak thwak thwak thwak thwak.*

They stopped, panting, sweat shining on their faces and between their breasts.

'Look at my hand,' Beth said, holding it up, palm vertical.

'Snap,' Gwen said. 'There's work for us as flags of Ulster, should we ever fall on hard times.'

'And what about Ansie?'

'Ooh,' Gwen said, pursing her lips as she stared at the spanked bottom before them. 'The flag of Japan?'

'Two flags of Japan, surely.'

'Yes, you're right. They could use one in the eastern hemisphere and one in the west.'

Beth blew on her spanking hand and stepped closer to Anna's bottom.

'Only in the tropics,' she said. She held her hand flat just above the spanked skin. 'Yes. Just feel the heat pouring off it!'

'It's not the only thing that's pouring,' Gwen said. 'The little beast is leaking at both ends.'

It was true: tears were trickling down Anna's inverted forehead and yelm was oozing between her half-closed thighs.

'How horrid. We can't have that.'

'No. She might slip when she's going across the pipe. End up hanging upside-down by her ankles.'

'Or she might get stuck to it. Stuck hard with dried yelm.'

The tears reached the fringes of Anna's blonde stubble, snaking left and right through the silky hairs, like hunting poodles in albino bulrushes, and dripped, falling away to the warm water flooding the floor two or three metres below.

'Listen,' Gwen said.

'For what?'

'Her tears, falling into the water.'

Beth listened for a few moments.

'Can't hear a thing.'

'Not a faint splik?'

'What's a "splik"?'

'The noise a tear makes falling into water. Can you hear it? Splik. Splik. A heartbeat after they drip from her head?'

'Nope. Not a thing.'

'Must be my imagination then. Oh well, back to the coalface.'

'Coal is hardly the word,' Beth said, taking up her position.

'Haematite?'

'Maybe. Is that red?'

'Very. Or so I've heard. On the count of three. One . . . two . . .'

'No, hang on. How many this time? Six of the best again? For each of us?'

'Yes, okay.'

'Or for each cheek?'

'To be on the safe side, let's say both. Six of the best for each of us *and* for each cheek. Which makes twelve.'

'For each of us?'

'Yes.'

'Or for each cheek?'

'Well . . . No. It's *tempting*, but no, let's not be greedy. We have a crossing problem to solve. We don't want to disable the little beast. Not permanently, anyway. Those spanked cheeks on that hot steel are going to hurt, you know. Hurt a *lot*.'

'Yes, I know. Isn't it good?'

'Yes. Very good. So, on the count of three. One . . . two . . . *three!*'

Thwak. Thwak. The blows began to rain again on Anna's once-white, still defenceless cheeks, and the trickle of tears quickened and thickened from her swimming blue eyes, dripping away unheard to the flooded floor.

Panting, they stood at ease, Beth flapping her spanking hand left and right, up and down.

'Whew,' she said. 'It's on fire.'

'It's not the only one.'

'You mean her poor little bottom?'

'Not just her bottom. Look at this.'

Gwen stepped forward, inserted a careless hand between Anna's half-closed thighs, and rummaged.

'Look.'

She turned back, holding the hand up.

'*Oozing* with it.'

'Let's have some. It might cool my hand down.'

'Be my guest.'

Gwen stood aside and Beth stepped forward to rummage between Anna's thighs.

'Any good?' Gwen said.

'Not *really*. But it's fun. And that's the important thing.'

'Yep. And more awaits us. Come on, Ansie, off the fence and let's get that piranha on its way. Come on, chop chop.'

Anna swallowed and sniffed.

'I've got cramp,' she said.

'We all have our crosses to bear,' Gwen told her sweetly. 'But it doesn't make *me* forget my obligations to others. Does it, Beth?'

'No. Certainly not. Nor me, does it?'

'No. Even more certainly not. But then you and I are of a generation that puts service before self. Unlike some, eh?'

'She's only a year younger than me, you know.'

'True, but far older in sin. For *her*, with her, it's self before service every time. Others might as well not exist so far as *she*'s concerned, the little beast.'

'Beast. Yes. A little blonde beast.'

'The worst kind. By far the worst. Well, if the Mountain won't come to Mohammed, Mohammed will have to go to the Mountain. Let's get her off the fence.'

They moved forward to take Anna off the railing, having to prise her fingers loose and lift her almost bodily, bottom glowing with heat as their hands and wrists, flanks and breasts brushed it.

'Oomps-a-daisy. Right, careful ... careful ... Okay, stand her up.'

They stood her up and moved back.

'Dizzy,' said Anna, and fell over. She struggled to sit up, barely managed it, then sat hanging her head.

'On your feet, Ansie. There's work to be done.'

'Dizzy,' Anna said again.

'You've always been dizzy. A little more won't make any difference. On your feet and get hold of that net.'

Anna looked up slowly. She stuck out her tongue.

'Bitches.'

Beth tutted.

'She never learns, does she?'

'She doesn't want to learn. That way she gets punished, and she likes that. You saw the way she reacted.'

Anna got slowly to her feet, thighs coming apart, culks glistening with yelm, cunt gaping pinkly.

'I can still see it.'

'She meant you to see it. She's nothing but a slut.'

'And a beast.'

'Nothing but a slut and a beast.'

'A beast-slut.'

'A slut-beast.'

'A bestial little slut.'

'A slutty little beast.'

'Just the kind I like.'

'Me too. Net, Ansie. Net. Good girl. Now, stand by.'

Anna had picked up the net in her gloved hands and stood red-eyed and waiting as Gwen crossed to the piranha tank and pressed the button set beneath it. Pressed it firmly. But nothing happened. She pressed it again. Still nothing.

'What the fuck's going on here then?'

'Try another one,' Beth said.

'Okay.'

She walked down the line of tanks to the one that held the water-plant and pressed the button beneath it. Pressed it firmly. But nothing happened. Pressed it again. And still nothing.

'Jesus Christ.'

She stabbed at the button set beneath the middle tank.

'Bet this won't work eith–'

And it all began to happen.

'Look, they're draining!' Beth said.

All the tanks were emptying simultaneously and Gwen saw that vents had opened in the floor of each, water pouring away through it. She heard the sudden splash and churn of water pouring into the main tank and beckoned hard for Anna.

'Quick, Ansie. They're all going to end up in the bottom tank at once. You'll have to be quick and get the piranha out.'

'Nooooo,' Anna moaned.

'Shut up and scoop. Now.'

With a flash of green the water-plant was sucked from its tank, appearing a moment later in the lower tank, forced deep into it by the water it had fallen with, then slowly rising to float at the surface. The water in the upper tanks was half-gone now and the two fish were having to swim hard to stay in their tanks. In another few seconds they would be sucked away into the vents and fall into the lower tank with the plant. With each other.

'Drag her over here, Beth.'

Beth obeyed, dragging Anna to the main tank.

'You little beast. She's dropped the net, Gwen.'

'Oh, for fuck's sake.'

The herbivorous fish looked animated for the first time, its eyes seeming to roll with surprise as it struggled to stay in its tank, which was less than a third full now. The piranha had begun to dart from side to side, seeking deeper water, growing more agitated as it failed to find it. And

74

then with a last comic gulp of surprise the herbivorous fish was sucked into the vent of its tank, vanishing for a second before appearing suddenly in the lower tank.

'Look, that fucking piranha will be next.'

Gwen stooped and picked up the net where Anna had dropped it, then forced it back into Anna's unwilling hand, holding her fingers closed so that she couldn't drop it.

'If you drop it again when I let you go, Ansie, your arse is going to be red-hot for the next hour. Trust me on this.'

'Fuck off. I'm not catching it.'

Gwen began to open her mouth to reply but she was interrupted by an urgent cry from Beth.

'Gwen! It's in!'

Gwen spun back to the main tank. The piranha had fallen and was now loose with the plant and the herbivorous fish. It was still agitated, making short darts from side to side, not seeming to realize the depth and size of the tank it was now in.

'Shit,' she said. 'How long have we got before they notice one another?'

'How long before the piranha notices food, you mean? God knows.'

'Come on, drag her to it. She's catching that fucking thing whether she wants to or not.'

'*Nooo!*'

Anna screamed as they began to drag her to the opening in the wall that let onto the main tank, pressing her feet hard into the floor and dragging herself back. It was futile, but they were losing precious seconds and the piranha was becoming less agitated all the time.

'Catch it!'

'No!'

Gwen wrenched Anna's net-carrying hand down and into the opening.

'You'll catch it if I have to move your hand for you, young lady.'

'No! Fucking get off!'

The net splashed as it touched the surface of the water in the tank, and the piranha darted towards the disturbance, jaw widening and large eyes seeming to swing wickedly forward to focus on whatever it was that had fallen into the tank.

Anna screamed and her bladder suddenly let go, a jet of bright yellow springing between her thighs, broken and splashing, the scent of it sharp and spicy in the humid air.

'You dirty little beast, Anna,' Gwen said. 'Look at me: it's all over my legs. Christ. Let her go, Beth. I'll have to do it. We'll settle with her later.'

They released her suddenly and Anna, still dragging herself backwards, lost balance and fell over, landing heavily on her spanked arse with a cry of pain. She struggled to sit up as Gwen, wiping disgustedly at her legs, bent and jerked the net from her paralyzed hand and turned back to the main tank.

'Here, fishie,' she said. 'Good little fishie.'

She put her hand into the opening and carefully lowered the net into the water. The piranha responded to the disturbance again, darting forward to examine the net as Gwen settled it into the water and turned the mouth of the net to face the fish.

'Good fishie,' she repeated. 'Have a closer look. Come on. It won't hurt you.'

She inched the net towards the piranha which, seemingly fearless, moved to meet it, peering into the mouth of white gauze that opened before it.

'Say when, Bethy.'

Beth stopped wiping Anna's piss from her own legs and stared into the tank.

'When.'

Gwen swung the net forward as quickly as she could and the piranha, suddenly sensing its danger, made a dart for freedom. Too late! As she raised the net from the water and pulled it from the opening, a furious slice of silver began jerking and jumping within, in a frenzy to escape. Gwen swung the net swiftly and smoothly to the tank sitting on the floor, tipped it, and the piranha was free again, darting venomously from side to side and end to end of its new prison.

'There,' Gwen said. 'Nothing hard about that, was there? So let's move to the next item on the agenda. The shocking disobedience and insubordination of our little blonde beast here. Look at her, Beth. Sitting on the floor in a puddle of her own piss.'

'Disgusting.'

'Still, her filthy habits are her own business, so long as she doesn't let them interfere with the lives of others. But is that the case here, Bethy?'

'You know it's not, Gwen. She didn't just piss on herself, she pissed on me too, and you. Look, it's all over our legs. And we have to walk on this floor too. How can we do that when she's pissed all over it? And what about breathing? I'd prefer to do so without having to smell her piss.'

'As would I. Very good points. She has interfered with us, so we can interfere with her. Anna, get the floor mopped up. Use that sheet of paper first, then your tongue, if that runs out. To be strictly honest, though . . .'

Anna swung onto her knees and crawled sullenly to retrieve the sheet of paper that had been in the tank now occupied by the piranha.

'What?' Beth said.

'I feel like a piss myself. Don't you?'

Beth was silent for a moment.

'Now you come to mention it . . .'

'Yes?'

'Yes.'

Anna had started to mop the floor with the sheet of paper, soaking up the splashes of her own piss.

'Stop that, Ansie,' Gwen said. 'We've decided we don't mind so much after all. I mean, it's only a bit of pee, isn't it? It's not as though it's *unnatural* or anything.'

'And it's not as though we mind you having a little accident very much,' Beth said.

'Under the influence of fear,' Gwen said. 'Even if the fear was completely uncalled for. No, it's not so bad after all.'

Anna looked up at them suspiciously, eyes still red with crying.

'Well, is it now?' Gwen said.

'I don't know,' Anna said.

'You should know, Ansie dear. It's not so bad after all. In fact, it's hardly bad at all. So we've decided not to punish you for it. Or even for your disobedience. To understand all is to forgive all. We understand all, and we forgive all. You were frightened. The piranha is a frightening fish. What is more natural than that, eh?'

Anna said nothing.

'Oh, dear, Beth, she doesn't look very convinced. She looks as though she thinks we're up to something.'

'Aren't we?'

'Well, yes, but nothing very serious. Nothing a young girl ought to object to having forced on her.'

'Forced?' Beth said.

'Did I say "forced"? A slip of the tongue. We aren't going to *force* Anna to let us do what we want to do to her. She should be happy to accept it. The air *has* got a little chilly, after all.'

'Has it?'

'I think so. Don't you?'

'Not noticeably.'

'Well, it could get chilly. Very chilly. So I really think we ought to warm Anna up. No, Anna, don't worry. I don't mean *that* again. Spanking is over for the time being. We want to warm you in another way. A natural, loving way. You can't have any objection to that, can you?'

Anna looked up at her suspiciously.

'What way?'

'Weren't you listening a little while ago?'

'No. You'd told me to do something and I was doing it.'

'Well, you've stopped doing it now, dear, and you can stay stopped, because we have something else in mind for you. Something that will warm you up, in a natural, loving way.'

'You've not said what way, yet.'

Gwen sighed.

'We're not going to say: we're going to show you. In a natural, loving way. With your complete co-operation, of course. Yes, dear, we're going to have your complete

78

co-operation. Whether you want to give it to us or not. Come on, come to Mummy. Catch her, Beth. Yes, that's right. Prepare her to receive my endearments. No, her head, you silly bitch. Her head. Turn it round. Hard, if necessary. That's right. Good. Right, Ansie, for what you are about to receive, may the Lord make you truly thankful.'

The jet of urine sprang and splattered, striking Anna in the centre of her forehead, an arc of gold breaking against marble. Beth's hands were clamped to either temple, locking her head in place to receive Gwen's bounty, and Anna's eyes were closed hard, her mouth sealed and grimacing. Gwen smiled and cruelly swung her hips forward, directing the stream down Anna's face, breaking now against the bridge of her nose, against the neat little bulb of her nose itself, against her mouth, her chin, then her throat, her breasts.

The stream began to falter and slow, coming in separate spurts, splattering more thinly, and stopped.

'Nice,' said Gwen.

Anna opened her eyes and blew hard through her mouth and nostrils, trying to blow droplets of piss off her lips.

'Bitch,' she said. 'I stink of piss now.'

'You stunk of piss anyway. Now, Beth, your turn. You may as well do it from where you are. Straight onto her head. That'll teach the little beast. Hold on. I want to put my hands into it, once you've started. Yes, okay. Piss at pleasure.'

Beth breathed slowly in, then out, and pissed, the golden stream falling neatly and directly onto the shaved centre of Anna's blonde-silked skull. Gwen inserted her hands into the stream, washing them together, breaking it so that it rained on Anna rather than flowed, a thousand glorious golden droplets, warm and richly scented, landing on Anna's white, slim body.

'Lovely and warm, Bethy. I wish you could piss for minutes, you know. Hours even. While away the golden hours, passing piss among the flowers.'

The look of concentration on Beth's face relaxed and she smiled.

'Me too,' she said. 'Pissing on our little pigeon.'

'Our little puppy.'

'Little pupil.'

'Little Pollyanna.'

'What's a Pollyanna?'

'An excessively cheerful individual.'

Beth chuckled.

'That's our Anna, alright. There. All done, nearly . . .'

A few last spurts and Anna's second aspersion was over. Gwen stroked her skull.

'Slick with piss,' she said. 'Yours and mine, Bethy.'

'It'll get sticky soon. Start to itch. All over. Come on, on your feet, Ansie. No rest for the wicked.'

They stepped away from her and Anna slowly got to her feet.

'What's that in your hand, you little beast?' Beth said.

'It's that paper,' Gwen said. 'The one she was mopping up with. Drop it, Anna. We've got a lot more to do to you, and then you've got things to do and places to go.'

'Across the pipe to the other side.'

Anna dropped the paper.

'Not there, you little beast. Out of the way.'

Gwen took a step forward to kick at it, then suddenly stopped and stooped over it.

'What's wrong?' Beth asked.

Gwen picked the paper up.

'There's more writing on it. Look.'

She unfolded the soaked sheet and held it flat, resting on both hands. Curious, Beth and Anna clustered in front of her, trying to read it upside-down. Gwen looked up with a frown.

'Ansie, you will stand at attention until you are told otherwise. Now. And don't touch that piss!'

Anna moved back, her hands falling guilty from the golden drops still beading her white body.

'Now, as I was reading when I was so rudely interrupted . . .'

She looked back at the paper. The frown returned to her face.

'What does it say, Bethy?'

Beth put her head on one side.

'Turn it a bit, so I can see properly.'

Gwen turned it.

ĀNΔ ĀOT ШENT ΥΠ OΥT OЧ ẐOAP, ANΔ ΔШEΛT IN THE
MOΥNTAIN, ANΔ HIC TШO ΔAΥTHTEPC ШITH HIM; ЧOP HE
ЧEAPEΔ TO ΔШEΛΛ IN ẐOAP: ANΔ HE ΔШEΛT IN A ΘAЧE,
HE ANΔ HIC TШO ΔAΥTHTEPC. ĀNΔ THE ЧIPCTBOPN CAIΔ
ΥNTO THE XOΥNΓEP, ŌΥP ЧATHEP IC OΛΔ, ANΔ THEPE IC
NOT A MAN IN THE EAPTH TO ΘOME IN ΥNTO ΥC AЧTEP THE
MANNEP OЧ AΛΛ THE EAPTH: ΘOME, ΛET ΥC MAKE OΥP
ЧATHEP ΔPINK ШINE, ANΔ ШE ШIΛΛ ΛIE ШITH HIM, THAT ШE
MAΧ ΠPECEPЧE CEEΔ OЧ OΥP ЧATHEP. ĀNΔ THEΧ MAΔE
THEIP ЧATHEP ΔPINK ШINE THAT NIΓHT: ANΔ THE ЧIPCTBOPN
ШENT IN, ANΔ ΛAΧ ШITH HEP ЧATHEP; ANΔ HE ΠEPΥEIЧEΔ
NOT ШHEN CHE ΛAΧ ΔOШN, NOP ШHEN CHE APOCE. ĀNΔ IT
ΘAME TO ΠACC ON THE MOPPOШ, THAT THE ЧIPCTBOPN
CAIΔ ΥNTO THE XOΥNΓEP, ẞEHOΛΔ, Ī ΛAΧ ΧECTEPNIΓHT
ШITH MΧ ЧATHEP: ΛET ΥC MAKE HIM ΔPINK ШINE THIC NIΓHT
AΛCO; ANΔ ΓO THOΥ IN, ANΔ ΛIE ШITH HIM, THAT ШE MAΧ
ΠPECEPЧE CEEΔ OЧ OΥP ЧATHEP. ĀNΔ THEΧ MAΔE THEIP
ЧATHEP ΔPINK ШINE THAT NIΓHT AΛCO: ANΔ THE XOΥNΓEP
APOCE, ANΔ ΛAΧ ШITH HIM; ANΔ HE ΠEPΘEIЧEΔ NOT ШHEN
CHE ΛAΧ ΔOШN, NOP ШHEN CHE APOCE.

'What fucking language is it in?'

'Looks like Greek. Hey, Anna! Stay at attention. This is nothing to do with you.'

'Then why can I read it and you can't?' Anna asked.

Beth raised her eyebrows.

'Good point, Gwen.'

'I love it when you do that,' Gwen said.

'What?'

'That with your eyebrows.'

'This?'

Beth did it again.

'Yes. That.'

'Let's not get distracted, for the time being. Show it to Anna if she can read it.'

Gwen held the paper reluctantly out to Anna. As Anna read it Gwen's eyes started to narrow.

'Why are you smiling?' she asked.

Anna looked up at her, her face blank and innocent.

'Smiling? I'm not smiling.'

'What does it say?'

'It's about what we have to do next. Instructions.'

'Yeah?'

'Yeah.'

'We'll have to trust her, Gwen. What else can we do?'

'Keep a damn close eye on her, and if she steps out of line take firm countermeasures. Very firm countermeasures. Finished, have we?'

'Yes, thanks,' Anna said. Gwen stared at her.

'Very firm countermeasures, Anna.'

'Okay. Shall we get on with getting out of this room?'

'When I say so.'

'Then say so. Please.'

'Right. We'll do it. You can get that tank across the pipe with the piranha in it.'

'Delighted.'

'We'll see how delighted you are when your arse is astride that pipe. Come on, Beth, let's get her on her way. Gloves on, Ansie, and straddle.'

The two of them shepherded Anna to the pipe and helped her climb astride it.

'Ow!' Anna said as her buttocks made contact, then her thighs, the smooth steel of the pipe searing into her soft skin.

'Hot, is it, dear?' Gwen asked. 'Just rest on your hands, then, while we fetch the tank for you.'

Anna rested her gloved hands on the pipe and slipped her thighs atop them, lifting her buttocks clear of the hot steel. Gwen and Beth picked up the tank and carried it back to her.

'Head down, Ansie,' Beth said. 'We'll pass it over the top of you, then lower it and you can rest it on the pipe. It should balance.'

Anna did as she was told and they passed the tank over her head. She slipped her thighs off the gloves, wincing again as her buttocks and thighs made contact with the hot steel, then helped them lower the tank to the pipe, balancing it precariously atop it. When it was balanced she put her gloved hands on the pipe again and slipped her thighs back onto them.

'Right, Ansie,' Gwen said. 'It looks as though the routine will be this. You'll have to lift the tank in your arms and shuffle forward on your bottom and thighs as far as you can. When the strain in your arms or the pain in your bottom and thighs gets too much or, hopefully, both, you'll have to balance the tank back on the pipe and rest before starting all over again. It's going to hurt a lot, I'm afraid, and your poor bottom will be very sore before you reach the other side, but it's all in a good cause, so neither I nor Beth is complaining. Right, off you go then. It should be easier on the return trip, when the tank is empty, unless you leave too much yelm on the pipe as you're making your way across. It might get slippery then. But still, it'll probably dry and crust very quickly, so perhaps it won't matter after all.'

Anna said nothing. She slipped off her hands, reached forward and underneath the tank, and lifted it, shoulders shaking with the strain.

'Shuffle now, Ansie,' Gwen said.

She shuffled, inching her left thigh forward, then using it as a pivot to inch her right thigh forward, the hot steel of the pipe searing mercilessly into her, her mouth open in a permanent moue of pain and effort, her heart beating faster, then faster still with the shame of what was happening in her cunt. The pain was exciting her. She would be smearing the pipe with yelm soon. Gwen watched her shuffle with sparkling eyes, already rehearsing what she would say as the first streaks of yelm began to appear on the shining surface of the pipe.

Eleven

'And day three?'

'No breakfast for her.'

'Why not?'

'Because she needs plenty of room for what's coming up, so she can sit and watch us eat breakfast instead. Eggs and bacon. Mountains of toast. Fresh butter. Strawberry jam. Hot, rich coffee with cream. How her little stomach will rumble! Big eyes on us as we stuff and stuff. Talking with our mouths full. Half-chewed pieces of bread falling carelessly to the white tablecloth. Lips glistening with butter, coated with crumbs as we stuff and stuff, till we're farting with satiation.'

'How crude.'

'Yes.'

'And disgusting.'

'Yes.'

'The vulgar little cow.'

'I agree. We'll have to put a stop to that rumbling stomach. And we will.'

'How?'

'*Les prisonniers.* Prisoners-of-war. A trainload of them is due to return to the motherland.'

'A trainload?'

'Yes. Two or three hundred. They've been away for years. Imprisoned without female companionship.'

'*Les pauvres.*'

'*Mais oui, certainment.* But we're going to make it up to them. Prepare a treat for them at the station. Our little *collaboratrice* is going to pay them lip-service.'

'Lip-service?'

'Yes. With her lips.'

'Just with her lips?'

'No, though that will be enough, for some. But tongue-service too, for the more eager. Throat-service, for the most eager of all.'

'I like throat-service best.'

'She won't.'

'Good. So what do we do?'

'We set up a little service depot. Three windows at the station, as though for tickets, but hip-high.'

'Hip-high?'

'Yes, hip-high. Which is cock-high too, of course. There will be a little picture at each window. One of me at window one, for I will be serving there, one of you at window two, for you will be serving there, and one of our little *collaboratrice* at window three, for she will be serving there.'

'What happens at your window?'

'Cocks are inserted one by one. I inspect them briskly but efficiently. If I am satisfied, I stamp them with water-proof ink and pass them to you.'

'Why water-proof?'

'Because of what you will be doing.'

'And that is?'

'Washing them. Cleaning them quickly but thoroughly with soapy water, douching them, drying them, before passing them to window three, where our little *collaboratrice* is kneeling on an inadequate cushion and waiting. Her window is much larger than yours or mine, and she can take three cocks through it at once, when necessary.'

'Three cocks at once?'

'Yes. Two men standing a little apart but side by side, with a third just behind them.'

'All of them erect?'

'Of course. Do you imagine our countrymen will not respond to the touch of a female hand, after all those years?'

'The third man will need to have a big cock.'

'They will all have big cocks.'

'I never doubted it. But what does she do with these cocks?'

'As I said before, she pays them lip-service. Occasionally tongue- and throat-service too.'

'Oh dear. You mean . . .?'

'Yes. She fellates them. Sometimes one at a time, sometimes two at a time, sometimes three at a time. Three cocks in her little mouth as she sucks at them frantically.'

'And does she spit or swallow?'

'She swallows. Every time, she swallows. That is what the little beast will be there for. To suck and swallow. That will teach her to let her stomach rumble while we are eating breakfast.'

'It will. But how many cocks will she have to suck?'

'Three at a time, when necessary.'

'No, I mean *in toto*.'

'*In toto?*'

'In all. How many cocks in all?'

'Oh, two or three hundred.'

'Oh no! *La pauvre petite!* And she'll have to swallow every time?'

'If a cock discharges while it's in her mouth, she'll have to swallow every drop.'

'Every drop discharged by perhaps two or three hundred cocks?'

'Yes.'

'But won't they discharge violently? After all, you say they will have been without female companionship for years. Without a female touch.'

'Or a female suck. Yes, they will have been deprived for years. Five years, in some cases. And yes, they will come with extraordinary violence. Torrentially, so to speak. A handful may come merely during the inspection or the washing. We must be careful of that. Erection must be our aim, not ejaculation. That should take place only in our *collaboratrice*'s hot little mouth.'

'Oh dear. *La pauvre petite*. Her stomach will be full!'

'Yes. If it is still rumbling after the first half-hour or so I shall be very surprised.'

'And I. Do you think it will slosh, when she stands up?'

'Her stomach, you mean?'

'Yes.'

'She won't be standing up. She will be servicing cocks. Sucking and swallowing.'

'But when she's finished that?'

'Well, when she's finished that, yes, I expect her stomach will be sloshing. Don't you?'

'Yes. And will her stomach be distended? With all that come she's swallowed?'

'That thick, creamy come, you mean?'

'Yes. That very thick, creamy come.'

'Spurting in hot torrents into her hot little mouth?'

'Yes. Spurting in hot torrents into her hot little mouth.'

'Half-choking her each time? Burning the delicate mucous membranes of her throat and fauces with its musky brininess? Or its briny muskiness?'

'Yes. Half-choking her each time. Burning the delicate mucous membranes of her throat and fauces with its musky brininess. Or its briny muskiness.'

'And what was your question?'

'Will her stomach be distended with it? That very thick, creamy come?'

'Oh, definitely. There will be a decided bulge in what was previously a slim, svelte little midriff. After all, she'll have swallowed positively gallons of it.'

'*Litres.* We're in France, remember.'

'Okay. *Litres. Litres de semence.*'

'Mmmm. I love the idea of it. The little beast swallowing litres of semen. Litres of come. Litres of spunk. Gulping and gasping it down.'

'Oh, she'll be doing a lot of gasping and gulping, alright. But I think gallons would be better for that. Gallons of semen. Gallons of come. Gallons of spunk. Gulping and gasping it down.'

'Yes, you're right. Swallowing litres, gulping down gallons. Oh, *la pauvre petite*! Do you think the taste of come in her mouth and throat will have started to fade a little by day four?'

'It's very unlikely, but it won't matter in either case.'

'Why?'

'Because there will be a train-load of prisoners to see off on day four. Italians, returning to the motherland.'

Twelve

The bright light shining from behind them swung and was extinguished as the door to the pipe-room closed, and for a moment they stood where they were, seeing what was ahead of them more clearly now. They were in a small room, with a long narrow corridor directly ahead of them. There was a dim but definite light shining down it, but the smooth lines of the walls were interrupted oddly by hanging shapes, as though horizontal candles had been set there that had softened as they burnt and drooped, extinguishing their own wicks and now hardened in permanent downward curves.

Like drooping candles or ... No, there were far too many of them for that. Far, far too many. The whole corridor was lined with them as far ahead as they could see. But Gwen found herself licking her lips before she spoke.

'Well, it's *avanti* again, isn't it?'

'But what are they?' Beth said.

They walked forward, seeing how narrow the narrow corridor was. They would virtually have to squeeze along it, brushing against the hanging curves. The oddly organic, hanging curves.

'Well, have a look,' Gwen said. They were close enough to touch one now, so Beth reached forward, taking hold of one, beginning to –

'Argh!'

She whipped her hand back with a shudder.

'It flexes,' she said. 'As though it's a piece of meat.'

'Bollocks,' Gwen said.

She reached out and took hold of the same one, but only for an instant. She whipped her hand back too and took a step backwards, wiping it on her stomach.

'Christ. You're right. It feels fucking obscene.'

'They're cocks,' said a small voice from behind them.

'What?'

They spoke almost in the same instant, heads turning to look back into the dark where Anna was standing.

'Cocks. Watch.'

Anna pushed past them, her skin sticky with their piss, and took hold of another of the hanging curves. They saw her shoulders twitch, but she didn't let go, and now her right shoulder began to flex up and down. She was working her hand over the thing, sliding up and down. Now she let go and stepped back.

'Look.'

They looked. The thing Anna had been manipulating had lost most of its curve: it was rising to the horizontal again. Swelling.

'It's a cock,' Anna said. 'Feel it. Feel any of them. They're all cocks.'

'It's not possible,' Beth said. 'Look how many there are.'

'They're cocks.'

'She's right, Beth. If it looks like a cock and feels like a cock and stiffens like a cock . . .'

'But what the fuck are we going to do? The whole fucking corridor's lined with them.'

'We squeeze our way past and hope there are no accidents. Anna, away you go. Come on, *avanti.*'

She kicked out, her toes sinking satisfyingly into Anna's soft backside, sending her forward with a squeak. She began to move along the corridor, body turned to one side, swaying to pass between the cocks lining the walls, and Gwen and Beth followed her, the flaccid cocks slithering over their bodies like small cool serpents, seeming to line the walls more and more thickly. No, definitely lining the walls more thickly. And ahead of them Anna had stopped.

'Move, Ansie,' Gwen said.

'I can't. They've started to stiffen ahead of me.'

'Don't talk rubbish. Just squeeze past them.'

'I can't. Look.'

Gwen squeezed up to her and looked over her shoulder. In the dim light coming down the corridor she could see the hundreds of cocks lining the walls ahead of them erecting, those nearest to them just lifting towards the horizontal, those furthest away almost fully turgid, projecting across the corridor left and right like a kind of grille.

'Christ,' she said. 'They're big.'

The nearest ones were half-way to erection now, and she realized erections were proceeding down the walls of the corridors in a slow wave that would reach them in a few seconds. Trapping them where they were. She turned.

'Beth, quick, go back.'

'I can't.'

'Why not?'

But she already knew the answer.

'They've got stiff from the other end. The ones we've already squeezed past.'

Gwen felt her heart throb uncomfortably in her throat and her stomach rolled. Caught in a trap. A cock-trap. The cocks to either side of her were on the rise, blunt, thick fingers lifting to point accusingly at her, and now hidden lights in the ceiling of the corridor were glowing to life, the light that poured from them cut and shadowed by the wall-cocks. She twisted to avoid the cocks as they rose at her, positioning her limbs and body between and around them, and snorted as she saw Anna and Beth doing the same.

'We're stuck, girls,' she said. 'Up cock-creek without a paddle.'

'What are we going to do?' Beth asked.

'Wait for them to go down, I suppose.'

'No. I've got a better idea. We can't go back and we can't go on.'

'Yep.'

'But Anna can. She can suck our way to freedom. Make them come and soften them.'

Gwen laughed.

'It has the simplicity of all great plans. Did you hear that, Ansie? Get sucking, sucker.'

'No.'

'Do it.'

'You do it.'

'Okay, I will.'

Gwen stopped, wondering if she had just said that. Had she? Yes. But for fuck's sake, why? Because she wanted to. And her cunt had known it before she had: opening stickily and beginning to ooze as she squeezed her way along the corridor, pulsing greedily now as she stood trapped by hundreds of big, stiff cocks.

She leaned forward to the most convenient of them, peeled its foreskin like a banana, put her mouth over the paradoxical plum of the glans, and began to lick and suck. After a moment she jerked back, spluttering with surprise. It tasted of strawberry. She dropped her mouth to the cock just below it, peeling its foreskin, popping the plum into her mouth, licking and sucking. She uncorked it from her mouth. Grapefruit.

'For fuck's sake,' she murmured. 'Beth . . .'

But what she had been about to say died in her mouth. Beth had her mouth over a cock too, sucking eagerly at it while her right hand worked at her glistening cunt. Gwen swallowed.

'Beth!' she said.

Beth's mouth came off the cock with a moist pop, leaving the glans shining purple, like a helmet worn by a fascistic papal guard. Her eyes met Gwen's, sleepy with pleasure.

'What?'

'Why are *we* doing this?'

Her mouth was already aching to return to one of the cocks it had been sucking. Unsteady with the desire to fellate, so that she almost stuttered as she spoke.

Beth shrugged. Her right hand was still working at her cunt; now she raised it and licked yelm off her fingers.

'Because it tastes nice. Because I want to. Don't you?'

92

Gwen turned her head and looked at Anna. She was leaning forward to the wall, an enormous cock buried deep between her lips, eyes closed, sucking lustily, the slim fingers of her small hands tweaking and twisting her nipples. She turned back and Beth had returned to her cock, hand working at her cunt again. Gwen snorted.

'Christ. But if you can't beat 'em . . .'

She put her mouth forward and over the first cock she had sampled. Strawberry. A cock-plum that tasted of strawberry. A cock-plum that started to leak strawberry pre-come as she shuttled her mouth slowly back and forth over it, licking, sucking, beginning to pump her mouth on it, her whole head moving backward and forward faster and faster, providing an oral cunt for the motionless cock to fuck. Big cock. And how big were the balls concealed behind the wall? Were they beginning to rise in their wrinkled sack, tightening in preparation for orgasm? Hardening as they readied themselves to hurl come into her working mouth?

She was almost forgetting to tease her own nipples, was almost forgetting to breathe, was almost unable to breathe, because she was accepting the cock so far into her mouth, and she realized suddenly she wasn't simply sucking, she was worshipping. Paying lip-service to a cock. Tongue-and throat-service too. A Cultrix of the Cock. Priestess of the Penis. Devotee of the Dong. Pleasuring herself by submitting herself totally to service.

The cock stiffened still further, trembled, and started to throb, firing come into her. She gulped it down eagerly, wanting gallons of it. Strawberry-flavoured come. She wanted to be choked with it, to be drowned in it, and her hands came away from her own tits and moved left and right to take other cocks and begin to masturbate them. The cock in her mouth stopped firing and she dragged her mouth off it, the desire to continue worshipping it only just overcome by the desire to take another into her mouth, and worship that too. Her mouth was a temple and she wanted to erect an eternal idol there. A Phallocrator, a Cock-Lord who would eternally rise, fall, and rise again.

The cock in her right hand began to spurt and she caught up the come and rubbed it clumsily into her tits, before reaching out for another one. Her mouth closed greedily over a second cock and sucked hard as it slid into her. Grapefruit. Christ, this wasn't enough. She wanted a cock in her cunt and arsehole too. One in each armpit, one between her breasts, one in each knee-hollow, one in her arse-cleft, one between her thighs, one between her calves, a dozen more sliding over her body. Coming continuously and being replaced, drenching her with come, choking her with it, filling not just her mouth and belly and arsehole and bowels but her nostrils and ears too. Soaking every inch of her.

She thrust herself backward, cunt burning and leaking between her thighs, feeling with her buttocks for a suitably positioned cock. Not that one, nor that one, yes, this one. Could she fit it? Could she get it in? Her mind, already directing her pumping mouth and pumping hands, coolly directed her arse as she straddled the smooth, glowing head of the cock with her arse-cleft and adjusted herself to present the velvet mouth of her arsehole to it. She wanted it up her arse. A cock in her mouth and a cock in either hand and a cock up her arse. It wasn't enough but it was the best she could do. The cock in her left hand began to spurt and she let go of it for another. A second later the cock in her right hand began to spurt and she let go of it for another, having to reach a little further now.

And behind her, she managed to lodge the cockhead in her arsehole and heaved backward. With a little shock of excitement and pleasure she felt the cock enter her arse, sliding up into her, shouldering aside her sphincter, hot and thick and solid. Just its presence was sufficient: another idol enthroned, another porphyrocephalic Phallocrator standing in a velvet-walled temple, another Cock-Lord cock-sure of blind obedience. She began to jerk her buttocks rhythmically, squeezing hard on the cock with the walls of her arse-chamber, milking it towards orgasm, when it too would begin to fire into her. The cock in her mouth stiffened still further, trembled, and spurted grapefruit-flavoured come. Her hands, switching to new cocks every thirty seconds or so, were dripping with come, so wet with it now that she had to grip hard at the cocks she was wanking, or her hands would have slid off. The last bolt of come pulsed into her mouth and slid down her throat like molten pearl, and she dragged her mouth off the softening cock and bent her neck to swallow another.

But even as she started to work on it something wet hit her face and her right eye was stinging furiously, splattered with a drop of come. A cock she hadn't touched was orgasming, and as she took her mouth off its third cock and blinked around her, trying to wipe her eye with a dry knuckle on her come-soaked right hand, she saw that many more cocks were starting to come and her back was being splashed by cocks discharging behind her. The cock she was still working on with her arse started to come, firing come into her bowels, filling her with warmth, and she sank back on it, allowing it to slide further up into her, a piston driving its own discharge deeper into her.

More and more cocks, untouched by any of them, were orgasming now, come showering down from both walls of the corridor as far in either direction as she could see from her watering eyes (the left had begun to weep in apparent sympathy with the come-splattered right). Beth and Anna were taking their mouths and hands off the cocks they were working on and looking around them at the discharges, the come hurled from dozens of throbbing cocks, splattering against the opposite wall and flowing downwards to pools on the floor of the corridor. Cocks that had ejaculated were beginning to soften and droop, resuming the curve that had puzzled them as they looked down the corridor before learning the truth. She leaned forward, sliding her arsehole off the cock that had spurted into it, feeling it slither from her arse, moist and softened.

'That's it, girls,' she said. When she spoke she felt the air sharpen the flavour of come inside her mouth. She gathered saliva and swirled it, then swallowed. Beth wiped come out of her eyebrows and off her scalp, shaking her hand.

'Yes,' she said.

They began to squeeze their way along the corridor past the softening cocks, feet splashing in the come that had flowed down the walls and gathered on the floor. A few cocks were still orgasming, like belated clocks in a horologist's workshop chiming the hour a minute late, into the brittle silence left by the massed chiming a minute before. The come underfoot seemed to be getting deeper and when Gwen looked down she saw that it was flowing. The floor was inclined, carrying the come with them as they walked.

'How far to the end, Anna?' she asked.

'Nearly there.'

She looked down Anna's wet back, following the trickles of come to her firm little arse, wanting to stoop and lunge forward, sink her teeth into it, lick off the come, explore the moist coin of Anna's anus with her tongue and nose. Anna's feet rose and fell from the come flowing along the floor, then lifted from it and didn't fall: Anna had stepped forward out of the corridor and down onto the floor of the next room. As Gwen stepped forward herself she saw that the floor was a foot or two lower than the floor of the corridor.

She jumped and turned to watch Beth jump too. Beth jumped but Gwen was no longer watching her. The come was flowing off the floor of the corridor and down the wall of the new room in three grooves that ended in three tall glasses held against the wall with loops of copper. The glasses were three-quarters full and rising.

Thirteen

'Day five,' Beth said.

'Yes. Day five.'

'Well. What happens?'

'A rest-day, maybe.'

'Certainly not.'

'But she will have been sucking cocks and swallowing come for the previous two days. Hundreds of cocks. Gallons of come. Her lips will be chapped, her sense of taste temporarily destroyed, her digestion badly upset. A day of rest and recuperation will definitely be in order.'

'It definitely won't.'

'Oh, I suppose you're right.'

'You know I'm right. So what happens to her on day five?'

'On day five . . .'

'Yes?'

'On day five we take her out into the garden. Of the *château*.'

'And?'

'We take her out among the flowers. In high summer. Just after sunset.'

'Not too soon after.'

'Okay. Maybe half an hour after. The air is still warm, of course.'

'Very warm.'

'Very warm. And thick with scent.'

'From the flowers.'

'Yes. From the flowers. And we strip her, of course.'

'Of course.'

'And set her exercising. Hard.'

'What kind of exercises?'

'Sit-ups. Press-ups. High-kicks. Squats.'

'I like the squats. Will we be able to see her clearly?'

'Oh yes. There's a full moon. Or we get floodlights set up.'

'Maybe floodlights would be better. More incarceratory. Like a prison-camp.'

'Yes. You're right. So, we set her exercising, among the flowers, under floodlights.'

'And the full moon too, maybe? No harm in icing the cake.'

'No, no harm at all. Okay then, under floodlights and the full moon. Sit-ups. Press-ups. High-kicks. Squats. At double time.'

'Why?'

'So that she sweats. The air is warm, remember.'

'Very warm.'

'The warmer the better. The warmer, the sweatier.'

'And then what? When we've got her sweaty?'

'That will take time. We want her not just sweaty, but drenched in sweat. Covered in hot, fresh sweat, so that it's positively streaming off her. So that her tits and arse are gleaming under the floodlights. So that rivulets of sweat are running between her tits and between her buttocks. So that her pubes are plastered to her mons.'

'I like it.'

'She won't.'

'That's a very big part of why I like it. What next?'

'Then we make her stand stock-still, legs apart. Arms raised, pointing upwards at 45 degrees.'

'Surely 34 degrees? And a bit?'

'We'd need a protractor.'

'They're not expensive.'

'Okay then, legs apart, arms raised, pointing upwards at 34 degrees and a bit.'

'Good. Legs apart, arms raised.'

'Yes. And pouring with sweat. Still panting with her exertions. Left tit visibly shuddering with her heartbeat.'

'And?'

'We pick flowers. Roses, to begin with. White roses.'

'And?'

'And we dismantle them. Plucking the petals. Cool white petals. So that we have handfuls of petals.'

'And?'

'We stand to either side of her with our handfuls of petals and we start to decorate her body with them, sticking them to her skin using her own sweat. We put petals up her spine, like a fountain bursting from her coccyx and flowering over her shoulders. Over her belly, up between her breasts. White petals sealed to her skin with her own sweat. Overlapping each other almost, like chain-mail, or the scales of a fish. But we leave her buttocks and breasts bare.'

'And?'

'While we are decorating her with this first batch of petals, we occasionally feed them to her. One by one. White rose petals soaked in her sweat. We make her chew them and swallow them, one by one.'

'And?'

'Another batch of petals. Red roses this time. We have laid the foundations of her cloak of many colours in white rose petals; now we add red. Red petals sealed to her skin with her own sweat. Then yellow roses. Pink roses. Slowly covering her skin, except for her buttocks and breasts.'

'Why?'

'That will become apparent shortly. For now, picture how her arse and tits will rise above her florated skin, round and full and white, like the full moon riding in the warm air above.'

'Yes. I can picture it. The moon is like a tit. Or an arse. But it's a bruised arse.'

'As hers will be.'

'I never doubted it. But what next?'

'We begin to complete the cloak of many colours. Other flowers are nodding in their beds, some closed for the night, others open and pouring scent. We pluck a selection of them, shredding them, detaching the cool petals, adding them to her skin.'

'What kind of flowers?'

'Marigolds. Carnations. Poppies. Pansies and violets. Cloaking her skin. Sealed to it with her own sweat.'

'But what if the sweat dries? Won't they fall off?'

'No. They will be sealed to it with dried sweat. But remember that the air is warm. She has just exercised vigorously. She will be sweating hard. Her skin will be very hot. Just as we wish it to be.'

'Why?'

'To release the scent of the flowers. She will be a living pomander.'

'I'm not so sure about her sweating, and will her skin really be hot enough to release the scents properly?'

'Yes, of course.'

'Are you sure?'

'Perfectly sure.'

'Precautions won't hurt.'

'Then why take them?'

'I'm sorry, I meant precautions *will* hurt.'

'What precautions?'

'Surely a little ginger . . .? Put where it will do most good?'

'Ah. I see. Yes, I see. And in fact, now you come to mention it, I do have to admit to a little doubt about her continuing to sweat quite as freely as she should. And about her skin staying quite as hot as is desirable. So you are right. A little ginger, put where it will do most good.'

'Describe what we do.'

'We take some raw ginger and make her chew it for us. Chew it to a pulp, though not for too long, lest it lose its vigour.'

'And we don't want it to do that.'

'Certainly not.'

'Then what? When she's chewed it to a pulp?'

'Then we make her spit it out in a small pot.'

'Yes. And?'

'We make her bend over, very carefully. Presenting her white arse to the white moon. Moon-arse gazing unto arse-moon.'

'Yes. Wonderful. And?'

'We lever the cheeks of her arse apart, exposing the pink petal of her arsehole. Sweat has flowed down her arse-cleft copiously and moistened it, but only on the outside.'

'Yes. Only on the outside.'

'So we work the sweat inside, with the handle of the little spatula we are to employ with the ginger. Thoroughly lubricating the passage.'

'Wonderful. And then?'

'And then, of course, we put the ginger up her arse. Raw, chewed ginger. Moistened with her own spittle, inserted into an arse lubricated with her own sweat.'

'Will it begin to work at once?'

'Undoubtedly. The delicate mucous membranes of the walls of her rectal chamber will report its presence immediately.'

'Ah. Please say it again.'

'Say what again?'

'What you just said. About her arse.'

'Okay. "The delicate mucous membranes of the walls of her rectal chamber".'

'Oh, yes. Again.'

' "The delicate mucous membranes of the walls of her rectal chamber".'

'Lovely. I can imagine them clenching on the ginger. Tightening harder as it bites deeper.'

'Oh, it will bite alright. It will burn and seethe. She'll feel as though the inside of her arse is on fire.'

'What if she tries to expel it? To shit it back out, I mean?'

'We won't allow that. We'll poke it well in with the handle of the little spatula. And we'll whisper frightful punishments into her ears, telling her what will happen if she shits it out. The ginger stays put, burning inside her little blonde beast's arse.'

'And what does that do?'

'What do you think it does? It makes her sweat harder. It makes her skin get hotter. Can't you imagine it? Raw chewed ginger up your arse? What it would do to you?'

'No. But I can imagine what it will do to her.'

'Then she'll sweat, won't she?'

'Yes. Sweat heavily.'

'And her skin will heat, won't it?'

'Yes. Heat a lot.'

'And that will release the scents of the petals decorating her skin. Make her into a living pomander.'

'Okay. What next?'

'Next we set to work on her pussy.'

'Oh, good. I was wondering when we'd get to her pussy.'

'She will be too. And it will be.'

'So what do we do?'

'She's still bent over, remember. We make her straighten, slowly, so that the ginger moves inside her arse, reaching parts of arse-wall previously unaffected by it.'

'Good. And?'

'When she's straightened, we make her open her legs wider. Feet wide apart. Very wide apart. Pussy bare and defenceless. We gloat over it for a while, then we peel back the lips and push petals inside it. One by one. Cramming her pussy with rose-petals.'

'Is she oozing?'

'Yes. To some extent. But we will use her sweat too, for lubrication.'

'How many can we fit in?'

'How many what?'

'Petals.'

'That's what we'll have to find out.'

'Dozens?'

'Quite possibly.'

'Hundreds?'

'If we're cruel and uncaring.'

'Hundreds, then.'

'Okay. Hundreds of sweat-soaked petals pushed up her unwilling pussy. Cramming it to capacity.'

'Then what?'

'Then tit-torture.'

'Great. But for any particular reason?'

'Do we need a particular reason?'

'No. I just wondered, that's all.'

'Well, as it happens, there will be a particular reason for her tit-torture. To moisten the petals in her pussy.'

'They're already moistened.'

'Only with sweat.'

'And some yelm. She's a pervert, remember. She will enjoy the ginger being put up her arse. She'll even enjoy the ginger *being* up her arse. But there won't be as much yelm in her pussy as we'd like. Nowhere near as much.'

'But why do we want the petals in her pussy moistened with yelm?'

'Because she's going to eat them. We're going to torture her tits very slowly and lingeringly, and because she's such a perverted little blonde beast, she's going to enjoy it a lot. She'll ooze like nobody's business. Thoroughly moistening the petals in her pussy. Then we hook them out one by one and feed them to her.'

'How do we torture her tits?'

'Nettles.'

'Yum-yum. But isn't the garden well-maintained?'

'Oh yes. But there'll be a good patch of nettles discretely tucked away somewhere. Rank and odorous. We'll stroke her tits with some big nettle leaves. Rub her nipples with them. Very gently. Because the gentler you rub, the more they sting. Then, when her tits have started to itch and swell, we'll rub them with rose petals. Smooth and soft and cool. Contrast, you see. When we stop, the nettle-sting will be worse than ever. That's when we start to tease her nipples. Tweaking and pulling them. Scratching her areolae gently with our fingernails. Blowing on them. Asking her if she wants them to be rubbed with the rose petals again, but refusing to do it. My, how she will ooze!'

'She will. Does she come too?'

'What do you think? With nettles on her tits and ginger up her arse, a disgusting little pervert like her?'

'Then she comes.'

'She does. And that's what we want, after all.'

'Why?'

'To macerate the petals in her pussy thoroughly. Just think of those pink velvet pussy-walls writhing and clamping on the petals. There's surprising strength in a pussy, you know. Especially a well-trained one. And she will be coming very hard, the little beast.'

'Why?'

'Because the torture will be so particularly pleasurable to her. Nettles on her tits. Nipples teased and tweaked and blown on, while her arse is on fire inside. Body aching with the strain of recent exercise. Oh, she'll love it.'

'How disgusting. What is the younger generation coming to?'

'I don't know about the younger generation in general, but I know about her.'

'Then what's she coming to?'

'She's coming to a heavy fall. But the condemned girl will eat a hearty breakfast. After her third or fourth orgasm, when the petals in her pussy are thoroughly macerated, we will remove them and feed them to her. *Pétales fraises au sueur et yelme d'Anna.*'

'And then?'

'Those nettles again. Remember, I said there was a rank patch of them close at hand. Dozens of plants, if not hundreds. And how many have we used so far? Maybe two or three, to supply leaves for her tit-torture. Well, we're going to rectify that now. We are nearing the climax of our session in our little *jardin des supplices*. We make her bend over again, presenting her white arse to the white moon. Then we leave moon-arse gazing unto arse-moon while we gather nettles. Bunches of them in well-gloved hands. Then we return to our little blonde beast, and gaze at her for a time. She's still coated in petals, her tits are still stinging and burning with nettle-rash, her pussy is still harbouring yelm-soaked petals, her raised arse is still on fire inside as it gazes at the moon.'

'And?'

'Well, her arse is on fire inside. What are we going to do about that?'

'Make it worse? Put more ginger up it?'

'No. We want symmetry of sensation. If it's on fire *inside*, we want it on fire where . . .?'

'I don't follow you.'

'Symmetry of sensation. If the *inside* is on fire, then so must the . . .?'

'Oh, I see. The *outside* must be on fire too. But how?'

'What have we just been gathering? What are we holding bunches of in our well-gloved hands?'

'Well, nettles. But you're surely not proposing we use *nettles* on her defenceless little bottom?'

'That is precisely what I am proposing.'

'But that's fiendish. It's bad enough rubbing her tits with them, but actually *beating* her with them. With an entire bunch of nettles. And no doubt you propose renewing the bunch when it's broken from the violence with which you've plied it on her buttocks.'

'That is precisely what I propose.'

'Then I can't go along with it. It's just too cruel. Fiendishly cruel. Beating her arse with nettles. That's going far too far.'

'Then you won't do it?'

'No. Of course not.'

'Under no circumstances?'

'None. Positively none. N-o-n-e. None.'

'Not a single, solitary one?'

'N– well, now you come to mention it, there is *one* circumstance in which I might consider relenting just a little of my principled opposition to the course you are proposing in defiance of all humanity and common decency. Just one circumstance, mind.'

'What is it?'

'That I get first go. While her bum is still white.'

'Granted.'

Fourteen

Gwen turned away from the glasses of come, wiping at her body and face, and looked at the new room. It was painted bright blue and was circular, about twenty metres across, high-ceiling'd, and perfectly bare but for three widely separated exercise bikes facing the centre of the room from just in front of the single, curving wall. She thought the bikes were equidistant, 120° apart. She walked over to the nearest. White enamel and steel. It looked just like the others except that one of them was red enamel and the other black. A plastic drinking bottle with a crooked steel drinking-tube sat on the handlebar, but when she tugged at the top and it came off she saw that the bottle was empty.

She replaced the top and felt the seat of the bike. White leather, oddly smooth beneath her fingertips. She swung herself astride the seat and glanced at the hodometer as she fitted her feet to the pedals. The needle, sitting ready at the left, went from 0 to 10,000 in divisions of 1,000 over the label *P/Sec*. 1,000s of what per second? Her feet were in the pedals and she pressed down hard with her right foot. Nothing. The pedals wouldn't budge. She swung off the bike and went to inspect the black-enamelled one. Her bike. She swung herself onto its black-leathered seat, rubbing her buttocks luxuriously on it for a moment before trying the pedals. They wouldn't move either. Beth was sitting on the white-enamelled bike by now, looking puzzled as she tried to move the pedals.

'Try yours,' Gwen called and Beth swung off Anna's and trotted over to try the red-enamelled one. She swung herself astride it, fitted her feet to the pedals, then shook her head.

'Nope. These don't move either.'

'Then what are the fucking things for? The pedals don't work, the drinking bottles are empty, and the speedoes go up in 1,000s. At least, mine and Anna's do. What about yours?'

'Yep. Mine does too. But 1,000s of what?'

'That's what I'm asking myself. Anna, any ideas? Hey, what the fuck are you doing?'

Anna, a look of disgust on her face, was carrying an overflowing glass of come across to her bike, holding it well in front of her so that the steady drips of come didn't land on her feet. She didn't reply, just walked to her bike, took the top off her drinking bottle, slid the glass of come inside it, and replaced the top. Then she stooped out of Gwen's sight and the pedal on Gwen's side suddenly began to move, turning a complete circle before Anna stood up.

'So that's it. Anna, you're a genius. Bring us our glasses and we'll get pedalling too.'

'Fetch your own.'

'You cheeky little bitch. Beth, we've got another insurrection to suppress.'

'Nah, forget it. We might have been puzzling it out for a long time if it hadn't been for her. Let's fetch 'em ourselves.'

Beth swung herself off her bike, cunt flashing a smile between her thighs, and went to fetch her glass of come. Gwen gripped her handlebars hard for a moment, staring at Anna, then gave in, swung off her bike too, and went to fetch her glass. As she lifted it from the wall and turned to carry it back to her bike she could see the shining trails of come-drops on the blue floor in front of her, one leading towards Anna's bike, one leading towards Beth's.

She created a third trail, carrying her overflowing glass to her bike, tugging the top off her drinking bottle, slipping the glass inside, replacing the top. The steel straw was sitting deep in thick come now, but she wasn't going to be sucking on it. Her mouth was still thick with the taste of the come she had drunk in the cock-corridor, and that was enough to be going on with.

But with the bottle full, her pedals ought to work, the way Anna's and Beth's already did. She swung herself onto the seat of the bike, put her feet to them, and pushed. They turned at once and she grinned, watching the needle on the hodometer jerk to life. She began to pedal harder and watched the needle climb toward 1,000. Anna and Beth were pedalling too: she could hear the sound, and she was about to glance up at them when Anna suddenly screamed.

She lifted her head fast. Anna had stopped pedalling and was staring at the floor in the centre of the room. A huge iris was opening there, revealing a pupil of deep black; and a door was sliding over the entrance to the cock-corridor. Beth had stopped pedalling too, staring at the centre of the room.

'For fuck's sake,' Gwen said. She stopped pedalling and swung off her bike. The iris had stopped opening now and as she walked towards the black pupil she saw it was the mouth of a circular pit. When she was a metre or so from the edge she went down on her knees and crawled forward to peer into it. Not just a pit: a very deep pit. The bottom was fifty or sixty metres away, a red circular floor at the foot of vertiginous black walls.

'Where's the pendulum?' Beth asked.

She looked up. Beth had got off her bike and was walking towards the pit too. As she approached the edge she went down on her knees and crawled to peer into it.

'Eh?' Gwen said.

'Edgar Allen Poe.'

'Oh, yeah. Well, if a pendulum is about to join us, it will come from up . . .'

She stopped speaking. Beth looked up and followed her gaze towards the ceiling. A grille had opened there and falling through it were hundreds of white, red and blue petals. Gwen moved back a little from the edge of the pit and stood up. The petals reached the air in front of her and began to fall into the pit, and she stepped forward and put out her hand to catch some.

'Careful,' said Beth. Gwen stepped back, examining what was on her palm. White, red, blue. Rose, poppy, violet.

'They're stopping,' said Beth. Gwen looked up. The shower of petals was thinning; in a few moments it would have stopped. She stepped forward again and shook the petals off her hand into the pit.

'Well, that solves the problem of the speedoes,' she said. 'They go up in 1,000s of petals per second.'

She turned and looked towards Anna.

'Anna, pedal again for a few seconds.'

Anna hesitated for a moment then started pedalling.

'Okay, that's enough!' Gwen said. She pointed upwards. 'Look.'

Another shower of petals was falling from the grille into the pit. White petals only, this time.

'But what's all this in aid of?' Beth asked. Gwen was about to reply when the floor shuddered and she stepped back from the pit.

'Christ, what was that?'

Anna stopped pedalling and swore under her breath behind them.

'It was the walls,' she said. 'They've moved inwards. The room has got smaller.'

Gwen looked at her, then at the walls.

'Are you sure?'

'I *saw* them, and my bike moved forward at the same time.'

'She's right, Gwen,' Beth said. 'The room is smaller. It *is* the pit and the pendulum.'

A final few white petals fluttered into the pit. Gwen shook her head.

'Where's the pendulum?'

'No pendulum,' Anna said. 'We've got petals instead. The room gets smaller and smaller until we have to jump into the pit. We've got to fill the pit with petals before then, or else.'

'Petals will be no good.'

'They will be if they're thick enough.'

The floor shuddered again and Gwen saw the walls move this time. Beth turned from the pit and ran back to her bike, calling over her shoulder as she went.

'What other suggestion have you got?'

Gwen shrugged, turned, and ran to her bike. The white petals were already falling again: Anna had started pedalling furiously as soon as she had worked out what was going on. Red petals were beginning to fall with them as she swung herself into the saddle of her bike and started to pedal herself. The floor shuddered again, reaching her even as she pedalled, and she felt the bike moving forward with the floor. The room was visibly smaller now, a band of blue iris contracting on the wide black pupil of the pit, staring up implacably into the shower of falling petals.

'Christ,' Gwen muttered. She pedalled harder, feeling herself start to sweat, the half-dried come on her skin beginning to moisten and flow sluggishly. Slug-slime. Come on her skin. The needle of the hodometer crawled towards 5,000. 5,000 violet petals a second. 5,000 poppy petals. 5,000 rose petals. 15,000 petals in all. Would it be enough? 18,000 would be better. 21,000 even better. She looked up, panting.

'Harder, Anna. Pedal harder. Beth, put your fucking back into it.'

Her legs were starting to ache, the first full trickles of sweat beginning under her arms, down her back, between her breasts and buttocks. And her throat was dry, her mouth drier. Pedalling was hard; pedalling thirsty was harder. If only the drinking bottle were full of water, not come. Full of iced water. Not come. She licked her dry lips, raising herself into her seat a little to drive her feet harder at the pedals. 6,000 violet petals a second. How many centimetres would that be? Would it even be a centimetre? Maybe it would be just enough to cover the floor of the pit, just enough to rise the pile of petals a fraction towards the ceiling.

Christ, her throat was dry and getting drier as she panted with effort, her whole body glistening with sweat

110

now. The needle stood at 6,500 and she stared at it, trying to send it higher by force of will alone. Her legs were already aching too badly for her to force them harder at the pedals. If only her throat wasn't so dry. If she could just moisten it she knew she could pedal harder. She stared at the drinking-bottle. It sat on the handlebars, stolid and unresponsive, full of salty come. If she sucked at it, it would just make her thirstier, in the long run. But the long run wasn't what mattered. If she could moisten her throat *now* she could pedal harder.

The floor shuddered again, and her resistance broke. She put her head down towards the drinking bottle, closed her mouth over the steel straw, and sucked. Come flowed into her mouth and she gulped it down. It tasted odd. Why? Because it had cooled. It was cool come now, not hot come. Not hot from a hairy scrotum.

She stopped sucking and drew her head back, rising in her seat again to force her legs harder at the pedals. It had worked: the needle was trembling at the 7,000 mark and somehow her legs weren't aching so badly now. Moistening her mouth and throat had done the trick. Even with come. And it hadn't tasted so bad, had it? It was better now it was cool. Cool come. Sitting in a bottle on the handlebars. Ready for her to drink whenever she chose. She looked up. Beth's head was just withdrawing from the steel straw of her bottle, her tongue licking at her pale lips.

Gwen grinned mirthlessly. This had the authentic tang of Bärengelt. She could taste him as clearly as she could taste the come in her mouth. The absurd situation, the pain, the effort, the humiliation. Drinking come to ease the ache in her legs. The needle wobbled as it reached 7,300 and she realized the ache in her legs was getting worse. She needed another drink. Another drink of come. Her throat felt narrow and tight, choking with dryness. She needed another drink. Even come would do.

She leaned forward, head going down, mouth sliding over the steel straw of the drinking bottle, and sucked, dismayed at the way her nipples and cunt reacted to the cool come that squirted onto her tongue and down her throat. She was enjoying it. Enjoying the taste. She sucked again, filling her mouth with it, then sat back, letting it trickle down her throat in jerks, her cunt beginning to ooze slowly onto the black leather seat of the bike.

The floor shuddered again, the bike moving forward another metre or so, and now Beth and Anna were half-hidden by the shower of petals falling into the pit. The edges of the pit were coated with petals that had fluttered sideways as they fell and she stared at them, trying to read the patterns they made as she let the last of the come in her mouth trickle down her throat. The ache in her legs was solid, but somehow pleasurable, left and right balanced on the glowing chalice of her cunt. She drew in a deep breath, savouring the tang of her own sweat and the musk of her leaking yelm. Her throat was closing again and she could hear herself beginning to wheeze, a sediment of light pain beginning to thicken at the base of her lungs. She needed another drink of come, but waited, enjoying the craving in her body and the dizziness of oxygen deficit.

Then she leaned forward and sucked on the steel straw. Thick, salty come. A male tang on her mouth and in her nostrils, overlaying the smell of her own sweat and yelm. She gulped it down and sucked in another mouthful, choking a little as the floor shuddered for the sixth time and the bike slid forward. She allowed it to flow down her throat in pulses, imagining that it was squirting hot and fresh into her mouth, then sucked in another mouthful and leaned back.

Beth and Anna were almost gone behind the falling petals, just a left foot and a right foot swinging up and down behind the fringes of them. If she knew how wide the pit was, she could work out how far they were from it. It looked like three or so metres. The floor would shudder two or three times more and then they would have to jump into the pit. How many petals had fallen into it? It must be hundreds of thousands by now. Maybe millions. The floor would surely be piled high with them. Roses and poppies and violets. A cool, deep bed to cushion their fall.

The floor shuddered again and she found extra energy to pedal with, the needle of the hodometer hovering midway between 8,000 and 9,000. Her throat was closing again, but she didn't want to torture herself any more, she just wanted to pedal as hard as she could and she put her mouth down to the steel straw and sucked hard. Come spurted into her mouth and she gulped it down and sucked again, disconcerted to hear the bottle bubble thickly, like a nearly drained milkshake. The come was nearly gone. She sucked hard, hearing the bubbling get louder, and swallowed the last of it, sucking for a final few seconds to make sure, then leaned back and pedalled.

The floor shuddered, and petals were falling just ahead of her now, white, red and blue, an endless descending curtain of petals that defeated the eyes' attempt to track it. Her throat was closing again, a faint wheeze in it, felt as yet rather than heard. No more come. She would have to do the best she could without it. Pedal and hope for the best. The next shudder in the floor might be the last. She gritted her come-coated teeth and pedalled. *Faster, you bitch. Faster.*

The floor shuddered again, carrying the bike forward to the very edge of the pit. If she leaned forward a little she would be able to see right down into it. Next time would be the end. She screamed breathlessly and pedalled, pedalled, pedalled, shaking her head from side to side to keep sweat from her eyes as she watched the needle crawl to the brink of 9,000. One more effort . . . and . . . yes! She grinned and then yelled with surprise as something landed across her defenceless arse, stinging fiercely. She left go of one handlebar and spun, clutching at her arse with the hand she had released. The wall directly behind her had opened in a vertical slot and something was turning in it. A wheel carrying bunches of nettles. Another was poised to fall full on her arse. She jerked forward, feet slipping off the pedals, then shouted with fear as the floor shuddered for what was surely the last time.

The bike slid to the edge of the pit and tipped forward. The bunch of nettles behind her fell, landing half on the sweat-and-yelm moistened leather of her seat, half on her arse, and the pain rose even through her fear. The bike was still tipping, firmly fastened to the floor, but obviously designed to tip until it was vertical and she had no choice but to let go and fall. White and red petals were diminishing in the falling curtain ahead of her – Anna had stopped pedalling too – but there were green petals there too now. Very large ones. Nettle leaves.

She looked back, saw the next bunch of nettles swing down towards her, and hopped her arse forward and out of range. The bike was at 45°, tipping relentlessly, and she could see down into the pit through the shower of nettle leaves and the last of the falling petals.

'Fuck it,' she said aloud. She swung her legs up and over the handlebars, turned, gripped the handlebars, let herself fall to the full extent of her arms, let go, and dropped.

Fifteen

As she fell the scent of the metres-deep layer of petals rushed up around her, overlaid with the tarter, greener scent of the nettles. She landed on softness, a resilient bed of nettle leaves that absorbed her deep into itself, cushioning the violence of her fall gently to nothing, and stinging her mercilessly for the privilege. She struggled upright on her elbows, her hands clasped protectively over her breasts, hissing with pain as she tried to look up into the continuing shower of nettle leaves. A white shape flashed downwards in the green to her left, only to be absorbed instantly into the bed of nettle leaves as though it had fallen into deep green water. Then a head emerged and a neck, then elbows struggling for balance as hands were clasped over vulnerable breasts too, and she saw it was Beth.

'Where's Anna?' she called through the soft patter of the falling leaves, and Beth jerked her chin upward.

'Hanging around while she waits to drop in.'

Waist-deep in nettles, Gwen let go of her breasts cautiously and cupped her hands around her mouth as she put her head back.

'Come on, Anna!' she shouted. 'It's safe. We're both okay.'

A wail greeted her from high above and suddenly a second white shape descended among the green, absorbed into the sea of nettles, fighting its way back to the surface.

'The gang's all here,' Beth said. 'Now what?'

Gwen was clutching her breasts again, shielding them from the shower of nettle leaves, her arse and legs and most of her body stinging fiercely.

'We sink and swim,' she said.

'Sink *and* swim?'

'Yes. Get below these fucking nettles and into the petals. Swim our way into them. There must be a door at the bottom of the pit somewhere. We've just got to find it.'

'Are you sure?'

'No. But what other suggestion have you got?'

Beth shrugged, hands still shielding her breasts.

'Okay,' said Beth, 'then it's carried. Get sinking and swimming. Anna, did you hear that?'

Anna nodded, her face blotched with nettle stings, small hands shielding her breasts.

'Then come on. At least those petals will be soothing.'

She took her own hands away from her breasts and began to dig into the nettles. It was going to hurt, but no pain, no gain. If they stayed where they were, they would soon be buried in the nettles anyway. She bent forward into the opening her hands had made, closed her eyes, and began to burrow, digging her way down through the deep seam of nettles for the deeper underlying seam of petals. Her breasts were stung at once, their delicate skin seeming to report every harsh hair that brushed against them, and her nipples and areolae blazed with pain, brighter beacons of sensation atop burning hills on the landscape of an entire body on fire.

She burrowed, eyes closed, nostrils filled with the scent of crushed nettle, hoping the seam wasn't too deep, that she would reach the petals soon, that the petals were not packed too tightly, that she would be able to burrow into them, out of this stinging sea of reeking nettles. The patter of the falling leaves continued above her and she could faintly hear Beth swearing, her voice dulled as it travelled to her through the nettles. How much deeper? Her hands were burning and she had to force herself to grab vigorously at the nettles. The more softly she touched them the more strongly they stung. If only she could crush her way through them, but she couldn't, she could only slide through them, her breasts supremely vulnerable, riding the sea of nettles like the breasts of a figurehead on a ship, kissed by its green waters with endless harsh, stinging lips.

She smelt the petals before she realized her hands were moving among them, their scent rising sweetly through the crushed nettle stink; and when she had smelt them she could feel them with her numbed hands, cool and gentle, already soothing the smart of the nettle stings in her hands and forearms. Christ, she wanted to get her breasts among them. Rub them in handfuls over the weals in the delicate breast-skin, crush them and smear them on her nipples. And with just a little more effort she could. She burrowed and dug, arms deep into the petals now, the scent of them stronger in her nostrils, strengthening her will to fight down harder, get her head down to them, so that she could finally open her eyes onto a strange green twilight and see better to work harder and faster and dig herself deeper into them.

The patter of leaves from above had stopped, or she was too deep to hear it now, and she could no longer hear Beth's swearing. Nothing existed any more but the sting of the nettles, the smell of the petals, and the joy of digging herself beyond one and into the other. Her breasts were finally safe, sliding against coolness and smoothness, and she had to fight the temptation to stop where she was and begin work on them at once, rubbing the petals against them, crushing petals and smearing them on her nipples. But she wanted her legs and arse out of the nettles too. She wanted to be entombed in petals: to lie safe, deep in them.

But the scent was stronger. Almost dizzying. Roses and poppies and violets. Perhaps it was the poppies. Like in *The Wizard of Oz*. The scent made her sleepy. Sleepier and sleepier, so that her burrowing got slower and slower, and when she was finally entombed, had finally burrowed into her bed of cool, smooth petals, was finally soothing her poor, nettle-stung breasts, she felt as though she was dreaming. She heard a giggle and jumped with fright as a hand clutched at her right knee.

'Who the fuck's that?'

Another hand clutched at her, fastening on her left thigh, and she felt stubble brush her stomach as a head dropped to her cunt and warm lips kissed it.

'Guess.'

It was Beth. She reached down for her, pulling her up among the petals so that they lay arm in arm, breast to breast. She ran her hands down Beth's back and took hold of her buttocks, rotating them, juddering them.

'And where's our little sister?' she asked.

'No idea. It takes a woman to satisfy a woman, so I was only interested in you.'

'But an *hors d'œuvre* is nice.'

She opened her mouth and drew in air, feeling the scent of the petals fill her lungs, dizzying her.

'Anna!' she shouted.

Beth kissed her neck and began to nibble.

'It's no good,' she said between nibs. 'She won't hear you. Forget about everything for the time being. Let's just fuck.'

'Suck first, fuck second. My tits are on fire.'

'And mine aren't?'

'You suck my tits, I'll suck yours.'

'It's a deal.'

Beth kissed her way down Gwen's throat, stabbing her tongue between her lips to leave little spots of moisture on Gwen's skin. She found the breast-cleft and began to lick in earnest, up it, down it. Gwen groaned in frustration.

'Tits,' she said. 'On them, not between them.'

Beth laughed softly.

'All in good time.'

But she began to kiss her way up Gwen's left breast, warm lips against warm, nettle-stung skin. When she reached the summit her kisses began to linger on the areola, spiralling the nipple without touching it. Gwen groaned again, her nipples hardening and lengthening to the puffs of Beth's hot, moist breath. The nipples were throbbing worse than ever, aroused but unsoothed.

'Lick them, you bitch,' she said between clenched teeth.

Beth's head came off her chest with mock surprise and Gwen could feel her staring up at her face in the twilight.

'What are you? A woman or a man? I don't charge like a bull at a gate at erogenous zones. I try to do things with a little more finesse.'

118

'Shut up and get on with it.'

'You always were butch.'

Beth's head dropped back and a little shiver of delight ran through Gwen's body as she felt the lips settle to her nipple, kiss it lingeringly, then seal slowly to it, sucking, pausing, sucking. The tongue emerged and licked, circling the nipple clockwise and anticlockwise, pressing at it, slowly rocking it. A trickle of heat ran down through her belly towards her cunt, pooling in the vee between her thighs, melting her cunt-lips apart, starting the ooze of yelm. As though by instinct Beth dropped her hand to the unfurling lips, fingertips stroking, squeezing, climbing slowly upward to the stiffening thorn of her clitoris.

Gwen released a long breath and drew in a fresh draught of petal-scented air. She was drunk on it, almost hallucinating on it, ready to drift away into an empire of dreams, clothed in stinging skin, but held pinned in reality by the glorious sensation of the tongue and lips on her nipple, the stroking fingers at her cunt. Another long breath out, another in. Her heart was thumping, applauding her on-coming orgasm as it rushed to breast the tape. Beth's hand dropped between and beyond her thighs, sliding easily on the yelm now sheening them, and returned with a handful of petals, feeding them between her cunt-lips, rubbing them over her clitoris.

Teeth began to nibble at her nipple, sending electric shocks of sensation through her breast, sharpening the heat in her stomach and cunt and heightening the sting of the nettles in her skin. She clenched her hands into the petals beneath her and released breath again, letting it shudder out of her, then letting it shudder back into her, filling her lungs, lifting her breast towards the cruel-and-kind mouth, sharp teeth, warm lips, moist tongue. Beth's yelm-smeared fingers, petals still clinging to them, began to work at her clitoris expertly, irresistibly, and her stomach swelled and hollowed simultaneously, opening a vacuum inside her that orgasm would abhor, that orgasm was already trembling to fill, that orgasm with a clash of sistra and a bacchantic shout was rushing up from her cunt and down from her nipple to overthrow.

She shuddered and jerked as it filled her, the tongue and fingers working more delicately now, prolonging the pleasure by feeding less of it into her, a whisper in Greek heard beneath a shout in Latin, a thread of incense smelt through thick fumes of burning wood. Beth's mouth left her breast, leaving a broad patch of spittle to cool there as she moved up her body to kiss mouth to mouth.

'Did you like it?'

'Loved it.'

'Good. Then I'll have the same, please. Heavier on the tongue, lighter on the teeth.'

'You'll get what you're given, my girl.'

'Is that a threat or a promise?'

'Both.'

She began to kiss her way down Beth's throat, waiting for her chin to touch the upper swell of Beth's breasts and slide between them, fitting snugly in the cleft. The skin beneath her lips was flushed and wealed with nettle stings, crusted here and there with dried come. Her chin brushed breast, touched breast, settled between the cleft, and slid. She kissed her way up the swell of Beth's left breast; reached the nipple and areola; began to breathe and puff at the nipple, sensing rather than feeling the way it swelled and stiffened to the moistness and warmth; then licked her way around the areola with short strokes of her tongue, left, right, circling it clockwise, counterclockwise, tasting the sweat, re-moistening flakes of dried come, tasting that too, two salty flavours that intermingled and were underlaid with the elusive Beth smell. The Beth-breast-smell. Delicious.

She laid her mouth on the nub of Beth's nipple. Nuzzled it. Licked it. Sealed her lips over it, sucking hard, and lifted her head, dragging the nipple up with it, letting it relax, licking it, sucking it. The flavour of Beth's skin was concentrated here, at the summit of her breast, tiny scent-glands oozing in the rich pink tissues as they were irrigated with blood. She opened her mouth in an 'O' and clamped her lips over the nipple and areola, breathing in and out, sucking in, blowing out, then returned to licking and sucking.

She was getting light-headed again, dizzy with lack of air, with the thick flower scent of the air she did have, and the hand she dropped to Beth's cunt seemed separate from her body, controlled by telepathy rather than nerves, for she could not feel her arm any more. She ruffled Beth's cunt-hair, feeling knots and beads of dried come in it, then brushed lower, down the silkier hair that fringed her swelling cunt-lips. Her wrist and lower forearm were re-reported, lying across Beth's cunt-hair, pricked by the dried come in it. Beth's nipple was a tower rising in her mouth, a ziggurat atop a tell.

She zigged and zagged her tongue at it, pink flashes of fat lightning, a goddess's pleasure and displeasure, then began to nibble at the blood-turgid morsel. Beth was trembling, little seismic tremors of excitement running up the plains of her thighs to die in the valley of her cunt. Gwen's fingers were moist with yelm, dripping with it, slipping and slithering as she worked at the lips and between the lips, dipping deep into the toothless, tongue-less mouth, all oozing gum, opening for a cock that never appeared, topped by the sharp little nose of the clitoris, raised and sniffing for pleasure. Time to give the clit some stick. To tease and touch it. Preside over the rising tide of Beth's orgasm as her own dizziness increased.

Beth began to rock and shudder, moaning into the thick twilight of the petals as they lay together below the nettles. Drunk with sex and scent, they grappled with each other, riding each other like surfboards on a sea of petals, fitting themselves to each other, settling head between thighs, head between thighs for mutual cunnilingus. And sucked. Licked. Sucked. And lost consciousness with fresh yelm on their lips and tongues.

High above them the nettle leaves had ceased to fall and those already fallen lay flat and thick and seemingly undisturbed, filling the whole bottom of the pit. A pink arm, puffed with nettle-rash, broke the surface, then a head, another arm, a torso, pink-and-white skin, puffed with nettle-stings, small breasts, pink-and-white too, nipples painfully turgid, squeezed and pulled between

121

slender fingers. Anna crawled and threw herself to the side of the tower and began to run the fingers of her left hand over the wall, right hand still working at her nipples, her mouth open and moist. Her face was harlequin: white and smooth, pink and wealed.

She found what she sought, fingers dipping into depressions in the smooth marble of the wall, tugging open a little door. She reached inside it, twisted at something, swung the door closed. A low moan filled the air, steadily getting louder, rising in pitch, and she looked up, rubbing at the weals on her face. The surface of the nettle-sea was starting to move, jumping and settling as though the air was plucking at it. Suddenly a small leaf left the sea completely, sailing upwards, joined even as it flew by half a dozen others, joined even as they flew by dozens, leaves large and small, sucked upwards on a rising shriek of air.

Anna put her fingers in her ears, pressed herself hard against the wall, and watched as the nettles were sucked upwards, hundreds of them, taking off in ones and twos and threes and fours, taking off in rafts, large and small, leaping upwards far faster than they had fallen, the sea evaporating far faster than it had risen. A sea floor of petals was exposed, sucked up among nettle leaves even more freely, feeding white, red and blue into their green. Something white was exposed as the floor of petals lifted into the air, a long slim something, white wearing a pink archipelago of nettle-rash, an Aegean of weals and blisters. Beth's legs, then Beth's buttocks, her back, head, shoulders, arms, unearthed by the stripping of the thick stratum of nettles above her, Beth lying atop another white shape, copper-stubbled head between its thighs. Beth sucking Gwen, Gwen sucking Beth.

Anna took a finger out of one ear and turned to re-open the little door, reached inside it, twisted. The shriek of moving air stopped and petals and nettles released in mid-flight pattered briefly on the exposed sea-floor of petals, landing across Beth's unconcerned white-and-pink back and legs. Anna swung the little door closed and got unsteadily to her feet, sinking shin- and knee-deep as she waded out to them.

'Beth,' she said.

She took hold of a buttock and rocked at it gently.

'Beth. Beth.'

The skin of the back tightened and shivered. Beth moaned. Her head came up, fell back, came up. One arm crocked, trembling spastically, propped in the petals, pushed up, lifting her so that she could look round at Anna. She blinked at her, face pink beneath the pinker splotches of nettle-rash.

'What the fuck's going on?'

'Time to get out of here. Wake Gwen.'

Anna waded shin- and knee-deep back to the wall of the tower and began to feel along it again, searching for the other door.

Sixteen

'Day seven?'

'Day seven is getting to grips day.'

'Getting to grips with what?'

'Getting to grips with her tits.'

'Ooh, I like the sound of that. How do we do it?'

'We make her think she is being released. That her punishment has been sufficient and her imprisonment is over. Today, she will leave the *château*!'

'And will she?'

'Yes. In the evening. But there are many hours to fill before then. So in the morning she wakes, tied to the small bed in an attic of the *château*, naked beneath an inadequate sheet, bottom still burning from the nettles, bladder full and aching, for you will remember how she sweated in the garden. When the session was over, we let her drink her fill. Now her bladder reminds her, throbbing painfully as she lies in the bed, unable to move, feeling the warmth of the day invade the little room through the black curtains at the barred windows.'

'Will she wet the bed?'

'That is what she fears. Normally, we are up to her very early, dragging her out of bed at six or seven o'clock to stand shivering on bare boards while we harangue her and tell her of the torments that await, and then stand watching and making crude jokes as she uses the white chamberpot under the bed. Today, it is eight o'clock or later, and we have still not appeared. How her poor little bladder throbs and aches, how she is tempted to surrender and let golden warmth flood the bed in a ecstasy of relief! But she dare not. She fears our wrath. She bites her pale lips and waits. How she waits, sweating, moaning softly, praying even!'

'To whom?'

'To *le bon Dieu*, of course. She is a pious little blonde beast. Those fat Teutonic cocks she sucked, those silver-ringed fingers she allowed to tickle her *con*, juicing her up for those fat Teutonic cocks to invade her, it was all in aid of her aged mother and sisters! She sold her body for food alone, deeming duty to *patrinomie* higher than duty to *patrie*, and she prayed furiously for forgiveness all the while, she performed so many penances!'

'Did they involve pain?'

'But of course. Her God is greedy for pain. He created her little blonde body, he has proprietorial rights over it, to sow and reap as he pleases.'

'Then does she not see us as an instrument of his pleasure?'

'No. For we openly enjoy what we do to her. We are instruments of the Devil, she is sure of that. She even accuses us, you will scarce believe, of trumping up the charges against her! "It is not I who am the *collaboratrice*," she claims. "You mistake me for another young blonde, or rather, you lyingly claim that I am she, that you might practise your perversions on me!"'

'As a later age will say, she is in denial.'

'But of course. The louder she protests her innocence, the more she proclaims her guilt. She has a clear choice: to confess all and absolve herself of her crimes, or prolong the pain she suffers. And by prolonging the pain she suffers, she provides more evidence of her depravity.'

'But does she not claim that the state of her pussy gives the lie to our claims that she laid nightly with our enemies?'

'*Pouf!* If her pussy bears no trace of the many cocks it welcomed, that is more evidence of her crimes. What but an expert pussy could absorb such violence? And in any case, it was a partner in her criminal enterprise, for she took her guests up the backstairs too, between those white globes of hers, through her pink arsehole.'

125

'Yet she claims her arsehole bears no signs of the depraved usage to which it must have been subject if our accusations are correct.'

'Again, *pouf*! She has a thousand whorish tricks to explain that away. Committed to her collaborationist course, she gave it her full energies and ingenuity. Do you not remember, before the war, how she used to work with the church among the whores?'

'Yes. Striving for their salvation.'

'And acquiring the expertise she would apply in the years of war that would immediately follow. To save others from sin, she must familiarize herself with sin. To guide the steps of the whore from the path to perdition, she must know the path the whore treads. Is it not so?'

'It is so.'

'But of course it is so. And now, she lies in her bed, praying to *le bon Dieu* on whose behalf she has always striven to work, bladder throbbing in the little blonde body that she has always selflessly given to the service of others. It is half past eight: no sign of us. Quarter to nine: no sign of us. Nine o'clock: no sign of us. The minutes begin to crawl, weighted with the bursting agony of her overfull bladder. Five past: no sign of us. Ten past: no sign of us. Quarter past: no s – but wait, what is that on the stairs? Footsteps! We have come at last and she will be relieved of her pain!'

'She will?'

'Yes. But not as soon as she thinks. The door of her little room rattles as it is unlocked, and we stride into the room, our heavy shoes crashing on the bare boards. She lies in bed sweating, blue eyes shining with a plea for release from the ropes that bind her. We sit on the bed, one to either side of her, and stroke her hot, moist brow, telling her that today she will be released. She trembles with impatience, fearing every second that her will will break even as we speak to her and she will gush into the inadequate sheet that covers her. She tries to speak, to interrupt us and plead to be untied and allowed to pee, but we do not seem to understand what she says and speak on.

Another five minutes pass! She is dizzy with pain and impatience! At last, we get up and begin to untie her. She springs out of bed in an instant and is already reaching under the bed for the chamberpot when she sees our looks of surprise.

' "May I pee, *mesdames*?" she asks.

' "But of course," we reply.

'She drags out the chamberpot, trembling with impatience, sets it on the floor, begins to squat over it.

' "*Un moment, ma fille!*" I cry and by sheer force of will she manages – just barely – to hold shut the bladder that another half-second would have opened and flooded without hope of control. Her eyes bulge with distress.

' "What is it, *madame*?" she asks.

' "I wish to inspect the chamberpot. We will have another prisoner in here tomorrow.

'Biting her lip with agony, she lifts the thing to my outstretched hand. I peer inside, turn the thing over, examine beneath it, turn it over again, scrutinize the rim.

' "It seems satisfactory," I say. The face of our little blonde beast breaks with relief. Another few seconds and she will be squatting, pissing, relieving the intolerable strain on her bladder.'

Beth laughed.

'But *I* have not examined it yet.'

'*C'est vrai.* You have not. And so, before the disbelieving eyes of our little *collaboratrice*, I hand it to you. And you examine it also.'

'Very carefully. Very slowly. Twice over.'

'Yes. And then I ask, "Are you satisfied?" '

'I reply, musingly, "Yes. It is satisfactory." And hand it back.'

'And I take it as though I am about to examine it myself for the second time. But it is only a tease, a last feint in our little game with our little blonde beast. In another few seconds either her bladder will have burst or she will have pissed on the floor. I hand the chamberpot to her.'

' "*Puis-je?*" she quavers.

' "*Mais bien sûr,*" I reply.

'She places the thing on the floor and even as she squats there is a loud thrumming of piss. A veritable torrent. *Une Niagara.* I raise my eyebrows.

' "But my dear," I say, "if your bladder was so full, you should have informed us sooner and we would not have inspected the pot till later.'

'She can only shake her head, filling the pot very nearly to the brim. Then she is finished.

' "Carry it to the bathroom, dear," I tell her. "There you may empty it and wash yourself before you dress and leave us."

'She eagerly obeys. In a minute, we are walking downstairs, the three of us, she as yet naked, of course, to a sitting-room of the *château* where new clothes are laid out for her over the arm of a *chaise longue*. We let her dress at once, telling her that a car will arrive for her in half an hour. She dresses and we order her to stand before us for inspection. She looks particularly well in the clothes, does she not?'

'Oh, yes. Delectable. What is it she will wear?'

'A white shirt, grey blouse, black skirt, white stockings, black shoes. She twirls in front of a long mirror, grinning with pleasure and relief.'

'And she is wearing knickers?'

'But of course. Red knickers beneath.'

'And bra?'

'Yes. A black lacy bra. It is a little tight, even on her, and she required assistance in doing it up.'

'From me?'

'From both of us. But as you watch her admire herself in the mirror, you have a suggestion.'

'I do?'

'Yes. Because she looks so well in her new clothes, you suggest she try a little jewellery. There is a jewellery box on the mantelpiece. We let her rummage in it and choose a pair of earrings. Amethyst drops mounted in silver. She slips them on and they are the icing on the cake, *comme on dit en anglais, n'est ce pas?*'

'*Mais oui.* She is now most toothsome. But we still have ten minutes to wait for the car, do we not?'

'Yes.'

'How to fill the time?'

'You are right. It is a problem. But wait! There is a pack of cards on the table that stands in front of the *chaise longue*. A little game, perhaps?'

'*Mais bien sûr*. Fifty *centimes* a hand?'

'Certainly. But she complains that she has no money. We muse over this problem, and suggest that she stake what she does have.'

'But she has nothing.'

'She has the clothes on her back. So we will play poker. Conventional poker for the two of us, strip poker for her.'

'Oh, dear. That suggestion does not go down well with her, does it?'

'Certainly not. It is evident she is harbouring dark suspicions of us as she sinks onto the *chaise longue* between us and I shuffle and deal the cards.'

'But we reassure her, of course?'

'Of course. We tell her that perhaps she will not lose, and besides, the car will be here very shortly. We play the first hand, and alas! what is this that has happened?'

'She has lost?'

'Yes. She has lost. And off must come one of her shoes. I deal again. She takes up her cards with a most unhappy face. Her dark suspicions are darkening towards certainties.'

'*La pauvre!* Will she ever know happiness?'

'Not while we are there to watch over her and keep her faltering feet on the path that leads upwards to salvation.'

'Which is as it should be.'

'Yes. But we have played the second hand and look, a second tragedy!'

'She has lost again?'

'Yes. Another shoe comes off, another hand is dealt. And of course, tragedy again!'

'A stocking this time.'

'Yes. A stocking. How happily she rolled it up and adjusted it barely minutes before! How sadly, how reluctantly she removes it now. Tears almost start to my eyes as I watch her.'

'And to mine. But the game must go on, must it not?'

'It must. And it does. Another hand. *Mais non!* It cannot be!'

'She has lost again?'

'She has. There is a devil in the cards. Another stocking comes off. My, this is a veritable plucking. Another hand. And oh no! Again it has happened! And this time, of course . . .'

'This time she must shed her skirt or her shirt.'

'That seems so, but she sees a third way.'

'It is illusory. It must be.'

'You are right. For she demands that the game cease: that we sit and wait for the car without playing cards.'

'But the car is already late, is it not?'

'Yes.'

'Then it might be badly delayed. It might not come at all. How to fill the time until we learn the truth?'

'How but by playing cards?'

'Precisely.'

'But still she seeks that third way: not to remove her skirt nor to remove her shirt, but to leave the game.'

'It is impossible. The game must be played to the end. Surely we made that clear to her at the outset?'

'But of course. It is only wilful stubbornness that makes her say otherwise. She must play. She must remove her skirt or her shirt. She refuses. We exercise our legitimate authority firmly, but fairly. She resists. We exercise our legitimate authority more firmly still. We drag the shirt off her back. *Oh, ces tetons!* Taut beneath that black bra, rising and falling as she pants. If her ill-luck holds, in another three hands, at most, the bra will have been stripped from her and those white breasts will be on open display. Our mouths dry and our pussies moisten at the thought of it. But first, the sixth hand. Can you believe it? We must force her cards into her hands! We must examine them for her and conclude, alas, that she has lost yet again!'

'There is, as you said, a devil in the cards. Her skirt, this time?'

130

'But of course. She unzips it herself, unwillingly, for she knows now that resistance is useless, and sits between us for the seventh hand. And of course, again she loses!'

'It is not a devil in the cards: it is Beelzebub himself. And this time, it is her knickers or her bra.'

'*Non*. Again she seeks a third way, the cunning little vixen.'

'Again, it is illusory, of course.'

'*Non*. For she argues that the *earrings* she wears are items of clothing, and that she may remove one of them in forfeit.'

'We do not let her, of course. This is Jesuitry – casuistry of the worst kind.'

'*Non*. I believe her case rests on solid foundations. Can you fault it?'

'Perhaps not. Very well, I agree. She may take off an earring.'

'Good. You go to the mantelpiece and return with the box for her to put the earring in. You open it in front of her. She takes the earring off. You are about to close the box and place it on the table when I cry, "*Un moment! Où sont les boucles de perle noire?*" '

'Where are the black pearl earrings? But they are unique, and most valuable. Surely they are in the box?'

'Surely not, for we now examine the box most carefully, and they are nowhere to be seen. How can this be? They were in the box that very morning, and we certainly saw them there as our little blonde guest chose her earrings earlier in the session.'

'*Oui. Les boucles d'améthyste.*'

'But now, they are gone. Suspicion suddenly clouds your face.'

'It does?'

'But yes. I question you and you suggest, most reluctantly, that *she* has had some hand in their disappearance. Literally so. We examine the pockets of the skirt she was wearing. Alas! your suspicions are confirmed. The earrings of black pearl are tucked away there, one to a pocket.'

'*La sale voleuse!*'

131

'It is so: she is a most filthy thief. She has repaid our kindness with theft and now compounds her crime by denial.'

'Even she would not be so wicked, with the evidence so clear at hand.'

'Alas, it seems we have scarcely begun to plumb the depths of her depravity. Despite the clear evidence she denies taking the earrings. She goes further: she accuses *us* of placing the earrings where they were found, in order to furnish ourselves with an excuse for further maltreatment of her.'

'She places herself beyond forgiveness.'

'No, I do not believe so. We must eternally forgive, that she may eternally transgress.'

'You are right, as ever. But forgiveness must be earnt.'

'Or paid for. In the only coin she possesses.'

'Pain.'

'Pain. And humiliation. If she was so anxious to carry off the earrings of black pearl – and how close she came to succeeding – how can we refuse her the chance to wear them?'

'We cannot.'

'It is as you say: we cannot. But *how* is she to wear them? You will remember, of course, that as yet she has removed but one earring of amethyst, leaving but one ear free.'

'But the earrings of pearl number two.'

'Of course. You have seen to the heart of it with your customary sagacity. One ear: two earrings. It is plain as the plainest possible pikestaff that two into one will not go. So, we have a little conundrum to solve.'

'We might, of course, remove the other amethyst earring, leaving another ear free, which would make *two* ears free.'

'A possible solution, but surely an inelegant one.'

'Then I withdraw it unconditionally.'

'And I accept your withdrawal. No, we must proceed with the game of cards and see what inspiration strikes.'

'Surely. The eighth hand.'

'As you say. The eighth hand. Which – can it be yet again? – she loses.'

'Knickers or bra, this time.'

'No. She seeks the third way. The second amethyst earring.'

'An earring is not an item of clothing.'

'I agree. What does she take us for? We are not hoodwinked by her casuistic reasoning. It must be knickers or bra. *L'une ou l'autre.*'

'*L'une.*'

'Yes. Some instinct tells her to postpone exposure of her breasts to the last of all possible moments. She slips down her knickers and sits between us, shivering, dressed only in bra and amethyst earring.'

'Only in bra. An earring is not an item of clothing.'

'Yes. You are right. Only in bra.'

'And why is she shivering? The room is not cold.'

'It is with apprehension. She shivers with apprehension as she sits between us, dressed only in a bra, watching me deal the ninth hand. She picks up her hand and there it is, for the ninth time, she has lost.'

'Beelzebub in the cards, did I say? No, it is all the devils from the pit, great and small.'

'You are right. But be that as it may, for the ninth time she has lost, and for the ninth time she forfeits an item of clothing. Her bra. It is tight, remember. Her breasts are crammed into it like the rich filling of a pie. She unclips it and it positively springs free of her breasts. They quiver with seeming delight at their release, in sad contrast to her whose they are. She, of course, continues her captivity.'

'And now the game is over?'

'Yes. It is over. We said no more than nine hands at the very beginning, did we not?'

'We did.'

'Then now the game is over. But her punishment is not. That has barely begun.'

'That has not begun at all.'

'You are right. And as she sits between us, completely naked but for that single amethyst earring, which does not count, an idea strikes you. Your eyes have been fixed on her breasts since the bra was stripped away. You have

133

licked your lips. And now, an idea strikes you. A cruel smile bends your shining lips. You lean across her to whisper your idea into my incredulous ear.'

'And what is it?'

'Who better to say than you?'

'I have forgotten.'

'Forgotten? Forgotten what the sight of those glorious breasts inspired in you, as you sat, eyes fixed upon them, licking your lips, *les boucles de perle noire dans la main*?'

'The earrings of black pearl? I have them in my hand?'

'Yes, but of course. Since you found them tucked away in the pockets of her skirt, you have held them there, as though for inspiration. And now inspiration has been provided you. An idea. A cruel idea. Which you whisper to me, leaning across her naked form.'

'*Ah, oui!* It returns to me now. The memory of her breasts was too powerful for a moment, but now it all returns. Those breasts, of course, have nipples.'

'Yes. Glorious pink nipples.'

'Highly sensitive.'

'But of course. As we have proved repeatedly over the week during which she has enjoyed our hospitality.'

'They grow blood-engorged on stimulation.'

'Yes. If one licks them, they swell. They are an excellent means of awakening the venerean appetite.'

'Then in all this, are they not like ear-lobes? Their relation to a larger whole. Their sensitivity. Their engorgement with blood upon stimulation. Their excellence as a means of, as you most felicitously put it, awakening the venerean appetite.'

'Yes. This is all true. There is a most exact analogy between nipples and ear-lobes. But it fails in one crucial respect.'

'Yes?'

'Yes. For one does not pierce nipples and suspend jewellery from them, does one?'

'No?'

'No. The idea is absurd.'

'Why?'

134

'It is self-evidently absurd.'

'No. It has the absurdity of unfamiliarity, which is no absurdity at all. For see how nature herself urges towards it. Can it be right that nipples and ear-lobes answer unto each other in so many respects, and yet not in this remaining one?'

'Expressed in those terms, I see the force of your argument. It cannot be right. Nature urges it.'

'As does fate. For here we have all the materials ready to hand. A fine pair of pink nipples on fine white breasts. A fine pair of pearl earrings. The pearls are baroque, and black. They will dangle most becomingly against those white breasts.'

'It is so. You have wholly convinced me. We must pierce those fine pink nipples and hang the earrings from them.'

'We must. And we shall.'

'In the afternoon? It will take some time to gather the instruments.'

'No. No time at all. For quite by chance, we have all that is necessary ready to hand. A bowl of ice-cubes sits on a nearby *armoire*.'

'For what?'

'I forget their original purpose, but now they will serve admirably to erect and numb her nipples.'

'That is so. But they will hardly be sufficient for the remainder of the task we have set ourselves.'

'This is true, but also we have at hand a selection of needles, for the piercing proper, and a bottle of medical spirit, for the sterilizing of her nipples, and a small laboratory burner, for the sterilizing of the needles.'

'Then you are right. It will take no time at all. Or so it would seem.'

'Seem?'

'Alas, yes, for we have neglected one item of all-importance.'

'Which is?'

'She to whom those fine pink nipples and white breasts belong. She has listened to you describe how, quite by chance, all that is necessary for the piercing is ready to hand. Now, as you stand to collect them and lay them on the table, ready for the operation, she protests.'

'Transgression piles on transgression.'

'Surely so. For each step of the road that brought her to this pass was wilful wickedness on her part. The collaboration with *les Boches*. The cocks she sucked, the cunt and arsehole she laid open to their unspeakable lusts, the honour and purity of Catholic womanhood that she defiled. This brought her to condign punishment at our hands. And then, when punishment is complete, when, out of the goodness of our hearts, we clothe her and prepare to send her on her way, she steals from us!'

'Disgraceful.'

'And now she resists just punishment for it. And this is what delays us a minute or so. While we overpower her and tie her to an armchair that sits also in the room.'

'The black armchair?'

'Yes. The armchair of black velvet. Her figure stands out most marvellously against it, like Andromeda on the black rock, awaiting those cruel teeth.'

'*La pauvre Andromède!*'

'*La pauvre Anna.* And now, we can begin.'

Seventeen

After she had stepped into the new room, Anna bent and began to brush petals from her shins and calves. Some of them were sealed to her skin with sweat and she had to scratch them off with her fingernails. She heard footsteps behind her and straightened, turning to watch Beth and Gwen come through the door, petals clinging to their bodies too, all over, from when they had fucked deep in the pile.

'Well, another room, another rumpus,' Beth said.

Gwen laughed.

'It looks like it,' she said. Anna turned and looked at the room with them. It was black and rectangular, narrow and very long, with a low ceiling and the lights studding the ceiling in an irregular pattern were very dim. Beth was peering down the room towards the far wall.

'What are those down there?'

'Let's see,' Gwen said.

They walked towards whatever was against the far wall and as they walked the lights began to brighten.

'Mummies,' said Beth. 'Glass mummies.'

Standing in a row against the far wall were three upright woman-shaped and woman-sized containers of clear, glistening glass. Or rather, one Anna-shaped and Anna-sized glass container, one Beth-shaped and Beth-sized glass container, and one Gwen-shaped and Gwen-sized glass container. The legs were fused together and the arms were fused to the body. As Beth had said: three glass mummies. Or:

'No,' Gwen said. 'Three iron maidens.'

They had stopped in front of the strange objects. Gwen had reached out and jerked a catch loose in the one on the right, the Gwen-shaped one, and the front had swung open.

'Three crystal maidens,' Beth said. 'One for you, one for me, and one for little Anna. But what the fuck is that in the tits?'

The breast peaks of the maidens were filled with what looked like clockwork: a complicated steel mechanism without a clear purpose.

'That's what puts the iron into the maiden, presumably. And what are those holes in the foot?'

Gwen stooped and looked. The double foot of the maiden was flush with the floor and there were two holes in it, where the right and left soles of a woman enclosed in the maiden would rest. Gwen reached inside the maiden and slipped her fingers into them, probing. She straightened, shrugging.

'Christ knows what they're for.'

'Well, I don't fancy getting into one.'

'Neither do I. Fortunately, we don't have to test-drive them, do we, Ansie? Hey, catch her, Beth!'

Anna had turned and begun to run but Beth was onto her at once, seizing her upper arms expertly and spinning her to face Gwen.

'Oh, Anna,' Gwen said. 'When will you learn? Come on, let's get her inside and see what happens.'

She stepped to the first maiden, the Anna-shaped, Anna-sized one, flicked the catch, and pulled it open. Beth forced Anna forward to stand in front of it, then she and Gwen swung her and pushed her inside, as she kicked and struggled and swore. Gwen stepped back and took hold of the front of the maiden, leaving Beth to keep Anna in place, still kicking, still struggling, still swearing.

'I can't slam it, so I'll have to get it as far closed as I can before you let her go. Okay?'

'Okay.'

'Right. Here we go. Watch she doesn't get a hand or a foot loose.'

'Right.'

Gwen pushed the front of the maiden closed as far as she could, then said, 'Okay, let go!'

They timed it well: the front of the maiden swung to the final few centimetres, the catch clicked back into place, and Anna was entombed in glass, unable to move and staring out at them in fury with her nipples pressed against the mysterious steel mechanisms in the peak of each moulded glass breast. Gwen laughed.

'All we need now are the Seven Dwarfs and a handsome prince and we've got all the ingredients for a happy ending.'

'Who wants a happy ending?'

'True. Calm down, you little beast. We can't hear a word you're saying, anyway.'

The glass in front of Anna's face had clouded as she shouted out at them. Suddenly her mouth closed and she seemed to be trying to peer downwards, her face mirroring alarm and disgust.

'What's happening?' Beth asked.

'I think we've got some action at last. Look: it's filling up with something. What is it?'

The foot of the maiden was filling with a thick white fluid that clouded the glass in a faint band just above itself as it rose over Anna's feet.

'Dear me,' said Beth. 'Is it what I think it is?'

'Yes,' Gwen said. 'It's come.'

Beth chuckled.

'Yeah, and it's clouding the glass the same way her breath did. It must still be warm.'

'Lucky Ansie. Look, it's up to her knees already. We'll have to get her out if it rises right to the top. We don't want the little beast to choke on it. Not for too long, anyway.'

'If we open it while it's full of come there'll be come everywhere. Beside, she'll be able to swallow a good bit before it gets above her nostrils. Let's wait and see how it goes.'

The white fluid, preceded by the faint band of clouded glass, was as high as Anna's thighs now, rising a little more slowly as the interior of the maiden widened, but with a quiet inexorability that suggested it would indeed fill the maiden in time. Anna would have to gulp frantically as it rose above her chin and threatened to reach her nostrils. How many seconds would that buy her?

'Her legs are about to go under completely,' Beth said. 'It must be all over her cunt. Oozing all over it. I wonder what it feels like?'

'It will be our turn soon enough.'

Beth grunted and glanced at her maiden.

'Well, as least we'll know what to expect. The uncertainty must be terrible for poor Ansie. Look, there they go.'

Anna's legs were submerged in come, hidden from view completely as the come rose inexorably on, sliding up over her buttocks and *mons Veneris*, reaching her waist and stomach.

Beth chuckled again.

'Look at the little beast. She's not enjoying this one little bit.'

'She's not here to enjoy herself. She's here to show us what happens before we risk it for ourselves. There goes her belly-button.'

'Yep. Shame, that. I've always liked her belly-button. Do you think we'll ever see it again?'

'Yes. What goes up must come down.'

'In this case it's what comes up must come down.'

Gwen laughed.

'She's getting her comeuppance.'

'Quite right too. Tits next.'

'And doesn't she know it. Lie back and think of England, Ansie. Things could be much worse, you know. It could be cold.'

'Urgh. Makes me shiver just to think of it. Being covered with cold come. This mustn't be too bad. A bit like an extra-thick herbal bath, really. Or bathing in ass's milk. Don't you think?'

'Hmmm. Could be. Or ass's yoghurt. There they go.'

The band of steam above the rising line of come had reached the lower swell of Anna's breasts. The come slowed a little as it filled the outward swell of the glass breasts, but in a few seconds Anna's breasts were covered, sealed in come along with the mysterious steel mechanisms.

'Bye-bye, babies,' Beth said.

'The smell must be much stronger now. Look at her face.'

'It must be getting humid in there too. All that warm come. She'll have to start gulping in a very little while.'

'And doesn't she know it. Cheer up, Ansie, it will be all over soon.'

'Not too soon, I hope.'

'Well, I suppose not. Not from her point of view, anyway, and that's the important thing. There goes her collarbone. Get that jaw loosened, Ansie. The wider you can get it the more come you can get down your neck.'

'What's wrong with her? She's frowning.'

'God knows.'

The come was nearly above her shoulders, filling the maiden solidly, entombing Anna's white body in its whiteness. The band of clouded glass was less translucent now: the glass must have warmed before the come reached it. Anna's face wore a puzzled expression, half-sleepy, half-worried. She shook her head, as though trying to keep awake.

'And there they go. Shoulders submerged.'

'Is submerged the word?'

'It's salty, isn't it?'

'Yes, but how about subsemened?'

'Subsperged?'

'Yes, that's good. Subsperged. Her shoulders are subsperged.'

'She's subsperged, practically. That little chin will be under in a moment. There's no escaping it: she'll have to start gulping.'

'And doesn't she know it.'

Anna's sleepiness had almost disappeared, driven away by the closeness of the come to her chin. Her mouth.

'She's trying to stand on tiptoes.'

'No room, Ansie. Get drinking.'

The come was just below her chin, still rising.

'There. It's touched her chin. Another few seconds.'

'Let's count them off,' Beth said.

'Okay. You first.'

'One.'

'Two.'

'Three.'

'Four.'

'Five.'

'Six.'

'S– yes! It's there!'

Anna's mouth was under: the come was rising towards her nose, was surely already cramming her nostrils with its thick masculine smell.

Beth laughed oddly.

'Get gulping, Ansie,' she said.

Gwen glanced at her. Beth's nipples were erect as she watched and one of her hands half-rose, fingers twitching. She felt Gwen's eyes on her and turned her head to meet them. They smiled at each other.

'Aren't we bitches?'

'Yes.'

Beth's head swung back sharply.

'Look! She's gulping!'

She was: frantically, frenziedly, furiously gulping the come as it rose inexorably on, threatening her nostrils, threatening to subsperge her completely. Beth's chuckles died away.

'Hadn't we better get her out? She might choke.'

'No. She's okay. She'll give up in a few seconds, let the stuff cover her completely, and I'll open the thing up.'

'There'll be come *everywhere*.'

Anna was still gulping, her eyes rolling with anxiety, but it was plain she was finding it harder to get the stuff down. Beth murmured something.

'What did you say?' Gwen asked.

'I said, "Poor little bitch." It's a hard life for her, isn't it?'

'Yep. And that's just the way I like it.'

Anna stopped gulping, forcing herself up as high as she could in the maiden to suck in a last few breaths of air through her nostrils.

'Okay,' Gwen said. 'When it covers the top of her head I'll open it.'

The come was lapping at Anna's dilated nostrils, lapping, lapping, covering, rising on. Her eyes glared out at them, bright blue and glistening.

'She's not going to forgive us for this, you know.'

'Stop worrying. We can handle the little beast, can't we?'

'I suppose so.'

The eyes blinked, closed, and were subsperged. The come was rising faster now that it was only having to fill the space around the head. In another few seconds it was rising above Anna's skull. She was subsperged, completely covered in come, encapsulated in it. Beth said, 'Okay. That's it. Let her out.'

Gwen reached for the catch, then stopped.

'No, look. It's sinking. It must be draining out.'

The come had reached the very top of the maiden, filling it completely, then almost immediately started to fall. Fall very fast. The maiden-head was almost a quarter empty and Anna's skull hadn't come back into view.

Gwen grunted.

'What the fuck's going on?'

Half-empty now, and Anna's head wasn't there any more. The come sank fast, leaving the head-cavity completely empty, beginning to empty out of the body-cavity, leaving it empty. No Anna. They stared at each other then back at the emptying maiden. It was two-thirds empty, the come sinking even faster now. Beth half-expected to catch a thick draining noise, like water leaving a sink. When it was shin-high, still sinking, Gwen undid the catch and swung the maiden open.

'Watch out for it.'

Beth stood to one side as come came pouring out, streaming over the black floor. They peered into the empty cavity of the maiden, the rivulets of come streaming down its glass sides. Beth tutted.

'Well, she's test-driven it and we're not much wiser. Me next, I suppose.'

She stepped over the come on the floor to stand in front of her maiden.

'Looks innocent enough, doesn't it?'

She tapped the glass.

'Yes,' Gwen said. 'All that glass, as though there's nothing to hide.'

'Except for those steel things in the tits. They look rather sinister. Do you think they were anything to do with what happened to Ansie?'

'They're something to do with something, definitely, but I don't know what. Her disappearing is Bärengelt playing silly-buggers. It must be like the vanishing lady trick. Now you see her, now you don't.'

'My thoughts exactly. And my turn now, too.'

Beth undid the catch on her maiden and swung it open.

'Bet you I gulp longer.'

'You've got a bigger mouth than she has.'

'Bitch.'

She turned her back to the maiden and stepped inside, swinging her body to slip it into her own pre-moulded shape.

'Does it fit?' Gwen asked.

'Like a glove. I wish it didn't, because the glass is bloody cold. Well, I'm ready, so swing it shut and watch the fun.'

Gwen swung the door shut and clicked the catch. Beth was shouting something but she couldn't hear what. She shook her head. Beth stopped shouting and tried to look down. Gwen looked down too. Come was pouring into the maiden, rising with a band of clouded glass just above it, rising around Beth's feet and ankles, her shins, up towards her knees and thighs. She looked back up at Beth's face. Beth made her mouth bend down with mock dismay.

'Jaw,' Gwen said, enunciating the word with exaggerated care. 'Jaw. Get practising.'

She pointed at her chin, opening and closing her mouth slowly. Beth stuck her tongue out. Gwen looked back at the come. It was over Beth's knees, rising inexorably to subsperge her. And would she vanish too, in the few moments it took for the come to fill the maiden to the very top? A thought struck her. Shit. Who was going to click the catch on her maiden? Well, Bärengelt had presumably thought of that. He would have thought of everything.

The bastard. Maybe that was *his* come, rising up to subsperge Beth. Maybe he had wanked daily for weeks, storing his come, refrigerating it until now, when he poured it out into the maidens, warming it just beforehand the way a chef warms refrigerated sauce. But there was too much of it, surely. One man would have to wank for years to produce that much. It was nearly at Beth's waist, rising a little more slowly now that it had more space to fill.

Gwen pointed.

'Bye-bye, belly-button,' she said.

Beth stuck her tongue out again. The glass in front of her face was faintly clouded with her breath. The come rose above her belly-button and Gwen waved goodbye to it. Not much longer now. She wondered what the warm come rising over her skin would feel like. Disgusting? Delightful? Six of one and half-a-dozen of the other? She couldn't see Beth's nipples: they were hidden by the steel mechanism in the peak of each moulded glass breast.

A few more seconds and she wouldn't have been able to see them anyway, because the come was rising over Beth's breasts now. Warm thick come on white, smooth skin. Beth opened her mouth, loosening her jaw ostentatiously.

'Good girl,' Gwen mouthed.

It was rising above Beth's collarbone. Warm, thick come on white, smooth skin. Nearly at Beth's chin now. Beth was trying to lower her head and lick at it.

'You slut,' Gwen mouthed.

Beth stuck her tongue out at her instead, then suddenly grimaced, as though something had hurt her for a moment. What had happened to Anna was happening to her. The come was at her chin now, above her chin, rising to meet her mouth. She was looking dreamy, half-asleep, but she suddenly shook her head and concentrated. She began to gulp, slowly at first, then faster, getting the come down her neck, filling her stomach with it, trying to win a few seconds before she had to surrender and let the come cover her completely. Gwen was counting under her breath. Anna had won about ten seconds. Beth was nearly there. Nine, ten, eleven, twelve, thirteen, fourteen, f . . .

Yes. She'd done it, but now she had to surrender, closing her mouth, dragging a last breath through her nostrils before the come reached them and rose on, filling the last few handfuls of space, covering every inch of her body, subsperging her. Gwen reached out for the catch. If it reached the top and didn't start to go down immediately she'd open the maiden and fuck the come getting everywhere. It rose above Beth's red-stubbled scalp, covering her completely, reached the top of the maiden, filling it, subsperging Beth in thick warmth – and began to go down.

Gwen relaxed, her fingers dropping from the catch. Beth's scalp would have re-appeared if she'd still been inside the maiden: it hadn't: she wasn't. The come descended, emptying the maiden, revealing nothing but glass streaming with come. Beth had gone. Now it was her turn. She stepped to the right and stood in front of her maiden. She had left the cover open and she could reach inside at once, running her fingers over the smooth glass inside.

As Beth had said, it was cold. She turned her back to the maiden and stepped inside, swinging her body as Beth had done, feeling the glass fit snugly over the curves of her arse and back, cold glass fitting like a glove, making her shiver. She reached forward and tugged the cover towards her. Would it shut properly? She'd have to swing it towards herself and get her hand inside the maiden before it closed. *One, two, three.* She swung, whipping her hand back inside the maiden, and the door clicked shut.

The catch had closed by itself. Bärengelt had prepared for this. She tried to look down at the come-vents in the floor, uselessly, because her feet would tell her when the come was rising before she could ever see it. Ah! It was rising. The soles of her feet were glutinously kissed with warmth, and a moment later she felt a thick fluid rising over her feet towards her ankles and shins. This was what it felt like: warm, thick come on her white, smooth skin. Neither disgusting nor delightful: six of one and half-a-dozen of the other. Disgusting because it was delightful; delightful because it was disgusting. She could smell it, the thick organic sludge-smell of it, and she knew now what she would have seen had Beth's nipples been bare beneath the moulded glass of the maiden's breasts.

Erection. Erect nipples as the come rose. As it kissed its way glutinously up her body, finding and filling every niche and cranny of her skin, glowing against her as though a thick, warm milkshake was drinking her rather than vice versa. It was above her knees now, starting up her thighs, a ridge of it lifted in the narrow gap between them by surface tension. How would it feel on her cunt? Breath shuddered in and out of her at the thought of it, clouding the glass in front of her face, veiling the room outside.

She jerked. What was that? Something had moved at the far end of the room. She breathed in hard, trying to clear the glass. What was it? Moving towards her. Striding towards her. Black against the black of the room. Christ. It was Bärengelt, tall and powerful in his body-suit of black leather, light winking from the horns of his blank-faced helmet.

The come reached and filled the crotch-gap at the summit of her inner thighs, kissing the pouting lips of her cunt as her cunt protruded into the gap, rising on, over her cunt, filling every nook and crinny, rising to cover her pubes, sucking every hair upright and into itself as though a hand were stirring through them. Bärengelt had reached her and stood motionless in front of her maiden, her glass mummy, as it was filled with white come against the black wall.

The come was lapping at her belly-button, rising, subsperging it, rising, rising. Soon it would be at her breasts, over them, rising on, drawing level with her collarbone, rising above it, climbing her throat, touching her chin, rising above it. It touched the lower swell of her breasts, rising into the crinny beneath them, lifting them on itself as it rose. Her nipples got stiffer, anticipating the glutinous kisses they would receive as they were subsperged. *Subsperges me. Subsperges nos.*

Ah. She gasped as it touched them, rose above them, and the glass in front of her clouded again with her breath for a moment. When it cleared, Bärengelt had gone. The come was sliding luxuriously up her back, over her shoulderblades, as it rose above her breasts, supporting them warmly and glutinously, heating her hardened nipples. Collarbone next. That was when Anna and Beth had both looked as though something had hurt them for a moment. What? Was it the steel mechanism in the peaks of the moulded glass breasts? What did it do? Another second and she would know. Another sec –

She gasped again. Her nipples had suddenly been pricked fiercely for a moment, both of them simultaneously, and there was a numbness in them, radiating out into her breasts. Her neck felt weak and she felt an urge to yawn. She was getting sleepy. What was happening? Had she been anaesthetized? Why? What was happening to her nipples, subsperged in the come? The thought of the come disciplined her wandering attention and she shook her head, feeling it around her neck, kissing at the point of her chin. She would be gulping it soon. Gulping it down to gain a few extra seconds before it rose above her nostrils and on, to fill the maiden completely.

But why? Why did she have to gulp? Why not just hold her breath? Not gain those few extra seconds: give them away, so that her ordeal was over more quickly? But she knew the answer to that. It was the same answer as the answer to all their ordeals, all their sluttishness, all their *bêtises*. Because it was Bärengelt's will. He willed that they perform for his voyeuristic pleasure. She lowered her chin, opened her mouth, and sucked at the come. It was not quite high enough and she had to suck hard for her first mouthful, making an obscene slurping noise, splattering the clear glass in front of her face with droplets of come.

But even as she sucked it was rising to her, rising high enough for her to gulp at it cleanly, taking great mouthfuls of it, swallowing, gulping more. How long would she keep it up? How much could she drink before she had to surrender and let it rise on? Her stomach felt full already and was beginning to bloat, and the rising come was inexorable. Inexhaustible litres, she thought, and just thinking it made her stomach feel fuller. Even her jaw was aching. She couldn't gulp much longer, couldn't, couldn't, and wouldn't. Yet something wouldn't let her stop, though it felt now as though her stomach was full to overflowing, that come was starting to back out of it, rising into the lower reaches of her throat, rising inside her in revenge at the way she had stopped it rising outside her.

Too much. She closed her mouth and dragged in a last long breath through her nostrils, feeling the come instantly reach her upper lip, rise over it. She sealed her nostrils and waited, her lungs filled with come-scent-saturated air. It was at her nostrils, rising above them, forcing its way into them a little, climbing her cheeks, rising around the back of her head, lifting her stubble away from her scalp the way it had lifted her pubic hairs, rising, inexorably rising. She took a last look out through the glass of the maiden at the black room and then closed her eyes tight. It would hurt a lot if any of it got in her eyes.

It rose over her eyes, kissing separately at her closed eyelids, over her ears, fitting itself snugly into their whorls and canals, rising above her eyebrows, her forehead, over the top of her head, above her, and she was completely subsperged, drowned in come, drained to the last drop by a warm thick milkshake, feeling nothing but come, tasting nothing but come, smelling nothing but come, hearing nothing but the thick warm silence of come all around her. The only thing that wasn't come was the numbness in her breasts, and numbness was nothing.

Eighteen

She found herself spluttering, a hand behind her back
trying to lift her up, and she tried to open her eyes.

'No,' Beth's voice said. 'Keep them closed. You've got
come all over your eyelids and face. It'll sting like buggery.'

She managed to sit up, keeping her eyes tight closed,
feeling a dull ache in her nipples.

'Where the fuck am I?' she said. 'And what the fuck has
happened to my tits?'

'In answer to question one: you'll see in a few seconds.
In answer to question two: they've been pierced. Here, hold
still.'

She felt a damp cloth wiping at her cheeks and eyes, then
along her eyebrows and forehead.

'You can open them now.'

She opened them. Beth was kneeling in front of her, just
lifting the cloth away. Behind her, face lifted with ecstasy
into steaming needles of water, Anna was standing under
a shower, her small, soap-foamed hands moving slowly
over her body. Gwen grunted.

'Here, give it to me,' she said. She took the cloth from
Beth and wiped the rest of her face, then threw it aside and
stood up. They were in a small shower-room, tiled
completely in black, with three silver-nozzled showers
controlled by sun-disk dials in the walls, and gold and red
towels hanging on one wall. Beth rose from where she had
been kneeling on the floor in front of her.

'Good, isn't it?' she said.

'It's fucking marvellous. To think it would come to this. But what were you saying about my nipples?'

She looked down at them, reaching up to touch them gently. They were swollen and hot, exquisitely tender to the touch.

'They've been pierced,' Beth said. 'Like mine. Like Anna's. That's what the steel mechanism in the maidens was for. Don't you remember the anaesthetic? It's wearing off now. That's why they've started to hurt.'

Gwen gently tried to squeeze one of her nipples, but winced and stopped almost at once.

'You're too right they've started to hurt.'

She looked up at Beth's breasts, seeing that her nipples were swollen too, a deeper pink than they had been before.

'C'mere,' she said. 'You suck mine, I'll suck yours.'

Beth stepped towards her and she lowered her head to her white breasts, opening her mouth and closing it over the swollen left nipple, drawing it gently in, licking it, slowly sucking it. She heard Beth gasp softly through the hiss of Anna's shower and took her mouth off the nipple. She looked up.

'Nice?'

'Nice.'

She put her mouth back to the nipple, circling it with her tongue, sucking at it, then came off it again, moving her head to the white right breast, the swollen right nipple. She licked it, sucked it, circled it with her tongue. Beth had gasped softly again and Gwen thought that if she lifted her hand between Beth's thighs she would find the lips of her cunt parting and swelling, just beginning to ooze fresh yelm. She took her mouth off the nipple and stood up.

'Your turn,' she said.

'Get that come off your tits first,' Beth said. 'If I have to taste the fucking stuff again before the fourth millennium it will be too soon.'

Gwen looked down at her tits again, noticing for the first time how thickly smeared they still were with come. It was moist and fluid, kept fresh by the humidity in the air.

'I don't usually do requests,' she said. 'But just for you, Bethy.'

151

She stepped to the nearest of the three showers, turned the longest ray of the sun-disk dial to WARM, and gasped with pleasure as needles of warm water flung themselves down at her from the silver nozzle in the black ceiling.

'Should have tried cool first,' Beth said. 'It turns white and solid in warm water.'

Gwen looked down at her body. The come had turned into thick white strands, clinging to her breasts and stomach in an irregular web. She scraped some off and dropped it on the floor.

'Yuck,' she said. 'It's like egg-white.'

'It's a heat-degradable protein,' Beth said. 'But soap helps. There's some behind you.'

She turned and saw a bar of fat green soap sitting in a niche in the wall. As she picked it up and started lathering her body, she said, 'Heat-degradable protein?'

'Yeah. Anna told me.'

'Is that true, Anna?' Gwen called.

Anna looked over towards her, face still blank with the pleasure of warm water.

'What?'

'That you told Beth come was a heat-degradable protein?'

Anna's mouth fell open in indignation.

'No! I never said that.'

As though opening her mouth had reminded her of what she could taste inside it, Anna tilted her head back, holding her mouth open in the needles of water. Gwen looked back at Beth.

'Well, did she or didn't she?'

Beth laughed and shook her head.

'No. But I think she could have done. You knew it before I told you, didn't you? I could tell by the look on your face. And you know a lot of other things about come too. Like me. Like Anna. And I'm fucked if I know how.'

Gwen opened her mouth and tilted her head back too, allowing the warm water to stream into her mouth, filling it, running over the left and right join of her lips and over her cheeks. She closed her mouth and swirled the water inside it, still thinking about what Beth had said. She lowered her head and spat.

'Come is mildly alkaline,' she said.

'With a normal pH of between 7·2 and 8,' Beth replied.

'It is essentially a medium for nourishing and facilitating the motility of spermatozoa.'

'Spermatozoon singular, spermatozoa plural. Yes, that's right.'

'It contains zinc, magnesium, phosphorus, potassium and calcium.'

'But not in any nutritionally valuable quantities.'

'It also contains sodium chloride.'

'Or salt.'

'As well as more complex chemicals such as glutathione and hyaluronidase.'

'Those are a mouthful. But you've missed something.'

'What?'

'The fructose.'

'Oh, yeah.'

Gwen raised her face to the needles of water again, filled her mouth, swirled, and spat.

'It also contains fructose,' she said, 'the power supply of spermatozoa.'

'Which are about one per cent of come by volume.'

'But a highly significant one per cent. For come is, of course, meant to be pumped reverently into a cunt and not shamefully wasted by diversion into any other vessel, such as an armpit or arsehole.'

'No. Disgusting thought.'

'Least of all it is meant to be diverted into the mouth.'

'No. Even more disgusting thought.'

'Come is not designed to be drunk, it is designed for the cunt.'

'Indeed again.'

'For come, as mentioned above, is alkaline, while the cunt is acidic.'

'Yin and yang.'

'And where the twain meet, there is neutrality. A well-spunked-up cunt is a blessed spot, God wot.'

'Most blessed.'

'And then there are prostaglandins.'

'Ah,' said Beth. 'Prostaglandins.'

'Proof positive of come's cuntophilic nature. For they arouse the uterus, assisting the spermatozoa forward to fertilization of the waiting egg.'

'That is what they do.'

'All in all, come is a miracle of biological engineering, a living fluid with one urgent and all-consuming task. Propagation of the human race.'

'Propagation. Propagation per prostaglandin.'

'And it is perverted beyond words, beyond the foulest and most depraved imaginings of the foulest and most depraved of men in their foulest and most depraved of debaucheries, to turn it aside from this sacred task and pump it instead into an unforeseen and unclean vessel.'

'Perverted beyond words.'

'A vessel such as an armpit.'

'Yes. An armpit. That would be unforeseen and unclean.'

'Or an arsehole.'

'Even more unforeseen and unclean.'

'Or a mouth.'

'Unspeakably foul. Most unforeseen and unclean of all. My stomach rolls just thinking about it.'

Gwen stepped out of the shower.

'See?' said Beth. 'You know all about come and I know all about come and I bet Anna knows all about come too.'

Gwen fingered her nipples carefully.

'She does?'

'I bet she does.'

'What do you bet?'

'I bet Anna.'

'And so do I. Anna, come here! We've got some questions for you.'

Anna still standing in ecstasy beneath the shower, looked towards them in surprise.

'What?' she asked.

'Questions, Anna. We've got some questions for you.

I'm afraid we've got rather suspicious about what's been happening to us. This continual misfortune.'

'And we explain it by sin. We are being chastised for some sin one of us has committed.'

'And it wasn't me.'

'And it certainly wasn't me.'

'Which leads us to suspect, if it wasn't either of us – and it was even more certainly not me than it was certainly not Beth' – 'Impossible,' Beth interjected – 'then it must have been someone else. That sounds reasonable, doesn't it, Beth?'

'Very reasonable.'

'And considering that there is no one else beside, well, you, dear, we thought we might investigate further. In short, and as I said previously if you cast your mind back just a few moments, we thought we might question you. Isn't that right, Beth?'

'Yes. We thought we might question you. That's it.'

'So come here. Now. Switch off your shower and come here and stand in front of us. Good girl. Now, arms behind your back. Head up. We want you to look us in the eye when we ask you these questions, because we have a strong suspicion that you have committed some serious sin. Some very serious sin indeed.'

'We suspect you've been playing with yourself,' Beth said.

'No, Beth, even more serious than that.'

'More serious than that? But what could be more serious than that?'

'Oh, Beth, you are naïve. You judge others by your own standards of purity and innocence. This little beast in front of you cannot be judged by those standards, I am afraid. We must plumb much greater depths to bring to the light of day even the milder of her depravities, I am afraid. And we are not talking about the milder of her depravities here.'

'No?'

'No. We are talking about something so foul that I seriously wonder whether it will not dim the lights when I speak of it.'

'Perhaps you should whisper it then? Into my ear?'

'No. We must bring this foulness into the light, that the light may expose it for what it is, and perhaps commence the slow and painful task of healing.'

'Slow and painful?'

'Slow and painful.'

'Just slow and painful?'

'To be strictly accurate, very slow and very painful.'

'I thought it might be.'

'You've made me lose the thread of my thoughts now. Where was I?'

'Bringing her foulness into the light.'

'Ah, yes.'

'To commence the very slow and very painful task of healing.'

'Yes. To do that. So, Anna, look us straight in the eyes and answer truthfully. What is the pH of come?'

Anna swallowed. 'Between 7·2 and 8, normally speaking.'

'And abnormally speaking?'

'It might rise above 8.'

'Making it even more what?'

'Alkaline. More alkaline than usual.'

'Thank you. Beth, do you have any questions for her?'

'I certainly do. Anna, name three metallic elements found in come.'

'Zinc, calcium and magnesium.'

'Name three more.'

'Phosphorus, potassium and sodium.'

Beth looked at Gwen.

'What do you think, Gwen?'

'The case is looking blacker all the time, I'm afraid. Anna, tell me, what is the chief sugar found in come?'

'Fructose.'

'And what purpose does it serve?'

'It provides energy for the spermatozoa.'

Beth broke in.

'And what is the singular of spermatozoa, Anna?'

'Spermatozoon.'

'Gwen? Surely that's the clincher?'

'No. We must carry on beyond reasonable doubt. Ask her some more questions about spermatozoa.'

Beth turned back to Anna.

'Anna, what is the name of the condition in which there are fewer spermatozoa than normal?'

'Oligozoospermia.'

'And the condition in which spermatozoa are present in normal numbers but have impaired motility?'

'As–' Anna started to say, then shook her head.

'Come on, spit it out.'

'Asthen– asthenozoospermia.'

'And the condition in which spermatozoa are malformed?'

'Teratozoospermia.'

'Gwen? Now that is surely it.'

'No. Let's be completely fair. One more question before the biggie.'

Beth turned back to Anna.

'Anna, name one more pathological condition affecting come and define it for us.'

'Azoospermia. No spermatozoa present.'

'Be more precise.'

'No living spermatozoa present.'

'Gwen?'

'Yes. It looks conclusive now. Anna, it only remains for me to ask one further question before we pass sentence. Have you been drinking come?'

Anna shook her head hard.

'No.'

'Not a drop?'

'Not one.'

'You've not even been thinking about it?'

'No.'

'Come on, now. You're a young and healthy girl. Are you seriously telling me you've not dreamed about sucking a big cock recently?'

Anna shook her head.

'About worshipping it with your lips and tongue? Taking it deep into your mouth? Even into your throat?'

Anna shook her head.

'No,' she said. 'Definitely not.'

'Till it bursts inside your mouth, squirting creamy thick come down your throat?'

Anna shook her head. Gwen glanced sideways at Beth.

'Then where, Ansie,' Beth said, 'have you acquired your expertise in ejaculate?'

Anna hung her head.

'Well?' Gwen said. 'Cat got your tongue, girl? Come on. Your expertise in ejaculate. Your comprehension of come. Your skill in semen. Where did you get it?'

'Your knowledge of nut-juice,' Beth added. 'Where?'

Anna's head hung lower still. Beth looked at Gwen.

'What do you think?'

'Condemned out of her own mouth. Or rather, not out of her own mouth. Her silence speaks volumes.'

'Guilty then?'

'Guilty as sin.'

Nineteen

The corridor began to widen, filling with a cold pearly light fused from three separate sources. Metal clashed ahead of them and Gwen felt her nipples stir. Her hands rose towards them involuntarily, fingers moving, and she had to force down, clench them into hard fists. Her nipples stang. Bastard Bärengelt. And her cunt wept. Bastard.

And now they could see what awaited them. The corridor divided, trivided, and there were three short corridors ending in closed steel doors, with waist-high cages of shiny steel jammed into them, up against the doors. One cage for each corridor. One waist-high steel cage. But a cage that was open at the top. And with wheels. And with a bar to push it with. A trolley. Three trolleys. Three supermarket trolleys waiting for them in a Schloss in the Black Forest. One trolley for each of them.

They stopped and looked at each other.

'What now?'

She wasn't sure who had said it: Anna or Beth. The voice was low and exhausted. Uncaring. They were both ready to give up now, both ready to give Bärengelt the satisfaction of winning. But she wasn't going to. Fucked if she was going to.

'We carry on,' she said. 'He hasn't won yet. He isn't going to. We'll find him. Too fucking right we will. Right?'

Neither of them answered her. She didn't care. She had enough will for the three of them. She didn't even care that neither of them moved as she walked forward and into the middle corridor of the three. She would lead and they would follow.

Close-to, she could see something was painted on the door at the end of the corridor. A Gothic *B*. B for Beth. On the door in the corridor to her left would be an *A*. A for Anna. And on the door in the corridor to her right, a *G*. G for Gwen. There was a small round window set into the door. Clear glass, letting through pearly light from a room on the other side. A large room. Maybe a huge room. Filled with rows of something. But she couldn't see what it was properly, and her thighs were beginning to hurt, pressed hard against the steel bar of the trolley as she tried to lean forward over it.

She stopped leaning forward and took hold of the bar. The trolley hadn't moved as she leaned against it. Was it jammed? She rocked the bar and a pair of little chains looped around it jingled, but the trolley itself didn't move. It was though it was glued to the floor. She shoved hard, trying to ram the trolley against the closed door. Not an inch. Not a fucking millimetre. She pulled. Nope.

She looked back, panting a little.

'Well, come on. Help me.'

Anna and Beth were still standing at the edge of the pearly light, pale shapes against the darkness behind them. Now they came forward, and as the light fell full on their bodies she saw the marks of sweat, the scratches on their breasts, the fresh bruises, barely visible yet, but ripening in their skin. In their disciplined skin. And their nipples, swollen and puffy. Anna's left hand was lifting and falling on a two-and-a-half-second rhythm, almost breaking free of her will, clenched back under control, wanting to rise and soothe those stinging nipples, but held back by the knowledge of what would touching them would do.

'Help me,' she said. 'I want to see what's on the other side, so let's see if we can get this fucking thing out of the way. If not, I'll climb over it.'

They came up on either side of her and took hold of the bar. Six white hands on one steel bar.

'Pull.'

They pulled. All three of them. And Anna and Beth were trying, she could feel it, could hear it from the way they grunted with effort, but the trolley didn't budge. Not a fucking inch. Not a fucking millimetre. Not half the width of Bärengelt's microscopic pecker.

'Okay, I'll climb over it. I want to see through that window.'

She lifted one leg up and over the bar, putting her foot down into the cage, then hoisted herself up and after it. Both feet in the cage now, their soft soles reading the network of the steel mesh, reading it harder as she released her weight fully onto them. She moved forward and knelt to look through the window, her knees reading the mesh instead.

For a moment she had to squint as her eyes adjusted to the light, then, as she absorbed the scene in front of her, she almost jerked back with shock, the discomfort of the mesh under her knees forgotten. Forgotten because what she was looking at was so shockingly familiar, and the next thing she saw would surely be shoppers pushing supermarket trolleys – and here she was naked, kneeling in a supermarket trolley and peering out at them.

Only the customers weren't there. No one was. The supermarket was empty. Huge and inviting and with rows of fully stocked shelves stretching to left and right as far as she could see, but empty. She looked back, unable to see anything for a few moments, her eyes blinded by the bright light through the window.

'I don't believe it,' she said. 'It's a fucking supermarket. Large as life. He's built and stocked a fucking full-size supermarket.'

Beth cleared her throat.

'Are you sure?'

'Yeah. Of course. Come and have a look.'

'Is it steady?'

'Yeah. It's being held in place. Magnets or something.'

She felt the trolley shake faintly beneath her. Beth was climbing onto it, moving up beside her, kneeling and crouching to look through the window. She heard her draw in breath.

'What the fuck . . .?'

'It's a supermarket.'

'No. It's not. *C'est un supermarché.* Look.'

'What are you talking about?'

'Have a look.'

'Ow!'

Their heads banged as Beth lifted hers away from the window and she put hers back down to it. She could hear the silky rustle as Beth rubbed her head.

'Stop whining. What were you talking about?'

'Look. Straight across there.'

Beth's head moved closer to hers, and her hand came up, tapping on the glass, pointing.

'The labels. They're in French.'

And they were. Directly across from the window, along the end of one row, was a stand of yoghurts. *Yoghurte.* With stylized pictures of young women's heads on the white plastic containers. The same young women. Three of them. A blonde. A red-head. A raven. Anna. Beth. Gwen.

'It's *us*,' she said.

'What?'

'It's us. It's us on the containers. Look. Me, you and Anna.'

Beth's head rubbed against hers as she looked through the window.

'You're right. A French supermarket with us on the logos. What does it mean?'

'It means that cunt's up to his tricks again.'

'So what's new?'

'Nothing. We just carry on.'

'How? This door is locked, isn't it?'

Gwen put her hands against it and pushed hard.

'Yep. Locked.'

'So how do we get through?'

The voice from behind them was so quiet that Gwen had to concentrate on her memory of it to understand what it had said.

'I think I know.'

She and Beth looked back, almost banging their heads together again.

'What? What do we do?'

Something was shining on Anna's face. Fresh tears. She felt her cunt stir at the sight of them, then had to bite her lip as her nipples stirred and stang. Bastard. That bastard Bärengelt. It would be days.

Anna choked. Swallowed.

'This,' she said.

'What?'

'This.'

Something chinked. Anna was lifting one of the pair of chains looped around the push-bar of the trolley.

'Look. There's a catch. It opens.'

She made it close and open with a minute chink.

'So what?'

'Two chains. Two catches. Two' – her voice choked again and when she carried on it was almost too faint to hear – 'tits.'

'*What?*'

'There's one trolley for each of us. Two chains on each trolley, one catch on each chain. When we put the catches through our nipples, the trolleys will move. The doors will open. You'll see.'

She heard Beth snort beside her and snorted too.

'You're raving, Ansie.'

'No. You'll see. We don't carry on until we're chained by our tits to the trolleys.'

And suddenly it seemed less unlikely. Less crazy. After all, look what Bärengelt had *already* put them through.

Gwen took hold of Beth's arm and tugged.

'Come on, let's get off it.'

Beth twisted her body awkwardly and started to crawl back down the trolley. Gwen slapped at her backside.

'Come on, move. Quick.'

Beth swore and moved quicker, climbing off the trolley, back onto the floor. Gwen followed her, nudging Anna out of the way and examining the chains looped around the push-bar.

'Fuck. She's right. Come here, Beth. This is your trolley, so let's test it on you.'

'Fuck off. Test it on yourself.'

'I would do but this is quicker. If it works on you, I'm going to have to do it too, so stop wasting time. The sooner we get out of here and see what we have to do next, the better.'

'The better for Bärengelt.'

'The better for *us*. He's not going to win.'

Anna spoke again, her voice very faint, trembling with strain, weak with resignation.

'I'll do it. It was my idea.'

'No. Beth can do it.'

'No, I will.'

Anna walked out of Beth's corridor and the two of them followed her, Beth putting out her tongue at her in triumph.

'Bitch.'

'Bitch yourself.'

They followed Anna into the first corridor and stood by her as she unlooped the chains from the push-bar of the trolley waiting in it.

'Here, come on, we'll help you. Help her, Beth. Put your hands behind your head. Tits out.'

Anna obeyed, a sparkling tear dropping from her cheek onto her left breast. Tender left breast, surmounted by a tenderer nipple.

'It's going to hurt, Ansie.'

'I know,' Anna whispered fiercely. 'Everything hurts. That's what he likes. I bet he's watching us now, and wanking. The cunt. The cunt. The cunt.'

Her body started to shake with sobs. Gwen took hold of her left breast and, as gently as she could, lifted and adjusted the nipple. She felt Anna's body tense and stiffen, the sobs quivering through it now, not shaking it. The hole in the nipple was raw and she could feel the heat in it.

'I'm going to do it now, Ansie. It's going to hurt, but it will be over quickly. Ready?'

Anna tried to speak and couldn't. She nodded.

Gwen opened the catch, positioning the two ends over Anna's nipple. If she got it right she could just . . . slowly . . . release . . . the catch . . . and . . .

164

Anna cried out. She was chained by one tit to the trolley.

'Sorry, Ansie. Sorry.'

And she was. But she wasn't. Her own nipples were stinging more fiercely than ever, swollen on the pleasure of causing Anna pain.

'Put the other one on, Beth. And be careful.'

But she could tell by the way Beth's hand trembled minutely as she lifted the catch to Anna's right tit that the same pleasure was exciting her. The same pleasure at hurting Anna. Even though they didn't want to. But Anna was the perfect victim. So tender, so trusting, so vulnerable. A lamb with two wolves. A fawn with two tigers.

Anna gasped and Beth said, 'Sorry, Ansie.'

And she was. But she wasn't. Gwen could tell from the tremor in her voice. Pleasure at Anna's pain. Her own cunt was hot and swimming with it and the walls of the corridor seemed closer, the air thickened and heated with the musk of her and Beth's arousal.

The chain wasn't on her and Beth was trying again. Anna bit her lip and then sucked in breath with pain. She was chained by both tits to the trolley. Gwen swallowed hard, turning away from her and putting her hand on the push-bar of the trolley between the two hanging silver arcs of the tit-chains.

'Is it moving?' Beth asked.

'Yes.'

She could tell as soon as she touched the bar that the trolley was free now.

'You push it, Ansie. Get out of her way, Beth.'

Anna's hands came up hesitantly and took hold of the bar. Small white hands on bright steel.

'Push, Ansie.'

The hands tightened, and pushed. The trolley rolled forward, butting up against the closed steel door with a faint clash. She took hold of Anna's shoulder (small, soft shoulder, trembling with pain and exhaustion) and squeezed it.

'Clever, clever Ansie. You were right. Will it open? Back up a bit and push at it harder.'

Anna backed the trolley a little and ran it forward at the door again. *Clash.*

'No.' Gwen said. 'I think maybe we'll *all* have to be chained by the tits before they'll move. So come on, Beth, let's get chained, then all go through at the same time. On my word of command.'

She and Beth left the corridor and half-walked, half-ran to their own, Beth's the middle one, hers the right one, and walked up to their trolleys to begin unlooping the chains. She could hear Beth's chains clinking the way hers did, a little clumsily, because she knew Beth's right hand was doing what her right hand was doing: ministering to an overheated cunt that needed release.

Twenty

It had hurt to attach the chains, hurt a lot, the pain rising through the after-seethe of her furiously provoked orgasm like sharp peaks of black, glossy, obsidianic rock through a warm green ocean, and she had to breathe in deeply twice before she was ready to speak.

'Are you ready, girls?'

She heard Beth call 'Yes', then Anna, drew in another deep breath, then shouted, 'Let's go!'

The trolley had come free as soon as her tits were attached. Now she drew it back a little and pushed it forward, and yes, the door ahead began to swing open for it, the Gothic *G* on it splitting in two, the bright light of the supermarket flooding out to meet her as she pushed the trolley through the door, onto the huge, aisled space that awaited the three of them.

'See?' she said, grinning at Anna and Beth as the three of them turned their trolleys towards each other, almost laager-like. 'I told you we'd get through. We'll beat him yet. Come on, let's find a way out. Look, it's there.'

She jerked her head to the right, to the row of empty checkouts and the huge sign above a rose-looped arch. *SORTIE.* She turned her trolley towards it and started pushing it hard, wanting to run, get to the exit as quickly as possible, get out of here, get on with tracking down Bärengelt and punishing him. Anna cried out softly behind her, and then she noticed it herself. The tingling in her nipples. Unpleasant tingling. Getting stronger and more unpleasant with every step. Then it quickened, on the brink of accelerating, racing towards a peak of agony, and she stopped dead.

It was gone. No tingling in her tits. She pushed the trolley forward an inch and gasped.

'What the fuck is going on?' said Beth's voice from behind her.

She turned her head cautiously and looked back. Beth had stopped two or three metres behind her, Anna two or three metres further back, both their faces apprehensive, uncertain, Anna's pale, her lips standing out clearly against her skin. Now she licked those lips and said (they shone in the lights of the supermarket as she formed the words), 'It's Bärengelt again. He wants us to shop. That's why we're chained to the trolleys. So we shop. And if we don't, he hurts us.'

Gwen cautiously began to turn the trolley, ready to stop at once if the tingling in her nipples returned. But no, it was okay: she was turning away from the exit, turning back to the job of shopping. She pushed the trolley back, stopping level with Beth's.

'She's right. Bärengelt wants us to shop. We'd better get on with it.'

She pushed her trolley on, sensing Beth turn her trolley behind her and follow her, walking after her to where Anna stood waiting. She stopped level with Anna's trolley.

'You're on a hat-trick, Ansie. Right about how to get those doors open, right about this. Bärengelt wants us to shop.'

'Shop till we drop,' said Beth, drawing her trolley up on the other side of Anna's.

'Come on then, let's do it. Shop till we drop. Yoghurt, anyone?'

She made for the display she and Beth had seen through the window of the middle corridor, the rows of yoghurts, logo'd with their own faces. The wheels of Anna's trolley squeaked faintly behind her as Anna turned and came after her.

'Look.'

She'd stopped in front of the display, feeling the cool air from the display fold around her, hoping it wouldn't peak her nipples as she reached out and took up a container of yoghurt with Anna's stylized face on it, blonde, pale, beautiful.

'Fame at last, Ansie. Your own brand of yoghurt.'

She looked back, smiling, hoping to see an answering smile on Anna's face. She turned the container in her hand to read the back.

'Top-quality, no doubt. Ingredients, or should I say *ingrédients* . . .'

She stopped speaking, her fingers tightening on the container, dimpling its smooth plastic. She read the words again, wondering if she was dreaming.

'What's wrong?'

Beth had drawn up beside her, silver chains leashing her to the bar of her trolley by her tits, coppery eyebrows raised. Gwen swallowed and held the container out to her, turning it so she could read what was on the back of it.

'Look,' she said. 'What does that say?'

Beth looked at it.

'*Ingrédients*, ingredients, *lait d'A* . . . Oh.'

'It does say it, then?'

'Yeah. *Lait d'Anna.* Anna milk. *Con streptococcus et lactobacillus.*'

Gwen put the container back in the display, picked up another one, one with a stylized picture of Beth on it, red-haired, pale, beautiful, and turned it to read the back.

'*Lait de Beth*,' she read.

'Let's see.'

She transferred the container to her left hand and handed it to Beth without looking back, already reaching for a third container, one with a stylized picture of *her* on, black-haired, pale, beautiful. Her heart was beating a little faster as she turned it and read the ingredients.

'Yours too?'

'Yep. *Lait de Gwen.*'

'I feel sick.'

She didn't reply, couldn't think of a reply, then Anna was pushing her trolley level with theirs, her blonde eyebrows raised the way Beth's had been.

'What's going on? What's wrong with the yoghurt?'

Gwen held the back of the container up for her.

'Read it. Translate it.'

Anna's eyebrows were still raised. Now, as she looked at the back of the container and her mouth opened ready to speak, they fell, quirking with doubt, then fell further, into a frown.

'What . . .? You mean . . .?'

'No. I don't mean. The container means. The containers mean. The whole fucking lot of them. He's made yoghurt from us. From our milk.'

'When?'

'When we were in the hothouse. Don't you remember? I told you. He did it to me.'

Anna shook her head.

'N . . . No. I can't . . .'

'You can. I think we all can. He's been milking us. Turning the milk into yoghurt.'

'Not just yoghurt.'

Beth's voice, from a little way off. Gwen turned and looked towards her, careful not to let the chains tauten against her nipples. Beth had moved her trolley a little further on and half-turned the corner to the aisle on the left.

'What? What do you mean?'

'Look. *Fromage*. Hundreds of different kinds.'

For a moment she didn't understand the word. *Fromage?* And then she remembered. Cheese.

'Careful,' Beth said. 'From the tingling in my nipples, he doesn't want us to leave the yoghurts until we've stocked up on them.'

But she'd already felt the tingling re-commence in her own nipples as she pushed her trolley past the corner and looked down the aisle. Hundreds of cheeses in waxed paper and silver foil, bearing the same little logos, her face and Beth's face and Anna's. *Fromage des sœurs Camberwell.*

'Jesus Christ,' she said.

'*Jésus Christ* indeed,' Beth said.

'Whatever. This is so . . . perverted. So sick.'

'So Bärengelt.'

There was a sound from behind her and she spun her head back to look at Anna. She was crouched on the floor, being quietly sick between the silver lines of her tit-chains. At the sight of it her own stomach rolled, but there was a gathering heat there too. Low down. Lower than her stomach, really. The outskirts of her groin. Gathering heat. Heavy, trickling heat. Trickling downwards.

She swallowed and said, 'Well, a girl's gotta do what a girl's gotta do.'

She pushed her trolley back to the display of yoghurts and reached out for a handful of them, putting them into her trolley, reaching out for more.

'Come on, Beth, you too. Which do you think we're supposed to take? Our own?'

'Three of each.'

Anna's voice again. Very quiet, almost inaudible. Resigned. She'd raised herself from the floor, tongue moving reluctantly over her lips, cleaning away the traces of vomit.

'How do you know?'

'I just know. Three of each. Then we choose some cheese.'

'Well, okay. You're the supermarket oracle.'

She had one too many Beth yoghurts, one too few Anna, three too many of her own, and she returned the excess to the shelves, picking up an extra container of Anna. She swallowed again. What would it be like to unpeel the top of the container, dip a spoon into the rich, fat, white yoghurt, scoop up some of it . . . and put it in her mouth? White yoghurt on a silver spoon. Or what would it be like to spoon the stuff onto the tits that it had squirted from, and lick it off them? Anna-milk-yoghurt licked from Anna's own tits.

Yes, the heat was definitely in her groin. Definitely trickling downwards. Down between the lips of her cunt. Puffing them and opening them. Waking and warming her cunt-musk, so that it wafted. Wakened, warmed, wafted. The perfume of her pussy. And that made her think of spooning the cool yoghurt onto Anna's cunt. Holding the pink lips apart and spooning it *into* Anna's cunt. Plain

171

unsweetened Anna-milk-yoghurt flavoured by Anna's own yelm. Christ. Jesus Christ. *Jésus Christ*.

She swallowed again and pushed her trolley forward again, to the aisle of cheeses, hoping that Anna and Beth wouldn't notice the tremor in her knees. The way she had already noticed the tremor in Beth's. Behind her, the wheels of Anna's trolley squeaked again as Anna pushed off after her, nine containers of girl-milk-yoghurt sitting upright on the steel mesh of the trolley-cage-bottom. What would Bärengelt call it? *Mädchenmilchjoghurt*.

Now the cheeses. *Les fromages*. So many of them! Sitting solid and rich beneath subdued golden lighting, little globes or blocks or drums of rich lacteosity wrapped in waxed paper or silver foil, sealed with fungal rinds, cloaked with dried herbs. Ready to be unpeeled, crumbled, sliced, slivered and sampled. Girl-milk-cheese. Laid on the tongue and savoured. Rows and rows of girl-milk-cheese. *Mädchenmilchkäse*. That was what Bärengelt would call it.

Beth asked behind her, 'What do we take, Ansie?'

Anna hesitated for a moment before replying.

'I don't know. I think, whatever we want. But lots. Lots of cheese. Bärengelt likes cheese.'

Gwen reached out and took up a fat drum of Camembert logo'd with Anna's pale face. *Lait Cru. V.C.C. Ingrédients: lait d'Anna*. She put it in the trolley, next to the nine containers of yoghurt (three Annas, three Beths, three Gwens) and pushed the trolley further down the aisle, pausing, picking up, hefting, reading the label, making a decision, replacing on the shelf or placing in her trolley.

Roquefort. Brie. Cantal. Vacherin des Camberwells. Bleu de Beth. Bleu d'Anna. Bleu de Gwen. Neufchatel. Pont l'Evêque. Gruyère. Poivre d'Anna. Poivre de Gwen. Poivre de Beth. All of them labelled *Fabriqué en Allemagne*. Made in Germany. *Ingrédients: lait*. Milk. Made in Germany from milk. Girl-milk. *Mädchenmilch*. Gwen-milk. Beth-milk. Anna-milk.

She stopped and looked back. Anna and Beth were two or three metres behind her, containers of yoghurt still outnumbering cheeses in their trolleys. She was about a third of the way down the cheese-aisle herself, but she thought she'd chosen enough. Time for the other side. She looked across at the display that faced the cheeses. Rows of hanging black bananas. Giant glossy black bananas. Or marrows. Or even dildos. That was what it looked like. But they were sausages, she thought, each bearing a little white circle of paper with a face on it. Her face or Beth's face or Anna's.

She turned the trolley and pushed it across the aisle, waiting for the tingling in her nipples to start again. No, it was okay. Bärengelt was satisfied with what she'd chosen, and now she could choose some sausages. Black sausages. She felt the air warm around her as she moved away from the refrigerated cheese-displays. Black sausages. Made from what? She reached out and unhooked one, an Anna-sausage, turning it to read the label on the back. *Ingrédients: menstrues d'Anna, herbes, sel.* She didn't understand. *Menstrues?*

Then it hit her and her hand tightened with sudden revulsion on the thick, firm length of the sausage. Only it wasn't revulsion. Revulsion would have dissolved her grip, made her drop it, made it thud as it hit the floor at her feet and lay like a black, over-ripe fruit. Not revulsion. Excitement. Anticipation. Longing. Longing to insert the black length of this sausage up where it had come from. Anna's cunt. The cunt that had bled the blood. Blood for the blood-sausage. *Menstrues d'Anna.*

A shudder ran through her. Sliding the blood-sausage in and out of Anna's cunt. Watching it begin to glisten with yelm. Listening to Anna's moans and murmurs of protest. Fucking Anna with her own cooked menstrual blood. Then cutting a slice from the sausage as it jutted from Anna's cunt, soaking it in Anna's yelm, and putting it to Anna's lips. *Take, eat, this is your body. This is your blood.* Then raising the slice to one's own mouth. Drawing in the scent of it. Biting off a sliver of it. Savouring it on one's tongue. The rich, iron tang of it. God. God. God.

She swallowed hard, forcing herself to relax her grip on the sausage and put it in her trolley, laying it full-length beside the heap of girl-milk-cheeses and the nine containers of girl-milk-yoghurt. A girl-blood-sausage.

Eine Mädchenblutwurst. She glanced across at Anna and Beth, squeezing her thighs together and trying furtively to smear flat the trickles of yelm that had begun to coat them. Could she put her hand down and . . .?

No. Anna and Beth had finished with the cheeses, were turning their trolleys, pushing them across to her, to the display of hanging sausages. Black sausages. Blood-sausages.

'What are these?' Beth asked.

Anna was silent, staring at her as though there was something strange in her face. Was she flushed? Excited-looking?

'Sausages,' she said. Gruffly. She was sure it was gruffly.

'Just sausages?'

'No.'

It was Anna. Answering for her. Still staring at her.

'No?'

Beth looked at Anna, then back at Gwen, frowning, trying to read what was passing between them. Anna knew. Knew what they were and what it was doing to her. How it was exciting her. Black blood-sausages from three white girls. *For* three white girls. To be inserted whence they came and used for fucking. Cunt-blood-cocks. Cocks made from cunt-blood.

Beth was reaching out for one of the sausages, unhooking it, turning it to read the label. She frowned, lips moving silently, then looked up.

'What are they?'

'Blood-sausages. Made fr . . .'

But Anna was folding to the floor again, tit-chains stretching tight, face bowing between the tit-chains as she threw up onto the floor again, creating a second little pool of clear, glistening vomitus. They hadn't eaten for a long time. None of them. So there *was* nothing to throw up. But Anna threw up nonetheless.

Gwen looked away from her, back at Beth.

'They're blood-sausages,' she said defiantly. 'Made from menstrual blood. Little Anna's here. And yours. And mine.'

A look of disgust started to flow across Beth's face, but some other emotion was riding with it, undermining it, overpower-

174

ing it. Excitement. Like her excitement. And Beth blinked. Glanced furtively at Anna, then turned back to meet Gwen's eyes. And both of them were thinking, *Are you thinking what I'm thinking?* And both of them were thinking, *Yes.*

Anna sniffed and stood up, tongue passing slowly and reluctantly over her lips again. She didn't meet Gwen's eyes, or Beth's, just pushed her trolley forward, placing her feet carefully to avoid the little pool of vomit, and reached out for a blood sausage. Beth-blood-sausage. Then an Anna-blood-sausage. Then a Gwen-blood-sausage. Laying them in her trolley beside the containers of yoghurt and the mound of cheeses.

'One of each, Ansie?' Beth asked.

'Yes. But we haven't finished on the other side.'

The wheels of her trolley squeaked as she pushed it away from the sausages, back toward the cheeses. Gwen laid the sausage she was holding into her trolley, chose another one, and another. Anna, Beth and Gwen. She swallowed, hoping her voice would be steady when she spoke.

'Yes, we have, Ansie. Let's see what's in the next aisle.'

Anna didn't stop or look back.

'We haven't finished with this one yet.'

Gwen exchanged glances with Beth. Beth's lips quirked. Her right hand fell to her cunt, fingers levering the lips gently apart, sliding up and down between and behind them. She lifted her hand and turned it for Gwen's inspection, fingertips thickly glistening with yelm. Gwen pushed her trolley forward, lining it up with Beth's, letting it come to rest beside it with a faint clash of meeting steel. Her own hand was busy at her own cunt-lips, harvesting yelm as she put her face forward, mouth opening, red tongue emerging to lick the yelm from Beth's fingers, then suck her fingertips one by one as her own hand completed its harvest and rose to offer five fingertipsful of yelm to Beth's opening mouth and red, emerging tongue.

Anna was moving along the cheese display again, reaching out, picking up, placing. Beth's mouth came free of Gwen's index finger with a faint pop.

'What's she doing?' she said quietly. 'We're stocked up on cheeses.'

Gwen gave a final lick to Beth's tongue, shrugging.

'No idea. Maybe she's come round to Bärengelt's way of thinking.'

She moved her face back and called out.

'Anna. Come on. There are the other aisles to do.'

Anna looked back, face expressionless.

'No. This side isn't just cheese. Come and look.'

They went and looked. Not just cheese. Ice-cream and butter too. Girl-milk-ice-cream. Girl-milk-butter. *Mädchenmilcheiscreme. Mädchenmilchbutter.*

Twenty-one

Anna had been sick for the third time before they reached the second aisle, trolleys half-full with yoghurt, cheese, butter, ice-cream and blood-sausages. They had collected the products of girl-milk and girl-blood. *Mädchenmilch-und-blutprodukte. Nun Mädchenpisseprodukte.* Now for the products of girl-piss. Rows of full-waisted glass bottles standing in a long chill-cabinet. Face-logos again, over-arched with *Eau d'Anna, Eau de Beth, Eau de Gwen* in elegant gold, red, black script, under-arched with *Aviné* in elegant gold, red, black script.

Gwen reached out and took down one of the higher bottles. The liquid in it had seemed clear in the chill-cabinet, but held to the light it was faintly yellow. She turned it, the glass cold beneath her licked-clean fingertips, and read the label on the back. *Ingrédient: urine d'Anna (100%)*. She put the bottle into a bare space in her trolley, between a little tower of butter and a blood-sausage, and reached for another, from a middle row, and another, from the lowest, the liquid in these progressively yellower, topaz and super-topaz. *Eau d'Anna, Eau de Beth (concentrée), Eau de Gwen (super-concentrée)*.

The wheels of Anna's trolley squeaked behind her and she pushed her own trolley further on down the aisle, towards where the chill-cabinet of bottled girl-piss ended and something else began. What? Salt. *Mädchen-pissesalz*. Girl-piss-salt. In packets and plastic containers, logo'd with their three faces, coarse-grained, fine-grained, powdered, in blocks, sun-evaporated, wood-fire-evaporated. She chose a packet and two containers, Anna-piss-salt, Beth-piss-salt, Gwen-piss-salt, put them into her trolley, and turned the trolley towards the row of goods on the other side of the aisle, the ones she hadn't understood when she turned the corner from the blood-and-milk aisle and first saw them.

She still couldn't understand them. *Champignons*. Mushrooms. How did they fit into the *Mädchenökonomie* of the *supermarché*? When she reached the display and looked at the logo on the clingfilm of one little container, she understood. It wasn't a face this time, but an entire little scene. A blonde girl in eighteenth-century costume, voluminous skirts and petticoats hoisted up to expose her slender white thighs, as she squatted to shit in the woods. *Champignons d'Anna*, the label ran above the little scene; and below the scene: *Cultivés dans sa merde*. Anna-mushrooms. Grown in her shit. Next to them were *Champignons de Beth, cultivés dans sa merde* and *Champignons de Gwen, cultivés dans sa merde*. Beth-mushrooms, grown in her shit. Gwen-mushrooms, grown in her shit. She chose one variety of Anna-mushrooms, then pushed on down the display, choosing another variety of Beth-mushrooms, then another variety of Gwen-mushrooms, sitting moist and fat in their little plastic containers.

She pushed on down the display, to the mushrooms that were being sold loose. Her mouth began to water at the heavy, rich, woody smell of them, and she twitched a little as she tugged and tore a paper-bag loose from the roll hanging ready for her, then filled it, cupping them in her hands before she let them fall into the bag. They felt a little like testicles. Smooth and heavy and moist. Sitting fat and complacent on the palm. Like Bärengelt's balls. She longed to squeeze them, crush them, dig her fingers into them, into their soft, vulnerable flesh, releasing the heavy scents of their dense, fleshy interiors – but she only picked them up and cupped them and dropped them into the bag.

When she had filled it, she chose another and began to fill it too, more slowly, choosing the mushrooms one by one. Funny to think that she was handling her own shit. Beth's shit. Anna's shit. Would the mushrooms be shit-flavoured too, or had they transmuted what nourished them by biochemical alchemy, turning malodorous girl-shit into savoury mushroom-flesh? The test would be in the tasting. Slicing the mushrooms. Frying them in girl-milk-butter. Sprinkling them slightly with girl-piss-salt. Spearing them on silver forks (why had she thought that?) and lifting them to mouths that already leaked saliva at the scent and sight of the frying. A dish fit for a king. Fit for a queen. Fit for queens. Queen Anna. Queen Beth. Queen Gwen.

She dropped the second filled bag into the trolley and pushed further down, to a row of bottles. *Champignons en saumure.* Mushrooms in brine. Pickled mushrooms. Pickled in girl-piss. She chose three bottles, Anna, Beth and Gwen, and put them into her trolley. It was three-quarters full now, noticeably harder to push. She looked across the aisle for Anna and Beth. Beth had reached the piss-salt, but Anna was still half-way down the *eaux urinaires*, the piss-waters, shaking her head faintly, perhaps unconsciously, with undiminished disgust and reluctance as she looked at what she had to choose. Now Beth was dropping a final packet of piss-salt into her trolley and pushing it across towards the mushrooms. Kept in the dark and fed on shit. Girl-shit.

Her head jerked up. Speakers had switched on, high in the ceiling of the supermarket. The sound of someone clearing their – *her* – throat. And then:

'*Votre attention, s'il vous plaît, votre attention, s'il vous plaît.*'

A woman's voice. A woman's voice they had heard before.

'*Le supermarché se ferme dans cinq minutes. Le super-marché se ferme dans cinq minutes. Merci.*'

She looked down from the ceiling and found herself looking straight into Beth's face, lips opening to mouth 'Who?'

She shook her head and shrugged, then suddenly realized that Anna was pushing her trolley across the aisle,

179

face shining with excitement and hope, tit-chains flashing as they swung between her nipples and the trolley push-bar.

'Gwen! Beth! Did you hear that?'

Beth nodded.

'Yes. It would have been hard not to. The supermarket is closing in five minutes.'

'No. Not that. The *voice*. Don't you know who it was?'

Gwen snapped her fingers.

'Madame Oursor.'

'Yes! *Yes!*'

And Anna was actually laughing, actually bouncing on her toes with excitement, her tit-chains tightening and slackening, swinging in silver waves. Gwen couldn't help smiling with her, infected with her excitement and joy, but not understanding them.

'Yes, it was her, but so what? She's on his side, remember? She works for him.'

'No. No. No. She *doesn't*. She's on *our* side. I've never told you. I saw her, here, in the Schloss. Before we were all in the hothouse. She's going to rescue us. Get us away from Bärengelt. So we can sue him. And now she's come back to do it.'

The speakers switched on again, and the voice began speaking again. Anna's head swung back and she gazed ceilingwards, as though at a vision of the Virgin Mary, relief and delight glowing in her face as though they caught and threw back the Marian robes and halo.

'*Votre attention, s'il vous plaît, votre attention, s'il vous plaît. Le supermarché se ferme dans quatre minutes. Le supermarché se ferme dans quatre minutes. Merci.*'

And off. Beth snorted.

'That doesn't sound much like a knight in shining armour to me, Ansie.'

Anna pouted.

'She's having to be careful. But she's here. She must have arranged everything. With the police, everyone, the way she said she would. She's got to be careful still, of Bärengelt. But she's here. You've just heard her voice. She's here.'

'Maybe,' Beth said. She bent forward to the display of mushrooms, picked up two containers, and put them in her trolley.

'Not maybe. Definitely. That was her voice. She's here to rescue us.'

'I'll believe it when I see it.'

'You'll see it.'

'Okay, then, the sooner the better. Have we got everything?'

'Yep,' Gwen said. 'Time for the checkouts, I think. Anna, come on.'

They wheeled their trolleys down the aisle towards the checkouts, turned the corner, and there they were. The checkouts. Only now one of them was occupied. Gwen heard a sudden rhythmic jingling of metal and looked back to see Anna jumping on the spot with excitement, face glowing with happiness and excitement, tit-chains swinging up and down, hitting the trolley push-bar with little clashes.

'Her! It's her!'

And as they pushed their trolleys near Gwen saw that it was: Madame Oursor sat at the checkout, looking towards them patiently and calmly, dressed in the white-and-yellow uniform of a checkout girl with a small red flower pinned over her left breast.

'*Bonjour, mes filles,*' she said as Gwen reached the checkout and began to unload her trolley. '*Comment allez-vous?*'

'*Bien, madame,*' Gwen said. Her own heart was beating a little faster and she glanced back at Anna to see that her face was flushed pink, her blue eyes fixed on Madame Oursor's face.

'I am very glad to hear it,' said Madame Oursor. She set the conveyor belt moving and the first items of Gwen's shopping slid towards her on its wide black tongue. Gwen felt laughter in her throat. Such normality, coupled with such absurdity. Three naked girls at a supermarket checkout, heads shaved, chained to their trolleys by their tits, the first of them unloading breast-milk cheese and yoghurt and

181

menstrual blood-sausage and shit-grown mushrooms and bottles of piss. As though she had read her thoughts, Madame Oursor looked up at her from the rolling tongue of the conveyor belt and said, '*C'est surreal, non?*'

Her long fingers began to dance on the buttons of the cash register and a white tongue of paper licked from it and began to curl longer.

'*Oui, madame,*' Gwen said. She started to say something more but Madame Oursor paused for a moment from her addition and shook her head.

'*Non, ma petite*, Gwen. We are observed.'

Gwen put the last items on the belt and pushed the trolley forward beside it.

'I have no money, madame.'

'It does not signify. You will pay for it in the usual way, to that madman.'

'With pain, madame?'

'*Oui, certainement*. With pain. And I am afraid I must take some of it now, on his behalf. Your chains, *ma petite*. I must remove them. Present them to me. *Non, pas comme ça.* Your breasts. Hold them out towards me. Yes, that is good.'

Gwen stood closer to her, thrusting out her chest, her stomach suddenly hollow with anticipation above a cunt that shifted and began to glow. Pain from those long fingers. Nipple-pain.

Madame Oursor reached out and took hold of the chains an inch or two below Gwen's nipples. Six or seven centimetres. Her dark eyes met Gwen's, cool and watchful. And then her fingers began to pull, to tug and twist, exciting a trickle of metallic pain in Gwen's nipples that thickened and flowed harder. Gwen gasped, feeling her cunt pulse once, then begin to swell with warmth and liquid.

The torturing fingers relaxed.

'Did it hurt, *ma petite*?'

'Yes, madame.'

'But it hurt well, *n'est ce pas*? So that you liked as it hurt you?'

'Yes, madame.'

'I am glad, *ma petite*.'

Her fingers rose up the chains and gently worked to unhook them from Gwen's swollen throbbing nipples, awakening the pain again in little sparks and threads.

'There.'

The chains fell free, but the fingers lingered at Gwen's nipples for a moment, rubbing, soothing, stroking, Madame Oursor's dark eyes still fixed on Gwen's, still cool, still watchful, but somehow amused now. Pleased. Gwen felt orgasm stir inside her, putting up warm tendrils from her cunt towards the pools of pleasure in her tits, but even as she felt it the pleasuring fingers were withdrawn.

'Enough, *ma petite*. For the time as it is. Here is your bill, *ma petite*. If you would check it, please.'

She tore off the white tongue of paper from the cash register and handed it to her. Gwen took it, glanced at it, looked harder, looked up at Madame Oursor, who met her gaze with a minute shake of the head.

'*Non, ma petite*. Say nothing. Please pack your shopping and prepare to take it. I must now serve *tes sœurs*.'

Gwen folded the bill, tucked it behind her ear, and pushed her trolley to the end of the checkout. As she began to pack her purchases into white and yellow bags, and stow them in the trolley, her mind was working over what she had read on the bill.

Twenty-two

'What did yours say?' Beth asked.

'What? My bill?'

They had left the *supermarché* and were pushing their heavily laden trolleys down another long corridor.

'Yeah.'

'Pretty much the same, I think. That she was organizing a rescue and we only had to wait.'

'I told you,' Anna said from behind them. 'I told you she'd help us.'

Gwen stopped pushing her trolley and looked back at Anna.

'What did *yours* say, then?' she said.

'The same as yours and Beth's. That she was organizing a rescue. That we just had to wait a tiny bit longer and it would all be over for good. That Bärengelt would get what he deserved, the bastard.'

'It said all that?'

Beth chuckled.

'Reading between the lines, Gwenchen.'

Anna stuck her tongue out.

'You'll see,' she said.

Gwen opened her mouth to reply but stopped. Beth had nudged her in the ribs.

'What?'

'Don't look now, but we've got company.'

Gwen swung sharply to look back up the corridor.

'I said don't look now,' Beth said.

'You try keeping your back turned when he's behind you.'

'You didn't know it was him.'

'I guessed.'

Beth sighed.

'And you were right, unfortunately.'

At the end of the corridor Bärengelt was waiting for them, his tall black shape clear and ominous against the white of the door behind him.

'He's holding that fucking cane again,' Gwen said. 'Well, we'll have to grin and bear it while Madame comes up with the goods. Come on.'

She started pushing her trolley again, moving reluctantly but resolutely down the corridor towards him.

'The bills,' Anna hissed from behind her.

Moving her lips as little as possible, Gwen said, 'What about them?'

'We can't let him see them, or it'll ruin everything.'

'She's right, Gwen,' Beth said.

'Shit. I know. We'll have to swallow them. Chew them thoroughly first. Okay?'

She heard Beth and Anna murmur 'Okay'.

'And try not to make it too obvious.'

She slipped her hand behind her ear as though she was scratching it. When she lifted her hand away the bill was tucked between two of her fingers. *Now, wait a few seconds. Keep walking, keep looking straight ahead. Okay, cough and put your hand to your mouth. Casually. Make it look natural.*

But Beth and Anna had had the same idea. Cough, cough. They were all coughing, all raising their hands to their mouths, all slipping their bills inside and chewing. Chewing, and tasting. It was a fucking farce and ... She couldn't help it: her head swung sideways and her widened eyes met Beth's widened eyes. What the fuck ...?

Because her bill tasted strongly of strawberry. Her head swung back and she looked up the corridor again, because Bärengelt's voices had come rumbling along at them from speakers in the walls.

'*Guten Morgen, Fräulein.* I hope you are all well and ready for lunch.'

As soon as he said it she felt her stomach start to rumble. She was ready. She was fucking starving. The door behind Bärengelt slid aside and he turned and walked through it. She paused for a moment, swallowing the bill, still tasting strawberry, and then pushed her trolley the last few metres to the door and through it.

'*Wilkommen*, Gwen. Please unload your trolley on the table next to your stove. It's the first you come to.'

She pushed her trolley towards the three stoves down one wall, trying not to look too hard at the large table in the middle of the room. A dining table with four chairs: one for her, one for Beth, one for Anna . . . one for Bärengelt? He was standing near the table, after all. The speakers rumbled out again, greeting Beth, and Gwen reached the first stove and began to unload her trolley onto the table that stood beside it. Mushrooms. Yoghurt. Cheese. Ice-cream. Mineral water. Blood-sausage. Butter. Salt. Lining them up beside the knives and chopping block and spatula. The speakers rumbled out for the third time, greeting Anna, instructing her to unload her trolley. Beth was already at the second stove, unloading hers. Gwen had finished.

'Okay, Gwen, now that you have finished unloading, you can start cooking. Mushrooms, first, fried in butter. Please stand with your legs well apart as you cook.'

Why? she wondered. But she already knew. She opened the bag of loose mushrooms, put a handful onto the chopping block, and took one of the knives from its stand. The mushrooms were plump and juicy. Or *champignons*. That sounded better. Sounded like what they were. She turned, looking towards Bärengelt as he stood beside the table.

'Master?'

'Yes?'

'What about washing them?'

'You do not need to wash them. Slice them and fry them. That is all you need do.'

She turned back and started slicing them, surprised by how sharp the knife was, then remembering it was the sign of a good kitchen. Sharp knives. As she was finishing she heard Beth begin slicing her mushrooms. Her *champignons*. Grown in her own shit.

There was a black frying pan hanging on the wall beside the stove. She took it down and put it on the single gas-ring. Butter. Girl-milk-butter. She unwrapped a block and looked for a table knife with which to cut a wedge off. She couldn't see one.

'Use your fingers, Gwenchen.'

She gouged butter from the block with her fingers and dropped it into the pan, trying to scrape her fingers clean on the rim of the pan. No good. Her fingers were still covered in it. She wiped them on her breasts, then turned the stove on. The gas lit automatically with a faint *pop* and she jumped, half with surprise at the sound, half with surprise at the colour of the flame.

'It's methane, Gwenchen. From fermented girl-shit. Fermented Gwen-shit. And please, remember to keep your legs apart.'

The finger-gouge of butter suddenly slid across the bottom of the pan, leaving a wide, melted trail behind it. It reached the side of the pan and stopped, already beginning to flatten and dwindle, melting against the hot iron of the pan bottom. She picked up the spatula and dabbed at the butter. Anna was slicing mushrooms now and there was a pop from Beth's stove as Beth lit it. The butter was nearly melted and she picked up the chopping board of mushrooms, ready to push them off and into the pan with the spatula.

'Use your fingers, Gwenchen. Where possible, always use your fingers.'

She picked up the mushrooms with her fingers, feeling their plumpness and juiciness. Fresh mushrooms, grown on Gwen-shit, fried in Gwen-butter on Gwen-flame. She dropped them in the pan, hearing them begin to sizzle immediately. Bärengelt's boots moved on the floor and she turned her head. He was walking towards her.

'Concentrate on your cooking, Gwenchen. I am merely going to season your blood-sausage.'

She turned back to her cooking and he loomed beside her, one black-gloved hand reaching down for one of the blood-sausages she had put on the table. Anna's stove popped faintly further along the wall.

'Legs wider, Gwenchen.'

She forced her legs wider, stirring at the mushrooms with the spatula as his boots sounded on the floor just behind her.

'Good girl.'

A gloved hand came up between her legs, feeling its way up her inner thighs to her cunt. She closed her eyes for a moment. Now he knew. Knew the way the cooking had began to excite her. Mushrooms sizzling in butter made from milk squirted from her own breasts. The sound and the smell of it. His gloved fingers vee'd her cunt-lips apart and she felt the head of the blood-sausage nudging at her.

'A little wider still, please, Gwenchen, and feet a little back.'

She obeyed, feeling her nipples harden and begin to throb. Bärengelt pushed the blood-sausage slowly into her. It was thick and hard and her cunt-walls oozed delightedly over it.

'Squeeze on it, Gwenchen.'

She tightened her cunt on it, surprised at the ease with which her cunt-muscles obeyed her, the power in them.

'Good girl. Now I am going to release it. Do not allow it to fall to the floor. Okay. Now, Beth, legs wider, please.'

He walked away from her, leaving the blood-sausage jammed into her cunt. The mushrooms were turning brown and beginning to shrink, sliding easily to and fro on the bottom of the pan as she stroked at them with the spatula. Maybe she should add another gouge of butter. She leaned over and dug her fingers into the butter-block, feeling the blood-sausage move inside her cunt. She glanced down. Half of its length was sticking out of her, black and solid, beginning to shine with threads of yelm.

'Good girl. Now I am going to release it. Do not allow it to fall to the floor. Anna, legs wider, please.'

She dropped the extra butter into the pan and stirred it with the spatula. They were going to finish cooking one after the other, all of them with blood-sausages jammed up their cunts. She looked at Beth, then leaned back a little to look beyond her to Anna. Bärengelt was kneeling behind her, lifting a thick blood-sausage up between her legs as one hand held the lips of her cunt apart. Anna had her eyes closed. Gwen swallowed and looked back at her cooking.

'Good girl. Now I am going to release it. Do not allow it to fall to the floor.'

She heard his boots move away from Anna, back to the table. A chair scraped back. He was sitting down. Sitting down at the dining table. Ready to dine?

'Gwen, how are your mushrooms doing?'

Yes, ready to dine.

'Nearly done, master.'

'Good. Bring them to me when you have finished.'

She cooked them for a minute more, then turned off the stove, lifted the pan, turned, and carried it over to Bärengelt. The blood-sausage jerked in front of her as she walked towards the table. It was covered in a white cloth and there was a silver candelabrum on it holding three absurdly small candles of dirty yellow wax. In front of the three empty chairs (hers, Beth's and Anna's) was an orchid in a small glass, but there was no orchid in front of Bärengelt.

'Good girl. Put some on my plate, then some on your own.'

His plate was huge, nearly a metre across, shining white porcelain anagrammed *AB* in Gothic script, with knife and fork sitting to either side of it. She pushed some of the mushrooms off the pan onto it.

'More,' he said. 'Okay, put the rest on your own plate.'

She moved along the table to the smaller plate monogrammed with a Gothic *G* and put the rest of the mushrooms on it. Her orchid was dark blue. Beth's was red, Anna's yellow. But if Bärengelt had no orchid, they had no knife and fork. Were they going to have to eat with their fingers?

189

'Okay, good girl. Take the blood-sausage out of your cunt and put it on the table beside your plate, then go and fetch your yoghurt and cheese. Beth, how are your mushrooms doing?'

'Done, master.'

Gwen reached between her legs for the blood-sausage. It slid out easily, slicked with yelm, and she laid it on the table beside her plate.

'Good. Bring them over to me.'

She carried the pan back to her stove. Beth was switching off her stove and lifting the pan from it, turning to walk towards Bärengelt and the table, her blood-sausage jutting between her thighs, jammed into her oozing cunt.

Gwen picked up some cheese and yoghurt and carried them back to Bärengelt. Beth was pushing mushrooms onto his plate. They glistened with butter. Melted Beth-butter.

'Okay, put the rest on your plate, take your blood-sausage out and put it on the table beside it, then fetch your cheese and yoghurt. Anna, how are your mushrooms doing?'

'They're ready, master.'

'Good. Then bring them to me.'

Gwen put the cheese and yoghurt on the table next to her plate.

'Sit down now, Gwen, and wait patiently for the meal to begin.'

She sat down, facing towards the stoves, watching as Anna walked towards the table, the black length of her blood-sausage ticking off her steps, up and down, jutting between her slim white thighs. Beth was picking up cheese and yoghurt, turning round and walking towards the table too, no blood-sausage between her thighs now, just a gleaming wash of yelm, as though her cunt were salivating hungrily. Anna was standing beside Bärengelt, pushing mushrooms onto his plate. His voices rumbled from the walls.

'More. Okay, put the rest on your plate and then do what I have already told your sisters to do.'

'Yes, master.'

Gwen swallowed saliva as Anna pushed the remaining mushrooms in her pan onto her own plate. Beth put her cheese and yoghurt on the table and Bärengelt's voices rumbled out again.

'Sit down and wait. Hurry up, Anna. You are holding everyone up, as usual.'

They waited. Beth was sitting directly across the table from her, Bärengelt at its head, sitting directly across from Anna's chair. She caught Beth's eye and raised her eyebrows fractionally. Beth raised her eyebrows too. Her throat noded and smoothed. She was swallowing saliva too.

Anna came scurrying back from her stove, arms full of yoghurt and cheese. She put them on the table beside her plate and sat down.

'Good girl.'

Bärengelt pushed his chair back and stood up, leaning forward over the table to the candelabrum and the three tiny candles. A silver lighter had appeared in his black-gloved hand. Clear yellow flame sprung from it, touched to the wicks of the dirty yellow candles one after the other.

'*Eine Kerze für ein Mädchen.* One candle for each of you, girls. *Drei Mädchenkerzen.* Three girl-candles. *Hergestellten aus deinem Ohrenschmalz.* Made of your ear-wax.'

He pushed the chair back further and stepped away from it, moving round the table towards her. The candles were burning with small, sickly flames, sending up thin trails of grey smoke. As the air disturbed by Bärengelt's movements reached them, the trails broke and swirled. A moment later she smelt it. The smoke of burning ear-wax candles. Her stomach rolled.

'And these, girls' – he was standing beside her and one hand reached out and nudged at the orchid sitting in front of her plate – 'are orchids I have grown from thick bulbs planted in your juicy arses. I extracted them only yesterday.'

His hand dropped to one side, leaving the orchid quivering for a moment, and he picked up one of the blocks of cheese sitting beside her plate. He stripped the paper wrapper off with strong fingers, put the cheese on her plate, and leaned down the table to pick up the knife next to his plate. He started slicing the cheese, leaving slices piled in a fan, then put the reduced cheese block back on the table and picked up the blood-sausage.

'Thick or thin, Gwenchen?'

She swallowed saliva, her stomach alternately rolling with nausea and grumbling with hunger.

'Thick, master,' she said.

He started to cut the blood-sausage in thick slices, arranging them in a fan beside the slices of cheese, counting each slice as he cut it away, cutting almost too quickly to keep up the count.

'*Eins, zwei, drei, vier, fünf, sechs, seben, acht, neun, zehn, elf, zwölf, dreizehn.*'

He put the blood-sausage back on the table beside her place, nearly half its length gone.

'Thirteen slices of girl-blood-sausage for you, Gwenchen. That will fill you nicely.'

He stepped around the table to Anna and began to unwrap her cheese. Another swirl of ear-wax candle-smoke reached Gwen's nostrils and she held her breath. Her stomach rolled and grumbled as she watched him cut the cheese. Anna-milk-cheese. *Annamilchkäse.*

'Thick or thin, Annalein?'

He was holding up Anna's blood-sausage.

'Thin, please, master.'

'Then thin it is.'

He began to slice her blood-sausage, counting off the slices, the rumble of his voices reaching Gwen's buttocks through the seat of her chair, carried up from the floor through the legs of the chair.

'*Eins, zwei, drei, vier, fünf, sechs, seben, acht, neun, zehn, elf, zwölf, dreizehn.* Thirteen slices of girl-blood-sausage for you also, Annalein.'

The speakers in the walls fell silent and he moved around the table to Beth. But the tremble of bass in the seat of her chair was still there. Still tickling at her buttocks. Reaching her cunt. Getting stronger. Because the seat of her chair was vibrating. Buzzing. Reaching her cunt through her buttocks and thighs. Rippling through it.

She shifted uneasily, simultaneously wanting the buzzing to stop and to get stronger. It got stronger. Anna shifted in her chair too. Was it happening to all of them? Bärengelt was picking up Beth's blood-sausage.

'Thick or thin, Betchen?'

'Thin, master.'

'Thin it is.'

She watched the silver knife flash as it cut away slices of the thick black blood-sausage. Fresh yelm was leaking between her thighs, about to stain the seat of the chair. His voices began rumbling from the walls and she shifted again as the vibration in the seat of her chair increased.

'*Eins, zwei, drei, vier, fünf, sechs, seben, acht, neun, zehn, elf, zwölf, dreizehn.* Thirteen slices of girl-blood-sausage for you also, Betchen.'

He put the blood-sausage back on the table and walked back to his own seat. He sat down.

'Now, girls, if you will each donate me one slice of blood-sausage and two slices of cheese.'

He lifted his huge plate and held it over the top of the table so that it rode the swirling trails of smoke from the ear-wax candles. Gwen picked up a slice of blood-sausage with her fingers and stood up to put it on his plate. Anna and Beth were doing the same. She picked up two slices of cheese and added them.

'Thank you, girls.'

He put the plate back on the table and sat down. It was only half-full, even with the three helpings of mushrooms, the three slices of blood-sausage and six slices of cheese. Their plates were crammed: mushrooms, cheese, blood-sausage.

'Grace, girls.'

What? But Anna was bowing her head and she realized what he had said. She closed her eyes and bowed her head.

'For what you are about to receive, may your master make you truly thankful. Amen.'

A soft murmur from Anna.

'Amen.'

Louder from Beth.

'Amen.'

'Amen,' she said.

'Good. Now, girls, one last thing before we begin. Please swap your plates. Anna, you take Gwen's; Beth, you take Anna's; Gwen, you take Beth's. Quickly, please.'

They looked at each other in confusion for a moment. Anna was looking sick.

'Quickly, I said.'

The little earwax candles were beginning to gutter and die. Beth stood up and held her plate across the table towards her. She passed Anna her plate and stood up to take Beth's. Anna passed her plate to Beth. Bärengelt was holding the neck of his bodysuit in both hands and tugging at it. What was he doing? Loosening his helmet?

Yes. She suddenly smelt aftershave and a patch of tanned skin appeared around Bärengelt's neck as the helmet loosened and he began to tug it up and off. His voices came rumbling from the walls, muffled as the microphone in his helmet moved away from his lips. Two of the earwax candles were out, the third nearly so.

'Eat, girls.'

The lights went out.

Twenty-three

She heard a groan and slowly opened her eyes. Her head was resting on one side and for a moment she couldn't understand what she was seeing, then she realized that it was the surface of the table, the white table-cloth crumpled and stained. She was still sitting in her chair, slumped forward on the table with her head resting sideways on it in something sticky and cold. She closed her eyes hard, re-opened them, and slowly raised her cheek from the table, trying to sit upright. Her stomach lurched and she groaned.

'Shut the fuck up,' said a voice from across the table. Beth's voice. She managed to sit up and blinked blearily at the table and the naked figure sitting with its head in its hands on the other side of it. The table was filthy, covered in streaks and pools of half-chewed food and vomit and fragments of broken glass and porcelain. Vomit was splattered on the floor and on her body: it was what her cheek had been resting in. Had Beth spoken or had she dreamed it? No, Beth groaned again.

'You shut the fuck up,' Gwen said.

Beth gingerly raised her head from her hands.

'Why should I? I was groaning first.'

It was too hard to come up with a response. She turned her head slowly to look at the end of the table where Anna had been sitting.

'Where's Anna?'

'On the floor.'

195

Gwen didn't want to lean back and look around the table to see.

'I'll take your word for it. Who's been sick everywhere?' Beth lowered her head back into her hands.

'You have and I have and Anna has,' she said, her voice muffled and distant. 'Now shut the fuck up. I want to suffer in silence.'

'My mouth feels like a vulture's jockstrap.'

'I know. After a wrestler's been shitting in it. Welcome to the club. Club rule number one is: shut the fuck up.'

'Where's Bärengelt?'

'Who knows? Who the fuck cares? And speaking of "fuck": shut it up. For fuck's sake.'

And she groaned again. Gwen knew why. The seat of her chair had started vibrating and as her cunt stirred her nausea got worse. She heard boots along the corridor outside and the sudden hum of speakers being switched on in the walls. And then the boots were inside the room and Bärengelt's voices were rumbling out at them.

'*Guten Morgen, Fräulein*. And a very good morning it is too. I hope you feel fresh and rested after your night's sleep, for you have a heavy day ahead of you. Come on, on your feet. Beth, if you would assist Anna to her feet it would be much appreciated. Oh dear, what is this? Why are you not leaping to obey my simple orders? I see I will have to liven you up, beginning perhaps with you, Gwen.'

She got out of her chair quickly and turned to face him as he strode across the floor towards her, the black leather of his bodysuit gleaming as sleekly as ever. What fuck had he done to them during the meal? Had they eaten everything and thrown it all up again? There was nothing in her stomach but nausea.

'*Gutes*, Gwenchen. The threat of punishment has brought you into line. Yes, Beth, that's it. Get her on her feet and line up with her. Come on, the three of you, lined up. I think I had better conduct a brisk session of callisthenics to get the red blood flowing briskly again in your veins.'

Gwen suppressed a groan and walked away from the table as fast as she could to line up with Beth and Anna.

The floor was splattered with streaks and smears of vomit and half-chewed food for metres.

'Not there, girls. Find a thoroughly clean space, if you please. You say in English cleanliness is next to Godliness, *nicht wahr*? In German, we say *Reinlichkeit ist die Tugend der Könige*, or "cleanliness is the virtue of kings". A useful insight into the Teutonic mindset, *nicht wahr*? So on the word of command, begin running on the spot. And the word of command is, of course, *los*. So: *los!*'

She began running on the spot, wondering dully how long it would be before she threw up.

'Faster! Knees higher! Knees higher, Anna!'

But slowly the feeling of nausea was beginning to wear off. Maybe the callisthenics would work. He didn't want them too ill for the heavy day ahead.

'And stop! Stop! On the word of command, squats, with arms held full-length in front of you.'

Squats. Arms held full-length in front of her.

'Slowly, Gwenchen. This is not an exercise for speed.'

She was starting to sweat, the smears of vomit on her skin moistening as she sweated into them. Less nausea now and her mind was focussing. So that she felt filthy. Covered in vomit, with bruises in odd parts of her body, and an aching cunt between thighs caked in dried yelm and come.

'And stop! On the word of command, touch your toes.'

She heard his boots move on the floor as he walked behind them. Why? He could examine their bodies from any angle using the cameras feeding the screen inside his helmet. Why did he need to walk behind them? So he could be near what he was feasting his eyes on? Their buttocks stretching and flexing, the flash of yelm-and-come-coated cuntlips between their thighs?

'And stop! On the word of command, you will move on the double out of the dining room and into the corridor. At the end of it you will turn left and proceed to the door that awaits you at the end of the left branch. You will go through the door, use the showers in the room on the other side, and then await further orders. So, on the word of command, on the double, run.'

Twenty-four

'Feeling fresh and well-cleansed now, girls?'

'Yes, master,' they chorused.

'I am very glad to hear it. Now, time to re-equip you for the ordeals ahead. Line up, all of you.'

They lined up in front of the desk, watching as Bärengelt slipped his fingers into a hidden pocket in his bodysuit and took out a small golden key on a silver chain. He turned the box sitting on the desk and inserted the key. Before he turned it, his voices came rumbling from the walls.

'I have taken something precious from each of you, as you still know. Several times, in fact, for what I took, you regained, till I took it again. And you will regain it yet again, slowly, but I wish to return it to you now, so that you have it immediately.'

He turned the key with a tiny, oiled click and lifted the lid of the box so that it lay open but facing away from them.

'Can you guess what it is, girls? Anna?'

'No, master.'

'Beth? You?'

'No, master.'

'Gwen? Can you guess?'

'Yes, master.'

'What then, Gwen? What?'

'Our hair, master.'

'Very astute of you, Gwenchen. It is your hair.'

His gloved hands took hold of the box on either side and spun it through 180° so that it sat in front of them with its interior open and seemingly empty. No, the floor was lined with red hair. Bärengelt reached inside and tugged at the hair. It came up in a mass. A wig. A wig of red hair. Real red hair. Beth's hair. The floor of the box was now lined with blonde hair.

'Anna,' Bärengelt's voices rumbled. He held out the red wig and Anna took it, two small vertical lines of puzzlement creasing the root of her nose. Bärengelt tugged at the blonde hair and it came up in a mass. A wig. A wig of real blonde hair. Anna's hair. The floor of the box was now lined with black hair.

'Gwen.'

Gwen took the blonde wig as he held it out to her. Now he tugged at the black hair and it came up in a mass. A wig. A wig of real black hair. Gwen's hair.

'Beth.'

Beth took the wig. There were three small oval mirrors lying against the bare, varnished floor of the box now.

'Now, girls, what was yours is yours again. You have instantly what would otherwise take you some time to re-gain. So please, put them on. Exactly as you have received them.'

Gwen flicked the blonde wig straight and lifted it to her head. It went on smoothly, easily, sitting comfortably on her scalp. After a moment's hesitation, Beth followed suit, flicking the black wig straight, lifting it, slipping it on, tugging it so that the hair didn't hang across her face.

'Come on, Anna. Gone yesterday, hair today. Put it on. Quick.'

Anna straightened the black wig with her fingers, lifted it, and pulled it on.

'Good girl. Good girls. Here, take one.'

He lifted the box and held it out to Anna as though it were a chocolate box.

'Take one.'

Anna took out one of the mirrors and Bärengelt swung the box to Beth.

'Take one.'

Beth took one.

199

'And you, Gwen. Now, adjust your hair, girls. We want you looking at your best for the rest of the day.'

They peered into the unfamiliarly familiar faces looking up and out at them from the small ovals of the mirrors. Anna's white face under red hair, Beth's white face under black, Gwen's white face under blonde. Bärengelt's voices broke in on their thoughts.

'Well, look at me. Do you like your new hair? Anna?'

'Yes, master.'

'That is excellent. And I like it too. I like it exceedingly. It is almost as though three new girls were looking up at me. Three fresh faces, with nine fresh orifices ready for service. Beth: what about you? Do you like your new hair?'

'Yes, master.'

'Excellent. And you, Gwen?'

'Yes, master.'

'Such sincerity, as always, Gwenchen. There is an odd, almost unsettling contrast now between what I know of your character and the hair that frames your face. Such purity and innocence in those blonde tresses; such black treachery and malice in the skull they adorn. Is that not so, my dear?'

Gwen said nothing for a moment.

'Well? There is no point lying to me. I know very well your feelings towards me. Is it not so?'

'Yes, master.'

'Good. At least you are not adding duplicity to your other vices. Your many other vices.'

Gwen looked at his blank black mask steadily.

'Nor cowardice, Gwen. You do not compound your vices with that, either. I have not yet broken you to my will, though I have had great pleasure in trying. Perhaps I should try again, this very moment. In celebration of your new hair. Yes, I think that is what I will do. Come here, girls. Stand away from the desk, over here. Yes, good. Now, in a line, facing this way.'

They lined up, backs to the desk, facing out across the bare centre of the room.

'There is nothing here, is there, girls? Nothing of interest. Until now, of course.'

Something moved in the middle of the floor. A section of floor was sliding open, revealing a trench about two metres across, about a metre long, two metres, three. Yes. There was a trench lying open in front of them and ... Gwen sniffed ... there was a thick, moist smell on the air.

'Move forward, girls. Examine the contents.'

Gwen walked forward, followed by Beth, then Anna, and they lined up along the trench, looking down into it. It was full of a white liquid that gleamed milkily under the lights in the ceiling, like molten pearl or white marble. The smell rising from it told them what it was. It was come. A trench full of come.

'What is it, girls? Gwen?'

She turned and looked at him where he was standing by the desk, the black cane raised and twitching slightly in his hand.

'It's come, master.'

'Good girl. Well-spotted. It is a trench, 377 centimetres long, 233 centimetres wide, and 145 centimetres deep. Or five feet four and a half inches deep. I know how you Brits cling to your imperial measures. And 233 centimetres is seven feet four inches, by the way. But I think Gwen can manage that.'

'Master?'

'You can manage it, Gwen. You can jump across the trench. So jump across it.'

'Yes, master.'

She took ten or so steps back from the trench, paused for a moment, gathering herself, then ran forward fast and jumped, feeling the come-smell swirl around her as she passed above it, landing with space to spare on the other side, turning and looking back. Bärengelt had moved to the desk and was stooping over it, opening a drawer, lifting something out. Ropes. Three ropes, about two or three metres long. A white one, a red one and a black one. He draped them over his shoulder and walked towards Beth and Anna. The ropes had silver balls at one end, maybe at the other too, but the other ends were hanging down his back.

He reached Beth and Anna and shrugged the ropes off his shoulder to the floor. Yes, silver balls at both ends. About the size of small oranges. Three of them at each end.

'Anna, pick the white one up. Tell me what it is.'

Anna walked nervously over to him and stooped in his shadow to pick up the white rope. She stood up, running her fingers down it, but Gwen knew what she was going to say before she said it.

'It's hair, master.'

'Whose hair, Annalein?'

'My hair, master.'

'That is correct. How useful your hair has proved to me. How pleasurable. I have taken it from you, causing you much pain and distress, and myself much pleasure. I have taken it from your nipples and cunts. Most of all, however, I have taken it from your heads. That long, glossy hair of which you were all three so proud. I have taken it from you several times, harvesting it again and again. I have made it into wigs. I have woven it into pussy-whips. Now, as you see, I have woven it into ropes. Very light but very strong ones. Come here, Annalein. Take hold of the rope with both hands. Good girl. Now watch.'

He took hold of one end of the rope Anna was holding, black-gloved hands clasping the silver balls, and lifted the rope vertically. Anna's hands went with it, lifting her arms above her head. She went up on her feet, on her toes, then left the ground, dangling a few centimetres above it, held up on the rope, her white body and red wig standing out sharp against Bärengelt's black leather bulk. Bärengelt suddenly let go and Anna fell back to the floor, stumbling, then recovering her balance.

'Good girl, Annalein. Do you see how strong the rope is?'

'Yes, master,' Anna said.

'That is good, because I want you to have confidence in it, for your *Tauziehen*.'

'Master?'

'For your *Tauziehen*, Annalein. For your tug-of-war. The tug-of-war you and Gwen are about to have.'

Anna's neck and shoulders stiffened. Gwen knew she had suppressed the urge to look round and at her, blue eyes suddenly frightened at the prospect of a tug-of-war between them.

202

'Yes, Annalein and Gwenchen, my two fine sportsgirls, a tug-of-war. And may the best – or should that be, the better? – girl win. Anna, come here. Stand so. Good. Here, hold this end of the rope.'

Anna took the silver balls in her small hands, a flicker of discomfort travelling across her face. They must be cold. Cold silver balls in Anna's cool little hands.

'Gwen, ready yourself. Catch.'

Bärengelt threw the other end of the rope across the trench and Gwen caught it, feeling the silver balls herself now. And they were cold. Cold and heavy. The rope was about three metres long, thin but strong, stretching in a shallow curve from her hands to Anna's. She couldn't understand why Bärengelt was doing this, unless there was going to be some handicap for her. Otherwise she would win easily, dragging Anna to the brink of the trench and over it, sending her splashing into the come that filled it. Poor little bitch. Up to her neck in come or deeper. And she was sure Bärengelt wouldn't leave it at that. The come wasn't just there to be fallen into. Bärengelt's voices began rumbling from the walls again and she shook her head and paid attention.

'Right, girls, now comes the next stage. Please put the first ball on your end of the rope up your cunt. Do you understand? Anna?'

'No, master.'

'It is perfectly simple, Annalein. The first ball on your end of the rope. Hold it up for me. Yes, that's the one. Now, please put it up your cunt. Just the first one, no more. Understood? Gwen?'

'Yes, master.'

But she didn't understand. How could they tug on the rope if the ends were held in their cunts? She got the first ball at her end of the rope ready and reached down for her cunt, parting the lips, putting the ball between them, pushing, sliding it in. It felt colder than ever on the delicate pink-and-red tissues of her cunt, sliding solidly between them like a ball of ice. It was up. Bärengelt had been watching, for his voices rumbled out again.

'Good girl, Gwen. Now, tighten on it. Hold it in place. Anna, hurry up.'

Gwen tightened her cunt on it, feeling its hardness between the walls of her softness. She supported the other two balls in her hand, not wanting their weight to drag the ball in her cunt free.

'Good girl, Anna. Now, as Gwen has done, tighten on it. Hold it in place. Good. Now, both of you, take your hands away from your cunts. Clasp them behind the back of your heads. Good girls.'

Gwen didn't want to let go of the two balls hanging outside her cunt, fearing they would drag the one inside free, because her cunt was surely too weak to hold onto it. She slowly let go of the balls, ready to grab back at them as they began to fall, but they didn't. Not a millimetre. She raised her hands fully and clasped them behind her head, watching Anna do the same. The hair-rope stretched between them, joining cunt to cunt, two silver balls dangling in front of Anna's cunt, two silver balls dangling in front of hers, brushing her skin with cold.

'Good,' Bärengelt rumbled. 'Now, listen carefully to what I say and wait for me to finish. Do not ask questions at any point, simply listen, and obey. The two balls that are outside your cunts. You must draw them inside. You will do this entirely by muscular contraction and manipulation of the walls of your cunts, moving the first ball up towards your cervix. I do not wish to hear that you cannot do this, I wish you simply to do it. Do you understand? Please nod if so without speaking. Gwen?'

She nodded. She understood what he had said but she didn't think she could do it.

'Anna?'

After a moment or two Anna nodded, looking unhappy. She had understood too, but she didn't think she could do it either. *That makes two of us, Ansie,* Gwen thought.

'Very well. Then do it. Now.'

Gwen focussed her attention on her cunt, but he might as well have told her to rotate her left nipple clockwise and her right nipple counterclockwise by sheer force of will.

She couldn't do that and she couldn't do this. Anna couldn't do it. Neither of them could.

Her head suddenly snapped forward and down and she stared incredulously as the two balls dangling in front of her cunt began to climb inside. The walls of her cunt were rippling under conscious control, drawing the first ball deeper, drawing the second and third balls after it. She looked up and saw Anna's balls climbing cuntward too. They could both do it. Somehow they could both do it.

She looked down again. The second ball nudged the lips of her cunt and began to slide inside, cold and smooth. She was doing it and she didn't have a clue how. Her cunt felt almost like a third hand, a third inverted hand flexing between her thighs, full of skill and power, and she felt her lips move, pronouncing an unfamiliar word. What was she saying? Cuntercise. Cuntercise. Only it wasn't so unfamiliar. It was the word Bärengelt had used to them as he lectured them on the flaccidity and idleness of their cunts in the hothouse, telling them how he would train them until they were worthy of his cock.

Her cunt-lips closed behind the second ball. It was inside her now, clasped securely between her cunt-walls, being carried deeper, drawing the third ball after it. Cuntercise. It looked as though Bärengelt had succeeded. Somehow, while they were hanging in the hothouse, he had trained them. Trained their cunts until now they *were* worthy of his cock. She looked up at Bärengelt. His cock. Worthy of his cock. The third ball brushed her cunt-lips and began to slide inside. The rope was tautening between them now, stretched from her cunt to Anna's.

'*Sehr gut*,' Bärengelt rumbled. 'Do you see what you can achieve when you do not question, you merely obey?'

The third ball was half-way into her cunt, her cunt-lips beginning to shut behind it. Only they wouldn't fully shut, because they were beginning to swell and pout. Drawing the balls into her cunt-chamber had aroused her. Feeling them travel into her, hard and cold and smooth between her cunt-walls. The ball was fully inside her, but her cunt-lips hadn't closed. Her cunt-chamber was aching with cold, but it was pleasurable, velvety walls lying on cold smooth metal. Three balls up her cunt.

She looked up. Anna had drawn the three balls successfully into her cunt and stood with her hands clasped behind her head, tits jutting, a faint blush on her face, her cunt joined to her eldest sister's cunt by a rope woven of her own blonde hair

'Good girls. Very good girls. Now, it is nearly time for the tug-of-war to begin. The rules are very simple. Each of you will attempt to drag the other forward to the brink of the trench and over it so that your opponent falls in the come with which it is filled. You will not touch the rope with your hands at any point, nor will you crouch or alter your posture in any other way. You will merely drag backwards as best you are able, holding the rope tight in your cunt. If the rope leaves your cunt, you lose immediately – and in addition to being forced to jump into the come, you will receive a dozen strokes of the cane. Do you understand? You may speak this time.'

'Yes, master,' she said, hearing Anna say it a second after her. Anna was looking worried. Good. That was a hopeful sign. Unsettling your opponent was half the battle and Bärengelt had already done it for her.

'Very well, then on the count of three, begin.'

She tensed herself, tightening the muscles of her thighs and buttocks, clenching her cunt even more tightly on the balls that lined it.

'*Eins . . . zwei . . . drei.* Go!'

Her left foot slid forward on the marble floor, swinging her body nearer the trench. Anna had begun tugging, taking small steps backwards, tightening the rope like a huge guitar-string. Christ, it wasn't going to be easy. Anna had the advantage of lack of height. She was tugging downhill: *she* would have to tug uphill. She adjusted her feet and tried to tug back at Anna. Yes. Anna's backward steps stopped and she looked worried again.

One of us is going to end up in that come and it's not going to be me, Ansie. You can bet your bottom dollar on that. And your bottom. She tightened the muscles of her buttocks and tried to take a small step backwards. Christ. Sweat appeared on her forehead as she realised the balls were beginning to slip out of her cunt. Christ. She sucked desperately at them by sheer muscular effort, trying to keep them in place, and managed to keep them all inside, but in the meantime Anna had begun to tug backwards again, taking small steps, her face set with determination, blue eyes unblinking as they gazed across at her.

You little bitch, Gwen thought. *I'll show you. I'll fucking show you.* But it was no use. She couldn't. At best all she could do was stay in one spot, but she couldn't begin to move backwards herself. There were only a few centimetres separating her feet from the brink of the trench and the smell of the come seemed to have increased, hanging in her nostrils as she fought to maintain her position, cunt clenched desperately on the three silver balls. Anna had a much bigger gap on her side: fifteen or twenty centimetres at least. Being able to tug downhill was an even bigger advantage than she had feared. Maybe if she swung her hips slowly she could . . .

She tried it, felt warm relief flooding her stomach for a moment, then gasped with frustration, feeling the relief curdle and cool. The balls were slipping out of her cunt again. What was fucking wrong with her? Why couldn't she do this? Anna sensed something was wrong and began to tug again, blue eyes unblinking, small white face set between the hanging wings of red hair. Gwen's feet slipped on the marble and another precious couple of centimetres was lost. Christ, her toes were almost hanging over the brink. Anna was fucking going to win. She was fucking going to win.

The thought gave her new strength and she managed to stop the balls slipping in her cunt. *Tighten*, she told herself. *Tighten.* Anna had stopped gaining ground. It was time for her to take the initiative, to take back some of what she had lost. But there was a new enemy now. Sweat. The sweat of effort and frustration. It was running down her back and flanks, in her titcleft, between the cheeks of her arse, trickling inexorably downwards, down her thighs and calves, onto her ankles, onto her feet, onto the floor.

Slippery sweat on the floor. She tried to take a small step backwards and almost cried out with anger as the sole of her foot slid on sweat. Her heart hammered. She had almost lost her balance. Anna would have taken advantage of it at once, dragging her to the brink and over, plunging her into the come.

She glared across at Anna. *Little bitch. Looking as though butter wouldn't melt in her mouth. But she was sweating too, her white body glistening with the same sweat that covered hers. Maybe she was going to slip too. Come on, you bitch, slip. Give me the chance to put you where you deserve to be, neck-deep in come.*

She tried another backward step and did cry aloud this time as her sole slipped on more sweat, because this time she did partly lose her balance, having to swing her upper body violently to counteract the loss of support from her foot. It would have been so easy with her arms free, but that was why Bärengelt had ordered her to clasp her hands behind her head. To make it harder for her. Easier for Anna. Because Anna had a lower centre of gravity.

And Anna had taken advantage of it, taken advantage of her slip, tugging her another centimetre or two nearer the brink. Almost all the way. Her toes were over it now, hanging over space. Anna was well back from the brink, blue eyes still unblinking, face still set with determination. Gwen glared at her, trying to intimidate her, trying to beam a threat into her disobedient little bitch's brain. Anna pouted and stuck out her tongue and Gwen's heart thumped again as Bärengelt's voices came rumbling out at them.

'*Brava*, Annalein! Do not let her frighten you. Drag her in. Let's see come fountain, as she plunges into it.'

Anna dipped her head as though in acknowledgment and began to take those small steps backwards again, those gut-hollowing, heart-twisting small steps backwards. Gwen set her teeth and clenched her cunt desperately, tightening her thighs and buttocks and stomach, but it was no use. She could stay still and let the balls be dragged out of her cunt, or surrender and let herself be dragged into the come.

208

A come-bath was preferable to a come-bath and a dozen strokes of the cane. She surrendered, letting her feet slide nearer the brink, nearer, toes fully over it now, nearer, nearer, losing traction, losing balance, taking a deep breath, dragged inexorably forward, forward until the inevitable was the actual and she was dragged into the trench.

Come erupted in a great white geyser, spraying up and out over the floor, catching even Anna as she stumbled backwards and sat down hard on her arse, white face lit by a smile now. Gwen had gone fully under; now she surfaced, gasping, come running down her face in streams, blonde wig soaked and plastered to her head, hands still clasped on her neck. Bärengelt strode to the edge of the trench and took hold of the rope where it lay slackly on the floor.

'Release it, Anna. Quick.'

Anna relaxed her cunt-grip and the three silver balls slid from her cunt, dulled with heat and moisture.

'Gwen, release them.'

Gwen shook her head, spraying come left and right, but she wasn't disobeying the order, merely trying to dry her face, for Bärengelt was hauling in her three silver balls, released somewhere beneath the come by her defeated cunt. Bärengelt tossed the rope to one side and held something out to Gwen as she stood breast-deep in the come. Anna was smiling now, delighted with her victory, and as she saw what Bärengelt was holding out her smile deepened.

A long stiff straw of transparent plastic.

'Gwenchen, the come is exactly one hundred and forty five centimetres deep. When you have lowered it a centimetre, you can come out.'

Bärengelt turned.

'But I don't know why you are smiling, Annalein. Even Gwen's stomach cannot accommodate that amount of come. You and Beth will therefore be called upon to help her from the edge. Here are your straws.'

He held up two more long straws of transparent plastic.

'Get cracking. A centimetre of come over that surface area is going to take a lot of sucking.'

Twenty-five

'Girls! A game!'

They crowded through the door into the rumbling echoes of Bärengelt's voices, but Anna stopped dead as she stepped onto the floor, then jumped, squeaking with pain as Beth banged against her arse, Beth grunting with pain too as Gwen crowded in behind her. Holding gingerly onto their buttocks, they stood as close to the door as they dared, staring apprehensively at the middle of the room. A large circular black table. Three medical couches around the table at 120 degrees, and 240 degrees, and 360 degrees, padded with white leather, with straps hanging loose down one side of each.

And the couches faced inwards, so that when a girl was lying on one, her head would be resting almost on the table and her buttocks – Gwen's cunt shimmered and began to melt as she saw Anna swallow and blink – her buttocks would be lying beneath just beside a drum of hypodermic needles held up on a jointed metal arm.

'Forward, girls.'

They heard Bärengelt's boots in the corridor outside the room and moved forward, half-turning so that they could watch doorway and table simultaneously. He came in, having to stoop a little to pass beneath the jamb of the door, and came towards them, black cane twitching in his left hand. They backed away, but he stopped two or three metres short of them, his right hand coming up and pointing.

'The game, girls. Watch.'

The drum of hypodermic needles beside the nearest couch began to spin, then slowed, slowed, stopped. Like a roulette wheel. The lowest hypodermic in the drum moved forward, paused, and sprayed some clear liquid that sparkled as it fell to the couch, leaving a dark stain on its white leather. The hypodermic withdrew.

'You might call this Prussian roulette, girls. Six hypodermics. Five of them are loaded with a mundane saline solution, one with something a little more . . . shall we say, exotic? When you are lying strapped to the couches, your buttocks will receive injections at random when you lose points in the little game we are about to play. The odds are five to one on that the injection will be saline solution, and five to one against that it will be that more *exotic* something. So onto the couches if you please, and I will explain the game to you.'

They didn't move for a moment, then – had Bärengelt begun to move, stilling the movement in the same instant as he saw the threat of it had worked? – walked forward reluctantly, none of them wanting to take the nearest couch and lie on the wet stain on the leather.

But without a word spoken, by some swiftly stilled dialectic of body-language, Anna took the nearest couch, climbing onto it, her eyes beginning to shine with tears. Beth moved left around the table, Gwen right, Beth climbing second onto a couch, Gwen climbing last. They settled themselves tits-down, resting on their elbows, waiting for Bärengelt to speak.

'Good girls. Let me explain the game to you.'

He walked forward, between Anna and Beth, and stood at the edge of the table, resting his right, black-gloved hand on it.

'Watch.'

His hand flicked at the table and the table began spinning clockwise beneath it, its black surface catching the light as it turned.

'A table that turns, girls. A turntable. That is the word, is it not?'

He was holding his hand horizontally over the spinning table, palm-down; now his middle finger dropped to it, pressing down and stopping it spinning. His other hand came forward – the cane had vanished – and opened to drop something onto it. Cards. A pile of cards.

'Anna. Take them.'

He flicked at the table again and it began to turn, carrying the cards towards Anna. His middle finger came down again and the table stopped. The cards were in front of Anna.

'Take them. Pick them up.'

Anna blinked, then reached forward and picked the cards up.

'Count them and name the card. As you do so, turn it and throw it onto the table.'

The first card landed on the table with a soft, flat click.

'One, ace.'

And Anna's face had reddened. She was blushing. Beth and Gwen suddenly leaned forward, trying to see what was on the card.

'Two, king.'

But it was too hard to see. Some shape. Not a traditional card. Not hearts or diamonds or . . .

'Three, queen.'

No. Not traditional cards. They relaxed and settled back on their couches. Bärengelt would let them see shortly.

'Four, jack. Five, nine. Six, eight. Seven, seven. Eight, six.'

And surely the pile in her hand was lessening just a little too quickly?

'Nine, four. Ten, three. Eleven, two. Twelve, ace. Thirteen, queen.'

Anna's soft, slightly lisping voice. Counting off cards that landed with even softer clicks now, as the surface of the table in front of her became paved with them. She raised one hand and brushed Beth's red hair out of her eyes, then carried on.

'Twenty, six. Twenty-one, five. Twenty-two, four. Twenty-three, three. Twenty-four, two. Twenty-five, ace.'

The hair was back, hanging across her face. She tossed her head.

'Twenty-six, king. Twenty-seven, queen.'

No good. She raised her hand again, brushed the hair back, carried on.

'Twenty-eight, jack. Twenty-nine, nine. Thirty, eight. Thirty-one, seven. Thirty-two, six. Thirty-three, five. Thirty-four, four. Thirty-five, three. Thirty-six, two.'

And that was it. The table in front of her was paved with brightly coloured cards in a loose crescent.

'Good girl. Thirty-six cards. Three suits of twelve, you see. One suit for each of you. Beth. Your turn. Take them.'

The table was spinning again, carrying the loose crescent of cards through 120 degrees to Beth. As they arrived in front of her and stopped, she looked down at them. One eyebrow rose for a moment.

'How many suits, Betchen?'

'Three, master.'

'Find an example of each. Hold it up.'

She reached forward and picked up a card.

'Here, master.'

She raised a card. A three. A three of . . . almost hearts. But not hearts. White curves, smooth, unmarked, almost marmoreal.

'The three of Buttocks, Betchen. Now choose another.'

She put the card back on the table and picked up another. She held it up. White curves again, firm little mounds, tipped with dark pink in little pools of lighter pink.

'The six of Tits, Betchen. Choose another.'

She returned the card to the table and held up another. White flesh again, cones of it, cones of splayed flesh with pink lips between them.

'The four of Cunts, Betchen. So those are your three suits. Buttocks. Tits. Cunts. Now, please place the cards together again neatly and put them back on the table. Do you understand?'

'Yes, master.'

'Then do it, please. Quickly now.'

Beth scooped the cards into a mound, hands sweeping them together from left and right, aligning them, picking them up as they formed a rough pack again, tapping them on the table so that their sides and bottom edges aligned. She put them back on the table in a neat pile.

'Good girl.'

Bärengelt's black-gloved hand reached out and put another pile of cards on the table.

'This is for you, Beth.'

He spun the table, waited a few moments, then stopped it, the cards in front of him carried smoothly through to Anna, the cards in front of Beth carried smoothly through to Gwen. He put another pile of cards on the table.

'And these, for you, Anna.'

He spun the table again, paused a few moments, stopped it. The cards that had been in front of him were now in front of Anna, those in front of Anna now in front of Beth, those in front of Beth now in front of Gwen.

'Check your cards. You should each have three suits of twelve, an ace, cards numbered two to nine, then jack, queen, king. Is that what you each have?'

They all reached out and picked up the pile of cards in front of them, leafing quickly through it. For Beth and Gwen it was easy: the cards were unshuffled and in order, but Anna's pack was the first Bärengelt had put on the table and it was partly shuffled.

'All present and correct, master,' Gwen said. She put the cards back on the table.

'Good. Beth?'

'All present and correct, master,' Beth said. Anna was still leafing through her cards, lips moving silently as she named each, trying to fix it in her memory.

'Good. Anna, why are you checking your pack?'

Anna blinked guiltily, her head half-turning as though she wanted to look at the hypodermics sitting ready beside her buttocks.

'Master, you t–'

'Can you never rely on your own initiative, my girl? You have already checked that pack. It is all present and correct. Three suites of twelve cards, ace, two to nine, jack, queen, king.'

Anna swallowed.

'Yes, master.'

'Then you have wasted our time, haven't you, Anna?'

Anna's throat worked again, but it was harder for her to swallow this time.

'Yes, master,' she managed to say.

'I do not like to have my time wasted, Anna. Particularly when it is entirely unnecessary. Particularly when a little thought – a little judiciously applied intelligence – would obviate the need for it. *Nicht wahr?*'

Anna's eyes were shining again. She nodded without speaking.

'Do you have nothing to say for yourself?'

'Yes, master.'

'Then what is it?'

A tear started down her cheek from her left eye, sparkling silver on white velvet between the hanging fans of Beth's red hair.

'I am sorry, master.'

'That is not good enough, Anna.'

The tear reached her chin and dripped, falling to the couch. Another appeared on the shining line it had laid down, sliding down her cheek. Gwen's cunt rippled and she felt her cunt-lips puff and begin to pout.

'I am very sorry, master.'

'How sorry?'

'Very, very sorry, master.'

Bärengelt strode around the table to stand alongside her as she lay on the couch, buttocks raised and defenceless. A black-gloved hand touched them, stroked up and down.

'Are you sorry enough to accept pain to expiate your fault?'

Anna's eyes closed hard. The second tear had reached her chin and dripped and a third and fourth were rolling down her cheek. Gwen slowly licked her lips. Anna opened her eyes and as she did so a fifth tear emerged from her right eye, creeping more slowly down her right cheek. Her mouth opened and her lips moved, but she was speaking too softly for Gwen to hear her.

'Speak up, Anna. Tell me again, are you sorry enough to accept pain to expiate your fault?'

'Yes, master.'

Almost a whisper. The black-gloved hand had returned to the curves of her buttocks, stroking, probing. Abruptly Bärengelt withdrew it.

'Then you are a good girl. Perhaps you will not have to suffer pain after all.'

He leant across her body for the straps hanging on the other side of the couch, his hands working to throw them across her, tighten them, fasten them. He strode around the table towards Beth.

'I only hope, Betchen, you can be as good.'

He threw the straps over her body, tightened them, fastened them.

'And you, Gwen. I hope you too will be as good as little Anna. So ready to accept pain to expiate her fault. Yes?'

Gwen flinched a little as the straps landed on her skin and Bärengelt tightened them hard, fastened them.

'Yes, master,' she said. Bärengelt was striding away to where he had stood before, halfway between her and Anna, directly across the table from Beth.

' "Yes, master" you say, Gwen, but there is no conviction in your voice. I know you of old, you bitch. You and Beth, you are only waiting for the opportunity to rebel, to take your revenge upon me, but little Anna, she is a true submissive. She knows her place, and her place is beneath her master's heel. She has learned to kiss the rod. To lick the whip. To bless the hand that bruises her. These are things you and Beth have not yet learnt. But I have hopes. Great hopes. Perhaps this game will open your eyes a little.'

He reached under the edge of the table and pressed or flicked something, and Gwen jumped a little as a square section of table in front of her slid aside and a short black pillar rose through it.

'It's an automatic card-reader, girls. Do you see where you place the card, face-down?'

'Yes, master,' she said. She did. The top of the pillar was sliced off at an angle and held a shallow pit lined with translucent glass. The pit was card-shaped. Card-sized. With a small groove at the bottom, so a finger could slip under a card that had been read and lift it away. She looked up and saw that identical card-readers had risen in front of Anna and Beth, and that a tree of video screens and miniature loud-speakers had sprouted in the middle of the table, its thin steel stem holding three video screens and three speakers. One screen facing her, one facing Beth, one facing Anna. One speaker facing her, one facing Beth, one facing Anna.

Bärengelt's voices rumbled out again.

'Okay, let's test your card-readers. Gwen, choose a card. Place it in your card-reader.'

She chose a card.

'No, don't look at it. Place it face down in your reader.'

She reached forward and fitted it into the pit. There was a flash of light from beneath it, as from the arse-readers they had inserted their buttocks into so long ago, and she looked up suddenly as a clear contralto voice said from the middle of the table, 'Three of Cunts.'

'Do you see, girls? It is all so simple. You simply choose a card and place it in the reader. It reads it for you and speaks the card aloud. Now, the game itself consists in this. You each have a pack of thirty-six cards. Let us suppose you shuffle the pack thoroughly, then choose a card at random from it, then return it to the pack, then shuffle the pack thoroughly again, then choose another card at random, and so on. Tell me, how long do you think it would take you, on average, to choose the same card twice? Remember, you are choosing repeatedly from the same pack and returning the cards you have chosen before choosing again.'

The odd question about something obvious. Because it *was* obvious, wasn't it? If there were thirty-six cards in the pack and you chose a card at random repeatedly from it, you would have to choose eighteen cards at random, on average, to get the same card twice. You could choose a card once and then choose again and get the same card at once, or you could get a different card every time thirty-five times, which meant that the next time you chose you would have to choose the first card. So it was simple. Eighteen cards, on average, to get the same card twice.

'Well, Gwen?'

'Eighteen, master. Eighteen cards.'

'Eighteen cards on average? That is your answer?'

'Yes, master.'

'Very well. And you, Beth, do you agree?'

'Yes, master. Eighteen cards. Eighteen cards on average.'

'Very well. And you, Anna? What do you say?'

'I don't know, master.'

'Your sisters say eighteen. Are you disagreeing with them?'

'No, master. I'm . . . I'm just saying I'm not sure.'

'But if you are not sure, you are disagreeing with them. For they *are* sure. Aren't you, Beth and Gwen?'

But now Gwen wasn't. It was a trick again. It had to be. Bärengelt had cheated or there was some trick in the question that they weren't seeing.

'Well, girls? Are you sure or not? Eighteen cards or not? Or, to put it another way, is there the same chance you will choose the same card before or at the eighteenth try as there is that you will choose it *after* the eighteenth card?'

Gwen thought about this. There had to be. Sometimes you'd get the card early and sometimes you'd get it late. Late was as likely as early, so yes, put that way, the answer was yes.

'Yes, master,' she said.

'And you, Beth?'

'Yes, master.'

'So, have we settled it then? Eighteen cards, on average, to choose the same card twice?'

'Yes, master,' Gwen said.

'Yes, master,' Beth said.

'Anna?'

'I'm not sure, master.'

'You are outvoted, Anna. Two to one. Eighteen cards it is. So this is how you will play. First, shuffle your pack thoroughly. Place it on the table and take the first card. Do not look at it. Place it on the card-reader in front of you. It will be read aloud and will appear on the screen that faces you. Return the card to the pack. Then, on my word of command, spin the table. Anna will receive Gwen's cards, Beth will receive Anna's, Gwen will receive Beth's. You will shuffle the cards again, place the cards on the table, take the top card and place it on the card-reader. And then as before. And then the whole thing again. And again. And again. If one of you chooses the same card *before* the eighteenth card – see how generous am I to you? – one of the hypodermics will inject its contents into her buttocks. And even then you may not truly lose. The odds are five to one on that its contents will be saline solution, five to one against that it will be something more exotic.'

Gwen cleared her throat.

'What is that something, master?'

Bärengelt was silent for a moment.

'There is still time to thrash you for insolence, Gwen. Remember that. The more exotic substance lying ready in one of the six hypodermics beside your arse must remain veiled for the present. But I promise you that if you are injected with it, you will not be left in ignorance for ever. Its effects will became unmistakably apparent in time. Any more questions?'

'Yes, master.'

'What is it?'

'Do we play the game only once?'

'No, Gwen, you do not. Each of you will be playing separately: it is the cards you choose that determine whether you win or lose. So one of you may lose twice while another may lose once or not at all. Therefore it is only fair that you all play a reasonable number of games. No, do not ask. It is for me to decide what a reasonable number of games is. Any more questions?'

She shook her head.

'No, master.'

'Good. Then I think we can get on with the game, or rather, the games. If you are all quite ready. Gwen?'

'Yes, master.'

'And you, Beth, and you, Anna?'

'Yes, master,' Beth said.

'Yes, master,' Anna said.

'*Wunderbar*. Then we shall begin. Shuffle your pack, each of you.'

Gwen picked up her pack and began to shuffle it. Her hands were clumsy for a moment then began to move with assurance. Not a perfect shuffle, but a practised one. Practised when? She glanced up and her hands carried on without uncertainty. Anna and Beth seemed to be shuffling their packs with almost the same assurance. She looked back at her hands and the cards being broken and re-assembled between them. Surely that was enough? Yes. Bärengelt's voices came rumbling out from the walls.

'Enough. Place your pack on the table. Choose the top card. Place it in your card-reader.'

She put the pack face-down on the table, lifted off the top card, and leaned forward to fit it into the pit in the card-reader. Light flashed beneath it, making her blink. She looked up. Anna and Beth were putting their cards in their card-readers. Light flashed in their faces, making them brighter for a moment. The speakers on the tree in the middle of the table came awake, naming the cards in the clear contralto voice.

'Anna: Five of Buttocks. Beth: Nine of Tits. Gwen: Four of Buttocks.'

And a single card had appeared on the video screen facing her. The four of Buttocks. Bass laughter rumbled from the larger speakers in the walls.

'We have begun, girls. Return the card to the pack.'

She put her finger into the small groove at the bottom of the card-pit, lifted the card out of it, and put it back on top of the pack sitting on the table.

'Now, girls, spin. Spin the table.'

She put her hands on the table and pushed it sideways, not able to use her full strength. It resisted for a moment, then began to move, slowly at first, picking up speed, carrying the pack away from her towards Anna, carrying Anna's pack towards Beth, carrying Beth's pack towards her. It was odd to feel it moving when she was supplying only a third of the force required to move it.

Beth's pack swung through the last few centimetres and was in front of her and she stopped pushing. The table stopped turning at once. Beth's pack. Ready in front of her.

'Shuffle as before, girls.'

She picked up the pack, feeling the warmth of Beth's fingers still in the smooth plastic of the cards, and began to shuffle them.

'Enough. As before.'

She put the pack face-down on the table, lifted the top card, and put it into the reader. Three flashes of light again, and the clear contralto voice naming the cards they had chosen.

'King of Cunts. Four of Tits. Ace of Tits.'

On the video screen facing her a new card was sitting next to the four of Buttocks. King of Cunts.

'Spin, girls.'

She took the card from the card-reader, put it back on the pack, and started to push the table sideways, carrying her-pack-that-had-been-Beth's to Anna, Anna's-pack-that-had-been-hers to Beth, Beth's-pack-that-had-been-Anna's to her.

'Shuffle.'

She shuffled.

'Enough. As before.'

She put the pack on the table, lifted the top card, put it in the card-reader. Three flashes of light.

'Nine of Buttocks. Seven of Buttocks. Jack of Cunts.'

'Spin.'

Three cards on the screen facing her as she pushed the table sideways. Her shoulders and wrists were starting to hurt and sweat was collecting under the plastic strapping that held her down on the couch. Beth's-pack-that-had-been-Anna's-that-had-been-hers arrived in front of her.

'Shuffle.'

The plastic was warm now. Warmed by three sets of shuffling hands.

'Enough. As before.'

Top card into the card reader.

'Five of Cunts. Nine of Cunts. Five of Buttocks.'

'Spin.'

Four cards on the screen in front of her. Who was that Greek guy? The one who pushed a rock eternally uphill? Sisyphus. She felt an unhappy smile quirk her lips.

'Shuffle.'

Shuffling. The pack wasn't just warm now, but hot. Hot with the hands that had held it, split, married it, re-split, re-married it.

'Enough. As before.'

Top card into the card-reader.

'Nine of Cunts. Ace of Tits. Six of Tits.'

'Spin.'

Five cards on the screen facing her. Her wrists and shoulders singing with strain. A new pack swinging on the rim of the table to end in front of her. Who had had it first of all? She couldn't think.

'Shuffle.'

Hot cards in her shuffling hands.

'Enough. As before.'

Top card into the card-reader.

'Seven of Cunts. Four of Buttocks. Two of Cunts.'

'Spin.'

Again. Pushing the table sideways. Sweat trickling down her flanks and soaking the leather of the couch beneath her. Beth's and Anna's faces shining with sweat as they pushed the table too. A new pack arriving in front of her.

'Shuffle.'

The cards were faintly slippery in her hands this time. Slippery with Beth's sweat. Or maybe Anna's sweat. Maybe both. Were the cards Anna and Beth were shuffling slippery with sweat too?

'Enough. As before.'

Top card into the reader.

'Nine of Tits. Four of Cunts. Jack of Tits.'

'Spin.'

Sisyphus. A labour of Sisyphus. Pushing a rock that would always need to be pushed.

'Shuffle.'

The cards were slipperier. More slippery. Almost falling from her hands. Shuffle.

'Enough. As before.'

Top card into the reader.

'Ace of Buttocks. Ace of Buttocks. Queen of Cunts.'

'Spin.'

She was distracted for a moment, then started pushing. Ace of Buttocks twice. Was that it? Would one of them be injected? No. It was the first time for both of them. Only the individual sequence counted. Hers, and Beth's, and Anna's. A pack arrived in front of her.

'Shuffle.'

Hot, slippery cards in her hands and a low, continuous ache in her shoulders and wrists, humming in the muscles and tendons, biding its time to flare higher as she pushed the table again.

'Jack of Cunts. Seven of Buttocks. Seven of Tits.'

She had already put her hands on the table and was pushing, thinking that Bärengelt's order would rumble out as she did it, but it didn't. No order, and the table was locked beneath her fingers. What was happening? Beth whimpered to her right and she realized.

'Spin.'

She pushed the table sideways. Beth had chosen the same card twice. Seven of Buttocks. Twice in nine cards. Losing the bet and having to play Prussian roulette. Being injected.

'Shuffle.'

She picked up the cards that Beth had chosen the fatal card from. The seven of Buttocks. Was the pack unlucky now, infected with Beth's misfortune?

'Enough. As before.'

Her heart was thumping in her throat as she lifted the top card and put it in the reader.

'Three of Buttocks. Three of Cunts. Queen of Tits.'

'Spin.'

Beth had started again. A new sequence of cards. She and Anna were still on their first sequence, working their way towards eighteen cards and safety.

'Shuffle.'

Anna had the unlucky pack now. The pack Beth had chosen from.

'Enough. As before.'

Card into the reader, heart thumping in her throat again, but less than before. Clear, contralto voice reading the cards aloud.

'Three of Buttocks. Three of Cunts. Queen of Tits.'

'Spin.'

Anna groaned to her left. They were a Sisyphus with six arms, rolling an eternal rock, soaking the leather of the couches underneath them with hot sweat.

'Shuffle.'

She had to wipe the pack on the table before she could shuffle it properly. A droplet of sweat stung her left eye and she closed it hard, still shuffling.

'Enough. As before.'

Card into the reader, heart thumping again, but less than before. And on it went.

'King of Buttocks. Jack of Tits. Nine of Tits.'

'Spin.'

She looked up at the screen facing her. Two rows of five cards and one card in the third row. Eleven. She'd chosen eleven cards.

'Shuffle.'

But this was the unlucky pack again. The pack Beth had chosen from. Hot and slippery with the sweat and hand-heat of all three of them, the cards sliding too easily in her hands as she broke and re-formed them.

'Enough. As before.'

Card into the reader, heart thumping hard in her throat. This was the unlucky pack.

'Five of Cunts. Four of Tits. Six of Tits.'

Followed by silence and Christ, Christ, the new card on the screen facing her was flashing silently. Five of Cunts.

Fatal five of Cunts. Out of the corner of her eye she caught dull flashes as the hypodermics rotated. Prussian roulette. She was playing Prussian roulette. The hypodermics stopped moving and she clenched her left buttock. Should she? Would that increase the pain? There it was: the sharp prick, the pain of it rising and fading in almost the same instant. Anna whimpered on her left. What the fuck? Had Anna lost too? Yes. Tears were trickling on Anna's face, half-way down her cheeks.

'Spin.'

Wrists and shoulders screaming with strain, sweat running off her in rivulets, a dull, spreading ache in her injected left buttock. Welcome to Bärengelt country.

Twenty-six

There was a buzz that sent Gwen's sleepy mind to the summer darkness of a café near Athens airport, where they sipped *ouzo* and waited for two hours with their agents, publicists and bodyguards while their luggage was hunted down for a connection to Japan. They had heard the same sound from a tree standing a little further down the street. That had been a cicada, but this was only a mobile phone. Only, but incongruously. Bärengelt was fumbling in a pocket of his body-suit, obviously surprised that the thing had started ringing. He raised the phone to his helmet.

'*Ja?*'

His voices rumbled angrily from the walls.

'*Ja ... Scheisse. Ist nicht wahr? Ja ... Ja ... Ich gehe.*'

She heard a door slide open in the wall. His boots sounded on the floor, almost running. The door slid closed. What the fuck was going on? Then more boots, outside, in the corridor they had been shepherded down, and her stomach suddenly burst with joy and relief. Voices. Speaking English. With English accents. The police. They were here! Here at last! Madame Oursor had come up trumps!

She tried to look up as the boots sounded just outside the door, then entered the room, but she was still too sleepy.

'Here they are, officers.' Madame Oursor's voice. '*Les pauvres petites*. He has been conducting his filthy business with them just barely a moment ago. But where is he?'

'He won't get away, madame.' A policeman's voice. Assured, reassuring. 'We've got the place surrounded and,

I promise you, when our lads get our hands on him they won't be gentle.'

She tried to look up again. Looming blue shapes in the room. Oh, Christ, she was so fucking glad to see them.

'I am glad to hear it, officer. He is a beast and must be treated so, must he not?'

She closed her eyes hard, blinked, looked again, then flinched suddenly as a hand was laid on her shoulder. Warm and solid. A male hand, but not encased in leather. Bare skin on her bare skin.

'Don't you worry, miss, you're safe. It's all over now.'

She heard a scraping. Metal on the floor. Metal feet. The policeman had dragged a chair across the floor and placed it just beside her. Where the fuck had it come from? She heard a weight settle on it and looked sideways. What was he doing? A clean-lined profile, a handsome young policeman, still wearing his helmet. He was holding a notebook, oddly small in a large, blunt-fingered hand, and was raising a pencil to his lips, moistening the tip with a red tongue.

'If I could just take a few details, miss, before we get the doctors to you.'

His voice had an odd effect on her, hollowing her stomach and starting a faint trickle in her cunt. It was the relief of rescue, the traumatized victim responding to her rescuer. That was it, surely. She heard other policemen saying nearly the same thing to Beth and Anna. Three young policemen sitting on chairs beside the victims of an outrage. Was this normal procedure? It must be. She licked her lips.

'Yes, okay,' she said.

'That's good, miss.'

He crossed his legs, nearest leg over furthest, as though her voice had made him a little uncomfortable. Perhaps that was why he wasn't looking at her. A decent young man, uncomfortable with her nakedness, doing his job as best he could, taking down the details of the crime he had rescued her from.

'Now, what can you tell me about what's just happened?'

She swallowed.

'Bärengelt h–'

'What was that, miss?'

'Bärengelt. It's the name of the owner of the Schloss. The one who's been doing all this to us.'

'Ah, yes, I remember now, miss. Could you spell it for me?'

'Uh, b-a-r-e-n-g-e-l-t. With those two little dots over the "a".'

'Okay, miss. B-a-r-e-n-g-a-l-t. With two little dots over the "a". Is that the first "a" or the second one, miss?'

'No, sorry, it's b-a-r-e-n-g-e-l-t. Only one "a".'

'Ah, only one "a". With two little dots over it. German name is it, miss?'

She couldn't reply for half a beat, annoyed with herself at the irritation the question aroused in her. But he couldn't be very bright, the poor bugger. Just an ordinary policeman, doing his job as best he could, embarrassed and uncertain.

'Yes, officer.'

'Not officer, miss. I'm just a humble constable, doing my job as best I can. You can call me Andy, if you like. That's m'name.'

And what an odd accent he had. As though he had lived in lots of different places. Sometimes northern, sometimes southern. Cockney vowels mingling with Liverpudlian consonants. Yorkshire and Devon.

'Okay, Andy. Yes, it's a German name. We're in Germany, you know.'

'Are we, miss? I thought as much, from the road-signs. But it's been a rushed job, very hush-hush. I was pounding the beat just yesterday morning, you know.'

He was painstakingly writing in his notebook. He glanced at her for a moment.

'Just one "a", you said, miss?'

Her irritation came back. Hadn't he even written Bärengelt's name yet? What the fuck was all this in aid of?

'Yes, Andy. Bärengelt. Just one "a".'

'Right-o. With those two little dots over it. I'll just add them.'

228

He added them, breathing heavily.

'Right, where was we? You'd been telling me about this here Bärengelt. Was he in here with you?'

'Yes. He got a phone-call, a few seconds before you came in. It must have been telling him about your raid.'

'Raid, miss?'

'Your raid on the Schloss.'

'Sloss, miss?'

'This is the Schloss. It's German for "castle", I think.'

The questions and answers were getting surreal. How were Anna and Beth getting on? She could hear the murmur of voices as they were questioned too. Were they dealing with policemen as stupid as this one?

'Right. The German for "castle". Could you spell it for me, miss?'

' "Castle"?' she said mischievously.

'No, miss.' His voice was as slow and stolid as ever. ' "Sloss", miss. Could you spell that?'

She suppressed a sigh of frustration, almost of anger.

'S-c-h-l-o-double-s.'

'Right.'

He began writing painstakingly in the notebook again, repeating the letters.

'S-c-h-l-o-double-s. Any of those double dots knocking about the place, miss?'

'No, I don't think so. Can you tell me where the doctor is?'

'He's on his way, miss. We'll soon have you all sorted out. Now, this here Bärengelt in the Sloss. You said he had a phone-call. Where's the phone? I didn't see one when we came in.'

'It was a mobile phone, Andy.'

'Ah, right. "A mobile phone".'

He started writing again. She wondered if he was going to ask how to spell it. No. But something was nagging at her. Something odd about the phone-call.

'Right, then, miss, so you say he had a call on his mobile phone and cleared off through a door that opened in the wall and then closed again.'

She paused again for a moment.

'Well, that's right, but I hadn't told you all that yet. Just about the phone-call. How did you know about the door in the wall?'

'Your sister over there's just been telling Bill.'

'Bill?'

'My colleague, miss. I'm Andy, he's Bill, talking with your sister with black hair, and that's Geoff, talking with your sister with red hair.'

'Oh,' she said.

'What're they called, miss? Might as well get all the details while I'm here.'

'Called?'

'Your sisters, miss. And you yourself, of course.'

'Aren't you going to ask me more about Bärengelt?'

'I've got all I need for the time being, miss, I reckon, and I'm a bit worried about more of those tricky German words, with those pesky umlauts. Two little dots, I mean, miss, begging your pardon.'

She wondered whether she was dreaming. How could she be having this conversation? And what was that nagging sense of something wrong about the phone-call? Bärengelt using his mobile phone. His voices rumbling out from the walls.

'Well, miss?'

'I'm sorry?'

'Your names, miss. You and your sisters.'

'We're the Camberwell Sisters,' she said, unable to keep the irritation out of her voice now.

'Oo, miss?'

'The Camberwell Sisters. We were all over the media a year or so back. Don't you remember us?'

'Can't say I do, miss. Never was much of one for the papers, you know. No, hang on, who was it you said you were? The Calderwhite sisters?'

'Camberwell Sisters.'

'Could you spell that?'

She sucked air into her mouth with disbelief. What the fuck was going on? What was this idiot doing? And she had realized what was funny about the phone-call. Why did Bärengelt need to use a mobile phone? And how could he have used a mobile phone with his helmet on?

'No,' she said, 'don't worry about that. I've just remembered . . .'

Something buzzed again, the same cicada-like note.

'Hang on, miss, I'm getting a call on me police radio. Excuse me for a moment.'

He bent his head towards his chest, flicked a pocket open, and lifted a small microphone to his lips. She could see a strand of hair sticking out from under his helmet, lying plastered to his smooth skin with sweat. Blond hair. The same colour as Anna's. Blond hair plastered to his smooth skin with sweat. Why was he sweating?

'Yes, sarge?'

The answer was too distorted with static for her to understand.

'Okay, sarge . . . right, okay . . . okay. Right, will do. Over and out, sarge.'

He returned the microphone to its pocket and buttoned it up. He uncrossed his legs and rose from his chair. She stared disbelievingly at his groin, at the huge bulge in the blue cloth. He had an erection. That was why he had crossed his legs. So she couldn't see. Couldn't see that sitting next to her had given him an erection. But now he didn't seem to care. His large hand came down and fingered the bulge, almost caressed it, as he called out to Bill and Geoff, 'Oi, fellas, that was sarge. The doctor's bin held up. We've got to examine 'em ourselves.'

The strong blunt fingers closed on the bulge and squeezed. He turned towards her and the hand lifted away so the bulge sat a few inches from her face as he said, 'Don't you worry, miss, it's not a truncheon in me pocket, I'm just pleased to see you. This is me truncheon.'

Something long and hard tapped at her arse, rolled along it.

'I could do a bit of good with that, eh, miss? But I'll just put it to one side while I examine ya. That's okay, i'n't it, miss? Don't you worry, we'll be gentle with yers.'

The voice was mocking now, stripped of the slow, careful phrasing and stupidity, and the true accent was near the surface.

'Yeah, we'll be gentle with yers. Or as gentle with yers as yers deserve.'

She heard Anna squeal with indignation and Beth shout, 'Get the fuck off me! What the fuck do you think you're doing?'

Andy's hand walked down her body, out of sight.

'What the fuck are you doing?' she said. 'You can't do this. You're here to rescue us. We'll sue your police authority for every fucking penny it's got.'

'That's okay, miss.'

A large, warm hand descended on her buttocks and started to stroke.

'That'll be a small price to pay for the privilege of handling an arse as superb as this one. And besides, now as you come to mention it, I'm not sure we're affiliated to any *particular* police authority. Isn't that right, Bill?'

'What's that?' said one of the other policemen.

The hand felt down her arse-cleft, then slid over her perineum and began to caress the lower juncture of her cunt-lips. Blunt, strong fingers. Warm, strong fingers.

'I was telling young Gwen here, about as how we ain't affiliated to any particular police authority, like as it were. In fact, come to think of it, I'm not sure as how we *are* police, strictly speaking.'

'No, you're right. We ain't. Not strictly speaking.'

Bill's voice sounded distracted. Anna squealed again. Was he feeling her cunt too? Prodding and squeezing at it with blunt, strong fingers?

'So as you see, miss,' Andy said to her, 'your threat don't really carry too much weight with the three of us. Seeing as how you might call us amateur policemen anyhows. Play-acting, as you might put it. Here, mind if I take my helmet off? I've bin sweating like a pig all the time as I's bin in this room, wondering when sarge was gonna make that call and I'd be able to get my hands on you.'

The hand lifted from between her arse and she realized with dismay that she didn't want it to. She wanted it back. Feeling her up. Feeling her down. Feeling her inside and out.

'There, that's better.'

The hand returned and she had to restrain a wriggle of pleasure. But she couldn't restrain the way her cunt-lips were puffing and pouting. The way she was beginning to leak.

''Ere, Andy,' another voice called. It must be Geoff's. The one working on Beth. Running his strong, blunt-fingered hands over her cunt.

'Yeah?' Andy said. He sounded distracted, the way Bill had done.

'What we gonna do about takin' their temperatures? We ain't got no thermometers, 'ave we?'

Andy's hand paused in its exploration of her cunt.

'You're right, there, Geoff. 'Ere, Bill, you heard that? What Geoff said?'

'What?'

Geoff spoke again.

'We ain't got no thermometers, for takin' their temperatures, like.'

'Temperatures?'

'Yeah. It's an important medical detail. Doctors always take temperatures. Stick a thermometer in the patient's mouth or up their arse.'

'You mean vets,' Andy said. His hand resumed its exploration of Gwen's cunt, slipping inside, fingering the first traces of yelm.

'Nah, doctors do that too. They have special rectal thermometers. Great big 'uns.'

'Yeah? But we ain't got no thermometers at all, Geoff, let alone great big special ones for sticking up someone's arse.'

'It don't need to be arse. Any orifice will do. Mouth. Even cunt.'

Bill snorted.

'But we ain't got no thermometers, you dozy twat,' he said, 'so what's the fucking point in talking about it?'

'We got the next best thing, ain't we?'

Andy's hand paused in its exploration again. She was oozing freely now, moistening his fingertips with hot, fresh yelm.

'What's that then?'

A zip buzzed down and when Geoff spoke again his voice was tight with excitement.

'Cocks,' he said.

There was silence for a moment, then Andy said, 'Fuck me, Bill, he's right. If you ain't got the correct tools for the job, what's the golden rule?'

Another zip came down, buzzing like a sleepy cicada.

'Improvise,' Bill said.

'That's right. Improvise.'

The hand left her cunt again and she heard Andy's zip come down behind her. Her cunt squirmed with delicious dread.

'But which orifice are we gonna use, Geoff?' Bill asked. 'This lass looks a bit small to take it up the arse.'

'Cunts, lads,' Geoff said easily. Something creaked. What was he doing? Climbing up on the couch behind Beth? 'Ain't you never heard of doggie-style?'

Andy laughed.

'Cunts it is,' he said. 'This un's well-greased up for it.'

'So's this un,' Geoff said. The couch creaked again.

'And this un,' Bill said. 'She might have squeaked, but she liked having a hand on her cunt alright.'

Anna's couch creaked now too. Bill was climbing up behind Anna, cock out. She blinked and tried to look across the table at them, seeing a dim blue shape with white around its waist climbing atop Anna's couch. White skin around its waist. Trousers partly down. Her own couch shuddered and then creaked. Andy was climbing onto it, trousers down, cock out. The straps slid on her skin and rattled. He was loosening the ones that held her legs and arse down.

'Who are you?' she said. 'Who the fuck are you?'

His voice was uneven with arousal. He had loosened the straps, was lifting her arse up, adjusting it, pushing her thighs fully apart.

'Just your friendly neighbourhood coppers, miss, giving our helmets an airing.'

'No. Who are you? Who are you really?'

'I've told you, miss.'

Her thighs were splayed and his hand was back on her cunt, feeling, veeing her cunt-lips apart.

'Just your friendly neighbourhood coppers. I'm Andy, that's Bill, and that's Geoff. I've got blond hair, Bill's got red, and Geoff's got black. That helps you understand, don't it, miss?'

The hand withdrew and the couch shuddered again. He was moving up, straddling her, lowering his thighs and pelvis to her. She tried to look behind. Something hot and sticky brushed the swell of her left buttock. The head of his cock. His hand returned to her cunt, holding the lips apart.

'Don't it, miss? That helps you understand, surely, who's about to give your pussy a right good seeing to. It's me, miss. Andy. Blond-haired Andy. That's Bill over there, red-haired Bill, just about to stick his cock up your sister's cunt, and that's Geoff, black-haired Geoff, just about to stick his cock up your other sister's cunt. Just three friendly neighbourhood coppers, miss, about to give our helmets the treat of their lives.'

He slid into her, huge and hot, shouldering aside the oozing walls of her cunt, filling her, and she felt her cunt close hungrily on him, gripping his cock with velvet walls as it slid inside her, deeper and deeper. The couch creaked as he began to thrust, working his cock hard against the suction of her cunt, drawing it slowly out, thrusting it slowly in, gradually quickening the rhythm and the power.

'Aye, the treat of a lifetime, miss,' he said, between gasps. 'We ain't none of us done owt like this before, miss. Fucking our own sisters up the cunt, like.'

Twenty-seven

She lay exhausted on the couch, cunt oozing a thick mixture of yelm and come. She could feel it dripping onto the leather of the couch. It must be leaving a puddle, slowly expanding in a darkening stain on the white leather. Brother-come and sister-yelm. She still couldn't believe it. She'd just been fucked by her own brother and she'd come. She'd come because she'd enjoyed it more than she'd enjoyed anything in her life. A big cock up her tight cunt. Thrusting. Working in a groove that worked with it, that worked back at it. Because he'd enjoyed it too. He'd been moaning almost as much as she had, lost in the ecstasy of working his cock in a groove that worked with it, that worked back at it. The whole room had filled with moans: hers and Andy's; Beth's and Bill's; Anna's and Geoff's.

Now there was a hot, heavy, satisfied silence, while their racing hearts slowly sank back to normal and the sweat dried on their skins. Andy had withdrawn from her almost gingerly, as though his cockhead had become tender and fragile, as though he might damage it getting it out. Breath had whistled out of him, almost with awe.

'Jesus,' he'd said. 'Jesus.'

Then the couch shuddered and creaked as he'd climbed off it. She heard the other couches creaking. Bill and Geoff had finished fucking too, and withdrawn from their respective cunts, and were climbing off the couches. Bill had whistled.

'What do you think of that, lads?' he'd said.

'Trained to perfection,' Geoff had said. 'Venus herself has no finer cunt than that.'

'Fancy another?' Andy had said.

'Give me chance to recover, for Christ's sake,' Bill said.

They were talking in middle-class accents now, all pretence of being policemen dropped, but as though Bill had read her mind he suddenly put the old, hybrid working-class accent back on, saying 'Yeah, chance to fucking recover. Let's go and have a fucking fag before we carry on. They'll still be waiting when we get back, won't you, eh, girls?'

She had heard the slap of a heavy hand landing on firm buttocks and Beth had sworn with indignation. Laughing, the three of them had left the room, leaving them lying on their couches, still strapped securely by their backs and waists, cunts oozing come and yelm. She looked up, trying to distract herself from the lingering pleasure in her cunt. The after-glow glee of having been given a right good seeing to.

'Gwen!' she heard Beth call softly. She could hear them just outside the door, laughing over some coarse joke.

'What?'

'Who the fuck are they?'

'You heard. Our brothers. Blond Andy, red-haired Bill, black-haired Geoff. One for you, one for me, one for Anna.'

'They can't be our brothers. Brothers don't fuck their own sisters.'

'Anything's possible in this place. God knows what they're going to do next.'

She realized with horror that there was no indignation in her voice when she said that: only pleasurable anticipation. She wanted Andy's cock inside her again. Soon. Another burst of laughter outside the door, almost drowning a soft gasp from Anna.

'What is it, Ansie?' she said.

'I've managed to get one of the back straps loose. I'll leave it hanging as though it's still in place.'

'What are you going to do?'

This wasn't like Anna. Anna should be the most accepting of all of them. Waiting meekly to submit to her fate. Especially because she had enjoyed being fucked too. Her moans had sounded clearly through the rest, timed to the creaks of her couch as Geoff gave her pussy a right good seeing to.

Beth snorted.

'Don't do anything stupid, Anna. We've got a chance to get properly out of this, now that Bärengelt's out of the way.'

'He *isn't*,' Anna said. 'He's still here. This is all a set-up. He'll be watching from somewhere.'

Gwen's lips quirked.

'And listening, Ansie?'

'Yeah, that too, probably. Hearing how you and Beth don't want to escape, how you're just lying there and waiting to have your pussies stuffed again.'

Beth gasped with mock anger.

'You hypocritical little bitch,' she said. 'I heard y–'

'Shut up,' Gwen hissed. They were coming back into the room, still chuckling over the jokes they had been telling. Or over the plans they had been making. For the three white bodies strapped to the three white-leather couches. She heard heavy male hands clap together heartily.

'Well, girls, have you missed us while we've been away?'

Andy's voice. Their boots sounded on the floor as they walked around the table, Andy finding her again, Bill finding Beth, Geoff finding Anna.

'We hope so, we really do. We've been looking forward to this for ages. Absolute ages. Getting to grips with our sisters for the first time. Really to grips. Skin on skin, girls. Though all the clues have been there, you know.'

He was standing beside her again.

'I mean, didn't you guess that there was more than one Bärengelt?'

His hands closed on her buttocks.

'He'd've had to be a fucking superman to do some of what he did. All that fucking in such a short time. Remember the time he arsefucked all three of you in the space of about an hour? Not just that, he did one of you twice. Who was it, Bill?'

'Beth. Very nice it was too.'

'Yeah. It was Bill who did Beth twice, but otherwise it was one apiece for me and Geoff. I did you, of course, Gwenchen, and Geoff did Anna. That's why there was always all that rigmarole with the electronically treated voices and the loudspeakers and that crap about wearing a leather bodysuit and helmet. To make it harder for you to realize what was going on. That there was three of us all the time. Still, we did think you might guess at some point. As I say, Bärengelt must have been superhuman to get through as many orgasms as he seemed to, in such a short space of time.'

Geoff interrupted him.

'Be fair, Andy. We did trick them over the time, a lot of the time.'

'Yeah. I suppose there was that. Because even with three of us, the amount of fucking *we* did and sucking *you* did took it out of us. We had regular breaks, leaving the three of you in, well, what would you call it? Hibernation? Hypno-sleep? Don't you remember how the cane used to appear and re-appear from Bärengelt's hand so mysteriously? No, it wasn't mysterious at all. It was just that you didn't notice when you lost consciousness and regained it. When I took a break and Geoff or Bill came on duty.'

'Hardly duty,' Bill said. 'Non-stop pleasure. I have some very happy memories of this arse and I hope to have some even happier ones of this cunt.'

'And me,' said Andy. 'But I think arses are next on the menu, you know, lads. If your cunts were anything like mine you won't be able to present arms for another half-an-hour at least, so I think we'll have to function with the aid of our trusty policemen's truncheons. What do you say? Get them to the stocks, lock them in, have a bit of anal relaxation with our truncheons before another cunt-fucking? Or a bit of fellatio?'

'Sounds good to me,' Geoff said.

'And me,' Bill said.

'Okay, then, let's get them unstrapped and to the stocks.'

She felt him working at the remaining straps, unfastening them.

'Come on, on your feet, miss.'

He slapped at her buttocks with his truncheon, letting it bounce up and down on them, and she struggled to raise herself and sit up. Her inner thighs were soaked with come and yelm and she wanted to wipe at herself, rub her fingers on the couch.

'Come on. Hurry up.'

She managed to sit up, shaking her head against sudden dizziness, then slipped off the couch to stand on the floor, still feeling unsteady. His blunt, strong fingers closed around the back of her neck.

'Right, let's get on our way.'

He shepherded her from the room. Her eyes were clearing now and see could see almost perfectly, but when she tried to turn her head and look back his fingers tightened.

'Just keep walking, Gwenchen.'

She could see his blue uniform out of the corner of her eye, and the long black shape of his truncheon, swinging up and down in his other hand. Anna and Beth were being shepherded along behind her: she could hear Bill's and Geoff's boots on the floor and hear them speaking. Telling Anna and Beth the same thing: just keep walking. Walking where? To the stocks, Andy had said. She had a sudden vision of a thief sitting with hands and feet locked in a stained set of wooden stocks, head and upper body splattered with filth. They walked down the corridor, boots tramping and bare feet slapping on the marble, and reached the open door of another room.

'Here we are, girls,' Andy said. It seemed strange to hear an unadulterated male voice, carried straight to her ears from his tongue and lips and mouth, rather than rumbling down at her from loudspeakers in the walls. She and Andy walked through the door and into a large room and she saw the stocks that were waiting for them in the middle of the room. Their hands and feet would be locked, and their heads too, but they wouldn't be sitting down: the stocks were designed to take their victims standing, feet locked into adjustable steel shackles on the floor, head and hands locked into an adjustable steel yoke standing between two uprights of gleaming steel.

'Standing room only, I'm afraid, Gwenchen,' Andy said. He shepherded her to the nearest set of stocks.

'Put your feet into them. Come on, no dawdling.'

She put her feet into the shackles mounted on the floor and he bent to adjust them and lock them. She looked over her shoulder. Bill was shepherding Beth across the room to the second set of stocks and Anna and Geoff were just coming through the door. The floor-shackles slid apart, carrying her feet in opposite directions, and she nearly lost her balance, having to put a hand on Andy's solid back. Warm blue cloth. Dark blue.

'Right,' he said, standing up. 'Hands and head now, Gwenchen. Just pop 'em through.'

He swung the top of the head-and-hands yoke open and she put her head and hands into the slots waiting for them.

'Good girl.'

He swung the yoke closed and a delicate shiver ran through her body as the cold steel kissed the skin of her nucha. He snapped locks, sealing her left hand into place, her head, her right hand, and then stepped back out of sight. She could tell by the sound of his boots on the floor that he was walking to stand directly behind her.

'Beautiful,' he said. 'A naked young woman in steel stocks, legs apart at just the right angle, and with just the right amount of power to resist assaults on her virtue. That is, none at all. It never fails to rouse my sincere, my very sincere appreciation.'.

She heard locks snapping shut on her right and turned her head to see Beth's head and hands sticking through the yoke of the second set of stocks as Bill locked it into place. Further along she could just see Geoff adjusting the yoke to the height of Anna's neck.

'Don't you think, lads?' Andy said more loudly.

'What's that?'

Bill stepped back away from Beth's head and Gwen heard him moving to stand behind her and admire her arse the way Andy was admiring hers.

'Naked young women in steel stocks,' Andy said. 'I was just telling Gwen here how the sight of one never fails to arouse my sincere appreciation.'

'Oh, aye. And mine. With an arse like that, how could it fail to?'

'It's spectacular, I grant you, but I prefer young Gwen's here.'

Locks had been snapping shut further along the line and now Geoff's voice joined the debate.

'Neither of 'em's got owt on Anna here. Now *this* is an arse. Just look at it, lads.'

She heard boots move on the floor as Andy and Bill moved further down the line.

'Don't you think?' Geoff asked. 'The curves of it. The symmetry. The whiteness.'

Bill sucked his teeth.

'Whiteness I'll grant you, but they're all very white. The curves ain't bad and the symmetry's top-notch, but I have to stick with Beth's here. Anna's got an arse, I'll grant you that, but Beth's got an arse-and-a-half.'

'If that's so,' Andy said, 'Gwen must have an arse-and-three-quarters. Come on, look at it.'

Boots sounded on the floor again as they walked to stand behind her and examine her arse.

'Look at the way it sweeps down to her thighs. Look at that crotch-gap and the perfect way her twat-lips complement her arse-cleft. And that fringe of silky black pubes. Perfect. Just run your fingers down her arse, lads, starting up here and ending on her twat. It's like a pilgrimage to paradise.'

His boots stepped forward and he fitted his actions to his words, running his fingers from her coccyx down her arse-cleft to finish twiddling on her twat, stroking her twat-lips and plucking gently at her pubic hair. The hand came away and the boots stepped back.

'Go on, try it.'

'We'll take your word for it, lad,' Bill said. 'But I never could stand legs apart at that angle, showing off all she's got between her thighs. It's distractin', when you've got a fine arse to admire. A peek of pussy's fine, but not the full monty.'

'Rubbish. Why did the good Lord put arse and twat so close together if he didn't want them to be admired at the same time?'

Geoff coughed.

'No, I'm with Bill on this one, Andy. The good Lord may have put 'em close together, but he gave us the free will to decide what to do about it and for the initial inspection, I choose to keep 'er legs firmly together. Otherwise it's like trying to drink two glasses of beer at once. Huntingdon's and Micklethwaite's, f'rinstance. You couldn't give either the attention it deserved and you'll not get the full flavour of either. Later on, mebbe, you can swing the legs apart and feast your eyes and hands on the pussy, but not straight off, not in my book.'

Andy grunted contemptuously.

'You're just a pair of stick-in-the-muds. Arses and twats were meant to be enjoyed together. Beside everything else, what about when you're whipping the arse and you get a bit bored? If her legs are apart, it's as easy as anything to introduce a bit of variety and put a couple of strokes up between them and over the twat.'

'But that's where you and us differ, you see,' Bill said. 'We don't get bored whipping our arses early on, so we don't need that bit of variety till later.'

'Speaking of which,' Geoff said. 'Where are the whips? I thought you'd brought them along earlier, Andy, ready for our session.'

'I couldn't find them – they weren't where Bill said they were.'

'They fucking-well were. In the desk in the come-trench room, with the ropes for the tug-of-war. You can't have looked properly if you missed 'em.'

'I did, and if I didn't it was your fault for making everything such a fucking rush in the l–'

'Lads, lads!' Geoff said. 'Let's not argue, let's just sort it out. The two of you can get along and fetch the whips while I stand guard over these three fine arses and see that they come to no harm.'

Bill chuckled.

'No premature harm,' he said. 'But you're right. Come on, you dozy twat, let's go and get the whips. I'll bet you nine strokes of Beth's arse to six of Gwen's that they're exactly where I said they were.'

'You're on.'

She heard their boots leave the room, only half-disgusted at how her cunt had responded to the way they had gloated over their prisoners. The come and yelm mixed in her cunt had trickled down her thighs as far as her knees, but her cunt was pouting and dribbling fresh yelm now too. She cleared her throat and opened her mouth.

'Ge . . .' she began, then closed her mouth with a click. Anna was speaking. What had she said? Geoff was asking the same question.

'What?' he said.

'I want to see it again. Your cock.'

'You will, soon enough.'

'I want to see it now. Please. To see if it's . . . it's as big as it felt. You know, when you' – her voice died to a whisper and Gwen had to strain to hear what she said – 'when you fucked me.'

Silence for a moment. Was Geoff swallowing? He coughed.

'You've talked me into it.'

A zip came down and then there was a moment of silence before she heard Anna gasp softly.

'It's bigger,' she said. 'Bigger than I imagined it could be. Please, can I . . . can I touch it?'

Geoff's gulp was almost audible this time.

'No,' he said reluctantly. 'I don't want to come yet. Not before we've whipped you all.'

'I won't make you come. I just want to touch it. I want to see if I can put my fingers round it. I'm certain I can't, but I want to see.'

Another pause. She imagined Geoff swallowing again. Swallowing hard.

'No.'

Even more reluctant this time.

'Please. I won't move my hand. Promise. I just want to hold it.'

Another pause.

'I can't. You're locked into the yoke.'

'Can't you let one hand free? You aren't frightened of me, are you? Just a little lass like me, against a great brute of a man like you. Armed with *that*.'

Another pause and Geoff coughed again, trying to disguise his lust.

'Well, one hand free. And you'll just touch. No movement. We've been waiting for this for months and I'm not going to let you spoil it.'

'Okay. I promise I won't. I just want to touch. I can't believe the evidence of my own eyes, you know. That's all.'

Gwen heard the click of a lock. Was he releasing one of Anna's hands? So she could put it down and touch his cock? Circle it with her hand. Yes: she heard his intake of breath and another gasp from Anna.

'Ooh, how hot it is. And I was right. I can't get my fingers all the way round it. It's too big. It's . . .'

'Hey! Stop that. You said no movement. I've a good mind t . . .'

'I'm sorry, Geoff. Really I am. I couldn't help it. My hand slipped. Please let me touch it again. No movement.'

'Promise?'

'Promise. Cross my arse and hope to cry.'

'Okay, here. Touch it again. And just *touch* it this time.'

'I will. What are you going to do with us, when Andy and Bill get back?'

'Ah. Yes. Just hold it. We're going to whip you. With whips made from your own hair.'

'Yes? And then what? No, don't draw back. I'm hardly moving my hand at all, am I? This is just soothing. I won't make you come. Promise. Go on, tell me what you will do to us next. Tell all three of us.'

245

'Jesus. You promise this won't make me come?'

'Of course not. I'm hardly moving my hand at all, am I? Go on. Tell us. Tell us what you're going to do to us after you've whipped our arses.'

'Jesus. Sweet Jesus. Don't get any quicker than that. That's okay. Yeah. Slow down a bit. Christ. After we've whipped your arses for you, we're going to have a bit of fun with our truncheons.'

'I bet you are. I would too if I had a truncheon this size, you great brute.'

'Ah. Yes. Christ. No, not our cocks, I mean our real truncheons. We're going to stick them up your arses.'

'All the way up?'

'Yes. Ah. God. God. All the way up. Hey, you're speeding up. Stop it.'

'I'm not. I promised not to. You're imagining things. What will you do to us next, after that? After you've stuck your big truncheons up our little bottoms?'

'Jesus. You've speeded up. I can tell you have. Then we're going to cuntfuck you again.'

'With your truncheons?'

'No, with our cocks.'

'Is that why you don't want to come now? You want to keep this big cock nice and stiff till then?'

'Yeah. Jesus. That's what I want to do, and that's what I'm going to do. Hey! What the f . . .'

Gwen heard a sudden sharp squirt and Geoff was suddenly sobbing and retching. From the way his voice sounded she thought he had fallen to his knees, face buried in his hands. The skin inside her nostrils prickled and she felt the urge to sneeze, then jerked in her stocks as Beth sneezed explosively beside her. Then she sneezed herself.

'What the fuck's going on, Anna?'

'I've pepper-sprayed the dickhead. I managed to get the pocket open in the other room without him noticing it but I thought it was no good when they brought us in here.'

She was panting as she worked at something. Her hand was free. Was she opening the yoke?

'Until Andy and Bill left us and I managed to persuade him to let my hand free so I could touch that great big cock of his. Silly cunt.'

Locks snapped open and Anna laughed. She must have got the yoke off. She started speaking again, her voice sounding muffled, as though she had bent down, working on the locks that held her feet in their shackles.

'Then I accidentally on purpose started wanking him and he got a bit carried away. Then when he managed to control himself and make me stop, I just reached down a bit further and got his pepper-spray out. One squirt and he was *hors de combat*. Still is. Can't you hear him?'

'Yes, so get a fucking move on and get out of those fucking stocks. The other two bastards will be back any moment.'

'I'm doing my best. There.'

Another lock snapped open. What had she released? One of her feet? Another lock snapped and a moment later Anna ran along the line of stocks to stand in front of her. She was free!

'Quick!' Gwen told her. Anna reached up and struggled with one of the locks on the yoke.

'They're fucking *stiff*,' she said. 'Ah. There.'

It snapped open and one of Gwen's hands was free. Anna ran back to Beth, saying over her shoulder, 'You'll have to do the rest with one hand, the way I did, while I help Beth.'

Gwen reached along the yoke with her free hand and got to work on the other locks. Snap. Her head was free. Snap. Her left hand. She levered the yoke up and off her neck and bent quickly to start work on her feet. How much longer had they left before Andy and Bill came back? God knew. Snap. Right foot. Snap. Left foot. She stepped out of the shackles and bent to work on the lock around Beth's left foot as Beth and Anna struggled with the locks of the yoke. One for all, all for one. She glanced sideways at Geoff. He was still kneeling on the floor with his hands over his face, swearing incoherently. The lock snapped open under her hand.

'Deal with him, Anna,' she said. 'They've got handcuffs. Handcuff him.'

'I've got a better solution. Get him into the stocks.'

'We can't waste time.'

Beth levered the yoke off and lifted her head and hands free. The lock around her right foot snapped open. They were all free. Gwen looked quickly around the room. Three truncheons were hanging by their straps on one wall. She ran to them and began to lift them down.

'Beth!' she called. 'Catch!'

She threw one of the truncheons to her and Beth caught it.

'Anna!'

She threw another. Anna caught it.

'Anna, get over to the door and see if you can hear them coming.'

Anna ran across the room to the door. She looked out, then turned her head and listened hard, looking back into the room.

'No, can't hear them yet,' she said. 'Hey, when they reach the door they'll see that we've got out of the stocks.'

Gwen crossed the room to the door too, took a step outside, then turned and looked back into the room.

'Yeah,' she said. 'They'll see the end one first. My one. Here, quick, this is what we'll do. I'll get back into that one as though I'm still locked into it. You and Beth stand by the door with the pepper-spray. We'll have to get that cunt out of the way. Beth, handcuff him and gag him with something.'

Beth ran to Geoff, put her truncheon on the floor, and began to search him for his handcuffs.

'Got 'em, Gwen,' she said, holding up a pair of shining steel handcuffs and waving them. 'Behind his back?'

'Yeah. Quick. Gag him too, then come and help me get back in my stocks.'

Beth took hold of his hands and dragged them from his face. He groaned, not seeming to realise what was going on. Beth neatly swung his arms behind his back and handcuffed him, then paused, looking around her.

'What's wrong?' Gwen said.

'A gag. What am I going to use?'

'Gwen!' Anna's voice, low and urgent from the door. 'I think I can hear them coming!'

'Shit. Beth, use his underpants. Get his shoes and trousers off as quick as you can. I'll have to do the stocks by myself. Then get over to the door. Are you okay with the pepper-spray, Anna?'

'Yeah. As the first one comes in he'll get a facefull of it. Trust me. I know what I'm doing.'

Gwen ran to her stocks and lifted the yoke, biting her lower lip softly with concentration as she fitted her feet back into the shackles, left and right. Beth had turned Geoff onto his back and was kneeling with his left foot in her hands, ripping at the laces of his shoe. She dragged the shoe off, flung it aside, and started on the right foot. Gwen lowered the yoke over her neck and left hand. She'd have to keep her right hand up by it as though it were locked in place. It wouldn't have to be perfect. They wouldn't be expecting anything.

Geoff's right shoe thumped on the floor and Gwen swallowed. She wanted to watch Beth stripping him. If she held the yoke up a little she could twist her head and look back. It wouldn't take a second to let it drop back into place when Andy and Bill were nearly at the door. She did it, looking back as Beth stooped over Geoff's waist, loosening his belt. Her head swung back and she hissed to Anna.

'Where are they?'

'A long way off but getting closer.'

Beth had his trousers loosened; she seized the hem with both hands and backed away from him, bringing them with her. They were off: she tossed them to one side, then realized they'd be visible from the floor, jumped towards them, and kicked them away from the line of sight of the door. She turned back to the bare-legged Geoff, seized the hem of his underpants, and whisked them off his legs. His cock was still half-erect, lolling drunkenly above the black bush of his pubic hair as he rolled on the hands handcuffed behind his back. She ran up his body and knelt at his head, twisting the underpants into a gag, fitting them over his mouth, lifting them behind his head, tying them. His face was puffed and reddened, his eyes screwed shut, streaming tears.

'Done,' she said.

'Is he out of sight of the door?' Gwen called.

'Just about.'

Beth ran back to his feet, grabbed hold of them, and dragged him across the floor, then spun, took two rapid steps, snatched up her truncheon from where she had rested it on the floor, and ran to join Anna. Andy's and Bill's boots were tramping down the corridor and she could hear laughter. She flattened her back to the wall just beside the door, trying to control her heavy breathing, clutching the truncheon tight. Anna was flattened to the wall on the other side of the door, truncheon in one hand, pepper-spray in the other. Gwen let the yoke fall back into place and waited, her heart beating faster. Another few seconds. Anna would have to put one of them *hors de combat* straight away with the pepper-spray or they'd have what was probably a losing fight on their hands. Boots just outside the door, then laughter again, then Andy's voice booming into the room as he stepped through the door, 'Here we are, g . . .'

It was cut through by the hiss of the pepper-spray and broke into gasps and sobs. Bill swore with surprise. Gwen wrenched the yoke up, lifted her feet left and right out of the shackles and spun to see what was happening. Andy was on his knees just inside the door, clutching his face with both hands, and Bill was struggling with Beth.

'Spray him, Anna!' Gwen shouted. She ran across the room.

'I can't. I might hit Beth.'

'Grab his legs. Get him on the floor and sit on him.'

Anna dropped her truncheon and dove at Bill's left leg. Gwen arrived a moment later and dove at his right. He tried to kick them off but they clung on, panting desperately, throwing their weight against him, trying to get him

250

off balance and topple him, the rough cloth of his trousers rasping against their arms and shoulders. He shouted with anger and surprise and began to topple.

'You little bitches. Just you fucking w . . .'

Over he went with a thump, Beth landing on top of him. She had cleverly raised a knee to his stomach, allowing her full weight to drive it home as she fell with him, and he gasped for air, completely winded. Gwen hauled herself up his body, adding her weight to Beth's, holding him down and helpless. She turned her head.

'Anna, give me the pepper-spray and sort out Andy. Me and Beth will deal with this. Handcuff him. Come on, quick.'

Anna handed her the pepper-spray and she took it, her heart singing. How the mighty are fallen! She lifted her hand to the swearing, reddened face, and her thumb closed over the button. *Pfffft.*

Twenty-eight

'Well, well, well. How the mighty are fallen, eh, boys?'

Anna giggled behind her. She turned and began to pace slowly down the line of stocks.

'Eh, boys? The tables are turned with a vengeance. And the arses.'

The stocks were occupied again, but not with girlflesh: with boyflesh. Andy, Bill and Geoff, trouserless, gagged with their own stripped underpants, heads and hands locked into the yokes, feet locked into the floor shackles, legs swung apart so that their cocks and balls hung between their thighs, supremely vulnerable. Gwen smiled.

'And your balls, boys. Are they full again? Let's see, shall we?'

She turned to Anna and Beth, her smile widening to a grin as she met their grinning faces.

'The truncheons, girls. They were going to use them on us, so let's us use them on *them*. But gently, to begin with. Very gently.'

She bent and picked her truncheon off the floor, then walked over to Andy, untied his gag, peeled the underpants away, and dropped them on the floor.

'How are your balls, Andy, dear? Filling nicely again, are they?'

She walked to stand behind him, put the truncheon between his legs, and began to nudge his balls from left to right with it.

'Left, right, left, right, your balls are swinging from left to right,' she told him. 'Do you like it?'

No answer.

'Do you like it? Answer, please, or I'll get rough.'

'No. I don't.'

'You don't? That's a pity, because I do. I like swinging them from left to right. But I like a lot of other things too, so that's enough for now. You still haven't told me whether your balls are filling again, you know. But perhaps I can tell for myself.'

She withdrew the truncheon, then swung it sideways and laid it horizontally against Andy's arse, fitting it in the gluteal crease where his buttocks met his thighs.

'Anna, come here a moment.'

Anna's feet pattered on the floor.

'Yes, Gwen?'

'Good girl. I want you to reach between Andy's thighs and take hold of his balls while I hold this truncheon in place. Then I want you to put his balls over the top of the truncheon, so that they're hanging down the other side of it. Then I'm going to let go of the truncheon and we'll see if it stays in place, held there by his balls. Okay?'

'Okay.'

'Are you ready?'

'Yes.'

'Then away you go. But be gentle with him. Remember, balls are very delicate organs.'

Anna giggled again and reached up to take hold of his balls.

'Ooh, Gwen, they're moving in my hand.'

'Then take a firm grip and stop them moving. I think he might be getting a little excited at the prospect of having his balls handled.'

'Okay. Firm grip. Then what do I do? Push them over the top of the truncheon?'

Andy snorted.

'Get the fuck off me. You're going to pay for this . . .'

'Gag him, Ansie. Quick, his underpants are on the floor.'

Anna picked up his underpants and stood on tiptoes to gag him. He was swearing at them, then his voice went muffled.

'I'll tie it,' Gwen said. She tied the underpants hard behind his head.

'There. Good. Now, where were we?'

'I was pushing his balls over the top of the truncheon.'

'Yes. So they dangle over the other side. Carry on.'

'Maybe it would be better if I did it from the other side.'

'Try it from this side.'

'Okay . . . No, the gap's too small. I'll have to go round the other side and . . .'

She had gone to the other side; now her voice broke off. Gwen's head jerked up.

'What's wrong? Don't trust the bugger an inch, Ansie.'

'I won't. But it's not an inch we have to worry about.'

'Whatever do you mean?'

'See for yourself.'

'I can't. I've got to hold the truncheon in place. Poke his balls over it and if it stays in place when I take my hand away I'll have a look.'

'Okay. Here goes.'

'Firm grip, remember, Ansie.'

'Okay. Firm but fair.'

'Forget about the fair. Just take a firm grip.'

'But you said balls are very delicate organs.'

'I know I did. It's at the forefront of my mind, all the time. That's why this is so much fun.'

Anna giggled again.

'I see what you mean. Well, firm grip, and here they come.'

Gwen watched as she tried to poke the balls over the top of the truncheon.

'Come on, just a little bit more.'

Anna tutted with frustration.

'It's no good. They're too big. Lower the truncheon a little bit.'

'No. It's in the perfect position now. I can't move it. Just try a bit harder.'

'What if he goes off in my face?'

'Whatever do you mean?'

'You'll see. Okay, trying again . . . No, still no good.'

'Try them one at a time. I can help with one hand while I'm holding the truncheon up with the other.'

'Okay.'

Gwen watched again as Anna tried to poke one ball through.

'Nearly there, Ansie. Keep trying. Yes, I've nearly got it . . . one more try. Yes, good. It's over and it's dangling. Try the other, while I hold this in place.'

She held the ball firmly between forefinger and thumb.

'Next one coming up,' Anna said. 'And I hope that's all that will be coming up,' she added under her breath.

'You *are* being mysterious, Ansie. What on earth is happening on your side?'

'You'll see. Here it comes.'

The second ball came slipping through the gap between truncheon and buttocks.

'Okay, Ansie. Keep pushing. I've nearly got it . . . nearly . . . Yes, I've got it. You can stop pushing now. I'll just arrange them so that they're dangling nicely and then I'll let . . . Yes! I've let go and the truncheon's not moving an inch.'

'Can I have a look?'

'Of course. It's your work as much as mine.'

Anna walked from in front of Andy to stand beside her and gaze at the balls as they dangled over the truncheon, holding it up against his buttocks.

'Don't they look silly?' she said.

'Of course they look silly. Balls always look silly.'

'Can I hold them?'

'Do what you like with them. He's ours to treat as we please, now.'

'Mmmm. They're lovely and warm. And . . . aren't they hard? His balls, I mean. Does that mean they're full of come?'

Gwen opened her mouth, then shut it.

'To be honest, I've no idea. Beth? Does it mean that?'

'Sorry, I don't know either.'

'Well,' said Anna. 'There's only one way to find out, and it won't take long.'

'What do you mean?' Gwen said.

'Just go round the front and see what I was telling you about. Ooh, I love the way they roll in my hand when I squeeze them together. Have a look at the front and see what happens when I do that.'

Gwen walked to stand in front of him. She tutted.

'Oh, dear. I see what you meant.'

'Does it move, when I squeeze them back here?'

Gwen watched.

'Yes,' she said. 'It twitches up a little bit. He's obviously very excitable, I'm afraid.'

'Just the way we want him,' Anna said. 'For our experiment.'

'What experiment?'

'To see whether his balls are full of come or not. Come and feel them, Gwen.'

'Okay.'

She walked back behind him.

'Go on, have a good squeeze.'

'Okay ... well, they're hard. They slide about in my hand. So what?'

'But does that mean they're full of come or not?'

'I don't know. How can you tell?'

'It's easy. We try and make him come. If he comes a lot, we know they must have been full of come. If he only comes a little bit, we know they mustn't have been.'

Beth laughed and clapped her hands together.

'Sheer genius. Anna comes up trumps again.'

Gwen nodded and let go of the balls she had been squeezing.

'I have to agree. So, what's our hypothesis?'

'If a man's balls are hard, that means they're full of come.'

'And a prediction from that?'

'They soften when they're emptied of come.'

'Okay. Well, how are we going to empty them?'

'Easy,' Beth said. 'We'll whip his arse for him, then stick the truncheon up his arse. If that doesn't make him come hard, nothing will.'

'Okay. Sounds good to me. Which whip?'

'Let's take it in turns,' said Anna. 'Someone can stand at the front and see how he's reacting. If he looks as though he's going to come, we'll give him a rest for a little while. That way he'll come much harder, in the end.'

'Okay. Who first?'

'Anna,' said Beth. 'If it wasn't for her none of this would be happening. Or at least, it would be happening, but it would have been happening to *us* instead of them.'

'You're right,' said Gwen. 'Perfectly right. Anna, you get first go, as a reward for your cleverness. You can use my or Beth's whip if you like. I don't mind. You don't either, do you, Beth?'

'No. Delighted, I'm sure.'

'It's okay,' Anna said. 'I'll use my whip. It's my hair, after all, so I think this has a certain poetic justice.'

Gwen laughed.

'It has justice to it, alright. It's just fucking perfect. Beth, you take first watch on the other side. I'll stand back here with Anna and monitor the state of his balls. As a secondary hypothesis, I predict his balls will get even harder the longer orgasm is delayed.'

'Don't squeeze them too much,' Beth said. 'Or you might make him come prematurely. Men are like that, you know.'

'Okay. Come on, Anna. Get a move on.'

Anna crossed to the whips that lay near the door, scattered in their struggle with Andy and Bill. She bent down and picked up the blonde one, then walked slowly back to the stocks, running its tails through her fingers, swinging it experimentally.

'Where shall I stand?' she said.

'About there. Yeah. That's it. Okay, have a few practice strokes.'

'Feet apart?' Anna said.

'Yes. But not too far apart. You want a steady base to work from. Just cast your mind back to how Bärengelt did it. Steady base allowing full, free and forceful movement of the whipping arm.'

Anna placed her feet apart and swung the whip. It hissed through the air. Beth laughed.

'His cock just jumped,' she said. 'He must be looking forward to this.'

'I hope not,' Gwen said.

'Then why did his cock jump?'

'With fright, I hope. This dirty bastard has been mistreating *our* arses for the past God knows how long, and now he's about to get a little of his own medicine.'

The whip swished through the air again, swung with real force this time. Anna was smiling harder and harder, her eyes starting to shine.

'A lot of his own medicine, you mean,' she said. 'Starting with me. Stand clear, Gwenchen: he's about to get the first mouthful.'

Gwen stepped back and to the side, watching with pursed lips as Anna adjusted her feet for the last time, swung her arm back, paused, and then lashed the whip forward with all her might. It hissed venomously through the air and landed on the male arse in front of them with a soft crack. Anna flicked it clear, her smile widening even further.

'You're enjoying this, you little beast,' said Gwen.

'Too right I'm fucking enjoying this. Aren't you? That would have been your *arse*, you know.'

'I know.'

Gwen gazed at the arse, her cunt rippling and beginning to melt at the red lines that had appeared on it. She stepped forward and ran her finger down one, her lips moving as she said, 'Whipmarks' silently to herself.

'Out of the way!' Anna called. 'I want to get a steady rhythm going here.'

Gwen stepped back. Anna swung her arm back, paused, and lashed the whip forward again, even harder if anything, sending it swishing through the air to land on the red-striped arse with another soft crack. Gwen feasted her eyes on the new marks, on the deeper red where the lines of the second stroke had overlaid or intersected the lines of the first. *Crack!* Anna landed a third stroke, the blonde whip leaping in her hand as though it were alive, and she was merely holding it aloft and ready for it to leap forward of its own accord.

Gwen swallowed, staring at the third set of lines, the scrabble of pink and red and deeper red marking what had once been a bare white arse. Her lips of her cunt were pouting and oozing and she wanted to put her hand down to him and finger herself, start wanking as she watched Anna dismantle a little more of his dignity with every fresh stroke.

'How's he doing, Beth?' Anna called forward.

'Stiffer than ever,' Beth said. 'When you land one his cock springs nearly vertical and stays like that for two or three seconds, then slowly drops back.'

'Good,' Anna said. 'I'd hate to think he wasn't enjoying this as much as I am.'

She swung her arm back, paused, lashed the whip forward. *Crack!* The once-white bottom was a maze of lines, a scrabble of whip-strokes, laid and overlaid and over-overlaid, beginning to melt together and merge, like firm brushstrokes in red watercolour on damp white paper, slowly spreading and merging.

'Two more, Gwen, then you can check how hard his balls are,' Anna said. She was puffing a little, sweat shining faintly on her face and breasts. Gwen half-raised her eyebrows. *Giving orders now, are we, Ansie? We'll have to see about that. Just because you've got us out from under doesn't mean the pecking order is going to change.* The whip cracked again, then again, landing twice more on the red-scrabbled arse. But Gwen said nothing as she stepped forward and began to test the balls for increased hardness.

'Careful, Gwen!' Beth said. 'His cock's twitching when you do that. He looks as though he's about to fire.'

Gwen squeezed more softly, the tip of her tongue protruding from her lips. She carefully released the balls and stepped back.

'Are they harder?' Anna said.

'Yes, they seem to be. Our hypothesis is standing up well.'

'So's he,' Beth said.

Anna laughed.

'I'll give him a rest for a minute or so,' she said, 'then give him another six strokes. Paced more slowly, this time. I'll give him plenty of time to think about them before they land.'

'Good idea. We want those balls nice and hard, and nice and high.'

'They can hardly get much higher. Look at the way they've bunched.'

'Hmmm. You're right. I think that's a sign of imminent ejaculation. How are things at your end, Beth?'

'It's twitching but it's not pointed quite as high as it was just before, when Anna was whipping him.'

'What angle do you reckon?'

'Oh . . . at a guesstimate . . . seventy degrees.'

'Well, keep a sharp eye on it and tell me if it swings again. I've got to do something about these bunched balls. The truncheon will slide out from under them if we're not careful.'

Anna shook the whip, then ran her fingers through its tails, smoothing them out.

'What are you going to do?' she said.

'I'll try to roll another truncheon over them. Like a rolling pin. That might bring them down a bit.'

She picked another truncheon from the floor and walked to stand behind Andy's red-scrabbled arse.

'If I start up here and *roll* downward . . .'

She pressed the truncheon flat and horizontal to his arse and rolled it slowly downward, but as she reached the swell of his scrotum and the truncheon began to roll across his balls she stopped.

'What's that noise?'

'What noise?' Beth said.

'I thought I heard a noise.'

'I didn't hear anything.'

'Must have been my imagination.'

She started rolling the truncheon over his balls again, but stopped at once.

'There it was again. It's him. He's groaning. Through his gag. Listen.'

She rolled the truncheon a fraction lower over his balls. Beth clicked her tongue in surprise.

'Yeah. You're right. He's groaning. I wonder why.'

'What's his cock doing?'

'Oh, Christ, I took my eye off. Jesus. It's . . . well, it's gone up another ten degrees at least. Pointing practically straight at the ceiling. To be honest, I don't think rolling his balls is a good idea, Gwen. He'll be coming all over the place if you do.'

'But what am I going to do to get his balls down?'

'Try cooling them,' Anna said.

'What with?'

'Lick them. The saliva will have to absorb heat from them to evaporate, so they'll cool down.'

'You lick them.'

'I'm doing the whipping, remember.'

'Chee–'

'Cut it out, Gwen,' Beth said. 'Anna's right. You're the one who's complaining about his balls being too high, so if you want to do something about it, do it yourself. Licking them sounds a good idea. Only be gentle. He's definitely on the brink and it won't take much to tip him over.'

Gwen harrumphed.

'*Et tu*, Bethy?' she said.

'And me. Get licking.'

She put the truncheon back on the floor and returned to the pair of balls hanging tightly bunched over the truncheon that rested in his gluteal crease. She put her face forward and blew at them, then jerked back as Beth cried out in warning.

'Stop! His cock just gave an almighty twitch. What did you do?'

'I blew at them.'

'Then don't. Just leave them alone. He'll come if y . . .'

'Fuck this for a game of soldiers,' Gwen said. 'I'm licking them. If he comes, he comes.'

She put her face back to the balls, opened her mouth, and drew them inside it, sucking hard, trying to close her lips around them and drag them down in their wrinkled bag of scrotal skin. They resisted and she lifted her head back, dragging harder.

'Jesus!' Beth said. Gwen ignored her and dragged harder. She licked at the scrotum, tasting sweat and masculinity, forcing her tongue up between the balls, feeling the ridge of skin that divided the scrotum in two neat halves, rolling the balls in her mouth like two large, hard sweets. Gobstoppers.

'He's going to blow,' Beth said. 'Another second and . . .'

She phooted the balls out of her mouth, moved back and stood up.

'It's okay. It wasn't doing any good. But I've moistened them nicely, so maybe that will have some effect.'

'He's dribbling,' Beth said. 'You've made him dribble. Come is dribbling from the top of his cock, running down the shaft, and dripping onto the floor.'

'As I said before, he's an excitable boy. You can't blame me for that.'

'It's stopped now. Christ, it's like watching a volcano about to blow, except the lava is white rather than red. I thought we had an eruption on our hands there, for a moment.'

'We will have, shortly. Once Ansie's got the strokes under way again. I reckon he'll blow on four, if they're intelligently paced.'

'They will be,' Anna said. 'I've got the hang of it now. But I say he won't come at all. You'll have to stick that truncheon up his arse first.'

'What if it won't fit?'

'It will. If you moisten it.'

'What with?'

'Yelm. You're making enough of it.'

Gwen opened her mouth to make an angry retort, then closed it, biting her lip. *Well, madam, if that's the way you want it.*

'Stop arguing,' said Beth. 'Let's stay united against our common enemy.'

'Our common enemy,' Anna said, 'is going to be in need of a common enema when I've finished the next six strokes. A truncheon-enema, lubricated with Gwen's yelm, and slid home firmly but fairly. Right, I think that's enough of a rest for the poor dear's arse. Let's get the next six strokes under way. Beth, yell out if you see any signs of imminent eruption.'

'Okay!'

Anna shook the whip, loosening its long blonde tails, and took up her position behind the red-scrabbled arse. Watching her, Gwen felt a trickle of apprehension. The way her blue eyes fixed on their target, coldly, calculatedly, mercilessly. This was a new Anna. The slim arm swung back, paused, and lashed the whip forward. *Crack!* Another stinging rebuke delivered to the defenceless bottom of their male victim, clear hot pain spurting through the seething glow of the previous strokes.

'Beth?' Anna said.

'It swung skyward but not for long. I think we're on schedule for the truncheon enema.'

'Okay.'

Anna inhaled deeply, exhaled, paused, her lips moving silently. What was she doing? Counting? Another deep inhalation, exhalation, then her slim arm swung back, paused, lashed forward, flinging the blonde tails of the whip at the now-scarlet arse. *Crack!*

Gwen shuddered with pleasure, feeling her cunt ripple more slowly as it savoured the sound and thought of the blow. Anna's lips were moving again, counting off the seconds to the next blow. Slim arm swinging back, pausing, lashing forward. *Crack!*

Gwen had to hold her hand away from her cunt by sheer force. How she longed to start wanking as she watched that defenceless male bottom redden more and more under the merciless strokes of the whip woven from the blonde hair of the slim, firm-breasted young woman who was wielding it. Anna's lips moving again. Slim arm swinging back, lashing forward. *Crack!*

'Beth?' Anna said.

'As before, Ansie. It salutes the blow by swinging skyward, then returns to its usual angle. No signs of imminent eruption.'

'See, Gwen?' Anna said.

'What?'

'You predicted he'd blow on the fourth stroke. That was it. He hasn't.'

'He might do on the fifth, or the sixth.'

'No. You'd better get that truncheon nicely slicked for insertion. Don't mind me.'

She shook the whip again, loosening the long blonde tails. Gwen felt a spot of heat in each cheek. Anna knew what she wanted to do. Knew that she wanted to wank as she watched the bottom redden under the blonde lash of the whip. She bent and picked up the truncheon lying on the floor. Her cunt was open and oozing freely. She put the head of the truncheon to one set of cunt-lips and stroked it slowly up and down. *Crack!*

She jerked almost guiltily, putting the head of the truncheon to the other set of cunt-lips. Sliding it up and down. Moistening the head of the truncheon with her own yelm. Anna's lips moving again, slim arm swinging back, pausing, lashing forward, crashing the blonde tails of the whip at the scarlet arse. *Crack!*

Gwen slipped the head of the truncheon between the lips of her cunt, into the cunt-chamber, rotating it, moistening it fully with yelm. She withdrew it, looking down to see a thread of yelm stretching between it and her cunt, stretching, snapping.

Panting, Anna turned to her.

'All yours, Gwenchen.'

Gwen made no move. The little bitch was going to pay for this insolence and very soon. She put the head of the truncheon back to her cunt, pressing it on her clitoris, rotating it. She shuddered with pleasure, then withdrew it and stepped forward.

'Take his gag out, Beth,' she ordered.

Beth silently obeyed, reaching up and around his head to untie the gag of his underpants. He groaned as the gag came away. With her free hand Gwen took hold of the truncheon being held up under his bunched balls and waggled it. He groaned again. She dragged the truncheon away, dropped it on the floor, and put the head of the yelm-moistened truncheon to his arsehole.

'Anna, get round the front and watch.'

A pause, then she heard Anna's feet patter as she obeyed. Good. Re-establish your authority, girl.

'Let's count down,' she said. 'From ten. Ready?'

'Yes, Gwen.'

'Yes, Gwen.'

'Okay. Ten . . . nine . . .'

They started saying it with her. She tightened her grip on the truncheon, taking hold of it with both hands. One solid thrust.

'Six . . . five . . . four . . . three . . . two . . . one!'

Her hands jerked forward, the head of the truncheon sinking without hesitation into his arsehole, the yelm-slickened shaft sliding smoothly and swiftly through it, sinking into his bowels. A single despairing groan burst out of him and she felt the truncheon shudder in her hands as the muscles of his buttocks and sphincter tightened convulsively. There was a splatter of liquid spurting forward in long arcs and falling to the marble of the floor. Beth gave a low whistle.

'Jesus Christ. They were full of come after all.'

Twenty-nine

'How far did it get?' Gwen asked. She let go of the truncheon and it stayed in his arse, twitching slightly.

'Nearly as far as the wall,' Beth replied. 'Come and see for yourself.'

She walked around the stocks. Beth and Anna were standing to either side of a wide, shining trail of come splatters that stretched towards the wall. Christ, Beth was right. It had nearly reached the wall. She looked at his cock. It was still erect, starting to droop a little. Beth was lining her feet up with the start of the come-trail.

'It starts here . . .' she said. She started to walk forward very slowly, bringing her feet forward one at a time, planting her heels against her toes, lips moving silently as she counted. When she had finished she turned round.

'Eleven-and-a-bit feet,' she said.

'Eleven-and-a-bit Beth feet,' Anna said.

'Well, mine are the biggest, aren't they?'

'Yes. Galumphing great feet. So that is some come achievement. Spraying it that far.'

Gwen heard a cough and turned. Andy was raising his head, a crooked smile on his lips, his eyes still streaming tears from the pepper-spray.

'Glad to be of serv . . .'

'Gag him, Anna,' she said. 'We don't want to listen to any boasting.'

Anna snatched up the underpants from where they were lying on the floor and scampered to obey, standing on tip-toes to push the underpants into his mouth and tie them around his head. Gwen walked over to her, knelt, and thrust her hands up between his thighs, groping for his balls. She found them, grasped and squeezed. Anna stepped back.

'Done it, Gwen,' she said.

'Good.'

She let go of the balls and stepped back herself.

'Are they still hard?'

'Yes.'

There was a sudden clatter on the floor behind him. The truncheon had fallen out of his arse but she noticed that his cock had risen again, pointing stiffly towards them.

'So does that mean the hypothesis is disproved?' Beth said. 'Even when they're not full of come, balls are hard?'

Gwen mused.

'No,' she said. 'We can hardly consider it disproved after a single experiment. We'll have to try another experiment on another experimental subject. Him.'

She pointed at Bill, gagged and yoked in the next set of stocks. His cock, which had been hanging half-erect beneath the burning bush of his red pubic hair, twitched upright as she spoke.

'Look at the dirty bastard, Gwen,' Beth said. 'He likes the idea.'

'He likes it despite himself, I hope,' Gwen said. 'I'll do the honours this time. Anna, you can take cock-watch while I whip him. Beth, you can stick the truncheon up his arse at the end. Fetch the whip for me, will you? I'll be borrowing your one.'

Beth's mouth fell open, then closed with a click. Gwen hid a smile and strolled back around the stocks to stand behind Bill, waiting confidently for her orders to be obeyed. *You've re-established your authority, girl; now re-assert it. Hard.* She heard Beth and Anna whisper to each other and smiled again. *Let them hate, so long as they obey.*

Beth walked to the door and the whips scattered on the floor near it. She stooped and picked up the one made of red hair. Her hair. She walked back to stand behind Bill. Gwen was adjusting one of the truncheons beneath his balls, allowing them to dangle over it, holding it up as it rested in his gluteal crease. She let go of it cautiously and it stayed up. She clicked her tongue with satisfaction and started to step back. The whip swished behind her and she smiled for the third time. Beth was testing it for her. It swished again. She started to turn her head.

Crack! She spun fully round, mouth open with anger and pain. Beth had whipped her! Caught her full on one buttock cheek. Her hand had clapped to it automatically, clenching at the red-hot lines of pain, rubbing, squeezing.

'What the fuck are you doing?' she said.

Beth shrugged.

'Keeping you in your place, Gwenchen,' she said. 'Anna and I don't take orders from you any more. Especially not Anna. She's right: you and I have treated her very badly up to now, and I want to make it up to her. Isn't that right, Ansie?'

'Yep. Gwen, you've got too big for your boots.'

'You . . .'

Gwen moved threateningly towards Beth, but she didn't retreat, merely lifted the whip and shook it.

'Fancy some more, do you? You'll be back in the stocks yourself, if you don't watch it. It won't take long to give one of them another squirt of pepper-spray and get him out and handcuffed while Anna and I wrestle you into his place.'

Gwen's heart thumped in her chest. Was this what all dictators felt like, when they were overthrown? When the downtrodden masses upped and started downtreading for themselves? Her eyes were locked on Beth's, amber pouring intimidation and threat into green, but the green eyes were steady and unflickering, absorbing everything and unconcerned.

'Bitches.'

She regretted the word as soon as she had said it. It sounded so weak, so ridiculous. The sort of thing Anna would say – would have said. And it got the reaction Anna would have got. Laughter. Anna laughed from the other side of the stocks.

'I think she's learnt her lesson, Beth.'

'She has. She's a good girl. So we won't punish her, we'll let her keep her job. You can keep sticking the truncheons up their arses, Gwen, once Anna and I have given them a good whipping. Okay, Ansie?'

'Yeah, okay. And we'll give her another privilege too.'

'What?'

'She can help us ask questions. The last session lacked a little something.'

'What do you mean?'

Gwen saw Anna advance on the stocks from the other side. She was standing on tip-toes again, reaching up for the gag. Her hands appeared around the back of Bill's head, untying it. It fell free and she heard it land softly on the floor a moment later. Anna stepped back.

'We want to question him as we whip,' she said. 'Get to the bottom of what's been going on.'

'Good idea, Ansie,' Beth said.

'It's an *excellent* idea,' Anna said. 'If I say so myself. Right, Bill, or whatever you call yourself, get your mind off that swollen cock of yours and get ready to answer some questions. We'll take it in turns, eh, girls? Ask one, then Beth can whip him straight afterwards to show him what's in store if he doesn't answer. Okay?'

'Great,' Beth said.

'Gwen?'

Gwen swallowed.

'Okay,' she said, knowing as soon as she said it that the tone of her voice had been wrong. Anna laughed delightedly from the other side of the stocks and Gwen hid a scowl. *Bitches.* But she didn't say it aloud this time.

'Right,' Anna said. 'Me first. Bill, dear, tell us: who the fuck are you three?'

Beth had set her feet on the floor, rotating her whipping arm, swishing the whip through the air. Now her arm swung back, paused, lashing forward, swinging the red tails of the whip at the bare white arse in front of her and Gwen. *Crack!*

Bill barked with agony.

'Well, Bill?' Anna said.

'We told you in the card-room. We're your brothers.'

'Bullshit,' Beth said. 'Even this fucking place isn't that perverted. Shall I whip him again, Anna?'

'No. Hold on for a minute. It might not be the truth, but it sounds as though he thinks it is. Bill, dear, tell me: what proof have you got of this thoroughly perverted claim of yours?'

Bill's head had fallen forward; now it lifted again.

'Abraham Bärengelt,' he said. 'Take the first two letters of each name and you get "abba". That's Aramaic for "brother".'

'Aramaic?' Anna said.

'It's a dialect of Hebrew.'

'What?'

'It's a dialect of Hebrew. Look, that's why you're called Anna, Beth and Gwen. It's A, B, G. Those are the first three letters of the Hebrew alphabet. And that's why we're called Andy, Bill, and Geoff. A, B, G too. It's all arranged, deliberately. Don't you see?'

'This is bollocks, Anna,' Beth said. 'Plain as the bollocks dangling in front of me. Tell him to prove it.'

'Hmmm,' Anna said. 'We've heard of Abba the pop group but we don't know anything about "abba" meaning brother. And this stuff about A, B, G. It's A, B, C, isn't it?'

Bill's head shook.

'Not in Hebrew. Alef, beth, gimel. Those are the first three letters. They're tattooed on your heads. Don't you remember, the coin-shaped patch of hair on your heads? You thought there was something important underneath it and you asked Bärengelt what it was. He told you. Alef. The first letter. Alef for Anna.'

'What? I thought he said "Alice".'

'No. It was alef. It was me playing Bärengelt that time, so I should remember.'

Anna was silent for a moment, then said, 'What do you think, girls?'

Beth snorted.

'He's just clutching at straws to preserve his perverted fantasy. I've got another question for him that will help us get to the bottom of it.'

'Okay. Ask away, then whip away.'

'Right. Okay, Bill or Bärengelt or whoever the fuck you are, here's your next question. Where is Madame Oursor?'

'Good question, Beth,' Anna said. Her voice had suddenly got softer. 'Now whip him hard.'

Beth nodded silently. Her arm swung back, paused, lashed forward. *Crack!* Bill barked with agony again and Anna chuckled.

'I see what you mean about the cock swinging skyward, Beth. I don't need to hear the whip land to know when it's landed. Right, come on, answer the question. Where is Madame Oursor?'

Bill groaned.

'She's here, now. Geoff played her. Oursor is French for "bear-gold". It's a translation of Bärengelt. That means "bear-gold" in German. She's n . . .'

'Shut up!' Anna shouted angrily. 'Beth, land another across his arse, for telling lies. Go on.'

'I'm not lying. It's the truth. Look at Geoff's face if you don't believe me. Geoff, it was you, wasn't it? In make-up? Look, he's nodding. It was him. There never was a Madame Oursor. It's all been a set-up, to get you here, to get you . . .'

His voice trailed off. Gwen pursed her lips.

'To get us what?' she said.

'To get us fucked,' Beth said. 'To get us whipped and buggered and pissed on and splattered with come. That's what it's all been in aid of, from the beginning. So okay, here's question number three and whip-stroke number three to help it on its way. Who's been behind all this?'

Gwen watched the arm swing back, pause, lash forward. *Crack!* The white bottom was scrabbled with scarlet and the balls had started to bunch, tightening under the ecstasy of the agony. Bill groaned.

'We have. It's been in preparation for years. Since all six of us were born. We're not just your brothers, we're your twins. Identical twin brothers. That's w . . .'

271

'That's impossible,' Gwen interrupted. 'You can't have identical twins of opposite sexes. They're like clones and you can't clone one sex from another sex.'

Bill's head shook.

'No. You can. But only in one direction. You can clone a male from a female. By throwing away genes. You'd have to add genes to do it in the opposite direction, so it wouldn't be a true clone. But we are clones of you. I am your clone, Beth, and Andy is Anna's clone and Geoff is Gwen's clone. We're your twin brothers. That was why Anna was so attracted to Madame Oursor. Because she was like Gwen. A masculine version of Gwen.'

Beth laughed.

'It fits, Ansie. And you haven't lost her if this is right: she's there waiting in the next set of stocks, equipped to fulfil your fantasies in wholly different directions.'

Anna was silent for a moment, then said, 'Okay, another question. If you are our twins, how can you have organized all of this? Go on, Beth. Whip. Hard as you like.'

Swing; pause; lash. *Crack!* Bill barked with agony and his face swung to the ceiling.

'Give his balls a squeeze, Gwen,' Anna said. 'Let's not neglect the gathering of experimental data.'

Gwen stepped forward, took a firm hold of his balls, and squeezed.

'Stop!' Anna called. 'That's enough. Are they hardening?'

'Yes.'

Gwen stepped back.

'Okay. Now, Bill, answer the question. If you are our twins, how can you have organized all of this?'

'We've been organizing the latter stages of it. We don't know who was behind it in the beginning. This Schloss was used during the Cold War for biological experiments. Cloning. We think there was research here during the Second World War. Maybe some of the German scientists stayed on, to work for West German intelligence. From what we've managed to discover, the six of us were an operation intended to test the possibility of creating a crack sexpionage team.'

'Sexpionage?' Beth said.

'Yes. Agents trained in the art of seduction. That's why they chose blonde, red and black hair. Why your builds and personalities are different. To appeal to as wide a range of tastes as possible. But then the Cold War ended.'

'And what happened?' Beth asked.

'The team h . . .'

'Shut up,' Anna said. 'Ask the question again, Beth, and whip him before he answers it.'

'Okay. What happened when the Cold War ended?'

Swing; pause; lash. *Crack!* Another bark of agony; another long look ceilingward before his head tilted forward and he gave his answer, choosing his words carefully as first, as though he was having to prise them from a brain overwhelmed with sensation. Pain and pleasure.

'When the Cold War ended the team here found it hard to justify its continued budget for cloning and future projects were scrapped. We were kept on, but for a different purpose. Experiments in mass psychology. They decided to use us to test certain manipulation techniques they had been devising. The three of us were first. We were one of the most successful boy-bands in Europe for three years. Apollo, we were called.'

'I knew your faces were familiar,' Beth said.

'We were never big in the UK, but we performed on *Top of the Pops* a couple of times. But we were just a preparation. For you. They wanted to see how big they could go. So they created you. The Camberwell Sisters. Complete with a unique medical condition. Lissestreicher's syndrome. No direct sunlight, or you'd die.'

He suddenly snorted with laughter.

'It was all nonsense, but the media lapped it up. You were massive, weren't you? By then we were working behind the scenes with the team in charge of promoting you.'

'Stop,' Anna said. 'What do you mean it was all nonsense? Lissestreicher's syndrome, nonsense? But we've all had it since we were kids. We can't go out in sunlight. Never.'

'No, it was all made. Complete fantasy. Y . . .'

'No,' said Beth. 'We *remember*. *I* remember. All of us do. When we were kids.'

'No. It's all made up. It's all been a set-up and we've been manipulating you every inch of the way. Can't you remember? We were in the audience of your chat-shows, sometimes. I asked you a question on the *Jerome Sprockett Show*.'

'I can't remember that,' Anna said.

'No,' said Gwen. 'I remember him. I remember his hair. How much it reminded me of Anna's. But he didn't have an English accent.'

'I didn't have much of an American accent either. Only Geoff is good at that side of things. That's why Andy and I were always wondering if you'd rumble us when we were playing Bärengelt, even with the electronic distortion. We never dared use much German: that was always Geoff. The fucking and the sucking were what interested us.'

'Glad to hear it,' said Anna. 'So let's have another question. Gwen, your turn.'

Gwen pouted, then shrugged.

'If the Camberwell set-up was fake, why do we have such perfect memories of our lives?'

'Good question, Gwen. Beth, whip away.'

Swing; pause; lash. *Crack!*

'That's six, Anna,' Beth said.

'Let him answer the question. Then Gwen can put the truncheon up his arse. Go on, Bill. What's your answer?'

His face was still lifted ceilingward; now it swung forward, shaking slowly from side to side.

'Hypnosis,' he said. 'You've been implanted with false memories. Your whole childhoods. The Emily McFadden books. They never existed. They couldn't. Don't you remember all the concealed meanings? All the anagrams of sexual terms? It was all a set-up. All of it.'

'Then where are our real memories?'

'Buried. You'll be given them back, when this is all over.'

'Over?' Gwen said. 'But it's over now.'

'No. It's continuing. This is the last act. This is the penultimate scene in the last act. The filming is still going on.'

'*What?*'

Both Gwen and Beth had said it.

'The filming. It's continuing. You've been filmed continuously since you arrived in the Schloss. We'll be releasing the videos in a staggered series. We'll make millions.'

'We?'

Anna's voice. Quiet and somehow deadly.

'The team. The team we've all been working for. You girls, without your knowledge, till now, and us boys quite willingly. Quite happily. Ecstatically, at times. Though I could have done without this last bit. Christ. My arse is *raw.*'

'Gwen,' Anna said, speaking quickly and angrily. 'Stick it up his arse. As hard and as far as you like. Don't bother lubricating it.'

Gwen stepped forward and put the head of the truncheon to his arsehole.

'Hey!' he shouted. 'Yelm it. Yelm the fucking th . . .'

His voice broke into a groan of surprise and pain. Gwen had slid the truncheon deep between his arse-cheeks; now she exhaled with satisfaction. She took hold of the truncheon more firmly and twisted it hard. He groaned again and she smiled cruelly as she felt the truncheon quiver in her fingers. The muscles of his buttocks and sphincter were tightening. He was coming. She heard the splatter of come landing on the floor.

Thirty

'Gag him again,' Anna ordered.

Beth dropped her whip on the floor and ran to the front of the stocks. She gagged him, ignoring his protests as she tied the underpants hard around the back of his head.

'Ungag number three,' Anna ordered.

Beth ungagged Geoff.

'Okay, get ready to whip him.'

Beth ran back behind the stocks, picked up her whip, and stood behind Geoff, waiting for the order to begin.

'Number three,' Anna said. 'We have just heard from number two that there is a team filming events within the Schloss. Where is the control room?'

Silence.

'Whip him, Beth.'

Crack!

'Number three, I am about to order Beth to whip at will as hard as she likes. When you are ready to answer the question and wish the whipping to stop, please simply nod your head. Beth, whip ad-lib.'

Beth grinned, stretched, rocked her shoulders, and began. *Crack! Crack!* Gwen watched the red tails of the whip land on the white arse, slowly moulding it to their own likeness. Red. Red arse under a red whip. *Crack! Crack!* On and on in a steady, untiring rhythm.

'Beth! Stop! He's nodded.'

Panting, Beth stopped.

'Okay, number three, what do you have to say for yourself?'

Geoff coughed and slowly cleared his throat.

'Fuck off.'

Anna laughed.

'Gwen, squeeze his balls for him. Hard as you like.'

Gwen stepped forward and took hold of his balls. She squeezed hard, then harder, and watched his buttocks tighten with pain.

'Stop, Gwen. Count ten, then do it again.'

She counted ten, then squeezed them again. Hard. Harder.

'Stop. Count ten, then do it again.'

She counted ten, slowly, enjoying the frustration of denying herself the delicious task that awaited her, knowing that it would arrive soon enough, then took hold of his balls again and squeezed. Hard. Harder.

'Okay, stop. Beth, continue whipping. Pace it. Allow the pain to join the pain in his balls. He wants to come now. I can see it in the angle of his cock. But we're going to deny it to him until he answers the question. So whip him.'

Beth shook the whip and began again. *Crack! Crack!* The same rhythm, but slower now, sending the whip against the reddened arse like waves marching steadily against a cliff of red marble. Gradually, they wear it away. Gradually, they undermine it. Gradually, gradually, until finally it topples.

'Stop. Gwen, squeeze his balls again.'

Gwen stepped forward and took hold of his balls, but as she began to squeeze he groaned, as though against his will.

'Gwen, stop. Number three, are you ready to exchange orgasm for information?'

No answer. His head was lolling on his neck, his black hair plastered to his scalp with sweat.

'Squeeze, Gwen.'

She squeezed. Hard. Harder.

Another groan.

'Gwen, stop. Number three, are you ready to exchange orgasm for information?'

Silence again. Gwen smiled and prepared to squeeze hard, then harder.

277

'Gw . . .' Anna started to say, then stopped. Gwen looked up with disappointment. The back of his head was moving forward and back. He was nodding.

'Yes. I'll do it. For God's sake, I'll do it. Just let me come.'

'Information first,' Anna said. 'Where is the control room?'

'Behind you. In the wall behind you. There's a secret door and . . .'

'Like in *Emily and the Ghost of the Towers*?'

'Yes. Like that. Now please, make me come. Please. Now.'

'Gwen, make him come. Stick the truncheon up his arse.'

'Lubricated?'

'It's up to you.'

Gwen drew the truncheon away from his arse and perfunctorily moistened the head between her cunt-lips. She heard Anna's feet run to the wall and Anna called, 'Beth, quick, come and help me look.'

Beth dropped her whip and ran to help her. Gwen raised the truncheon from her cunt and put it to the arse of number three. Gwen serving Geoff. G servicing G. GG. And he was about to come like a horse. How appropriate. She thrust the truncheon into him and smiled as she heard him groan with humiliation and ecstasy, then heard the first splatter of come fired forward from his cock.

'Gwen!' Anna called. 'Come quick and – oh, fuck, he's just fucking splattered me.'

Gwen walked around the stocks. Beth was running her fingers over the wall, searching for the hidden trigger that would open the door to the secret room behind it, like in *Emily and the Ghost of the Towers*. Anna was wiping her arse and back with both hands. Geoff had spurted far enough to hit her. Then she put her hands back on the wall and continued to search.

Gwen joined them. Hands to the wall, fingers sliding on its smooth marble, searching for the hidden trigger. Then Anna shouted triumphantly and a section of wall was sliding open in front of her, revealing steps that descended steeply into darkness.

278

'Come on!' Anna said. 'There'll be a light at the bottom, like in *Emily and the Ghost of the Towers*.'

She stepped forward and began to run down the steps, holding her hands out to either wall to keep her balance. Beth followed her, then Gwen. Down, down, down. Down into the darkness below the Schloss, like Emily in *Emily and the Ghost of the Towers*. After a dozen or so steps it was pitch-dark and Gwen put her arms out too. Down, down, down.

Then the air began to lighten. They were nearing the secret room. The secret room deep beneath the Schloss, the control room where the videoing of all that had happened to them was co-ordinated. Anna cried out in surprise ahead of her and she heard Beth's feet speed up, pattering down the last few steps. She moved faster too, blinking as the full brightness of the light began to hit her. She jumped down the last few steps and ran forward. Beth's body was outlined in the doorway of the secret room ahead of her, as she stepped through it after Anna. Gwen ran to the doorway and stepped through it too.

And they were all three in the secret room, standing behind a black-leather swivel chair that faced a wall of video screens. And there was someone sitting in the swivel chair, the top and horns of his helmet peeping over the back of the seat. Beth screamed. Gwen felt her heart start to beat hard and resisted the urge to step backwards. The chair was turning to meet them and there, sitting in it, the blank, eyeless mask of his helmet gazing coldly at them, was Bärengelt. Bärengelt again, sitting deep beneath the Schloss, facing them as video screens flickered behind him with all the obscenities he had subjected them to since they had entered the Schloss.

Anna cleared her throat and Gwen jumped with surprise. She realized she was tense with apprehension, waiting for speakers in the walls to rumble into life with Bärengelt's mocking voices. Andy and Bill and Geoff had lied to them. Or maybe they hadn't known the truth themselves. Maybe they had played Bärengelt, but all the time there was a fourth one. A fourth Bärengelt. The real one.

'Who are you?' Anna asked.

Silence. Gwen jumped with surprise again. The chair was turning back towards the video screens, but Bärengelt hadn't moved. Beth murmured something.

'What?' Anna asked.

'It's automatic,' Beth said. 'It's moving by itself.'

The chair turned again, swinging Bärengelt back to face them. Anna stepped forward, reaching for the helmet, and Gwen tensed, waiting for his arms to swing up and seize her, and his voices to come rumbling finally from the walls. But the arms didn't move. Anna took hold of the helmet and tugged upward, slipping one knee onto Bärengelt's lap to help her. But the trousers of the bodysuit collapsed under the weight of her knee, and as the helmet came loose in her hands and she lifted it away, the chair began to turn again, swinging back to face the video screens. But Gwen had seen what was underneath the helmet.

Nothing. The bodysuit was empty. Anna was reaching inside the helmet.

'It's still warm,' she said. 'It's still warm inside.'

LEXICON

anch: tr. vb. to crush or squeeze the balls painfully.

birze: itr. vb. (of the buttocks) to grow hot during spanking or whipping.

blenk: to blink with pain (and then close the eyes).

campher: (the skin of) the inner thigh.

chillick: tr. vb. to lick (spanked buttocks) with an ice-chilled tongue.

cockcrown: the papillated rim of the cockhead, sitting directly above the cockditch (qv).

cockditch: the narrowing of the cock behind the cockhead, directly beneath the cockcrown (qv).

cockplum: a cockhead swollen and empurpled by erection.

crinny: n. one of the narrow patches of skin exposed by the lifting of the breasts or folding to one or another side of one of cunt-lips.

culk: n. the hollow in the inner surface of a female thigh.

deswiff: tr. vb. to shave or pluck the swiff (qv).

dreckle: itr. vb. (of sweat) to flow down the cleavage or the buttock-cleft.

flur: a movement caught out of the corner of the eye, esp. one that is impossible to assign a cause to, and draws the eye involuntarily to it.

freck: tr. vb. to pluck at the skin of the scrotum.

gleft: n. the female perineum.

golm: tr. vb. to lick the sweat or other fluids collected in a crinny (qv).

hulf: tr. vb. to drop molten wax onto a sexual part.

hulver: n. a large candle used for dropping molten wax onto a sexual part.

mockle: n. a freckle or other mark on or near the cunt.

naxter: n. the hollow behind the knee.

olf: (of the cunt) to smell.

oozle: to ooze a little, ooze slowly.

pre-swiff: n. the hair found on the perineum of a young woman.

quervil: n. combed and/or trimmed pubic hair.

quimpf: itr. vb. (of the cunt) to ooze under sexual frustration.

slatch: n. the semen-and-piss slot in the head of the penis.

smlash: itr. vb. portmanteau of 'smash' and 'splash'.

splitch: (of sweat) to spray in minute (and invisible) drops.

sprong: itr. vb. (of an erect nipple) to return elastically to the horizontal when pressed out of alignment.

sprongle: itr. vb. frequentative form of *sprong*.

swiff: n. the (silky) hair found around the arsehole of a young woman.

swiffhulf: itr. vb. to drop molten wax on to the swiff, as before deswiffing.

swiflet: n. one of the (silky) hairs around the arsehole of a young woman.

tenge: adj. the pink of a young woman's sphincter.

thrape: to force the penis deep into the mouth of an unwilling fellatrix (portmanteau of *throat* and *rape*).

thrickle: A strong trickle of arousal in the cunt.

tithulf: tr. vb. to drop molten wax onto the nipples.

tweng: tr. vb. to squeeze a nipple between the second joints of the index and middle fingers.

twengle: tr. vb. to squeeze and pluck a nipple between the second joints of the index and middle fingers, as though playing a musical instrument.

twilf: hairs around the nipples. Cf. twilfet.

twilfet: a single nipple-hair. Cf. twilf.

under-rein: the *frænum præputii*, or small flap of skin leashing the foreskin to the underside of the cockhead.

waftage: the distance over which an aroused cunt can be smelt.

yamble: tr. vb. to tongue the balls.

yelm: n. sexual secretions from the cunt.